Welcome!

The inspiration for these stories springs from the mists of Irish prehistory. Celtic legends are the oldest surviving works in British literature, predating the Arthurian cycle and *Beowulf*.

The tales of the ancient Celts embody the spirit of a fierce and passionate people who valued the strength of women as highly as that of men. The legends are romantic and vivid, with an irresistible interplay between reality and fantasy. The world they depict is fraught with danger, yet also aglow with intense beauty.

We invite you into a place of dreams and desires, where trees have souls; swords and stones can speak; and where men and women discover that love is the most powerful magic of all.

Roberta Gillis

Barbara Samuel

Morgan Llywelyn

Susan Wiggs

EARLY IRELAND

ULSTER

Emain Macha

MEATH   Dagda's Sidhe

CONNAUGHT

Cruach

Brugh na Boinne

Leenane   An Fhairche

Bri Leith

Uaman   Boyne   Tara

Sraith Salach

Galway

Galway Bay

LEINSTER

MUNSTER

0   50 miles
0   50 km.

IRISH MAGIC

SUSAN WIGGS
MORGAN LLYWELYN
BARBARA SAMUEL
ROBERTA GELLIS

Kensington Books
Kensington Publishing Corp.
http://www.kensingtonbooks.com

KENSINGTON BOOKS are published by

Kensington Publishing Corp.
850 Third Avenue
New York, NY 10022

First Trade Paperback Printing: March, 1995
First Paperback Printing: February, 1996

10 9 8 7 6 5

Printed in the United States of America

Contents

Galway Bay

by
Morgan Llywelyn

For Michael, who knows that the borders between reality and fantasy are very thin indeed.

BEFORE

The priest crouched in the bushes, his eyes riveted to the scene on the riverbank. He knew he was committing a grave sin but he could not help himself. He had to know.

And having once seen her, he had to stay.

She stood naked at the edge of the water. He had never seen a naked woman before, except in sneaked glimpses at pictures in wicked books. This was Ireland in 1960. The West had long since created the atomic bomb, the East had countered with the Iron Curtain. But rural Ireland still lived in an earlier time, and a boy marked for the priesthood was kept as pure as possible by his proud parents.

Yet even the Church could not legislate his dreams, and at night he had dreamed of this woman as he dreamed of the gods and goddesses who once walked Ireland in all their pagan glory, casting an enchantment over the land. Compared to the heroic high summer of Cuchulain and Finn Mac Cool, or the radiant magic of the Tuatha De Danann and Nuada of the Silver Hand, the era in which he lived was dry as dust and grey as winter.

He felt the lack of magic in his life. The rituals of his faith were not sufficient recompense, hedged round as they were with stern prohibitions.

The woman on the riverbank accepted no prohibitions. She stood as naked as she was born, with her arms upraised and her full young breasts quivering.

"*Manannan Mac Lir!*" *she cried, summoning the ancient Lord of the Sea.*

The water stirred as if troubled from beneath.

"*Manannan!*" *came the call again.* "*Attend me!*"

And then the priest thought he saw—though he was never quite sure afterward—the crests of Manannan's white horses on the waves of the bay beyond the estuary. They turned in unison and flowed, against all logic, toward the river. He heard the sound of a great shell blown like a trumpet, and the air sparkled like water.

The man crouched lower, his heart thundering in his chest.

He had followed her out here meaning to speak sternly about her rumoured heresy, her adherence to the Old Way. It was whispered in Galway that she used magic to heal when modern science failed. People had begun surreptitiously seeking out her little cottage by the crossroads, where she supposedly brewed all sorts of potents and nostrums to restore milk to the cows of local farmers or potency to human loins withered with age or disease. But she was very young and very beautiful; such claims might be the spite of jealous rivals.

Now he knew better. Now, watching her, he knew they were all true. He should run out and grab her and drag her away, chastise her, shame her, force her to abjure and repent. Save her soul.

But he could not even save his own. He could only tremble and stare at her body and feel forbidden passion rise in him, threatening to break free.

The white crests flowed up the river toward her and the shell trumpet blared wild music not heard in this land for centuries, and the woman on the riverbank threw back her head, her long hair swinging, and laughed with delight.

"*Manannan!*" *she called,* "*Bring the one I love to me!*" *She threw a sacrifice into the water, a tiny figure carved from bog oak. The water leaped upward to catch it, and the willows on the riverbank sighed and danced a pagan dance.*

She danced with them. Her body gleamed like May morning dew. The wind brought him the smell of her, warm as summer, sweet as honey mead. He could not help himself. He parted the bushes and stepped out into the light and she laughed when she saw him, laughed with her teeth like pearls of the sea.

And she who never went to confession confessed that she loved him. And he who never touched a woman reached for her.

chapter 1

Galway Bay was a disappointment. Eileen had envisioned a crescent of sandy beach as soft as sugar, a full moon paving the sea with silver, and thatched cottages overlooking the bay with Tralee roses wreathed around their doors. An Irish harp would be playing sweetly in the background. This was the scene her imagination had painted whenever she heard a tenor warble "Galway Bay," and it never failed to bring a nostalgic lump to her throat for a land she had never seen.

But when she arrived in Ireland for the first time nothing was as she had imagined. The version of "Galway Bay" she knew was an American version, she discovered as soon as she turned on the radio in her rental car; there was an Irish song of the same name that was altogether different. The Rose of Tralee was a highly commercial beauty contest, and most of the houses she saw around Galway were of relatively modern, if unfamiliar, architecture. Thatched cottages seemed to be in short supply. This wasn't the Ireland she had dreamed about when she leafed through the travel brochures.

Life had held a lot of disillusionment for Eileen Costello. The real Galway Bay had a beach of dark stones the size of hens' eggs instead of white sand, and raucous rock music was blaring out over sullen gray water from a nearby amusement arcade at Salthill as Eileen parked her rental car in front of the bed-and-breakfast. The air smelled of stale popcorn and beer; a watery sun was half-obscured by a threatening fringe of cloud like a dirty beard on the face of the sky.

Eileen felt like crying. But she was a big girl now, with a business of her own and . . . and no man of her own. The memories came stabbing back. Bob coming out of a family movie with two little boys and a woman who carried a sleeping toddler. Bob taking the sleeping child from the arms of the woman who was obviously his wife, then looking up and seeing Eileen standing there on the sidewalk staring at them.

Bob acting as if he didn't even recognize her and hastily shepherding his family away, then glancing back over his shoulder and trying to give her some message with his eyes . . .

"No!" she told herself sternly as she got out of the car and wrestled her suitcase from the back. Talking to herself was a habit she had fallen into recently. "Don't think about it, Eileen, it's ancient history, over and done with. You're in Ireland for your first vacation in years and you're going to enjoy yourself.

"You're going to enjoy yourself if it kills you," she added with grim determination.

Yet the pain lay waiting in her like a deep pool—pain compounded of stress and anxiety and too many locks on her door, too many bills on her desk. Taxes and pollution and crime. Red tape and frustration and loneliness. Too much to do and never enough time.

Pain for her stillborn dreams, so easily slain by a man who did not care in spite of all his protestations of undying love.

The B & B the travel agent had booked her into was neither thatched cottage nor romantic castle. It was a large, depressingly modern bungalow with plastered, pebble-dashed walls and a series of picture windows across the front offering views of Galway Bay. Hundreds of similar houses dotted the area, providing an additional income for the people who lived in them by offering tourists an affordable alternative to hotels.

When Eileen introduced herself to the red-cheeked couple of indeterminate years who owned this particular bed-and-breakfast, they nodded as if they recognized her name. "Costello," the man repeated, putting the accent on the first syllable in a way she had never heard before. "You'd be Irish yourself then?"

"My father was Italian," she replied. "And we pronounce it Cos-TELL-oh. I never knew it was Irish too."

"It is Irish, there's lots of Costellos here in the West," he assured her cheerfully. "I'm called Malachy Moore, myself, and the wife is Breda."

Hovering at her husband's elbow, the wife spoke so softly Eileen could barely hear her when she said, "Will ye come this way now?" She led their guest to an immaculately clean bedroom, furnished with mahogany reproductions instead of the authentic Irish country furniture Eileen had hoped to find, and proudly declared there was a "bath en suite," which proved to be no more than an adjoining bathroom but was obviously considered something of a luxury.

Well, Eileen told herself, I did tell the travel agent I wanted inexpensive accommodations.

She had a supply of traveler's checks with her, but most of them were earmarked for purchases. Once they had represented her savings for a trousseau . . . no! Don't think about it! In New York she owned a tiny shop specializing in cottage crafts for the interior design trade, and she hoped to bring back some unique items from Ireland to help her keep the shop going for a little longer. If it failed—as seemed likely—what would she do?

So after she had unpacked her suitcase and washed the

travel from her face, she asked her hosts to recommend a restaurant for dinner that would not be too expensive. She was very tired from the flight and knew she was fighting jet lag, but she was determined not to waste her first evening in Ireland by going to bed while it was still daylight.

"Is it American food you're after?" Malachy Moore inquired tentatively, as if expecting her to demand hamburgers and Southern fried chicken.

When she replied, "I want Irish food," his expression changed.

"Corned beef and cabbage?" he said. "That's what most Americans think is Irish."

His choice of words was a giveaway. Eileen smiled. "I'm not most Americans. My mother's mother was actually born here—well, in County Clare—so I have some Irish blood. From her I learned that real Irish people eat cabbage with bacon rather than corned beef. Bacon as in ham, not bacon as in rashers."

His round face burst into a smile and he twinkled at her; positively twinkled! Eileen had never seen anyone twinkle before. "And am I not after telling the wife that you're an Irish lass if ever I saw one?" Malachy Moore promptly reached across the highly polished coffee table in the living room, or "lounge" as his wife called it, caught one of Eileen's hands and squeezed it like a fond uncle.

In New York she would have snatched her hand back and looked for the nearest cop. In Ireland the gesture seemed innocent and welcoming, part of the ambience she had flown three thousand miles to find.

"The place for you to eat tonight is Chokkie Dalyuh," he said with conviction. "You'll feel right at home there, herself that runs it is a Clare woman too."

"Chokkie . . ." Eileen struggled with the unfamiliar name and he laughed. "It's the Irish," he explained. "It translates to Daly's House, and you'll be wanting Mrs. Daly. Tell her about your grandmother."

Her head was whirling. "Where is . . . uh, Daly's House? Is it near the bay?"

"Merciful hour! Why would you want to eat there, what with the young ones running wild up and down the promenade far later than they should? No, the restaurant I'm sending you to is on a nice quiet country road. There's a little inlet just across the way, so you'll have water to view if you want, and on a long summer's evening like this you'll probably see swans settling down for the night."

Eileen was charmed. "Where do I find this place?"

Her host continued to beam at her. "It's just past the pub," he said, then raised his eyebrows when she laughed.

"Just past the pub," Eileen had already learned, was a standard Irish direction. Armed with a road map, she had driven out of the car rental zone at Shannon Airport late that morning determined A) to master the intricacies of right-hand drive, and B) find her way to Galway and her night's accommodations without help. She had partially succeeded in the former, but she had been forced to ask directions several times.

Every answer had seemed to involve at least one pub. And one cheerful man walking a brace of huge greyhounds had laughed outright when she confessed to being lost. "Sure, how can you be lost?" he had asked with great good humor. "You're here, aren't you?"

Now, following Malachy Moore's directions, she made her way along a frighteningly narrow road between impenetrable briar hedges, "past the pub," and at last pulled up in front of a very plain building covered with plaster painted a startling mustard color. Over the door was a red-lettered sign: Teach na Dalaigh.

"Chokkie Dalyuh?" Eileen murmured to herself as she got out of the car.

"It is that," replied a resonant voice. She whirled to find herself facing a tall man dressed in cords and a sweater. His eyes were an improbable dark green, like deep sea water, and below their surface was a glow that held her transfixed.

"I'm looking for Mrs. . . . uh, Daly," Eileen said. Any man as good-looking as this one shouldn't be allowed out in public, she told herself. He made it all but impossible for a woman to think clearly.

He smiled; a slow, courteous smile. "My mother. Come inside and I'll introduce you." His accent was Irish, soft and musical, but unlike any other accent she had heard so far. Before she could stop him he had cupped her elbow in a very old-fashioned way and was steering her into the restaurant.

It took a moment for Eileen's eyes to adjust to the lack of light. The interior of Teach na Dalaigh was quite dim, the only illumination coming from candles glimmering on the tables. The restaurant appeared to consist of one medium-sized room, with perhaps a dozen tables, each covered with a crisp white linen cloth. Instead of flowers there were piles of seashells in the middle of each table, and the walls were draped with fishing nets suspended from hollow glass balls.

A mouth-watering odor wafted from a half-open door that must lead to the kitchen.

"Will you sit here?" suggested the man, pulling out a chair for her.

Eileen sat, suddenly dazed with fatigue and not a little disoriented. When she looked around, she discovered that she was the only diner in the room. Was it early, then, for the evening meal in Ireland? Half-turning in her chair to ask, she intercepted a hand reaching over her shoulder with the menu. The hand was masculine, beautifully shaped, with strong white fingers and nails that gleamed even in the dim light.

Eileen looked up into sea-green eyes and smiled. "Thank you," she said as she took the menu, a large folio in limp leather.

He replied with a little bow of such old-world courtesy, she smiled again.

In the dim light she had to lean very close to the candle to read the listings. Everything seemed to be some sort of seafood, even the appetizers, which were called "starters" but all sounded delicious. Eileen found herself mouthing the names in delight. Ballyvaughan mussels. Clarinbridge oysters.

Over her shoulder, she asked the green-eyed man, "What would you recommend?"

He chuckled, a deep warm sound that went right through her. "Everything is delicious here—if you like the products of the sea."

"Oh I love the sea," she assured him. "That's why I came to Galway first, I wanted to be close to the water. I can never get enough of it. From the window of my apartment in New York the only water I see is the tiniest slice of the river, but I used to dream of living out in . . ."

"Sorry!" exclaimed a female voice. "I didn't realize anyone was out here." A lean gray-haired woman came bustling out of the kitchen, wiping her hands on her apron. "We don't usually get the dinner trade quite so early."

"That's perfectly all right," Eileen assured her. "Mrs. Daly, is it?"

The woman responded with a nod, pleased to be called by name.

"Well, Mrs. Daly, your son has looked after me already and given me this." Eileen held up the menu, open to the page with the starters listed.

Only then did she realize that he was no longer standing behind her. She turned in her chair and swept her eyes over the room, but in spite of the dimness, she could see that she and Mrs. Daly were quite alone.

"My son." Mrs. Daly repeated the words with a deliberate lack of inflection.

Eileen was disconcerted. "He said he was . . . he was here just a minute ago . . . a tall man with smooth brown hair and green eyes . . . ?"

"My son," Mrs. Daly said again in a very different tone of voice. "It was him of course, and right he was too to bring you in and seat you. Now then, what will you be having?"

Together they consulted on the menu, and together they decided Eileen would have the mussels, black sole on the bone, and something called a dulsc pudding for dessert. "It's a sweet made from seaweed, very good and good for you," Mrs. Daly claimed. Eileen was dubious, but agreed to give it a try to please the woman.

Mrs. Daly proudly informed her all the food was cooked fresh, to order, so there would be a little wait. Meanwhile she provided a basket heaped with warm brown bread so chewy and delicious that Eileen found herself gobbling it down with great smears of sweet butter. It was the first time in months she had been really hungry.

Still no one came into the restaurant. Eventually Mrs. Daly emerged, flushed, from the kitchen, to report, "It will be another few minutes. Perhaps you'd like to walk across the road and enjoy the view? I'll come for you when your meal is ready."

To avoid eating any more of the bread, which probably contained a thousand calories a bite, Eileen followed her suggestion. As she stepped outside she glanced around in hope of seeing Mrs. Daly's son again, but he was nowhere in sight.

Probably gone home to his wife, Eileen thought bitterly.

A few feet below the shoulder of the road damp grass sloped down to a small inlet. Beyond the reedy backwater flowed a stream, a tributary of Galway Bay. Remembering Malachy Moore's words, Eileen looked eagerly for swans but saw none. Yet as she gazed at the water she felt an unfamiliar tranquility steal over her, a sense of being so far removed from New York, and pressure . . . and heartbreak . . . that it felt as if knots were being untied in her soul.

She drew a deep breath. Sweet air, moist air bathed her lungs as it was bathing her skin.

"Ireland," she said softly to herself. "I'm here. I'm really here."

She was struck by the realization that no one knew exactly where she was—no one but the Moores. She could vanish without a trace. Who would notice?

Who would care?

Eileen shook her head, impatient with herself. She must be very tired indeed to give in to such self-pity.

A mist was rising from the inlet. Just beyond the reeds the surface was disturbed by the sudden emergence of a smooth, round head, dark against dark water.

Eileen strained to see what it was, but the mist thickened, obscuring her view. The shape she had glimpsed was wrong for a water bird and strangely immobile. What could it be? A trick her weary eyes were playing? She stared hopefully as the mist swirled away for a moment, revealing the surface of the water, but the round object was gone.

Then she heard Mrs. Daly calling to her.

Though the evening was warm, Eileen felt a shudder ripple across her shoulders as she stepped through the doorway of Teach na Dalaigh. She turned back to look toward the water, but there was nothing to be seen; nothing but the mist.

chapter 2

Afterward, Eileen could never remember what that dinner tasted like, though she had the impression it was the best meal she'd ever eaten. The atmosphere in the restaurant was relaxing to the point of being hypnotic. A few other people arrived and ordered dinner but their presence did not disturb her mood. She felt as if she were floating, an effect heightened by the wavering candlelight and the nautical theme of the decor. The other diners were seated in the shadows; if they spoke to one another their voices were so low Eileen could not hear them.

She was content just to sit there, drifting. In a world apart.

By the time she made herself get up and pay the bill, thank Mrs. Daly—who seemed to fulfill all functions, from hostess and cook to cashier—and leave Teach na Dalaigh, night had fallen. Eileen stepped into a luminous purple twilight as soft as gauze. The lapping of the nearby water was clearly audible.

She scolded herself for not having left sooner. She was in an unfamiliar country driving an unfamiliar car; it would have been smarter to make her way back to the B & B while there was still light.

As she opened the car door and the dome light came on, she heard a splash. The sudden brightness had frightened some creature on the bank, making it dive into the water. She was reminded of the round shape she had glimpsed so briefly.

On an impulse she closed the car door and went back into the restaurant. Mrs. Daly was just accepting payment from the last couple to leave. Eileen waited until they were gone, then asked, "Are there any seals around here?"

The woman behind the counter was putting credit card receipts into a drawer. "Seals? Here?"

Eileen gave an embarrassed laugh. "I suppose that's foolish."

Mrs. Daly closed the drawer firmly and locked it with a key. "Do you know anything about seals?"

"Only what I've picked up watching nature programs on public television," Eileen admitted. "But while I was waiting for my dinner I saw something out there . . . in the water . . ."

"And it looked like a seal to you?"

"Like a seal's head, maybe."

"There are seals on the coast," Mrs. Daly told her. "They range from Donegal to Kerry, I believe, though I really pay no attention to such things. But I can't think why a seal would come this far inland."

"This isn't far inland, we're still close to the bay."

"We have no seals around here," Mrs. Daly assured her. "You must have been imagining it."

Eileen began to doubt herself. "Probably," she agreed.

Mrs. Daly heard the regretful note in her voice and gave her a long look. "Are you all right?"

"I am, I'm fine. Just tired, that's all. I'd better get back and go to bed."

"Don't forget to come back," the older woman replied with a smile of such genuine warmth Eileen felt as if she were bathed in a golden glow.

She helped herself to some mints from a dish on the

counter and went out into the night. This time when she opened her car door, nothing splashed.

The drive back to the B & B was uneventful. To her pleased surprise, she had no difficulty finding her way. As she turned onto the main road running beside the bay, a full moon was paving the sea with silver.

"That's more like it!" Eileen said to herself with a laugh.

She parked the car and stood looking out across Galway Bay.

She was so tired she was numb, yet there was a strange exhilaration in her. Eileen wanted to fling her arms wide and embrace the night and the shimmering sea.

She did not even hear the rock music blaring from the amusement arcade.

She did not even see him watching her from a distance.

He did not think of her as beautiful. Physical perfection was not one of his requirements in a woman. He was looking for a combination of strength and vulnerability, a delicacy of soul and toughness of spirit that might not show in face or form. If the American woman possessed these qualities only time would tell.

But he had time. He stayed at a distance, following her, every sense alert to her.

Eileen slept restlessly that night. The moment her head touched the pillow she sank into a turmoil of confused dreams that left her red-eyed and exhausted by morning.

At breakfast both the Moores fussed over her while she picked at an awesome meal of eggs, sausages, bacon, two odd round patties called black pudding and white pudding, grilled tomatoes and mushrooms, buttered scones which were the same almost as American biscuits, orange marmalade and a steaming pot of tea. Eileen was staggered by the food; so much of it on her plate killed her appetite.

"You let yourself get too tired yesterday, that's your problem," Mr. Moore asserted. "We know the signs. Tourists try to do too much on their first day. You should have stayed here and let us order you some takeaway for your dinner, there's a nice Chinese in Salthill. Or the wife could have made you some soup and sandwiches, no bother on her."

"No, that restaurant you sent me to was lovely. Perfect, just what I wanted."

He suggested, "You should be gentle with yourself today. Why not rest here a while, then take a nice stroll around the city, see the sights?"

"I would like to do some shopping," Eileen said.

Mrs. Moore leaned closer, making it easier to hear her soft voice. "Galway's a grand town for shopping, so it is."

Her words proved true. Eileen fell in love with the town, with its narrow, crooked streets, its colorful shops, the swirl of young people that thronged the sidewalks. Galway was vibrant and alive, intensely Irish without being overly quaint. She found a number of shops selling the sort of merchandise she wanted to purchase to take back with her, but wisely refrained from buying anything substantial until she had more chance to look around.

Her most extravagant purchase was a book entitled *Irish Folk and Fairy Tales Omnibus*, by Michael Scott, which she planned to read in bed that night to acquaint herself a bit more with the magical spirit of Ireland. Tucking the fat volume into her capacious hobo handbag, she sauntered through Galway, enjoying the contrast between modernity and antiquity which characterized the busy little city.

When her leg muscles began aching, she wandered down to the picturesque Spanish Arch and seated herself on a bench in the sun. A broad sheet of water glimmered in front of her; the river that connected Lough Corrib with Galway Bay.

She thought her eyes had only been closed for a moment when she felt someone sit down beside her. Eileen tensed, with all her streetwise antennae quivering, and turned to glare at the intruder. But her glare faded when she saw his homely, pleasant face, as innocent of menace as a baby's. His hair was flaming red and he was covered with freckles from the tips of his ears to the backs of his hands. In the open throat of his shirt, what Eileen could see of the skin beneath the freckles was as white as milk. He appeared to be in his late thirties, and had round blue eyes and a pipe clenched in his teeth. When he saw her staring at him he withdrew the pipe. "Do you mind . . . ?" he asked politely, holding it up.

"Not at all," she assured him as she caught a whiff of his tobacco, pungent and masculine. "I don't smoke, but I rather like the smell of a man's pipe."

She had bought Bob a pipe once, as a surprise . . .

She pushed the memory away resolutely as her seatmate said, "There's not many will admit that these days, but I'm too stubborn to give it up. It goes with the image."

"The image?"

"Professor. I teach folklore at the university. And you're American?"

Eileen laughed. "Does it show?"

"It does," he replied. "American shoes identify you anywhere. And then there's your accent, of course."

"I don't have an accent!"

It was his turn to laugh. "You do in Ireland!"

The sun was warm, he was easygoing and did nothing that could be construed as coming on to her. She had never met a man who looked or acted more innocent. Even his soft Irish accent was reassuring. But Eileen had been taught in a hard school. When at last he stood up and said he was going for a coffee, would she care to join him, she asked crisply, "Are you married?"

He laughed again but his face flamed behind the freckles. "You Americans certainly are blunt," he commented. "I am not married, never have been. Teaching and my own studies take up most of my time, or have until recently. I've just begun a year's sabbatical to do some work on a book. My name is Barry Hynes, by the way." He held out his hand and shook hers as if they were being formally introduced.

Now Eileen was embarrassed. To make up for her rudeness she agreed to join him for coffee and soon found herself in a tiny little shop close to the Spanish Arch, listening as Barry described the book on Irish folklore he was writing. She did not mention the thick paperback volume on the same topic which she had tucked in her handbag, but privately she relished the coincidence.

Barry Hynes seemed to have a full measure of Irish charm, but she felt no physical attraction toward him. He was the exact opposite of dark, smoldering men like Bob, the type to whom she was invariably drawn. Barry's amiable freckled face was one she could forget the moment they parted.

However Eileen found it pleasant to be chatting comfortably with a man with whom she could not possibly get involved; a man who could not hurt her.

"Banshees and leprechauns are all I know of Irish myth," she told him, "but I would like to learn more. I hope to take some native crafts back to the States with me to sell, and I think it would help enormously if I could, well, import a little of the magic with them, you know? So I'm lucky to have met an expert on Irish myth. Before today I never heard of pookas and Ron and . . ."

"They are not myth," Barry interrupted. "Folklore is not the same as fairy tales, and even the fairies are not myth, not in Ireland."

At first she thought he was joking, but his face and eyes were serious. "Our history is unlike that of any other country," he told her. "The dividing line between what you would call fantasy and reality has always been a thin one here. The early Irish were Celts, descendants of the druids, people who believed in the spirits of trees and stones and water.

"Ancient Irish history is folkloric; it existed only in the oral tradition until the coming of Christianity, and was handed down by the bards, generation after generation. Some of the most splendid and detailed of those stories tell of the Tuatha De Danann, the Magic People who were defeated by iron-age weaponry and remained in Ireland to become spirits of place.

"Fairies," he elaborated when she raised a questioning eyebrow. "The Little People. They are still here, you know."

Eileen gave him an incredulous look. "You really believe in them?"

"I would not disbelieve," he said firmly. "I've spent my life studying folkloric history and I'm convinced a great amount of it is true, if highly colored.

"Even today, people—especially in the country—are careful not to say or do something that might anger the fairies. They call them 'The Good People' to keep from insulting them, and a lot of building contractors in the West will warn you against building a house on a fairy road, or bulldozing a fairy fort."

"But that's just superstition!"

"You wouldn't think so if you had spent all your life in the West of Ireland as I have. Not long ago I interviewed an old woman from Clare who once heard the banshee cry. Thirty years had passed since then, but when she spoke of the banshee it might have been yesterday. The expression in her eyes . . . no one could see that and not believe."

"The expression in an old woman's eyes is hardly proof of anything," Eileen argued.

"She was genuinely frightened, even after so long a time."

"She probably heard the wind howling and blew it up in her own imagination."

Barry gave her a grave look. "You speak of imagination as if it's a sin. Have you none yourself?"

Eileen busied her fingers with pleating her paper napkin, and her eyes with watching them. "No more than any sensible adult," she replied in a low voice.

Studying her thoughtfully, the Irishman took a final long pull on his pipe. "Perhaps you're the sort of person who has to see something with their own eyes to be convinced. That's an American trait, I believe. We have more faith here."

"Not everyone, surely!"

"No," he agreed, "not everyone. I myself had to . . ." He stopped abruptly.

"Had to what? Did you see something, is that why you're so convinced? Oh do tell me! Was it a leprechaun? Did he wear a little green coat and pointed shoes?" Eileen laughed to show him she was willing to enter into the game.

Barry knocked the embers from his pipe into a glass ashtray on the table, then withdrew a tissue from his pocket and wiped out the bowl. It gave him, Eileen observed cynically, time to think.

"Not a leprechaun," he said at last. "But I do have some firsthand knowledge of the Ron."

"You mentioned them before and I told you I've never heard of them. What are they?"

"Stories about the Ron are found in almost every culture along the Atlantic seaboard; their range is quite extensive," Barry replied in a professorial tone she could imagine him using in the lecture hall. "The Scots call them Selkies, or Cuilein Mairi, meaning Mary's Whelps. There is one charming nursery tale that accredits them with being fallen angels, though the truth is considerably blacker.

"The Ron are the seal-people."

Eileen leaned forward over the dirty coffee cups. "What?"

"Seal-people. Creatures operating under an enchantment. Human souls trapped in the bodies of seals, if you will, but capable of reverting to their human form under certain circumstances."

He was still serious. Eileen began to think he might be mad. When she said as much he shrugged good-humoredly, taking no offense. "You Americans *are* blunt. But you come from a different culture, perhaps more different than you realize. Just because we each speak a version of English doesn't mean we have all that much in common."

"But seal-people; really! Next you'll be telling me you believe in mermaids."

"No, because I've never seen one. But perhaps they are variants of the same species."

Now Eileen was certain he was having a joke at her expense. "Are you implying that you've actually seen the . . . what do you call them, the Ron? If you have, you show me one!" she challenged.

Barry regarded her somberly. "Someone living under a curse is not to be summoned with a snap of the fingers for a tourist's amusement."

"That's just what I thought," Eileen retorted, pleased with her small victory. "You can't show me one of the seal-people because there's no such thing."

He stood up and dropped a few coins on the table to pay for their coffee. "I didn't say that. I can show you the Ron, if you want. It just won't be easy, and perhaps not even safe. But you Americans are supposed to be adventurous, aren't you?" he challenged her in turn.

Against her better judgment, Eileen found herself agreeing to meet Barry Hynes late the next afternoon.

But she was determined to check him out before she met him.

When she mentioned his name to Malachy Moore, she got an instant response. "Och, we know the man well. A fine lad he is too, one of the professors at the university. He's called in on us the odd time, hasn't he, Breda? He's always collecting stories, and our families have lived here for a thousand years, so we're good subjects for him."

"Is he married? He doesn't wear a ring."

Breda Moore gave a delicate sniff. "That doesn't mean so much these days."

"I asked him and he said no."

Malachy Moore chuckled. "I'd say that gave him a start! No Irish lass would ask such a question. But he told you the truth; in as far as I know he has no wife, no family. And he's not the worst man in Ireland either, if you're interested."

Eileen shook her head. "I'm not the slightest bit interested, not that way. He kindly offered to show me some of the seacoast and I think I should take advantage of the opportunity; after all, I came here to see Ireland. But I just want to be sure I'm not getting into anything."

Breda Moore's face lit with the ardor of the born romantic. "Yourself only here the one day and walking out already!"

Eileen was not familiar with the term "walking out," but she could guess what it meant. "We're just going for a drive along the coast," she said firmly. "And I'm doing the driving."

Malachy Moore exchanged a knowing look with his wife.

chapter 3

When Eileen called for Barry the next afternoon she was surprised to find that his "flat" near the university was in a very modern apartment building, painted Mediterranean blue but possessing an American-style balcony. "I'd expect a professor of folklore to live in a huge old house filled with antiques," she told him laughingly.

"Not at all. I spend enough time in the past. When I come home and close the door behind me I need the modern world for balance."

"Yet you don't drive a car?"

"I do not. Never bothered to learn. In Galway you can walk everywhere you need to go, like most towns in Ireland, and of course I have a bicycle. For longer distances I can always find someone with a car. Or take the bus. Or use my thumb."

"Is it safe to hitchhike?"

He grinned at her. "Everyone does it here. Little old ladies hitchhike home from the grocery with the week's shopping."

Eileen shook her head. She was making a number of discoveries about Ireland, not the least of them being that a lot of people did not have telephones. "We aren't on the phone," someone had said to her without embarrassment in Paddy Kavanaugh's Pub the night before.

Irish pubs were another revelation. Not simply bars as in the American sense, they were more nearly social clubs. They served wonderful toasted sandwiches and bowls of thick delicious soup. People brought musical instruments which they played spontaneously to an appreciative audience. Others sang. Parents brought their children. The occasional dog came with its master and lay complacently at his feet, while the other customers stepped over the animal without complaining.

And Mrs. Moore was not the only person with a soft voice Eileen could hardly hear. By American standards most Irish voices were inaudible. In the pub she had visited last night, Eileen was mortified to discover she could readily identify her countrymen, those holidaying like herself, by the fact that they seemed to shout all the time.

Today with Barry Hynes she was making a constant effort to pitch her voice more softly.

At his direction they were driving south from Galway, toward Clare. For a man who did not drive, Barry was a good navigator, skillfully directing Eileen through the intricacies of the Irish traffic circle. They followed a major roadway for a short distance, then turned onto a series of back roads distinguished only by astonishing potholes. At any moment she expected to break the axle of her rental car, but when she complained Barry just smiled. "These are not bad at all," he assured her. "I've seen holes where you could catch a salmon."

She was not certain if he was joking or not.

They began their drive at four in the afternoon—"A couple of hours before teatime", as Barry said—for a specific reason. "If you want a look at the seal-people we had best catch them basking in the sun, and they tend to do that in the late afternoon."

"You're talking about real seals, then," she chided him, "and not these mysterious Ron of yours at all."

He did not rise to the bait. "Wait and see," was all he said.

They seemed to be circling Galway Bay. Eileen noticed town names on signposts: Irish names, such as Roevehagh and Killeenavarra. One beautiful vista after another appeared, with low rolling hills, stretches of deserted beach—sometimes the white sand of her dreams—and sparkling dark blue water.

She kept waiting for Barry to make a pass. But he remained, as her mother would have said, a perfect gentleman. Not even the smallest innuendo, the most subtle double entendre.

At last he directed her to "Turn in there." Obeying, she found herself on a rutted dirt road facing a closed farm gate. Barry jumped out of the car and opened the gate for her. "Drive on down toward the water," he instructed. "I'll follow you on foot."

A hundred yards ahead the muddy trackway came to an abrupt end. Eileen let the car crawl forward in low gear, then halted and pulled up the hand brake. A tumble of boulders confronted her. Beyond them the land fell away sharply toward the sea.

The sweep of Galway Bay lay before her, as innocent as the first day of Creation. Even the houses on the opposite shore appeared to be no more than distant pebbles glinting in the mellow light of afternoon. There was no nearby amusement arcade, no rock music, no traffic noise. Seagulls swooped and soared. The wind sang. The sun shone in a cloudless sky, and the wavelets transmuted its light into a million flashing stars glittering on the surface of the bay.

Eileen sat with her hands idle on the steering wheel, staring out across the breathtaking view until Barry's gentle knock on the window snapped her out of her reverie. "Get out and follow me," he said.

Skirting the boulders, they made their way down a

steep slope toward a tiny, rocky cove. Barry gestured to her to proceed slowly. "Don't make any noise," he whispered, his voice almost lost in the wind off the sea.

In spite of the sun, Eileen felt cold. She was wearing a heavy sweater over her turtleneck and jeans, but even this did not seem enough, so close to the water. Accustomed to the summer sizzle of New York, she was astonished to find herself shivering in July.

Suddenly a strong hand grasped her arm. "Don't move," Barry whispered. "Look. There."

Following his pointing finger, she saw what at first seemed no more than another cluster of rocks at water's edge. But when she squinted she realized they were seals. Half a dozen sleek rounded shapes lay close together, some with their heads resting across the backs of others, their flippers splayed out from their bodies.

Eileen drew in her breath sharply. They didn't have to be Ron, she didn't believe that story anyway. It was sufficiently exciting to be standing at the edge of the sea looking at a flock—herd, pod, bunch?—of seals basking in the sun. Even as she watched, two more emerged from the water to join the group on the shore. The newcomers were greeted with a chorus of grunts and barks that reminded Eileen in a curious way of friends calling greetings to one another in Paddy Kavanaugh's Pub.

He was aware of the intensity of her gaze. He was aware of the strong shape of her shoulders under the heavy woolen sweater; the self-control of her body as she held herself immobile; the rise and fall of her bosom over good big lungs.

He was aware of many things. The warmth of the sun, the coldness of the sea. The smell of salt and fish and seaweed. The light of the land, the darkness of the water.

Soon enough he would have to go back into the water and the

cold. Back into the darkness and the depths. But ah! the joy of
taking this one with him, down, down, to . . .

Abruptly Eileen sneezed. It happened so fast she did
not have time to pinch her nose closed or cover her
mouth to muffle the sound. The sneeze was like a gun-
shot and the response of the seals was instantaneous.
They were there, then they were gone. Simply—gone.
Without a splash. Vanished.

Eileen turned apologetically toward Barry. "I'm sorry,
I didn't mean to do that."

"Of course you didn't, it's all right."

"Will they come back?"

"I doubt it, not this afternoon."

"How quickly they disappeared! I wouldn't have
thought they could do that, I mean, I would have expected big fat animals like that to be clumsy, to splash as
they went into the water no matter how startled they
were."

"Seals do splash going into the water," Barry replied
gravely.

"These didn't."

"No."

"Are you trying to tell me they weren't seals, then?"

"We should go back," he said, "if you're getting cold. It
would be a shame to get sick on your holiday."

"Answer my question. Are you saying those were . . .
were seal-people? As magical as banshees and leprechauns?"

"Isn't that what you came out here to see?"

Eileen was exasperated. Part of her was convinced he
was teasing her; part of her was surprised he hadn't made
any sort of a pass, the way the men she knew would have
done in similar circumstances. Barry, however, didn't
seem to see her as a desirable woman at all.

And another part, some deep atavistic sense she could not identify, was frightened. Wanted to leave this place right now, and not because of Barry Hynes.

By the time they got back to the car the light seemed to have gone out of the sky. The sun was still shining, but the pinpoints of dazzling light were gone from the crests of the waves. Galway Bay looked dark, sullen.

When Eileen started the engine she turned on the heater.

Barry did not comment.

"Are you disappointed?" he finally asked as they drove back toward Galway.

"I'm . . . no, I suppose not. I don't know what I expected, so I can hardly be disappointed."

"We were lucky to find them at all, you know. I've gone there many times without catching a glimpse of them."

"Ah," she replied noncommittally, concentrating on her driving. Soon they would be encountering more traffic, and she was still coping with the strangeness of right-hand drive and being on the left side of the road.

Barry said, "As far as I know, there is only one group of them on the bay."

"I take it you mean one group of seal-people, as opposed to one group of seals?"

He chose not to take offense at her obvious sarcasm. "There are plenty of seals if you know where to look," he assured her.

"I know, I think I saw one myself the other night."

"One seal, as opposed to one seal-person?" Now he sounded sarcastic.

Eileen was suddenly contrite. Barry Hynes had been nice enough to try to give the American tourist a bit of a treat and a touch of magic, even if it was all make-believe. The least she could do was go along with him. "How would I tell the difference?" she asked. "If those . . . those creatures back there hadn't vanished into the water so silently, how would you have identified them as Ron?"

Now he was wary. "Do you mean that as a serious question?"

"I do," she assured him solemnly.

"I've lived here all my life. There are certain signs you get to recognize; it's like identifying Americans by their shoes. The Ron have a peculiar luster to their fur, different from that of normal seals. And the shape of the head is slightly different, too. The look in the eyes . . ."

"How could you possibly get close enough to one to look in its eyes?"

He hesitated. "I've made them a lifelong study," he said at last.

She had a strong sense that he was keeping something back. "Why, Barry? Why seal-people in particular?"

Instead of answering, he asked her a question. "Aren't you curious as to what turns a human into one of the Ron?"

"Why . . . yes, I suppose I am. Do you know?" She took her eyes off the road long enough to glance at him for a moment.

His freckled face wore an expression of sadness. "I told you the Ron were operating under an enchantment. In a few instances it is whispered they have actively sought the enchantment, bringing it upon themselves by choice for whatever reason. Perhaps the life of a seal lying fat and lazy in the sun seemed preferable, to some overworked farmer locked in his own life of drudgery. If he could find a witch who had access to ancient sorceries, he could escape.

"But a curse called down in anger is the usual way one becomes one of the seal-people. A person so cursed is a tragic figure, I think; an outcast from the society in which he was born. He—or she—must watch from a distance, while life goes on without him."

"Rather like the Flying Dutchman," Eileen said.

"Now that," Barry Hynes replied with conviction, "*is* a myth."

"But the Ron are real?"

"Oh yes."

"How can you be so sure?"

Eileen's question resulted in another discovery. An Irishman would prefer to tell a story in a pub rather than in an automobile. It was not until she and Barry were ensconced in his "local," or favorite watering hole, with a pint of Guinness as rich and dark as velvet in front of each of them, that he was willing to divulge his personal involvement with the Ron.

She had to admit the story sounded better with the right atmosphere.

"I grew up on a small-holding not a million miles away," Barry began, taking a deep and appreciative drink from his glass. "My parents had one cottage, my aunt and her husband had the cottage just across the road. The two families were close, as people are in rural Ireland. They knew everything about each other.

"Almost everything," he added reflectively, taking another drink.

Eileen sipped from her own glass. Though the thick collar of foam on the Guinness looked like whipped cream, the stout beneath it was bitter and curiously refreshing.

"My aunt had married a much older man; I gather she had been pressured into it by her family, who thought she was running a bit wild. They seemed happy enough by all accounts, but after a few years her husband became seriously ill. He was away in hospital for a while, then she brought him home to die. It took him a long time to die, however. Eventually the neighbors stopped calling in to see how he was. It looked like Uncle Frank might live forever, a helpless invalid. The only person who continued to call—religiously, you might say—was the parish priest, Father . . . well, never mind his name. Suffice it to say he visited my aunt every day, rain or shine.

"And her husband lying paralyzed and useless in the bed upstairs."

Eileen almost choked on a mouthful of Guinness. "Do you mean he was . . . they were . . ."

Barry nodded. "I mean the priest comforted my aunt to the extent of getting her pregnant. This was the rural Ireland of thirty-five years ago, mind you, and it was a great scandal. When Uncle Frank could bear it no longer he conveniently died, leaving a bit of insurance, but that was not the help his widow needed most.

"She went to the bishop, so family legend goes, and demanded that he release the priest from his vows so he could marry her and be a father to his child. But the bishop refused.

"Then she begged the priest to run away with her, defy convention and live openly with her, but he refused. He even intimated someone else might be responsible for her condition.

"This is my father's sister we're talking about, a strong woman with a temper. My father had the same temper, you'd not care to cross him. When her lover rejected her, Aunt Mary resolved to bring down a curse upon him in the old way. She was what the local people call 'wise' and her knowledge of magic and Celtic spells had been passed down to her from generations of ancestors on the west coast of Ireland.

"One day close to the summer solstice, a time of potent magic, Aunt Mary somehow persuaded her priest to go out in a boat with her. They were well out on the bay when she went into labor. At the same time, a storm blew up. Storms on the bay can be very sudden and savage. As the priest struggled to keep the boat afloat, my aunt gave birth to a son. Then she called on Manannan Mac Lir, the

ancient Irish god of the sea, to punish the man who had
sired her child.

"Having the priest in the boat made him vulnerable to
Manannan, but Aunt Mary was forgetting the powers
possessed by a man of the cloth. While she was calling
down Manannan's curse upon him, and thunder rolled
across Galway Bay, the frightened priest began to cry
aloud to his God for forgiveness."

Eileen sat frozen as Barry's narrative drew toward its
inevitable conclusion. She forgot all about her pint of
Guinness. In her mind's eye she was watching a small
boat on the raging bay, with a woman screaming a pagan
curse while she held a newborn infant in her arms, and a
priest kneeling in the bottom of the boat frantically pray-
ing to the heavens for mercy.

"What happened to them?" Eileen whispered.

"No one knows for certain, but at some time during the
storm the priest fell overboard. When his body washed
ashore days later it was terribly burned; the authorities
concluded he'd been struck by lightning. Aunt Mary and
the baby were miraculously untouched, however, and
were subsequently rescued. No one could make much
sense out of her ravings; she was put into a mental hospital for a while, but after a few months they released her
and let her go home to raise the boy.

"Throughout my childhood I remember them living
just across the road, shunned by everyone except my
mother, who sneaked over to see them sometimes."

Eileen's eyes were huge. "What a dreadful story! No
wonder you grew up with an interest in the old tales, in
folklore and . . . where do the Ron come into this, Barry?
You said you had a personal connection with them."

"I do," he replied softly. "The curse my aunt called
down upon the priest was meant to place him under an
enchantment which would not be broken until he atoned
for what he had done to her. She implored Manannan

Mac Lir to turn him into one of the Ron. But he died before the curse could take effect, and his desperate prayers deflected the curse onto another victim instead. She could not undo it; she could only cast spells, not break them.

"My aunt's newborn son fell victim to the enchantment meant for his father. I know; I grew up just across the road from him.

"My own cousin is one of the seal-people."

chapter 4

So captured was Eileen by the spell the Irishman wove, that she could not shake it off. Even after she had returned him to his apartment—and smilingly declined an invitation to dinner, pleading exhaustion—she kept envisioning the scene in the boat all those years ago.

Yet she knew it was only a story. How could it be otherwise?

This was not ancient Ireland but a modern nation, a member of the European Union, with jet airports and cable television and computer industries.

Wasn't it?

Having refused Barry's offer of dinner, Eileen ate a solitary meal in a brightly lit, tile-walled, fish-and-chip shop within walking distance of her B & B. She took the paperback omnibus out of her handbag and read snatches from it as she ate, allowing her mind to wander without having to keep up conversation with a dinner partner.

Eileen felt, as she had so often felt these past few months, that she would rather be alone than with anyone. Since Bob, she had been sinking into a gentle melancholy that was becoming increasingly comfortable. The day's adventure, if one could call it that, with Barry Hynes had been too much; too much fresh air, too much excitement, too much like taking part in life.

She wanted to stand aside from life instead, out of harm's way.

Or perhaps she was just tired.

Very tired. Tired to the depths of her soul.

"The rigors of travel are catching up with you, my girl," she told herself as she toyed with the remains of her "chips"—French fries in the States. "It's back to the Moores and an early night for you."

In spite of her good intentions, however, she found herself wandering down toward the bay instead, lured by a soft warm wind and the onset of twilight. Turning her back on the harsh lights of the amusement arcade and the noise of a group of teenagers racing their motorbikes up and down the road, she left the sidewalk and picked her way down across the stony beach. From time to time bent to pick up a glittering fragment of quartz, or examine a frond of seaweed.

Eileen had never really looked at seaweed before. The tide cast it onto the shore in a hundred different shapes, from something as delicate as an asparagus fern to great racks of leathery branches like antlers, redolent of iodine. She examined the latter curiously, and when she dropped them found herself licking the salt taste from her fingers with a curious hunger.

Her feet kept carrying her toward the water as if they had a will of their own.

He had been watching her ever since she left the bed-and-breakfast, content as long as she stayed within his range. If she left the area of Galway Bay it would be more difficult; he could not follow her far, unless she kept to the coastline.

But she was a tourist and an American. Probably she would

want to go to Dublin sooner or later, which would mean going straight across the country. Away from the Atlantic.

He must act before that could happen. Once he was certain, really certain, that she was the one, he would have to make his move.

Would she be frightened? Probably. Nothing in her world could have prepared her for his.

If he had possessed an ordinary human conscience he would have had qualms about what he was planning. Yet a great silent need in her had called out to the great silent need in him, and he must answer at whatever cost to them both.

He must follow her, watching her, until the time was right.

Eileen stood for a long time at water's edge, letting herself experience the sea. America seemed very far away. Even the nearby town of Galway did not intrude itself on her awareness; there was only the bay, the great, gently heaving presence of the sea lying in the half-embrace of the land like a lover in the bend of the loved one's arm.

The water hissed softly as it ran in to the shore. Tiny waves left crescents of white foam, like Irish lace, like the foam in a glass of Guinness, on the stones at Eileen's feet.

Lace on the hem of Manannan Mac Lir's robe, she thought to herself. The fanciful imagery surprised her.

Eileen tensed, staring out across the water. Almost at the farthest reaches of her vision was a small black circle rising above the waves. Something about the size of a human head. Though she could not make out any features, she was somehow certain it was looking at her.

I should be afraid, she thought, and was surprised to find she felt no fear at all. Her only emotion was an irresistible curiosity.

Balancing on one leg, she stripped off her shoe and sock from the other foot, then reversed the process. Without looking, she tossed her footgear and handbag onto the beach behind her and began wading into the water.

It was icy cold; her common sense told her it was icy cold. Yet it seemed as if there was the thinnest cushion of warmed air between her bare flesh and the water. She did not feel the cold. She felt wonderfully insulated from all discomfort . . . from all unhappiness . . .

Eileen waded farther, smiling.

He watched her. It was not time to go to her and claim her, not yet. She must take the first steps on her own. She must make the choice. But he could call to her, he could do that much. From the depths of his being he could gather all his longing and loneliness and hurl them through the space between. If she was the one for whom he had waited so long she would hear him; she would respond. What she did in the next few moments would tell him all he needed to know.

He gathered himself, holding his breath, while she took another step.

And then another.

Someone was shouting at her. Someone was running down the beach and splashing into the water, yelling, but she would not turn around. Whoever it was had nothing to do with her. She hurried deeper into the water, feeling the rocky shelf fall away under her feet. In another moment she would have to swim.

A male voice shouted right behind her and a hand clamped, hard, on her shoulder, pulling her backward. She tried to fight it off, but the hand and the force behind it were too strong. Eileen half-turned to face her attacker, at the same time struggling to keep her feet under her and get some sort of purchase with her toes on the seabed.

But she had gone too far. She tumbled backward into a gulf of water with no floor to stand upon, no solid surface at all. At the same moment the man shifted his grip to try and get a better hold on her, and she fell away from him, falling free into black water.

The sea closed over her head.

For one heartbeat she made no effort to save herself. As if she had always known this was what she intended, she surrendered to the water without a struggle.

Then her body took over, fighting for itself. Her arms thrashed, her legs kicked, almost against her will she churned toward the surface, gasping and spluttering when her head broke into the open air.

And he caught her.

Eileen tried to scream, but her mouth and throat were full of water. As she choked he began dragging her relentlessly toward the shore.

A desperate frenzy seized her. She had never been raped in a New York alley but she knew women who had; she had listened with dry mouth and pounding heart to their stories, trying to imagine what she would do. Use karate, a knife, mace? Scream for help or surrender to save her life?

Now she discovered what she would do. She fought with all the strength she possessed.

But her attacker was stronger. He dragged her up onto the beach and threw her down like a sack of potatoes, then crouched over her.

"Missus, missus! Are you all right? Merciful hour, what were yez tryin' to do to yerself out there?"

The voice was so young it cracked in midsentence.

Eileen opened her eyes, blinking with the sting of salt water. A boy in his late teens crouched anxiously over her. Seawater was running off his sodden leather motorcycle jacket. A cluster of his pals gathered around them,

staring down at the spectacle of their friend and the sui-
cide he had rescued from Galway Bay.

"Yer a bleedin' hero, Mickey," one of them breathed in
admiration.

Eileen had never been so embarrassed in her life.

Some time later she returned to the Moores' B & B,
only to have to explain all over again to her host and hostess, who were understandably upset at having one of
their guests delivered to them in a police car with a blanket wrapped around her shoulders.

"I wasn't trying to kill myself, I would never do such a
thing," she reiterated after the policemen left. "That boy
misunderstood. I was just wading out into the water—
and why shouldn't I? I didn't see any signs prohibiting it.
Isn't that what people do at a beach?

"But this young lunatic saw me and came running out
to 'save' me. In point of fact, he nearly got me drowned
instead. He frightened me, coming at me like that, and I
fell off the shelving into deep water.

"I tried to explain it all to the police, the . . . what do
you call them here?"

"The Garda Siochana," Malachy Moore said as his wife
pressed a hot whiskey into Eileen's hand. "Guardians of
the Peace, which you disrupted for certain tonight."

"Ah, but are they not used to the ways of tourists?" Mrs.
Moore asked in her soft little voice, as if Eileen was some
strange species of animal in a zoo whose habits were
being discussed by normal folk.

Eileen gulped the whiskey, letting it burn on the back
of her throat. "It was all a misunderstanding," she said
again, biting back anger. Who were these people to judge
her?

Then she looked at their gentle, concerned faces and
was instantly sorry. They only meant well. The teenager

who had run into the sea after her only meant well, abandoning his motorbike in the middle of the road to risk his life, or so he thought, for a stranger.

It had taken a great deal of self-control to watch without interfering, but he could not claim her yet. This he knew. The rules of magic which bound him were as inexorable as the tides of the sea.

When she disappeared from his view behind walls, he waited. He must be content with waiting. For now. He must be as deep and patient as the sea.

That night Eileen lay sleepless in her bed, trying to sort through her tangled thoughts and emotions. In spite of what she told the police and the Moores, she was not certain of the motivation behind her actions. She had seemed to be in a trance, almost, acting without conscious volition.

Was it possible I did mean to kill myself? she wondered as she lay wide-eyed in the night, staring at the blank rectangle of the window beyond her bed.

The thought was frightening, but she could not dismiss it totally. If nothing else it was an indication of the depth of her unhappiness, which she had tried to keep hidden even from herself.

Swinging her legs over the side of the bed, she got up and padded to the window. Lace curtains hanging on either side did not obscure her view of the bay with the moon floating serenely above, framed by wispy clouds.

By moonlight Ireland was still the magical land of thatched cottages and harp music. Manannan Mac Lir and seal-people. Ancient curses. Modern apartments. Leather-jacketed boys on motorbikes and bitterness and mistrust and loneliness . . .

With an impatient gesture Eileen drew the lace curtains across the window, shutting out the view of Galway Bay.

chapter 5

In the morning, by the cold light of an overcast day, Eileen took a serious look at herself in the mirror above the little mahogany dressing table.

"Perhaps you should go home," she told the face she saw reflected there. The skin looked wan and drawn, the eyes weary.

"Ireland may not be safe for you," she warned herself. "You're too far away from everything you know. You should go back to New York and find yourself a good therapist, even if it means selling the shop. You can always start again later, when you have your feet under you."

Have your feet under you . . . a memory returned of herself wading senselessly out into the bay, and the feeling of the world suddenly dropping out from under her as she stepped off the shelving and sank into deep water.

"Definitely, Eileen Costello!" she said aloud. "Go home. Now!"

But when she fumbled in her handbag and got out her ticket, she read a warning that changing her flight would involve a penalty.

She sat on the edge of the bed and held the ticket in her hand for a long time, staring into space. She could ring the airline and see just how much the penalty would be.

Surely not very much; not more than she could afford, if she went back to New York immediately and spent no more money in Ireland.

But she did not ring the airline. After a time she put the ticket away, finished dressing and went out.

She found a day of soft rain quite unlike New York rain. Instead of individual droplets the air simply oozed moisture, like water being gently squeezed from a sponge. No one, Eileen noticed, was carrying an open umbrella.

It seemed like a good day to finish her tour of the Galway shops, checking out a number she had noticed earlier but not taken time to enter. At the back of Eileen's mind was the thought that tomorrow she would drive on, perhaps—make her way down to Killarney. Or over to Dublin. She had no particular itinerary, having decided when she planned this trip to leave most of her time open.

She had longed for freedom from plans and pressure. Now she had that freedom. But it was hard to know just what to do with it. She thought about talking with Barry Hynes and asking for his suggestions. It would seem rude to vanish without at least speaking to him again.

She spent her morning shopping, then collected her car from the bed-and-breakfast and drove over to his apartment building. It occurred to her that she might have walked, the distance was not so great. Everyone seemed to walk, a car was almost an inconvenience.

Americans, Eileen reflected sourly, drive everywhere, then spend a fortune on exercise classes. In Ireland the only fat people you see are tourists.

When she reached Barry's apartment she was disappointed that no one answered her ring on the doorbell. She was just turning away when an upstairs window opened and a head popped out. "Sorry?" called a woman's voice.

"I was looking for Barry Hynes."

"Ah, he's gone out to the mother's. You'll find him there. Do you know the way?"

"I don't but . . ." Before Eileen could explain that she had no intention of going to his parents' house, the woman in the upstairs window went rattling on giving directions.

"Why, I know where that is!" Eileen cried in surprise. "I drove out that road the other night looking for a restaurant."

"Then off with you now. He'll be that glad to see you and to show off his visitor from Amerikay." The window banged shut.

I'll do no such thing, Eileen thought to herself. What would Barry think of me showing up unannounced and uninvited on his parents' doorstep?

The pervasive damp had grown damper, almost qualifying as real rain. Eileen returned to the B & B, uncertain what she wanted to do next. She only knew she did not want to stay indoors, did not want to sit in the lounge in front of a coal fire and endure the feeling of life passing her by. That was all right for the Moores, who were old.

But she was young.

Youngish.

And the blood still ran warm in her veins.

When she went to her room to change into dry clothes Mrs. Moore waylaid her in the hall. "You aren't going back out without taking a bite of something, sure you're not," the woman said with conviction. "And yourself not eating any breakfast!" She clucked her tongue in motherly disapproval.

At the thought of the huge meal she had avoided by leaving the B & B early, Eileen groaned inwardly. "I couldn't eat a thing, really, Mrs. Moore. I'm not hungry."

"No wonder you're so thin! There's not a pick o'meat on your bones."

Eileen was astonished. "In America I'm too fat, I'm always dieting."

"Well this is Ireland, and here we'd call you too thin. You wait right there now while I go in the kitchen and make you some nice soup and sandwiches. And I have a nice apple tart—with some cream?"

With a great deal of effort, Eileen managed to talk Mrs. Moore out of feeding her a meal that would have left her overstuffed and drowsy for most of the day. People in Ireland were relentlessly hospitable. It seemed to be part of the national character; even shopkeepers in Galway urged a cup of tea and a plate of cookies on customers if there was not a crowd in the shop. Perhaps, Eileen thought to herself, she should have gone out and met Barry's parents. They might genuinely have enjoyed welcoming the visitor from America.

But there was no point in encouraging anything there. She was not the least bit interested in the man; only in the glimpse he had given her of Irish magic and folklore. She found herself thinking again of the seal-people, the Ron, and the strange tale of the woman and the priest.

She put the car in gear and began to drive.

The road she had followed two nights before was easy to find. Yes, there was the pub, and beyond it Teach na Dalaigh. A mile or so farther on she came to a crossroads set amid stone-bordered fields, with the gleam of the bay plainly visible in the distance. A pair of cottages faced each other across the road; cottages with thatched roofs, and a bicycle leaning against the gate of one. The name on the gate said, Hynes.

But it was the other cottage that drew and held Eileen's attention. No name identified it; if Barry's tale were true, it was probably shunned locally. There were indications of occupancy, however. Curtains at the windows, smoke coming from the chimney, that achingly nostalgic scent she had already learned was the smell of burning peat.

It seemed strangely fitting that a woman who had borne a child to a priest, and then supposedly lost that child to an ancient curse, should live in a thatched cottage and burn peat in her fireplace.

Eileen sat in her car and gazed at the house, trying to will herself into some knowledge of the life lived inside. This was far removed indeed from her experience. If she ignored the car surrounding her she might have been in the Ireland of a hundred years ago. No modern sights intruded, there were not even telephone wires overhead.

Just silence and the soft rain gleaming on the golden thatch of the cottage roof.

A movement at the corner of her vision caught her eye and she glanced around in time to see a curtain fall back in place at one of the Hynes's windows. Eileen suddenly felt guilty, as if she had been caught spying. Hurriedly she put the car in gear and drove off.

She had gone another mile down the road before common sense took over and she realized she must have looked even guiltier for driving away like that. Barry, if it had been Barry peering at her through the window, must think by now that Americans were very odd indeed.

She had almost persuaded herself to turn around and go back when she noticed a tiny shop at the side of the road, half-hidden by a broken stone wall and a tangle of briars. "Country Crafts," announced the hand-lettered sign over the bright blue door.

On impulse Eileen parked and went in, and was delighted to see it was just the sort of place she had hoped to discover. Small, dusty, packed from wall to wall and floor to ceiling with bits of authentic Irish country furniture and bric-a-brac. Hand-carved pine cradles nestled beside massive cupboards. Yellowing Limerick lace, fine as cobwebs, was draped over blanket chests and the backs of sugan chairs. A massive copper washtub held a precarious stack of rare lustre ware and fine sponge ware.

There was no sign of a proprietor. Astonished that any-one would leave such a treasure trove unlocked, Eileen made her way around the room, exclaiming under her breath at one discovery after another.

Then she saw the seals.

A shallow pine cabinet held shelf after shelf of them, tiny carved figures of some dark, glossy substance that Eileen's tapping fingernail confirmed as too hard for wood. Each little seal was different, with unique features in an expressive face.

They looked almost human.

As she stared at them, bemused, someone cleared their throat behind her.

Eileen turned, half-expecting to find such a shop pre-sided over by a wizened crone with the features of a be-nevolent witch. Instead she found herself facing a lovely woman with a glowing Irish complexion and a mop of lustrous brown curls. "Are you interested in animal carv-ings?" she inquired.

"Not particularly," Eileen replied. "I mean, I'm inter-ested in all sorts of crafts, but . . . these are seals, aren't they?"

"They are," the shopkeeper confirmed. "They're bog oak, semipetrified wood taken from the peat bogs and carved in Galway by a local artist."

Looking at the faces of the seal figures, Eileen said, "Are they supposed to represent the Ron by any chance?"

The other woman stiffened perceptibly. "What do you know about the Ron?"

"A charming man named Barry Hynes was telling me about them. He's a professor of . . ."

"I know Barry," the shopkeeper interrupted in the un-mistakable tone one woman uses to warn another woman off her preserve. "We practically grew up together. And I cannot imagine him discussing the Ron with a stranger."

Oh dear, thought Eileen. Even though she had no interest in the redheaded man she felt a sudden wrench, a sense of yet another door being slammed in her face.

"I only met him the other day," she emphasized.

"I see."

"We got to talking about folklore, and he happened to mention the Ron together with all sorts of other things, banshees and pookas and . . ."

"I see," the other woman said again as if she did not believe a word. Then responding to the distress in Eileen's face, her tone softened. "I'm sorry, I didn't mean to sound so abrupt. It's just unusual to have an American wander in here in the first place, and then to have you know about the Ron, and Barry—I was just surprised, that's all.

"Forgive me," she added, holding out her hand. "My name is Moya Hennessey and I'm not at all the monster you must think me."

The abrupt change disarmed Eileen completely. Before she knew what was happening, she found herself seated at a tiny table at the rear of the shop, sharing tea poured from a Georgian silver teapot while Moya Hennessey chatted about Irish weather, country furniture, her own holiday in America two years before, and, at last, local legends.

"The stories about the seal-people go back centuries," she told Eileen. "There is a long history of sealing on the west coast of Ireland, both for fur and oil. But if you've ever seen a seal up close you know how appealing they are: those huge liquid eyes are as innocent as a child's, they would break your heart. Perhaps that was the start of the legend, the idea that human souls were trapped inside those bodies."

"Ron referred to them as Mary's Whelps."

"That's one version of the tale, the belief that they are under the special protection of the Virgin Mother. In Ireland it's helped save them from the worst of the slaughter their species has endured elsewhere, I think.

"But the best known story about the Ron is the one about the skin. Supposedly the seal-people, on certain moonlit nights, meet on the land and take off their sealskins so they can dance in their human form. It is said that a man fell in love with a maiden he saw dancing and stole her sealskin, so she couldn't return to the sea. She married him and bore him children and they lived quite happily together, until one day she found the skin he had hidden away behind a stone in the wall. The heart inside her broke with longing for the sea at that moment, and she put on her skin and went into the water with her babes in her arms. He never saw any of them again."

Eileen had been watching Moya's face with fascination during this recital. "You believe it?"

The Irish woman dropped her eyes. "I don't disbelieve," she said, as Barry had done.

"And this story Barry told me about his aunt—you know the one? Do you think it could be true?"

Moya met Eileen's eyes with a strange, intense stare. "He told you that too, did he? About the curse?"

"He told me that the woman who called down Manannan's curse did not mean the enchantment to be broken until the priest made up for what he had done to her. But when he was apparently struck by lightning and died, Manannan . . ." Eileen paused. It sounded too improbable, in this cozy, warmly lit shop with a steaming cup of tea in front of her.

Moya finished for her, "When the priest died, Manannan Mac Lir's enchantment fell on the newborn baby instead. Indeed."

"Barry's cousin?"

Again that strange, intense stare. "Is that what he told you? That it was his . . . cousin . . . who became one of the Ron?"

Eileen felt a cold finger draw a line up her spine. "Wasn't it? What are you trying to say? Was it Barry himself?"

Moya's gaze held hers, letting the idea sink in.

Eileen wanted to laugh. In America no one would think of trying to convince her of such a mad notion.

But here in Ireland—with the rain drumming softly on the roof and the dust of centuries lying thickly around them—

"The Ron are drawn to humankind," Moya was saying. "At least some of them are. They are able to shed their skins and spend long periods of time among land-people, although eventually they have to return to the sea. If the priest's son can find a human woman who will love him, and with whom he can atone for the wrong his father did his mother, then he may be able to throw off the enchantment and live the rest of his life as a normal man."

Moya's eyes bored into Eileen's. "The love he would offer a mortal woman would be very special, you must understand. The exact opposite of his father's. Instead of rejection and betrayal, absolute and total devotion every minute of every hour of every day. Only that would balance the scales."

"I should think any woman would be overjoyed to have such a love," Eileen replied feelingly.

"Really? There are some who might feel smothered by it. This is the twentieth century, after all. Women, even in Ireland, are no longer mere extensions of their men. Some of us work, some of us have businesses of our own and lives of our own and would be reluctant to give them up."

Eileen nodded. "I suppose so."

"I should think you as an American would understand better than most."

Suddenly Eileen did understand. The version of the story that Moya had just told was specifically crafted to

frighten her off, to make her forget about Barry Hynes—
whom she had never wanted anyway! She almost
laughed. But part of her was angry at the presumption of
this total stranger, who thought, with tea and fairy tales,
to bewitch her.

She stood up. "Thank you for the tea, and for your
time," she said coolly. "I appreciate both, but I must be
going. I would like to buy one of those—what did you call
them? Bog oak?—seals if I may, as a memento of this afternoon. How much are they?" She was already opening
her handbag.

It was as if a glass wall had been dropped between the
two women. Politely, Moya accompanied her to the cabinet of seals to make her selection. Politely, Eileen paid for
it, waiting while Moya produced change for her traveler's
check. Then they smiled, exchanged a few meaningless
pleasantries, and Eileen found herself outside the shop
with a small paper-wrapped parcel clutched in her sweat-
ing palm.

"The nerve of that woman!" she muttered to herself as
she got into the car. She dropped the wrapped figurine
on the seat beside her and put the automobile in gear.

If nothing else, the peculiar exchange and the anger it
engendered had stimulated her appetite. As she drove
back toward Galway she resolved to keep an eye out for
Teach na Dalaigh.

When she drove through the crossroads with the two
thatched cottages, she kept her eyes straight ahead and
looked at neither one of them, though she was aware that
the bicycle no longer leaned against the gate marked
Hynes.

chapter 6

As she approached Teach na Dalaigh, Eileen glanced at the clock on the dashboard. The watch she used to wear had been a gift from Bob; it had been left behind in New York, pushed to the back of a bureau drawer.

It was really too early for dinner, she decided. But when the familiar mustard-colored building loomed on her right she slowed down and turned into the parking lot.

There were no other cars.

The front door of the restaurant was ajar, however, and she caught a glimpse of someone moving around inside.

Teach na Dalaigh was open for business.

When Eileen got out of the car she glanced automatically toward the water. Galway certainly was the kingdom of Manannan Mac Lir. Even when she could not see the bay she was aware of its dampness in the air, its light reflected against the sky.

No wonder Mrs. Daly specialized in seafood.

Suddenly Eileen was ravenously hungry. To her delight, marvelous smells were wafting through the open doorway of the little restaurant, odors that might have been tailor-made to tantalize her particular tastebuds.

"Mrs. Daly must be a mindreader," she murmured to herself as she locked the car.

Then she realized she was probably being foolish; why lock a rented car with nothing in it, in a deserted parking lot on an empty country road? It seemed a paranoid, American thing to do.

With a twist of her wrist, as if to announce defiantly that she was in Ireland now and had nothing to fear, Eileen unlocked the car door again. Then she went into Teach na Dalaigh.

The restaurant was just as she remembered. So was Mrs. Daly, bustling forward to welcome her as if they were old friends. "And will you be wanting your usual table?" the gray-haired woman inquired.

Eileen smiled. My usual table. She liked the phrase; it indicated an established presence, a permanence. She belonged here.

Barry Hynes had called his favorite pub "my local," she recalled, summoning that same image of territorialism.

These are not rootless Americans, Eileen reminded herself as she sat down at "her usual table." People in Ireland have a sense of place. Many of them have lived within a ten-mile radius for generations, gone to the same churches, the same schools; learned the same legends their great-grandparents knew.

On impulse, Eileen said to Mrs. Daly as the woman stood beside her table, "Have you always lived in this area?"

"I have indeed. Born just down the road, I was, and when I die my bones will go into the earth just up the road in the churchyard."

Eileen felt a wave of envy. "I lived in seven cities before I was ten years old," she confided. "My father was a chemical engineer and his work took him from California to Connecticut. When he died we buried him in Salt Lake

City, but when my mother dies I suppose she'll be buried in Boston."

"And yourself, where is your home?"

"I live in New York for now. I don't really have anyplace I call home. I chose New York, I suppose, because there are so few native New Yorkers; everyone there is from someplace else, like me."

Mrs. Daly shook her head pityingly. "Ye poor things," she commiserated.

Eileen managed a bright smile. "Oh it's wonderful, really. I love New York. It's very exciting."

"Is it excitement you're wanting? You should be out on the bay with a storm blowing in from the ocean; now that's exciting," Mrs. Daly told her. "Just yourself and God out there and Himself not watching."

Eileen puzzled over that last remark as she chose her meal. Mrs. Daly had not complained of the hour, but assured Eileen, "I'll cook up whatever you want, it just takes a bit of time. But the Lord must love time, He made so much of it."

As before, Eileen wandered out to enjoy the view while she waited for her meal. The rain had stopped, leaving Ireland drenched and sparkling, its multitude of greens so intense they hurt the eye. Even the air smelled green. When a breeze came up and stirred the leaves one could easily imagine a tiny man in a little green suit scurrying through the bushes.

"Leprechauns," Eileen said to herself, smiling.

Warm wind ruffled the surface of the reed-hemmed inlet. In the distance a fish leaped, falling back into the water with a slap. The soft gray overcast had been replaced by a dazzling blue sky, fresh-washed, with a bank of brilliant white clouds to the southwest looking like an Armada in full sail.

Eileen's imagination leaped like the fish, recalling some of the stories she had read in the omnibus of folklore. How easy it was, in such a setting, to believe them all true.

But they weren't true, American common sense asserted. "Don't keep falling under Ireland's spell," she warned herself. "Snap out of it!"

She resolved to leave Galway in the morning; pack her things into her rented car and set off in some other direction, anywhere as long as it was away from the bay. Explore other parts of Ireland, buy things for the shop, go home.

Go back to New York. Away from the seductions that fed on the imagination of a lonely, unhappy woman.

As she turned and strode purposefully into the restaurant, she did not notice the sleek dark head rise above the surface of the water and fix soulful eyes on her back.

She was making it easy for him. She stayed within sight of the water, either the bay or one of its countless tributaries and inlets.

He was beginning to be sure of her, certain she was the one.

With difficulty he had resisted the temptation to seize her when she waded into the bay. She was not ready yet; not quite, as her subsequent reactions showed. He must not force her.

But oh, the waiting was hard!

Even among his own kind he was singular, marked by the confusion that had distorted his enchanting. The others pitied him. They were content with their lot, most of them, only occasionally yearning for a landlife. But he ached every waking moment for the existence he had been denied from birth.

The time he was able to spend out of the water was a rapturous torment to him, rapturous in that it gave him a semblance of normalcy for a while, and tortured because it showed him what his life could have been like. When the change began in the cells of his body and he knew he must return to the water or die, he sometimes shook his human fists at Galway Bay and cursed Manannan, but that was as futile as cursing the sea itself.

The ancient gods were indifferent to human emotions. They had no more conscience than the elements, being woven from the same threads of creation in the dawn of the world. They could be placated, and manipulated to a very limited extent, because they too were controlled by specific and irrevocable natural laws . . . but not the same laws as those for human beings.

Caught between two eras and two worlds, the Ron must make a choice. Most of them opted for the old way, living out incredibly long but not immortal lives in that version of paradise still inhabited by the animals, when man does not trespass with his cruelty and killing.

Only a few wanted to escape enough to do anything about it.

He did. He thought of little else. He had devoted a lifetime to learning everything he could about ancient legend, ancient magic, in hopes of finding the key that would set him free.

Then when he did find it, he discovered it would require someone else.

For a long time he had despaired of finding her. He could not simply take what he wanted as his father had done before him. To break the enchantment he must be as generous as the priest had been selfish; he must give to the woman what she wanted most.

That was the secret; she had to want what he could offer, want it more than anything else in the world.

He had tried before, with other women. In the beginning he had been overeager, even desperate, and made mistakes. Had it not been for the help of his few friends he would have, in his darkest days, gone seeking release from a sealer-hunter's club.

Yet he had hung on somehow, waiting. And now she was here.

He must be very careful. If he frightened her away there might never be another so perfect for him.

But it was getting harder to control himself.

When Eileen finished her meal, she took the last bit of bread from her plate and wiped up the few smears of sauce that were all that remained from a salmon poached to perfection. "If I ate like this every day, in a month I would weigh a ton," she remarked to Mrs. Daly as the woman began clearing the table.

"Not at all, child. It would do you good to put some flesh on your bones, the winters are cold here when the wind comes roaring off the sea."

"I'm afraid I won't be here in the winter," Eileen replied. "So I won't need that extra insulation."

The older woman asked, with what sounded like genuine regret, "You're leaving us, then? It's sorry I am to hear it."

"I have to, I'm just here on vacation. If I'm going to see more of Ireland than just Galway Bay, I'd better get started. I plan to go in the morning."

"And where would you be going?"

"Ah . . . Dublin, I suppose," Eileen said, offering the first name that came into her head.

Mrs. Daly assured her, "You won't get fresh seafood as good as this in Dublin, you know."

Eileen smiled. "I suspect you're right."

To the delight of Mrs. Daly she ordered a second helping of dulsc pudding. "Hang the calories," she muttered to herself. "I'll never have this again, so why not enjoy it while I have the chance?" Even in New York she had never seen the seaweed concoction on any menu. It looked rather like a blancmange, but tasted like a creamy blend of delicate, exotic fruits that lay sweetly on the palate without being cloying. "I don't suppose you'd give me the recipe?" she asked her hostess.

"'Twould do you no good, you can't make that anywhere but here, with dulsc gathered fresh on the beach in the morning. Ah, you'll find a lot of things in Ireland you'll find nowhere else," the woman added.

Even when the food was gone and she had drunk more coffee than was good for her, Eileen found herself lingering in the soothing atmosphere of Teach na Dalaigh. She had no sense of time passing. It was like being underwater, drifting along in a flickering light. For a second time she had to force herself to leave.

After Eileen paid her bill the two women chatted for a while, then Mrs. Daly walked with her to the door. The older woman did not venture outside, however. Instead she looked left and then right, as if watching for more customers. But the only car in the parking lot was Eileen's rental.

And astonishingly, twilight had fallen. Eileen turned to Mrs. Daly in disbelief. "Have you got the time? I couldn't have been inside for so long!"

"Ah sure, I never wear a watch. They won't run on me."

"It's so much later than I thought it was, I really must be going," Eileen said. She waved good-bye as to a friend, and watched Mrs. Daly go back inside the restaurant. Then she got into the car, shut the door, fastened her seat belt. Looked at the clock on the dash and discovered it was indeed evening.

Glanced down to find the small parcel still waiting on the seat beside her.

Suddenly she thought of offering the carved seal to Mrs. Daly as a way of saying thank you for her hospitality. She was out of the car and approaching the restaurant with the package in her hand before she realized, ruefully, that every household in the area must contain at least one of the bog-oak figures already. From her own experience artisans sold their wares to all their neighbors before venturing out into the wider market.

She did not really want the figure either, she admitted to herself. She had only purchased it to get past the awkwardness of the moment with Moya Hennessey. The human expression carved onto the seal's face was too wistful, reminding her of terrible images on television, gangs of men clubbing helpless baby seals to death on bloodstained snow. As much as she loved animals and nature programs, those were pictures she could never watch.

On a sudden impulse, she walked across the road and hurled the bog-oak seal as far out into the water as she could.

The water leaped upward to catch it.

Eileen gasped and clapped her hand over her mouth. Her heart was beating wildly in her throat, choking her. For a moment she thought she would faint. She screwed her eyes shut as if to negate what she had seen, then opened them again.

The water in the inlet lay calm and shining, undisturbed.

"Nervous breakdown," the frightened woman whispered to herself. "I'm building up to a nervous breakdown."

She hurried to her car and fled back to her B & B as if pursued by demons.

chapter 7

Eileen could hardly wait to get to her room and collapse on the bed. But the Moores, who appeared determined to treat her like a personal friend instead of a paying guest, met her in the lounge and pressed a glass of sherry into her hand before she could frame a polite protest.

"What a wretched day it is," Malachy Moore said. "Not fine weather at all, you'll be getting the wrong idea of Irish weather entirely."

His wife spoke up in her soft little voice. "She'll be getting the right idea of Irish weather entirely. You have to love rain to love Ireland."

"I love the rain," Eileen told them. "I used to go walking in the rain when I was a child, it always made me feel good."

"And are you feeling well now?" Malachy asked. "After your adventure in the sea the other evening?"

Everyone seemed concerned about her health. Does it show? Eileen wondered. Do other people think I'm about to fall apart?

She assured the Moores, "I'm fine, I really am. You've been wonderful to me and I'm grateful."

They beamed at her like two solicitous leprechauns. It would be hard to leave them, too. But she must go.

She must.

An increasing sense of urgency gripped her, as if black clouds were massing on the horizon, and she must get away before the storm broke over her head. By the time she was able to escape to her own room, her nervousness had increased until her hands were shaking. Had it not been so late in the day, she would have thrown her suitcase into the car and fled.

But that was foolish. She had no place in particular to go and no one expecting her, she had not booked any accommodations for herself beyond Galway. It made sense to wait until morning. "Only a hysterical woman on the brink of a nervous breakdown would run off in the night for no reason," Eileen told herself sternly. "And that isn't me."

She undressed and put on the flannelette nightgown she wore when she felt in particular need of comfort. Switching on the lamp on the bedside table, she got into bed and settled down to read. She had bought some magazines and she reached for them now as a distraction, but instead her hand picked up the omnibus of Irish folklore.

After punching up her pillows to make a backrest for herself, Eileen began to read.

Within a few minutes she was lost in another land and time.

She did not know when the words began to blur; when her eyes drifted closed and the book slipped from her hands. She would never remember switching off the lamp, or getting up to open the bedroom window so that a wash of salt sea air flooded the room.

She was calling him, calling him plainly now. The heart leaped in him.

His long wait was almost over.

* * *

As they prepared for bed in their own room at the other end of the house, Mrs. Moore stopped creaming her wrinkled face long enough to ask her husband, "Should we look in on the American, do you think?"

Malachy was sitting on the edge of the bed, unlacing his shoes. "Why would we do that?"

"She seems so troubled."

"And aren't we all after being troubled, one way or another? Let her rest, it's the angels' own cure." Breda Moore obeyed her husband, but she lay awake for a long time, listening to the sibilant inrush of the tide in Galway Bay. All her life had been spent on the shores of the great bay, her rhythms attuned to its beating heart. She knew without thinking whether the tide was in or out, and one glance at the light in the sky told her more about approaching weather than all the meteorologists on the telly.

On this night, the air was disturbed. Breda could feel it.

Eileen awoke with a start. The room was dark, but enough moonlight filtered through the lace curtains over the open window to allow her to see grainy gray shapes. The curtains were billowing in a stiff breeze and the room was cold.

There was something else, too; an unaccustomed odor, a fragrance . . . she sniffed, trying to identify it. Could it be pipe smoke?

She sat up in bed, clutching the covers to her body. Her eyes darted one way, then the other, peering into the shadowed corners. But there was no one; nothing moved. She was alone.

Yet there was a lingering smell in the room that definitely had not been there when she went to bed. A male smell, not unpleasant but distinctive. And the air was curiously disturbed, as if someone else had just left the room.

"Hello?" Eileen said tentatively.

The only answer she got was the voice of the sea beyond her window. Even the noise from the amusement arcade at Salthill had long since ceased. Ireland lay at peace under a full moon.

She threw back the covers and went to the window.

Her earlier anxiety had eased. She could look back on what must have been a panic attack, and feel only wonder. In this gentle land with its old world courtesy, what was there to hurt her? She had been shown only kindness; even Moya Hennessey had meant her no harm, merely wished to warn her off Barry Hynes.

"You're a fool, Eileen Costello," she scolded herself. "You're going to turn into a classic old maid if you're not careful."

Something moved a few yards from her window. She cupped her hands around her eyes and peered into the night. Was someone walking across the parking area? "Hello?" she called again.

Whoever it was, stopped.

"That was stupid of me," Eileen muttered. It was probably another guest, there were at least half a dozen people staying at the B & B. Any of them were entitled to walk around outside if they chose without being challenged by a voice from the darkness.

Then she heard the crunch of gravel as footsteps came across the parking area right toward her open window.

Leaving the water was always hard. No matter how much he longed for the landlife, there was a moment of intense pain as the sealskin loosened from the connective tissue that held it to muscle and tendon. Next came the sensation of his body being compacted

*in some ways, elongated in others, the bones wrenched apart like
the pelvis of a woman giving birth.*

*He had long since learned to grit his teeth and endure. The
worst of it came after the pain had passed, when at last he stood
upright on human legs, on solid earth. There was always a nauseating sense of dislocation as his sense of self was stripped from
him and a new image was imposed.*

*During that time he was as helpless as the proverbial fish out of
water.*

*Fortunately, it did not last very long. Soon his head cleared,
his senses normalized. He could see, hear, feel like a human, he
could walk instead of rowing himself along with his front flippers, he could talk instead of barking and grunting. Invariably
he experimented with his voice, trying a few murmured words to
be certain he sounded normal. He had a lingering fear that one
day his voice would not change with the rest of him, so that when
he started to speak he would reveal himself as an impostor.*

*Metamorphosis complete, he bent, marveling as he always did
at the clever mechanism of the human knee, and picked up his
discarded sealskin. He folded it very carefully, then secreted it in
a small stone cairn disguised as part of a field wall.*

*There were a number of such caches around the bay, if one
knew where to look.*

*At last he straightened and turned his face resolutely in her
direction.*

Eileen drew back from the window, suddenly afraid
that whoever it was would see her. She wished now that
she had thought to close the window but it was too late.
The footsteps were only a couple of yards away.

She stood holding her breath and saw a dark shape
outside hesitate, then move on past.

The tension drained out of her so suddenly it left her
limp. She sank down on the bed.

Then she heard the doorbell.

"Of course, you fool, it was just some late arrivals!" she told herself, crawling back under the covers. But she could not help trying to listen. Her straining ears detected the sounds of muffled voices, then the front door being opened, followed quite clearly by an exclamation of surprise.

Then nothing.

Eileen lay wide-eyed in the dark for a long time, torn between the desire to get up and learn what had happened, and a desperate need to stay huddled in bed and feel safe.

She did not remember falling asleep. When she awoke it was bright daylight, and the luscious fatty fragrance of one of Breda Moore's massive Irish breakfasts was permeating the house.

Eileen confronted her hostess in the dining room. "Mrs. Moore, was anyone in my room last night before I came home?"

"In your room? Why, no; no one but meself earlier, seeing to the linen."

"A man, perhaps? A man who smoked a pipe?"

The woman stared at her blankly. "No one here smokes. I don't like it in my house, the smell gets into everything."

"Then . . . who was it who arrived in the middle of the night? I heard the bell."

Mrs. Moore looked contrite. "I'm so sorry if it disturbed you. Funnily enough, it was no one. I mean, my husband went to the door, but when he opened it no one was there. A strange thing to happen so late at night, wouldn't you say?"

Eileen did not reply. But she was absolutely, chillingly certain someone had been there; someone who perhaps had been in her room earlier, taking advantage of the unlocked window.

Since it was to be her last morning with them, she sat

down at one of the small tables crowded into the Moores' dining room and let her hostess serve her tea and brown bread, though she refused the fried food. Elsewhere in the room a couple of families, obvious tourists like herself, were tucking into the huge breakfast. A little boy speared a circle of black pudding on his fork and held it up to his nose, sniffing suspiciously.

"It's blood sausage," his mother informed him in a German accent.

Mrs. Moore bustled over to Eileen's table with a crystal bowl filled with coarse-cut orange marmalade. In her wake, her husband carried a fresh pot of tea. "Would you like some more bread," he inquired, "since you're not eating anything else?"

"No, I'm fine, really. I don't want to drive on a full stomach, it makes me sleepy. I'll be leaving right after breakfast, you see," Eileen explained.

Breda Moore and her husband exchanged glances. "Where will you be going?" the man asked conversationally.

"I don't know yet."

"Then why not stay with us a few more days, give yourself a chance to . . ."

"To what?" Suddenly Eileen felt her streetwise New York antennae quivering. "Why do you want me to stay?"

The couple looked abashed. "Just for your own sake, just to enjoy more of your holiday in Galway," Malachy Moore replied.

But to Eileen's ears the assurance did not ring true somehow. There seemed to be undercurrents she did not understand . . .

She choked down a few bites of buttered bread, gulped her tea, and hurried back to her room to pack. Run! urged the voice of irrational panic inside her.

The Moores appeared bewildered by her abrupt departure. She tried as best she could to assure them it was due to no failure of their hospitality—"You've been just wonderful," she asserted several times as they stood awkwardly together just inside the front door. "But I must go, that's all. I simply have to go."

Then she was striding across the graveled parking area, her heavy suitcase banging against her leg. Malachy Moore had tried to carry it for her but she would not let him. "I'm used to doing it for myself," she insisted.

Modern woman, she thought under her breath. Liberated woman.

Lonely woman rushing off to nowhere.

When she was in the car she locked the door before she fastened her seat belt. Once the engine was running she let herself look at them, standing together in the doorway of their immaculate bungalow, waving good-bye to her like fond parents.

Sunlight gleamed on the plastered walls and sparkling windows. Eileen's stomach growled with tardy regret for the uneaten breakfast. Curiously, she felt like an ungrateful child running away from home. But she could not help herself. She put the car in gear . . .

. . . just as a shadow darkened the window on the passenger side and someone tapped at the glass.

Eileen was so startled she killed the engine.

The face looking in at her was amiable and freckled; one hand was holding a pipe. He had tapped the window with the pipe stem. "Where are you going?" Barry Hynes mouthed at her.

Her resolve washed out of her, leaving her trembling. She sat with her fingers clenched on the wheel as he came around to her side of the car. Even though she kept her eyes fixed on her hands, she knew he was making winding motions, indicating she should roll down the window.

At last, with a sigh, she did as he wanted.

"Where are you going?" he repeated.

"Dublin."

"Ah. Right now?"

"Yes."

"Have you time for a cup of coffee first, or are you in a great hurry?"

The question was so ordinary, asked in such a normal tone of voice. Glancing past him, Eileen could see the Moores still standing in their doorway; two nice, normal, ordinary people, whom she had tried to invest with sinister overtones as if they were characters in a gothic novel.

Sitting in the car with her hands on the wheel and a pleasant, freckle-faced man smiling in at her, Eileen could see it all so plainly. She had fled to Ireland seeking the magic that was missing in her life, seeking the dreams she should have outgrown long ago. When she did not find what she sought, her overwrought imagination had begun producing it for her.

They were all harmless, the people who had been so kind to her. She had done them a great wrong.

Barry Hynes obviously liked her, at least enough to come looking for her this morning. No matter how Moya Hennessey felt about him, he was showing interest in Eileen. If she did not want to return to New York—and to be honest with herself, she knew she did not—she could stay here in Ireland, get to know this man, perhaps eventually marry and settle down and have a nice ordinary normal life and raise a brood of redheaded, freckle-faced, ordinary kids.

What more could she want?

What more could she hope for?

He was not her ideal man, but he was decent. After all, the Moores had vouched for him.

Feeling as if she had been offered some sort of reprieve, she looked from the Moores to Barry Hynes. She would smile at him, say, "I'm not really in a hurry, and I would love a cup of coffee." She was already preparing the smile and the words when her eyes inadvertently slid past him to the shimmering expanse of Galway Bay spread out in front of the B & B like a picture in a dream.

Until that moment the sun had been shining brightly, but even as she looked, it disappeared behind a cloud and the entire bay turned dark. A wind came sweeping in from the west, from the ocean, blowing the waves in front of it so that they leaped and tossed their white crests like the manes of white horses.

The white horses of Manannan Mac Lir.

The smell of a strange man in her room.

The Moores vouched for him.

In one swift motion, she turned the key and threw the car into gear. She drove out of the parking area with screeching tires, spraying gravel. Barry Hynes jumped back with a cry of astonishment.

When she looked in the rear-view mirror she could see him standing there, staring after her.

She drove straight through Galway, miraculously not getting lost on the narrow streets, until she found a sign pointing the way to Dublin. Following its direction she went on to a traffic circle, but this time she did not take the route east to the Irish capital.

Instead, for no reason she could identify, she went south toward Clare.

Off to her right lay Galway Bay beneath the gathering storm.

chapter 8

She drove with neither a sense of purpose nor of direction; just drove, going as fast as the roads would allow. At some point she discovered she had left the main road that connected Shannon to Galway, and was lost on some by-road. But she did not turn around and go back.

Go back to what?

The road became narrower, turned into a lane between hedges. For a while she thought it was the road she and Barry had followed before, but then it made a sharp right-hand bend she did not remember, and she found herself facing a muddy farmyard and a herd of dairy cows. A farmer in Wellington boots was staring at her in surprise as a black and white sheepdog ran forward, barking a challenge. With an apologetic nod to the farmer, Eileen backed up in the narrow space and turned around. She made her way back the way she had come until the road branched; she took the left. Soon a vista of fields opened up ahead of her, and beyond them dark water.

It seemed as if she had been driving for a long time, yet she was still within sight of Galway Bay.

* * *

He could follow her because she wanted him to follow her. She never went out of his range.

He had to hurry but he did not mind. At last he was hurrying to something; to his changed future.

The storm blew at his back, urging him on. Manannan was not cruel, if all the conditions were fulfilled he would not maintain the enchantment out of spite. Manannan was ancient and powerful and aware and indifferent, but even the gods could not break the laws that bound them, any more than the earth could of its own choice fly apart into trillions of individual specks of matter. Everything was caught in a web of being, and the threads of that web were destiny.

The wind howled and the waves leaped and for a moment he gloried in their power, in the world of the sea he had known since birth. Did he really want to give it up?

This was not the time to ask that question, which had never bothered him before. This was his chance, his one best chance.

The storm was growing worse. Torrents of rain poured down the windshield, obscuring her view. Eileen was afraid to drive when she could not see, so she parked the car but did not turn off the engine. She left it on and switched up the heater instead, feeling the chill of the storm.

"What are you going to do now?" she asked herself. She had to raise her voice above the pounding of the rain on the roof of the car. Then she laughed. Why shout at oneself?

The laughter relaxed her. "Okay, Eileen, you've just made a fool of yourself. There's nothing to be done about it. Sit there until the storm lets up, then turn around and go on to Dublin. What you need is a real city again, then you'll be all right."

A real city. The words seemed to have no meaning. She

sat staring at the flooded windshield, listening to the wind howl.

She had the curious sensation of being alone and underwater, caught in a bubble of time and space. Perhaps the world beyond the car was not real at all. Perhaps the real world was the one in the folklore omnibus, peopled by enchanted swans and faery maids. If she closed her eyes and wished very tight, then flung open the car door and jumped out, she might somehow break through to that magical kingdom where there were, occasionally, happy endings . . .

Before she knew she was going to do it, Eileen had opened the car door and stepped out. The wind hit her like a fist. It drove the breath from her and lashed her hair into her eyes. Rain beat down on her unprotected head with a savagery she had never experienced before. Its silver spears were probing for hidden weaknesses.

She screwed her eyes tightly shut and stood there, letting it happen. Enduring as if enduring a test.

The wind eased.

The rain stopped. Stopped all at once, as if someone had turned off a tap.

Eileen opened her eyes. She was soaked and shivering but it did not matter.

Over the bay the clouds were breaking up as swiftly as they had gathered. Rays of golden light stabbed between them, gilding the surface of the water. A huge panorama of misty beauty spread out before Eileen, clean and pure as it had been in the dawn of creation when the old gods were young.

"I can't leave," she heard her voice whisper. "I won't."

As if a weight had fallen from her shoulders, she felt her spirit rise. There would be countless problems ahead, endless complications as the world she knew tried to impose its rules on her and keep her trapped, but she could break free. She *could*, if she wanted it enough! There was no spell binding her.

Her mind began to race, planning how to sell the shop in New York, find someplace to live here . . . would she be an alien resident? What would her mother say? What about taxes? How would she live? Maybe she could arrange to export crafts to someone in the States. Moya Hennessey might be a good contact to begin with, she would know about sources. Maybe she would be willing to consider a partner, once Eileen convinced her she had no interest in Barry Hynes.

The idea was overwhelming and terrifying and thrilling.

"I really have gone mad," Eileen Costello said aloud. But if so, the idea no longer frightened her.

Besides, she did not think she was mad. She felt more sane than she had in a long time; more in control of her life. All it required was courage.

In the distance she saw a man walking up the road toward her. Had this been New York, and she alone, she would have jumped into the car and locked all the doors.

But this was Ireland.

"I'm not going to be afraid any more," Eileen promised herself.

She stood and watched him come. Perhaps he was from a farm nearby, someplace where they would give her a hot cup of tea and let her warm herself by the fire. Gentle, generous, hospitable people.

But as he drew nearer, she realized he was not a local farmer. His was a form she recognized even before he was close enough for her to see his green eyes; even before he was close enough to reach out and put his arms around her as if it were the most natural thing in the world.

"I've been waiting a long time for you," said Mrs. Daly's son.

after

If you are looking for souvenirs, there are a number of interesting shops in the Galway area. Those in town offer the usual attractions, china and crystal and knitwear, but the more adventurous shopper may prefer to venture along quiet country lanes in search of something unique.

A few miles out of town is a little shop called Country Crafts, half-hidden by a broken stone wall and a tangle of briars. It does not advertise and is not easy to find, almost as if the owners do not want the world to beat a path to their door. But inside are treasures. Many of them come from the sea. There are always numerous sea shells, both common ones from the western coast of Ireland and more exotic shells that have surely been carried back from far places and distant climes. Glass balls used as floats for fishing nets are popular with tourists, and children take a special delight in little figures carved from bog oak, depicting whales and fish and gulls on the wing.

After an hour or two of browsing, you might find yourself with an increased appetite. If so, there is an excellent restaurant specializing in seafood not too far away. They do not advertise either, but the place is easily recognizable; it is the only mustard-colored building for miles. Teach na Dalaigh is worth a visit if only for the view of the inlet beyond the road, and the tranquil, healing atmosphere one finds within.

One family has interests in both establishments. They draw enough income to supply their needs for part of the year, when they live in a charming cottage with a thatched roof and roses around the door. A low stone wall surrounds the cottage and the path to the door is lined with seashells. The door itself, like the frames of the windows, is painted bright blue, which Irish country people believe keeps away evil spirits. People driving by like to stop and take photographs. Sometimes they will glimpse someone inside peering out at them through the lace curtains.

But for half the year the cottage is closed, with shutters over the windows. During that time, the neighbors will tell you, the family that lives there goes to the sea.

the harper's daughter

BY

Barbara Samuel

For Susan Brown, who brought me Irish pebbles, and Susan Wiggs, who is even more generous than she is accomplished. Many, many thanks.

Part One

a dangerous Beauty

Already the bards are telling my story around winter fires, and it has not yet been even a score of years since that time I was a girl and Cathbadh, the fair druid, made his predictions of my fate. The bards tell it as if all those predictions of Cathbadh's came true.

I admit it annoys me no small part.

'Tis sure history will blame me. It will be men, after all, who sing of what happened. They'll be wanting to warn their daughters and wives to do as they are told. They'll be wanting to show the king in a good light—and if they tell the truth, Conchobar will look small and mean.

Which he was, for a time, though it makes him no less a hero for all the other things he did in his life. We all have moments of weakness. I was that moment for the good King Conchobar.

For that reason, for the sake of his good name, I thought to let the false tale of my tragic end alone—it makes a good story. But one afternoon, I saw a tangle of young girls bunched around the feet of a bard who spun the yarn of the seductive and evil Deirdre. Equal parts amusement and annoyance warred in my breast, and I paused to listen. The girls were all known to me, and I to them. None connected the crone I've become with the girl in the tale, of course—such is the arrogance of youth.

One girl in particular caught my eye as I watched in silence from behind. She bore the early mark of what would be great beauty in her angular, dark face. I admired her supple skin, her long thick hair, with the same happiness with which one admires the sky or a flower.

And all at once, I was angry that one day, that poor child would come to believe that she was to blame for the way men treated her. I no longer wished to hold my tongue. For that girl-child, and all the others who follow her, I tell my tale, as it was, not as the bards have told it.

As you see, I am not dead. Not yet. And much of the rest is wrong as well.

chapter 1

Noise overwhelmed her.

Voices and drums and harps rang against the stone walls of the rath; a dozen feet moved in whispers against the floor; a score of hands rustled the air. Deirdre wanted to weep at the onslaught, cover her ears, run away.

She had been raised in a forest grove, alone but for her foster mother. She could hear the sweep of a deer's long lashes as it blinked, and the low voice of the earth, moving and shifting ever so slightly with each turn of the hour. She could hear the soft singing call of the oaks turning up their leaves to the rain, and the scrabbling huddle of little animals in their dens. Thus had she been trained.

At the court of King Conchobar, all those small, precious sounds were obscured. Their loss left her feeling disoriented, out of step, unable to cope. Every moment of her years she'd been readied for this wedding that was to take place six days hence, and yet Deirdre could not even eat.

Leborcham, her foster mother, spoke in low tones to the king. "The child needs time, my lord. None of us gave a thought to how hard it would be for her to join the world when she has been so long hidden away, alone."

Behind the king stood Cathbadh, the great druid who shadowed the king wherever he went. He stared now at

Deirdre with hostility. "It is another omen, sire," he said, "that she is not ready for this wedding. Send her away— you imperil your warriors by bringing her here."

Deirdre shrank back. Cathbadh made her think of a wolf; there was in his eyes that feral beauty. And it was, after all, Cathbadh who'd cursed her at her birth. Deirdre had been told the story many times.

Her father, the king's harper, had discovered a wounded sorcerer in the forest and taken him to his wife to be healed. When the old man was healed, he offered the traditional granting of some need or wish. The harper asked that the child his wife carried be as beautiful as a queen. This the sorcerer had granted, though he warned there would be a high price to such greed.

Deirdre had been born at the height of a great feast, and the midwife brought her out to the hall for King Conchobar's blessing.

The king, delighted with such a good omen, called for the warriors to celebrate the child's birth. The warriors gave what brooches and jewels and snippets of ribbon they could, till the girl was nearly rich as the king himself.

The harper was well pleased, till Cathbadh, the great and handsome druid who was the king's right hand, came forward. He stood before the babe and midwife and stared down at the child with a grim expression. The room went silent as all waited his pronouncement.

At last the druid said, "It is not my wish to cause you grief, Fedorich, but the portents show the price you pay for this child will be high. Her beauty will outshine the very sun, but that beauty will turn the rivers of the land red with blood."

Cathbadh turned toward the gathered soldiers. "Because of this child, great warriors will die."

In the hall, there was a growling fear. "Kill the babe now, then!" spoke a soldier, drawing his sword with a burly arm.

"Nay!" From her place at the dais rose Scathach, a tall and noble woman adorned in hauberk and leathers, who wore a longsword at her side. "I see portents, too," she said in her deep, strong voice. "It will not be the beauty of the child that will shed blood, but the lust of the men who want her."

All stepped back to let the great sorceress pass. They feared her, for not only was she a powerful warrior woman, but she had trained the finest soldiers in all the land at her secret island.

Now she approached the midwife who held the babe in her arms. All watched her long-limbed, easy movements in admiration. Down her back curled her long red hair, tied in a leather thong to keep it from her face, which was eternally young, though twice over her sons had lived full lives.

She studied the babe, touched her cheek lightly, and said, "Her name will be called Deirdre." From her hauberk, Scathach lifted a smooth violet stone on a silver chain.

"I'll add a prophecy to the vile one uttered here today," Scathach said. "I cannot change her beauty, nor halt the punishment men will inflict upon her, but I may add that if one man loves her true, the prophecy will be ended."

Bending low, Scathach put the stone over Deirdre's head. The babe gurgled softly.

Now the king rose. "Hide the girl away, Fedorich," he said to his harper. "When she comes of age, I myself will take her to wife."

Thus had Deirdre come to stand in the King's hall, clutching her foster mother's hand, with the druid's feral eyes fixed upon her. After a moment, he bent and spoke to the king's ear. Leborcham took Deirdre's hand. They waited with held breath for the king's decision.

The king.

Because he had saved her life, Deirdre had grown up imagining Conchobar to be a kind, wise man. She carried in her imagination the picture of a hale warrior, in the prime of his life. It was a pleasurable, if vague vision.

The night before the warriors had come to fetch her to Emain Macha, Deirdre had dreamed of a man with hair black as raven's wing, cheeks ruddy like blood, eyes bright as the morning sky. When she awakened, she had run to Leborcham to ask her if her vision had shown her Conchobar.

Pity and a fleeting fear had touched the old woman's eyes before she shook her head. No, not the king.

The king was *old!*

Oh, once he might have been handsome. Deirdre could see that in the fine bearing, the red-gold of his hair, the sea-wild shimmer of his gray eyes. But silver dulled his hair, his belly swelled his tunic, and a wreath of lines made a nest around his eyes.

Old!

She did not know how she could lie with him. Did not know how she could bear it.

As if he'd sensed her reluctance, the king made his pronouncement. "We will marry at week's end," he said gruffly. "Leborcham, you were charged with making the girl ready. You'd best see you've done your work."

Hearing the dulcet threat in his words, Deirdre took Leborcham's thin arm. "Come," she said quietly. "I will do as I'm expected, as you've taught me."

The king grunted in satisfaction, and the druid stepped aside to let them pass. They left the hall, walking hands entwined to a grove of trees on a hill beyond the ramparts. Deirdre found peace there, in the silence of the ancient arms of the oaks and birches that grew atop the green hill like a crown.

"Here," she said, sinking to the ground, "will I come

when it grows too wild in there. A bit at time, I will learn to like the noise."

"I am uneasy," Leborcham said. She walked the circle of trees, peering toward the horizon in all four directions. "There is brewing here something I do not like."

Deirdre touched the knot of guilt in her breast. " 'Tis my own reluctance that makes you worry." She lifted her head. "My dream."

Leborcham paused. On her face showed an intent and secretive look. "No, child. You cannot be faulted for dreaming of young men." She resumed her pacing, lifting her head as if to scent the wind. "It is the way of all girls."

Deirdre wondered if all girls dreamed of the same handsome man she had—a man born of the elements, shaped of earth and sky and rain, his eyes merry with much laughter.

On the wind came a sound. Deirdre jumped to her feet, skirts clutched in her hands, hearing them an instant before her stepmother spoke.

"Horses! Hide yourself."

Tucking the skirt of her tunic between her legs, Deirdre shimmied into the sheltering arms of an ancient oak. Through the new green of the leaves, she peered toward the rough road from the south.

Over a rise came a trio of horses, their heads as proud as the warriors they carried. Bright ribbons were braided into their manes, and tiny bells rang from collars around their necks. The warriors, too, were splendidly attired in richly woven cloaks of six colors.

" 'Tis the sons of Uisnech," Leborcham said, ducking close to the tree to hide herself. "The king's favored warriors."

Deirdre peered through the leaves of the tree, careful to stay in the shadows as she made a window to see the road and approaching warriors.

As if each animal and the man who rode it had been born together, their colors matched. Two of the brothers rode reddish horses—a sorrel and a chestnut, to match the magnificent fall of their thick copper hair.

But the brother in the middle snagged Deirdre's gaze. He rode high and straight on a high-stepping black horse. His hair, as black and shiny as the raven's wing, fell to shoulders wide and strong. His scarlet cloak was cast back, showing a broad chest covered with a tunic dyed a blue as clear and true as the noontime sky. As Deirdre stared through a frame of leaves and branches, he made some jest to his brothers, and all three laughed. Deirdre watched the dark brother, watched his wide-cut mouth curve to show teeth whiter than snow.

It was the man from her dream.

Now he was below her, sun glinting hard from the crown of his head. And then he was gone on, and Deirdre crouched still in her place, stricken.

"You marry the king in six days," Leborcham said quietly. "And here, in Naisi, the king's warrior, is your test— do not make the grim prophecy of the druid come to life."

Deirdre climbed down, subdued. "No," she whispered. "I shall do as I am bid." Thoughtfully she fingered the polished stone that hung from a chain around her neck. "But it is true I dreamed of him. What does that mean?"

"I don't know, child. Beware—there are forces evil as well as forces for good."

Dutifully, Deirdre bowed her head, but she could not quell the sweetness singing through her blood, nor the eagerness she felt to look again upon the beautiful face of the raven-haired man.

He was alive and real, not a dream at all.

chapter 2

It was nearly time for the evening meal when Naisi and his brothers came into the king's court, washed and rested after their long journey from the shadowed isle of the warrior woman Scathach. The smell of roasting meat filled the air, mingling with elusive notes from the oiled bodies of beautiful women, and the sweet odor of the fire itself.

They were here for the wedding feast of the king. In spite of the *gessa* put on him—Scathach had mysteriously and abruptly forbidden him to have sex with any of the women at Emain Macha—Naisi was in high good spirits.

His brother Arden nudged him, lifting a discreet chin toward a girl nearby the hearth. Her blond braids reached her knees and were hung with gold ornaments. She smiled at the brothers.

"Mine," Arden said quickly.

"Unless that brute beside her changes your mind," said Ainnle, laughing as a muscle-bound warrior crossed his arms and glared at the three.

"Best look elsewhere, Arden," Naisi said, clapping a hand on the youngest's shoulder. "Come, let's greet our king. Time enough for women later."

They found Conchobar in a curtained alcove, listening with gravity to the druid Cathbadh. When Naisi flung aside a well-woven woolen curtain, the king looked up angrily. "I told you—!"

"What, no friendly word for your devoted warriors?"

"You!" Conchobar came to his feet with a roar. He embraced Naisi fiercely. "Ah, my boy! A fine sight you are for these tired eyes." In turn, he kissed the cheeks of Arden and Ainnle, and gestured toward a servant woman. "Bring wine and bread!"

Naisi raised his hands. "No, my lord. We'll wait for that meat we smell. We only came to greet you."

The king lifted a brow. "And meet my bride?"

"Aye." Naisi smiled at the preening vanity of an aging man who took a young wife. "They sing of her beauty all the way to the Shadowed Isle."

Cathbadh moved forward. "And one day they'll sing only of the blood that beauty spilled."

"Enough!" Conchobar roared. "Scathach herself said the child need only find one man who loved her true to halt the bloodshed. I am that man. No more of your doomsaying, do you hear?"

The druid lifted a dark brow. "If a man chooses not to see an omen, that does not mean it does not exist."

"Go, Cathbadh. Breathe your bleak visions in someone else's ear for an hour or two. Let me enjoy the evening with my young friends here."

With a mocking bow, Cathbadh said, "As you wish."

But as he was about to exit, there came a soft, rustling stir from the hall behind the three brothers. Naisi heard it on his skin before the sound reached his ears.

It was a moaning sound, like the wordless disquiet of a dog. It came from many throats at once, almost inaudible, and deeply chilling.

Naisi turned to scan the room for danger, his hand going to his sword instinctively. And at first, he did not quite see what the stir was about. Two women moved through the hall, heads down modestly as they wound around the edges of the room. One was bent and old. Her bony hands lifted her skirt. The other was young, dark-headed, and almost entirely concealed by a deep-bordered woolen cloak fastened with a large gold brooch.

It could only be the king's betrothed. Naisi had no doubt it was she who caused the odd, subvocal sound in the room. She seemed very afraid, her shoulders hunched, her head down.

"There is Deirdre," Conchobar said.

Naisi looked at his king in surprise, for his voice was peculiar. As if to underscore the strangeness, there was in Conchobar's eye a fixed and unseemly lust.

Head still lowered, the girl came to stand by the king. Her face was shadowed by a fall of hair, her body draped by the rich folds of her beautiful cloak. All Naisi could see was the supple curve of a white cheek.

"By the gods, girl!" Conchobar swore, and roughly tugged the fabric of her mantle. "Stand proud in your beauty—you'll soon be the queen of Ulster!"

A little unbalanced by the sharp gesture, Deirdre staggered toward the king's broad chair. She caught herself on the back, and her cloak, drawn by the king's greedy hand, fell away. Deirdre was unveiled.

She straightened, almost defiantly tossing her noble head to send her undressed hair cascading over her back. Naisi's gaze caught first on her smooth long throat, and the defiant thrust of that chin. She took a breath, the long-suffering annoyance of youth, and Naisi was reminded of a mare who bore the scrutiny of her masters but would much prefer the open meadow.

Amused by her youth and impatience, Naisi grinned. "Proud we'll be to call you queen," he said, bowing toward her with a courtly gesture.

She looked at him. His amusement died.

Her eyes were the color of evening and filled with the fine pleasures of sex. He could not have said why it was so—only that there was something in the long, heavy-lidded eyes that called up sweat and musk and exquisite pursuits. Her mouth was lush, shaped for the dark taste of men, her breasts high and pointed, her legs long as a colt's.

As the sooty-ringed irises fixed upon him, Naisi saw that his lustful perusal disappointed her.

Ashamed, he looked away.

The king stood and draped an arm around the girl. "Fulfills the prophecy, I'd say," he said with a leer. One hand dangled close to her breast and Deirdre shrank from him. Conchobar laughed and groped at places he should not have been touching on a virgin or on any woman of honor. Not publicly.

Deirdre made a small mortified sound and yanked away. Her cheeks were bright red. The king grabbed her again, and Naisi saw the red marks of Conchobar's fingers on her smooth white skin.

The king of Ulster liked his women—and his ale and his food—with the same lusty pleasure as all Celts, but Naisi had never before seen him lewd. He wondered if the king was drunk.

She was no whore, but a queen. Naisi could not bear it. "My lord," he said. "She is young."

At the gentle reproof, Conchobar seemed jolted from some private dream. "Aye," he said roughly, and let Deirdre free. With a glare at the druid, then at Deirdre, he wiped his hand on his tunic. "Too much drink I've had this day."

Deirdre retreated, shrinking close to her woman. With pleading in her face, she looked to Naisi as if he could rescue her. All at once, he saw her for what she was—only a girl, young and very afraid. A protectiveness roused in him.

"I'm off to my bed, young Naisi," the king said. "I

charge you with the care of my bride. You'll see 'tis not only me who swells with lust at the sight of her."

"Perhaps she should stay in the women's quarters till the wedding, then," Arden suggested.

"Nay. Soon or late, men will need to grow used to looking upon her." He touched Deirdre's shoulder. "Forgive me, child."

She kept her head down. The king took her hand and led her to where Naisi stood with his brothers. Into Naisi's hand the king settled Deirdre's slim fingers. "The sons of Uisnech will care for you this night," the king said. "They'll guard you well."

Her flesh was cold against Naisi's palm, and Naisi instinctively covered the long fingers with his own to warm them. She still did not raise her eyes, but silently curled her fingers into his grasp. Standing so close to her, Naisi could smell herbs in her hair, hair that swirled around her in a glossy mass of colors, catching torchlight in a blaze of reds and golds amid the mahogany strands. She was much smaller than he, almost too thin, but for the weight of breast and curve of hip.

Ainnle stepped forward. "Sire, do you think it wise to—"

The king waved away the objection. "I'm to bed."

He moved from the room. With a single, blazing glower, Cathbadh followed him.

Arden and Ainnle stepped close to Naisi. "Brother," said Ainnle, "I like not the spirit in this room."

Naisi raised his head. "We'll sing, then, and soothe it."

"Scathach has put you under *gessa*," Arden warned. "You may have no woman till she grants it."

Holding Deirdre's warming fingers in his own, their clasp buried in a fold of his cloak, Naisi said, "You worry overmuch."

Arden shot a malevolent glance toward the girl. "I think not."

Deirdre tugged her hand from Naisi's. "I am weary of everyone speaking about me as if I am without brains," she said crossly. "I have ears to hear with, and a mind to think with and a mouth to speak what thoughts are in my mind." Her chin rose, and again Naisi thought of a proud, beautiful mare. "I'll not cause your brother any harm."

Arden and Ainnle stared at her. Her voice held the golden honeyed notes of mead, almost unbearably intoxicating.

"You must speak more often, my lady," Naisi said with a chuckle, "Rare it is my brothers are speechless."

Her smile was swift and sweet and unsure. Naisi took her hand again, as if to safeguard her. In truth he wanted again the feeling of her fingers against his own. "I think you will sing a beautiful song with us to still the unrest in this room."

Her fingers tightened around his. "Aye."

Naisi wanted to throw up his cloak and make some magic to hide her from the men in the room, who whined like a pack of hungry dogs at her skirts; he wanted to hide her even from the king. She captivated him.

There was a spark of mischief in those long eyes as she spoke of her life in the forest. It made him laugh and lean forward and ask to hear how she had spent her days before she came to Main Macha.

And like some forest creature, she was simple and strong and quietly cunning. She ate with gusto, and laughed easily, and sang with the sweet clear voice of a lark.

When most in the hall were deep in their cups, Deirdre and Naisi sat alone. By then it had grown late, and the guards were falling asleep, their cheeks flushed with too much beer. In dark corners were the sounds of rutting—

Naisi didn't look but knew Arden was among them; he had found a way around the barbarian guarding the pretty woman he wanted.

Deirdre sat next to Naisi, silent, fingering that round stone at her breast over and over again.

Naisi lifted his hand and covered hers, and there was a look in her eye then, a pleading look, a hungry look, something he knew. Nervously, she fingered the round, time-polished amethyst she wore around her neck, and Naisi could see she was trying to calm herself down and make peace with the way things were for her.

With a queer start, he recognized the necklace she wore. The stone was clasped in a fanciful setting—the paw of some animal, perhaps a wolf or a dog, quite unusual. Naisi reached below his tunic and drew out the necklace Scathach had given him a few days before.

"Look," he said, holding it up.

They matched. Naisi's stone had a blue cast; Deirdre's a more reddish hue, but when they brought them together, it was as if they sparked a fire between them, for a soft glow stirred in both stones.

Deirdre smiled at him. "Mine was put on my neck when I was only a babe. Leborcham told me it is protection from the great warrior woman, Scathach."

"Scathach gave me mine, too," Naisi said. "Perhaps to remind me of my loyalties."

"Your loyalty to the king."

"Aye," he said, but he was not sure. He looked back to Deirdre, frowning. "I don't know."

"You are my fate," she said, softly. "I dreamed of you before I came here."

"No!" Angrily, Naisi drew his hand away. "You are the king's betrothed, and I am a trusted warrior!"

Quickly, her head dropped and he saw with a pang the bright bands of color that stained her cheeks. "Yes, that's true," she said. "And I will do as I must."

She made to rise to her feet, and Naisi halted her with his hand on her arm. "My lady, let's walk. If we do not stray far from the yard, we'll be safe. Then I will see you to the women's house."

For a long moment, she paused, her head bent, as if listening. Then she nodded and placed her slim fingers trustingly into his palm. Girding himself against the base thrust of desire the movement gave, Naisi stood and led the way into the night.

chapter 3

Out in the night, away from the noise of the diners and the fire and the mating, Deirdre clung to Naisi's hand. He made her feel safe. Like a wary stag alert to the scents and whispers of man who would kill him, he gave off a bristly warning.

He smelled of firesmoke and horse and the tang of a man, a scent wholly unlike the smell of women. Deirdre felt a wide array of things, walking next to the warrior Naisi, about whom songs had already been woven.

It was wrong, the way she felt. And the quiet way they had escaped the hall and the others so they might be alone—that was wrong, too. Deirdre's heart ached with excitement and regret.

And then Naisi dipped into the deep shadows along the wooden wall, and used his multihued cloak to hide them. Naisi, beloved of the king, pulled her close to him.

Deirdre could see nothing in the velvety darkness. A lock of his cool hair touched her cheek and she smelled a moist waft of fennel on his breath when he spoke her name.

She lifted her hands to his face, the face it seemed now that she had known always. His flesh was smooth over the bridge of his nose—a big strong nose—and the high hard round of his cheekbones; it grew coarse along the edge of his jaw. In silence, he let her explore him, but she felt his restraint in the slight trembling of his arms around her, in the rushed sound of his blood in his neck below her fingers.

She touched his mouth. He sighed then, and bent his head to hers, nestling her close in the overly warm place below his sheltering cloak.

He kissed her.

There were no words for the feeling she knew then, that wild and calm and charmed feeling. With Naisi holding her close, his mouth and hers together, she thought that it was for this moment she had been born; there was reason to all that had happened, if only they could decipher it together. He kissed her and kissed her and kissed her, until she was breathless, until they sank against the wall in a close tangle.

Naisi made a sorrowing noise and put her away from him. "No more," he said. "Else I'll shatter every promise I've ever made and lead you to betray your king."

Shame filled her, and she turned away from him. "The prophesies . . ."

"The bards sing stories of you already." He took her hand and touched her fingernails with the pad of his thumb. Slowly, he quoted, " 'More blood that has ere been spilt on this soil, will Deirdre of the sorrows cause.' "

"Yes." In a rush she lifted his hand to her lips. "Farewell."

Then she gathered her skirts and ran from him, ducking into the women's quarters without looking back. Leborcham awaited her there, and caught her foster daughter to her thin chest.

"Shh, child," Leborcham whispered. "Shhh. You've done well."

Deirdre wept a long time into Leborcham's soft linen shift. The depth of her sorrow alarmed the old woman,

Deirdre knew, but she could not herself explain it. At last, she slept, and it was fitful, and restless.

Toward dawn, she started awake and saw the faint gray glow at the edges of the sky. Weariness dragged her back into an uneasy doze, her head cradled upon Leborcham's bony shoulder.

She dreamed. King Conchobar stood on a rampart holding high the severed head of Naisi. From the neck dripped fresh blood, and it stained the king's hairy forearm. In the dream, Deirdre screamed.

The horror jolted her awake. Leborcham slept on, undisturbed, so the scream had been in Deirdre's mind alone. Blinking, hands shaking, she crept from the bed. On the rushes, was her cloak where she'd dropped it the night before. She knelt in the damp early chill to pick it up and went outside, walking in the dawn stillness to the copse of trees from which she'd first glimpsed Naisi.

It was very early. She could not even hear the sound of pots or the whisper of stable boys. She pulled her cloak tightly around her and carefully drew the hood around her face. All had warned her to beware of even the king's guard; she'd been warned she could not be alone, not even for a little time.

And yet she could not bear the press of bodies around her all day again, the irritation of so many voices, so much motion and activity, without some quiet stolen for herself this morning.

In the sheltering circle of trees, she sank to the earth, unable to rid herself of the bleak shadow of the dream. Conchobar's fierce grimace of joy was what frightened her most. She knew how much he loved Naisi. Hadn't she seen the way the king put her hand into the keeping of the warrior?

A quickening beat in her belly at that—at the remembrance of that hand, the quick strange glitter in his eyes. The sympathy that replaced his lust endeared him to her, the kindness in him, the song in his voice . . . the pair of them seemed destined to mate. Why else would—

But no, the dream was plain. It was for her that Naisi would die at the hand of his king.

And yet, had she not dreamed of him before Leborcham and Deirdre came to Emain Macha? And Scathach had given him a necklace to match hers, knowing he would come here and find her. Why?

Deirdre rubbed her temple and whispered a prayer to the goddess of the forest. "Flidhais, guide me!" She promised she would make an offering at dusk, when the shy deer spirit would appear at the edge of the waters to drink.

The silence was enough to strengthen her for the rest of the day. Later, as the growing crowd of warriors played war games in the yard, and shouted and let go of big, booming laughs, Deirdre stayed away from Naisi and his brothers. She and Leborcham sat close to the king and his druid all day, cheering when the king—still vigorous—knocked warrior after warrior from his mount.

It appeased Deirdre a little to watch the king like this, to see that in spite of his age, he was a vigorous man, trim enough if one didn't count the belly. He unseated nearly all his warriors.

Except Naisi.

She tried not to think about that.

The afternoon grew hot, and the men shed their tunics in the sunny day to play games of war in the yard, and drink vast amounts of beer, and tell ribald jokes and grab the women who drank with them.

The king got drunk, too, but not Naisi.

It was painful to watch him. It seemed to Deirdre he sat straighter on his horse than all the other men. His shoulders seemed broader, his chest deeper, his legs longer. About his hair, there was no contest—his was the blackest, and thickest, and glossy as a pool in moonlight. All the women commented upon Naisi's long and beautiful hair.

And they took bets over who might seduce him. When he shed his tunic with the other men, the women in a knot nearby Deirdre went silent with admiration.

"Ah," said one, finally.

It made Deirdre's stomach hurt with jealousy. One of them, one day, would have the warrior who'd snared her heart, while she would lie with the fat, old king. It wasn't fair.

Such thoughts frightened her, and she tried to avoid even looking at him, but she couldn't help it. He stood there as strong and tall as a pine, his skin gleaming with health, his hair caught in a leather thong so it wouldn't fall in his face. His muscles moved sleekly in his chest and buttocks and thighs as he swung an axe with one hand, easily, rhythmically, that most of them had to use two hands to lift.

And she knew he watched her, too, that he was aware of her gaze upon him.

When the fires had been lit, and the chill of the early spring evening chased everyone into the hall, Deirdre snuck away. She told Leborcham that she was off to empty her bowels, and headed toward the small building that housed that place, then veered off toward the women's quarters where she might be alone.

As she neared the door, a shadow startled her. From behind the building stepped Naisi, his tunic unlaced at the neck to show some of his chest, his hair tousled from the games all day.

In his hand, he held a cluster of blooming twigs from an apple tree. "I found them and was told I should give them to you," he said, "since you and the blossoms have no equal."

Deirdre didn't speak. There was a little twinkle in his eye, a sideways quirk of his mouth that stole her breath.

She reached out for the twigs, and he captured her hand in his own.

"Who told you to bring them to me?" she asked, curling her fingers over his.

"The king."

"No."

"I swear it," he said softly, and his eyes were sober, steady. "I've seen you watching me today, but the king saw nothing. Why is that?"

She shook her head slowly.

Naisi put her hand, palm down, upon the exposed skin of his chest. It almost burned her, the sensation of that skin, and she made a soft, lost sound. Before she knew she would do it, she swayed forward and put her lips to the place, too.

In a trice, he swept her into the shadows between the building and the fence around the yard. "I cannot bear to leave you, Deirdre," Naisi said. He touched her face, smoothed a hand over her hair—paused, and covered her breast with his hand. A hard pulse shot through her.

"I cannot think of it," she said. "It cannot be."

"No," he whispered, "it cannot." And he kissed her, open-mouthed. She kissed him back and let their bodies melt, one to the other.

"So we'll kiss," she said, adrift.

"Yes. I'll kiss you till morning without pause," he said, and covered her mouth. "Till morning."

So they were when Arden and Ainnle, looking for Naisi, found them. Deirdre didn't hear them approach— only heard the sharp, furious intake of one brother's breath. "Naisi!"

With an abrupt movement, he was torn from her arms, as if his brothers had shoved him. Angrily, he shook them off. "Leave me be," he growled, and reached again for Deirdre, who hung close to the wall of the women's quarters in fear.

Ainnle slapped his arm. "Fool. Think with something besides your cock and you'll see the error of your ways."

Naisi lifted his chin. "This is not what you think it is."

"No?" Ainnle returned. "Whether it is that manhood you vow it isn't or some deep love, I don't care. You betray your king with it, a king who loves you as a son."

Deirdre turned her face away. That was true, and there was no way around it. "Go," she said, and heard the word sounded harsh.

"Deirdre!" Naisi caught her arm, shaking his brothers from him with the authority he commanded. "There is madness in this, but I vow it is not . . ." he glared at his brothers, "what my brother so elegantly said. I swear it."

She touched his face, looked deep into the deep blue eyes. "You are not like the others. If I could, I'd lay my worldly goods at your feet and follow where you led. But your brothers are right. You may not lead and I may not follow."

Arden and Ainnle, appeased by her words, backed off a little.

Naisi lifted her hand to his mouth and pressed a hot kiss to her palm. "With first light, I'll go."

His mouth against her skin was warm and mobile. "Be well," she said, and drew her hand away.

Then he moved backward away from her, and his brothers took him, gathering him almost as if they wanted to shield him.

Deirdre lifted her head proudly. From between her breasts she took the purple stone Scathach had put around her neck when she was a babe, and kissed it, her eyes locked with Naisi's. He kissed the amethyst he wore around his own neck.

And he was gone.

chapteʀ 4

Again, just before dawn lit the sky, Deirdre dreamed.

From the south came three ravens, carrying honey in their mouths. Behind them came three gray hawks. When Deirdre peered closely at the hawks, who were such an odd deathly color, she saw blood on their beaks. And she knew, in the way of dreams, that it was the blood of the ravens, who lay on a deserted and barren beach, their necks broken. In the cold gray wind, Deirdre wept over the slaughtered birds, but naught could bring them alive again.

She awakened with pounding heart. Around her, women slept on, oblivious, their snores thick with the effects of the mead all had drunk the night before. None would stir before full noon.

Except Naisi and his brothers. Wrapping herself in her cloak, she went to sit by the small window, hoping to catch sight of them as they left. It was a small hunger. Surely the goddess would grant so small a need as one last glimpse of her beloved.

A tiny jingle sounded in the fog. Deirdre lifted her head. Several indistinct shadows moved through the gray, men and horses. The thick curtain of mist thinned a little and Deirdre saw the sons of Uisnech . . . first Ainnle, then Arden, and at last, Naisi, his face a grim mask as he mounted his fine horse and settled his multi-hued cloak around him.

She started to her feet, gripping the unshuttered opening to the yard.

Naisi paused. In the quiet light he shone like the moon in a dark sky. His brothers rode out and were swallowed by the fog, but still Naisi paused atop the restless horse, looking toward the women's quarters. He caught sight of Deirdre's face at the window, and for the space of a dozen heartbeats, they stared at each other.

He was leaving before the prophecies could be fulfilled. And Deirdre had to let him go. Her heart ached with it.

But then—oh, then . . . Deirdre who had learned to hear even the small sound of a bee's legs on the pistil of a flower, heard Naisi's breath leave him on a sigh of infinite longing and sorrow.

She did not think. Gripping her cloak, she turned away from the window. By the door were her slippers, and she picked them up but didn't pause to put them on her feet. Into the damp cold morning she ran, her toes sinking into the mud of the yard.

At first she couldn't see him, for they had ridden on. Deirdre had to run, silently, carrying her shoes, until she was through the gates. Even then, she dared not cry out, for the fog hid her form but it would not disguise her voice.

Holding her cloak over her head with one hand, her shoes in the other, she ran for a long time. It was no hardship—her feet were leathery from her days in the forest, and many had been the times she'd run with the deer for miles over rises and into valleys and ditches carved by streams.

At last, she saw the indistinct forms of the brothers ahead on the road. So far from the king's court, she felt free to shout. "Naisi!"

Instantly, he halted. He whirled. "Deirdre! What are you doing?"

"Ignore her!" Ainnle shouted. "She's a temptress, Naisi, and will cause all our deaths!"

Deirdre stopped in the road, suddenly mindful of her unbrushed hair, her dirty feet, the smell of last night's fire on her. She stared at Naisi helplessly.

He rode to her.

"Naisi, come," Arden said urgently. "You mustn't pause. Come with us, now."

Ignoring them, he bent down and put a palm against her cheek. "What is it, sweet Deirdre?"

"Why did you go?" she whispered, putting her hand over his own.

He didn't answer, but Deirdre saw it in his eyes. "To avoid me," she said, and backed away, humiliated. "And here I've come running after you like a cat in heat."

"Naisi!" Arden called, his voice urgent.

"Leave me be," he shouted over his shoulder, and turned back to Deirdre.

Seeing the untenable position she'd put him in, Deirdre kissed Naisi's hand and let it go. "Forgive me," she whispered. "I mean you no harm."

She whirled. Lifting her skirts in her free hand, she started to run, blindly, for her eyes were filled with tears. It didn't matter. She'd as soon die as go back to the king. Perhaps she could melt into the forest, there to live as she had for so many years—happily and in peace. Surely if she hid away, the prophecies could not come true . . . surely not even magic could be so unkind as to cause wars simply because a woman was *born*.

What had she to do with that?

And then Naisi was behind her, bending from his mount to sweep her into his arms. "I cannot leave you."

He kissed her, and Deirdre met the kiss with a little cry, putting her hands on his face—his dear and beautiful face. For once, Ainnle and Arden were silent, though she felt their gaze fixed upon them. She didn't care—it was right she should be with Naisi—whatever else there was in life, this was the right thing.

Then he lifted his head, and in his dark blue eyes she saw no shame, only determination. "She goes with us," he said gruffly, and it was plain he would not argue the point.

Ainnle and Arden said nothing at first. In a moment, Ainnle said, "What if we all die over this, Deirdre?"

"It isn't her," Naisi said, shifting to make a comfortable place for Deirdre to ride. " 'Tis the lust of men that makes her beauty evil. They were ready to tear her to shreds at Emain Macha—the king, too—and you know it as well as I."

"What of the *gessa?*" Arden asked. "Have you no fear of Scathach's powers?"

Deirdre felt Naisi's breath against her neck. He brushed his lips over her ear, and his voice was soft. "I've not broken the *gessa.* Nor will I till Scathach gives word."

Arden and Ainnle exchanged a glance. "Then we'd best make for Scathach's camp straight away."

"The better to defend our position, as well, for woe be to us if Conchobar's warriors find us before we have her help."

"Aye," said Arden gravely. "And kill us all if he can."

Deirdre thought of her dream of the king holding Naisi's head up high, fresh blood spilling out. She looked at Naisi. "You must never again come close to the king, do you hear me?"

His smile was sad. "Aye. But, however much Conchobar would wish it, it is not I that would die in such a battle."

"Beware arrogance, my Naisi." She pressed her fingers into his cheeks. "I dreamed your death at the king's hand, just as I dreamed you would come to me."

"All right, Deirdre," he said, but she could see he didn't believe her. "For now, we ride on, and quickly. The king will set his soldiers upon us as soon as it is seen you and I are gone together."

part two

the island of shadows

I am Naisi, oldest son of Uisnech, of Ulster. I am a warrior.

As long as I can remember, it was my will and my wish to be a soldier to the great king of Ulster, Conchobar, he of the hale laughter and bright eyes. I loved Conchobar, always.

But I loved Deirdre more. It was so sudden and swift it caught me unaware. The men in the room, whining like a pack of hungry dogs at her skirts, the king himself grappling at her like she was a camp whore and not the woman who'd been raised to be his queen. Like a small child, she roused my protectiveness.

And other things, I admit it.

Like all the others, I ached to touch her—yes. I wanted to taste her ripe breasts and nestle deep between her thighs. I am a man, that's the way we think, and especially when we think of women like Deirdre.

I liked so many things about her beyond that base thrust. There was a spark of mischief in those long, perfectly colored eyes. I liked the simpleness of her smile and her gusto with her food. When she forgot about the men staring at her, forgot that she was the king's betrothed, and laughed—like any young girl—at my jests, I ached for the sorrows awaiting her.

I could not bear it.

But it was the first night, when I kissed her, that I knew we would live or die, but it would be together. And it took a day for me to work my mind around to the betrayal I would be forced to deliver to my king.

In the end, I was the coward, and Deirdre the wise one. She followed her heart and came after me when I would have run away.

chapter 5

Naisi saw plainly the resentful glances his brothers cast toward Deirdre as they rode. He understood them. Because of Deirdre they had to ride away from Emain Macha and willing women and a grand feast.

And, although both had slaked their hungers at the rath, it was as hard for Arden and Ainnle to look upon Deirdre as it was for any other man. They had told Naisi as much, last night over the fire in their room, when he expressed his need to be with her at any cost. They told him Deirdre was enchanted, that there was no resisting her for any man, and Naisi was not feeling love, only the lust of the magic.

That there had been very powerful magic uttered over her there could be no doubt, but Naisi felt more than enchanted. As he held her close to him now, lust was far from him. He wanted only to have her near, where he might listen to her sweet singing, where he might catch a glimpse of her smile.

A small doubt lingered, deep in the center of his chest, a tight nut of fear that he was only acting under some spell. What if, when all was finished, he found he was only a pawn in some game of priests and sorceresses and the gods?

Deirdre, as if sensing his thoughts, looked up at him.

"What will Scathach think of me?" she asked, and he saw the fear in her face.

"I know not."

"What is she like?"

Naisi smiled. "It would be hard to even tell you. There is not another woman like her in all the world."

Ainnle fell back and said, "She has red hair, curling and wild, to her hips."

"Aye, and she's as tall any of us," said Naisi.

"Likely stronger, too!"

Arden, ignoring them, rode face forward, his mouth in a tight line.

Ainnle tugged up his sleeve to show a harsh scar on his arm. "It was Scathach who marred me thus, wielding a sword bigger than I've seen a man lift."

"Then I should be afraid," Deirdre said.

"Nay," Naisi said gruffly. "There is no doubt she has some plan for you, some need or wish, else she'd not have gone through so much trouble."

"What could it be? I am a very simple girl."

Naisi scowled. Perhaps she, too, was a pawn in some game of magic between the mighty ones. "I cannot say."

Deirdre turned her face toward the forest, and didn't speak again for a long time.

The rain did not cease all day, as if the sky itself had made a judgment upon them. By twilight, all of them were soaked to the skin and miserable, but afraid to stop. Deirdre pointed out a path into the forest. Arden and Ainnle, resentful and boorish, refused to listen at first.

She got down from her mount and knelt against the ground, putting her palm to the leaf-cushioned earth. "There are many riders behind us. We *must* take shelter."

Naisi looked at her, and felt his brothers look, too. Even grimy from the riding, a smear of dirt on her cheek, her feet blackened with the mud of the morning, she was astonishing. Naisi thought her beauty was like the sweep of the stars against the night sky—he could get used to it a little, but suddenly the sharp painfulness of it would sweep through him anew.

"Naisi," she said quietly. "Tell them. I do not lie, and have lived my life in this forest. There are places for us to take shelter for this night, places we may rest."

"Follow her," he said.

His brothers gave him mutinous glances. A little guilt touched him again. Not only he and Deirdre, but his brothers, too, would be exiled and pursued. Perhaps there would never be rest for them again.

And yet, without question, they pulled up the hoods of their cloaks and followed a small, strong woman into the darkness of the forest. Because Naisi, the eldest brother, told them to.

It pierced him.

She led them to a secluded place, deep in the forest, where rocks provided a small cave, and a stream sang silver in the darkness. Trees, unimaginably tall, reached over the clearing to give a roof. It was still and silent and perfectly circular.

Ainnle was afraid of the fairy folk and he hung at the edges of the circle. "My lady," he said, his voice for once not harsh with her, "do you know this place? Is it safe for us?"

Deirdre smiled at him and held out her hand. "Aye, it's safe here. We must only thank Flidhais for her sanctuary, for it was she who led us here."

At the mouth of the rocks, where the stream came out, Naisi saw a flash of a deer's tail before it disappeared.

"What offering do we have to give her?" Deirdre asked.

Arden dismounted and took from the pouch on his girdle a bag of acorns. He walked into the clearing and gave it to Deirdre. All of them knew it was an offering of thanks to Flidhais, but also a peace offering to Deirdre herself.

For a long moment, she held the soft doeskin pouch in her palm, loosely as if to allow him to take it back. Naisi kept still.

At last, Deirdre turned and slipped into the waiting silence of the trees, a wraith against the gloom, and Naisi let out his breath on a sigh. Dismounting, he went to his brother and clapped his shoulder. "Thank you."

She returned with forest greens and a sweet-smelling herb she tossed on the fire Naisi had started. The scent of it made Naisi momentarily dizzy. "What is that herb?"

"Only something my mother showed me," she said. "It will not hurt you, but it will make it harder for our enemies to find us."

Her vagueness annoyed him a little, but he let it pass. They ate in silence, huddling close to the fire. Beyond the cave the rain fell steadily, sometimes so light as a drizzle, other times, like a torrent. Naisi rubbed his damp feet and held them close to the fire.

Deirdre sat a little apart from them, as if she knew she had to give them time to include her in their old patterns. Tortured by his doubts, Naisi watched her as cautiously as he'd watch a wild cat.

The magic of her beauty was powerful indeed. Against the firelight her hair gleamed, and her skirts covered her coltish legs with alluring drapes of soft fabric. Her skin gleamed pale and luminescent as a pearl.

It was all-too-easy to imagine the curves uncovered, her breasts pointed and strong and ready for his touch, her lips quivering—

With a soft groan he left the cave and went into the rain, hoping to wash away his longing, his lust—this wretched enchantment.

She followed him. "Go, Deirdre," he said. " 'Tis from you I retreat."

"And that is what you must not do," she replied. "It is from our joining the curse will be broken."

"I am under *gessa*, Deirdre! I cannot lie with any woman till Scathach gives me leave."

"So we will not lie together," she said. "Won't you let me sit and talk with you?"

In her voice was a certain loneliness, and Naisi cursed himself for the beast he was. It was not her fault he longed for her so desperately. And she'd followed him, risking life and comfort to be at his side, leaving behind all that was familiar.

He took her hand. "I feel that I am enchanted," he said quietly. "That it is not true emotion that drives me, but some magic that will lift."

She began to sing, softly, and somehow the sweetness of the song eased him a little.

"I'd forgotten your father was a harper," he said.

"He used to come sometimes to the cottage, when I was a little girl, and sing to me." Her voice was wistful. "I loved him very much."

"But it was his greed that set the curse upon you."

She nodded. "Yes. But I'll tell you, Naisi, until I came to Emain Macha, I didn't feel cursed. I felt like all the other creatures of the forest, with my place, as they all have theirs."

Again her simplicity made him ache. He took her hand. "I vow you'll know that peace again, my Deirdre."

"You are not angry with me?"

"No." Ruefully, he smiled. "I only want to get to the island so Scathach can lift the *gessa* and I might make love to you."

Deirdre bent her head and pressed her mouth to his palm. Her hair fell like liquid silk over his hand. "That will be a fine day."

He pulled her close, and she nestled her head into his shoulder and they rested that way a long time.

chapteR 6

They crossed the sea to Alba. At first it frightened Deirdre
to be tossed on the water so vigorously, but she quickly
learned to shift her joints and body to accommodate the
movement. Ainnle spent the journey quite ill, a fact over
which his brothers teased him when they at last rode on
solid ground once more.

Nightfall found them at the dun of a young prince,
who took them in cheerfully. It was rare for him to have
visitors, and news of their betrayal had not traveled so far
north.

Hooded and cloaked, Deirdre kept to the back of their
little group, hoping to go unnoticed. Already, after so
short a time, she was wary of men; afraid of the way they
would treat her. The brothers seemed to sense this, and
unlike King Conchobar, felt no need to show her off. As
they were led into the hall, Naisi took her hand and bent
close. "I will tell him you are our sister."

Deirdre nodded and drew her cloak more closely
about her.

The hall was a big, cold place, strangely silent after the
noise of Emain Macha. Deirdre wondered if most halls
were like this one; for after all, there had been a wedding
to celebrate in Erin. At the rough tables were clustered
rough, bearded warriors in crude furs, their legs tied

about with strips of leather. There was no friendliness in their gaze as they examined the knot of visitors coming into their realm.

Deirdre looked to the women, longing for someone in whom to confide her fears, ask advice. But there were only a few and none seemed likely to be the sort that would listen to a young girl, fleeing the riches of a king. These were women as rough as the men; their teeth, gapped and blackened; their faces hard as the north wind. With even deeper suspicion they viewed the group.

Leaning into Naisi's shoulder, Deirdre whispered, "Is this not on the path to the warrior woman's island? Surely they have seen such men as you and your brothers before now!"

"Perhaps." He eyed them carefully. " 'Tis wise to be wary of strangers."

The prince seated them at his table. A young man, stuck in the outer beyond, and hungry for news, he was handsome in a ruddy, hale way if it had not been for the wet red lips, overly ripe in a spare face. His gaze flickered over her, uninterested.

Relieved, Deirdre stayed covered, her eyes down as she ate. A harper came in and began to sing.

At first, she paid the song little notice, but when the man was a little way into it, she heard her name. The ballad of Deirdre! And in it she was painted in an evil light indeed. Abruptly, she lifted her chin in outrage, about to give protest to the harper.

Three things happened at once. She lifted her head, and the hood fell back. The prince reached for a cup of ale and knocked it sideways. One of the other women jumped up to avoid the ale and stepped hard on Deirdre's foot.

She yelped and ducked and grabbed for the hood, but it was too late.

Too many times already had she seen this transforma-

tion on men's faces; one minute they were simple creatures, laughing and uncaring; the next there came a light
in their eyes, pointed and strong and terrifying. It said
more than they wished of their characters, and Deirdre
thought they didn't even know it, didn't know how they
looked when they came undone this way. It made her ill.

His eyes licked her as his tongue licked his lips, making
them wetter and more disgusting than ever. "My good
men, you didn't tell me your sister was so beautiful! Bid
her take off the cloak."

"My lord, she is only a girl, and very shy." It was Ainnle
who came to her defense.

Arden added slyly, "She is in training to be a priestess,
and has much magic in her purse."

The woman beside Deirdre, hearing all this, yanked at
the fabric of the cloak. "Oh, let's have a look at her."

Before Deirdre could move, Naisi was on his feet, his
broad, heavy sword drawn, the tip barely touching the
woman's chin. "Leave her be," he said in a voice dark
with warning.

The woman backed away. " 'Twas only a game," she
muttered.

The prince, lifting one amused brow, waved a hand at
the woman. " 'Tis not worth dying about. There are
beautiful women besides this one." To Naisi he said, "I'll
send a woman to sleep with her."

Naisi lowered his sword. "We are protective of our sister," he said, and sat down warily.

After a minute, the eating resumed, but there was no
comraderie to be had. Deirdre lifted her hood and hid
herself. Bleakly she wondered if there would ever be
peace for any of them.

When they had eaten, a woman showed Deirdre to a
small chamber and gave her water to wash with. "I have

other chores," she said, "but will return to sleep on the pallet there beside you."

Uneasily, Deirdre settled in, wary of every small noise and rustle. When no sound marred the night, she at last settled on the bed below the window, and covered herself with her cloak. In her sleeve, comfortingly cold against her wrist, was her dagger.

In spite of all her wish to remain alert, the day's journey had been long and she ached for sleep. The woman did not return. Twice she dozed off and jerked herself awake a few moments later, heart pounding.

The third time, she fell deeply asleep. She had no idea how long she'd been so far into the dream world, but it was an unpleasant sensation that woke her, a roughness on her thigh—

With a shout, she awakened and tried to jerk away. A fat hand came down on her mouth, and a rough hand grasped her wrist. "Shhh, pretty," came a drunken voice in the darkness. "Be still and I'll be gentle."

Wet lips closed over hers. Deirdre gagged and fought against the weight upon her. She turned her head from the evil thrust of the prince's tongue in her mouth. He grabbed her chin, straddling her now, with his body heavy on her stomach, and kissed her again. With one rough hand, he kneaded a breast, squeezing as if her flesh were a loaf of bread. She could not shift enough to get her dagger into her hand, for his knee held her arm at the wrist.

Still she struggled, first with steady, furious resistance. Her arms and body and legs were thrashing against the onslaught, but it only seemed to inflame him. He tore her bodice and pawed her nakedness and shoved up her skirts.

Suddenly, as if frightened, Deirdre went limp.

The prince laughed. "It will not be so bad if you calm down, little filly. I'm a big man and give big pleasure." He freed himself in the darkness. Deirdre felt a new sensation against her leg and knew what it must be.

His leg came off her arm. With a swift move, Deirdre let the dagger slip into her palm. Giving a loud scream, she slashed the blade over his face. He cried out, his hands instinctively going to the wounds, and Deirdre rolled away from him, jarring her arm on the stone floor as she fell. A bright shock of pain shot through her wrist and elbow, but she scrambled to her feet, heading for the door.

And there was Naisi, wearing only trousers—his sword in his hands. He thrust Deirdre behind him and with a wild yell, went after the prince.

The two men grappled for only a moment. Naisi was by far the better warrior, and the prince had already been wounded. Deirdre, breathing hard with fear and pain, felt a thrill of savage pleasure when the prince lay dead at Naisi's feet.

She bent, knelt, and picked up her dagger from where it had fallen, and took her cloak from the end of the pallet. Naisi had already moved toward the door, holding an arm out to beckon her. "Are you hurt?"

She held her injured arm close to her chest, below the cloak, and shook her head. "Only a little. We must make haste to flee—you've killed the prince!"

"Aye," Naisi said. His voice was heavy with regret.

Their eyes met. Deirdre heard the old, old prophecy ring in her ears. "Blood enough to turn the rivers red," she said quietly. "So it begins. Perhaps you should leave me here, Naisi, so you are not drawn into my fate."

He took her hand, his mouth grim. "Your fate is my fate. And I would not trade it."

The sounds of their struggle had awakened some of the others and now there were rustlings and stirrings, and a wordless buzz in the rooms. "No time to tarry," Naisi said, just as his brothers appeared, already dressed, Naisi's tunic and cloak in their arms.

They fled before dawn, once again.

chapteR 7

The approach to Scathach's island warrior camp was shadowed with powerful magic and could not be breached unless she wished it.

So what Deirdre saw as they approached the coast was a thick fog, pearly in the lowering light of late afternoon. A choppy sea washed at a shore of gray and black pebbles.

For one, cold, terrified moment, Deirdre thought of her dream of three ravens, broken and dead on such a beach. She clutched Naisi's fingers in her own, afraid to speak, but equally afraid not to. What if her dream had been an omen?

Deirdre had not seen the beach except in that dream, any more than she had seen Naisi but saw him in her dream. She turned to him, thinking of the third dream, the dream of Conchobar holding Naisi's head high—

All at once, the fog parted to reveal a path in the stones on the beach. In her astonishment, Deirdre forgot her need to warn the brothers of her dream. Between two boulders on the rocky path, calm waters were spanned by a wide wooden bridge; all were bathed in a warm light, as if it were full summer and not damp spring.

They rode on the bridge, and the horses' hooves made a hollow clomping. In wonder, Deirdre stared at the gentle waters below, at the soft greens furring the land at the end of the bridge. A cluster of people began to gather at the sound of their approach; young warriors, and women in beautiful tunics with deep borders embroidered with bright-colored thread, their hair laced with ribbons.

Convulsively, Deirdre gripped Naisi's hand. She felt his laughter against her back. "Fret no more, little flower, for now we are in Scathach's protection." He kissed her neck in jubilation, and kicked the horse into a faster pace. "Now we may be joined."

"Wait!" She wanted to ask him what would happen if Scathach forbade them to mate, but he rode exultantly toward the island. "Naisi!"

Heedless, he gripped her close around the waist, his arm strong. Deirdre clasped her hands over his and held on tight, staring toward the bank for her first glimpse of Scathach.

The bank led up a small hill. Naisi rode through the clustered onlookers with a wave; Deirdre barely saw them in the blur, but heard their murmurings of surprise and excitement and dread.

And then Naisi pulled up sharply before a wide clearing. A woman stepped onto the wooden ramparts just in front of them, her long red hair sparking yellow and crimson in the bright sunlight. She was tall—easily as tall as Cathbadh or more—and the way she held her body left no doubt that she was as strong as any of the warriors clustering now to see what would happen.

With a single graceful movement, the woman leapt into the air, easily clearing the pointed stakes that would have impaled a lesser warrior, and landed nimbly on her feet before the horse.

Deirdre gasped.

"The salmon leap," Naisi said with a chuckle. "Well done, mistress!"

The woman didn't acknowledge him. Her gaze, a bright sharp blue, settled on Deirdre. Deirdre's hand flew to her throat and the talisman that hung there—it felt warm suddenly, as if it were magically linked to the warrior woman.

Scathach was beautiful; her skin was like milk, and the thick sparked hair hung to her knees. The legs were long and slim, her bust full. Deirdre wondered that any could call *her* beautiful when this woman was so clearly the most magnificent woman in all the world.

"So you are Deirdre of the Sorrows," she said at last, her countenance showing neither pleasure nor dismay. "I have waited a long time for this day."

Naisi helped Deirdre dismount, and she knelt in a submissive posture before the intimidating woman. Words failed her, so she simply bowed her head and waited for Scathach's judgment.

"Stand up straight, girl," Scathach said, poking Deirdre's shoulder with the broad cane she carried. "Only the gods know to what purpose you were born, but you may be sure there was a purpose to your beauty, and the sorrows, too. Lift up your head proudly."

For the first time since arriving at the court of Conchobar, Deirdre lifted her head without shame. Here, she heard no rumbling growl among the men, nor felt the heat of blunted stares. Relieved, she stood up. "I am proud to meet you at a long last."

For a long moment, everything and everybody in the grove fell under a strange hush. The birds did not cry out, nor the trees rustle. Not a sword clanked against the buckle of a belt. Even Scathach was motionless.

A new ripple of fear touched Deirdre and she glanced over her shoulder to Naisi, who had dismounted and stood behind her. He reached down and gave her his hand.

Scathach looked at their linked hands. "You will bring trouble upon my camp, Deirdre of the Sorrows. Are you worthy of the battle we will fight for you?"

"Nay." Deirdre said quietly, thinking of the spilled blood of the prince, of her dreams of Naisi's severed head. "And yet, my fate seems to have brought me here."

"I have brought you here," Scathach said with a lift of her strong chin. "In the morning, you and I will go alone to a special place. There will I learn your mettle."

Arden and Ainnle and Naisi said in one voice: "No!"

Scathach almost smiled, and Deirdre caught the ironic lift of a brow. "What's this noble protest? You doubt my judgment?"

"Nay," Arden said. "It's only that her arm is broken . . ."

"And she fights—we've seen it," Ainnle said.

Now there was definitely a glimmer of amusement in the dark blue eyes. "You've bewitched them," she said to Deirdre. Her expression sobered as she looked to Naisi. "If I find her unworthy, I'll kill her myself."

"No!" Naisi stepped forward. "Or kill us both."

"Are you worthy of him, Deirdre?"

"I long to be so. Whatever I must do I will do."

Scathach nodded and stepped close to remove the woolen fabric of Deirdre's cloak from the girl's arm and touched it lightly. Birch splints held the arm immobile, but it was swollen and blackened around the wrist. Apologetically, Deirdre said, "I had not the herbs I needed to tend it properly," she said. "Does fairy moss grow here?"

Scathach looked up in surprise. "You know of this treatment?"

Deirdre nodded.

The warrior woman smiled, full on, this time, her teeth white and even, against her red lips. "I am pleased. More than you know."

Abruptly, she moved. "For now we will feast! Everyone will eat well tonight!"

* * *

Naisi walked with Deirdre to the room she was given, and waited for the servant woman—a warrior in training—to leave them. When she was gone, he leaned close to Deirdre and pressed himself into the soft and giving warmth of her form. "All day I have been hungry for you," he whispered and took her head in his hands. " 'Tis only hours now till we can lie together."

She gave out a small whimper as his mouth took hers, a little roughly though he tried to keep it light.

He touched her long back, and curved his palm over her hip. Dizzy, he smoothed upward, the fabric of her tunic rumpling under his hands. Need made him stiff as dried leather; against his will he pressed himself against her thigh. She sighed, softly, so softly, and opened her mouth, lifting her arms. All of her, all of her was open and damp. He groaned. "By the gods, I can't bear this!"

She made a sharp, quiet noise and arched into him. "Touch me," she whispered.

Lost—they were lost. Putting his hands up, he touched her breasts. She gasped but melted against him, and he kissed her throat, her chin, her shoulder, wildly, tasting the flesh as his hands weighted and marveled at the—

A sudden bleak and bloody vision bolted into his mind: his own head, severed from his body, held high by Conchobar. Nearby lay Deirdre, dead, her beauty mutilated in gruesome ways by the king's knife.

They broke apart and stared at one another in shock. "Oh, Naisi!" she cried. "What will we do?"

Grimly, he straightened. "We must not do this until Scathach says we may."

Deirdre, eyes wide, nodded.

He lifted her palm and pressed a kiss to the firm center, tasting a hint of salt. He brushed his tongue over it, and drifted, tasting then the tendons of her wrist and put himself next to her to taste the thin white skin of her inner arm.

Gently, she pulled away, making a low keening sound. "Stop, Naisi! Oh, stop!"

Sickened at himself, he pushed away. "I'm sorry," he said and left her.

He stalked across the grounds and stormed into Scathach's chambers. "Remove this *gessa!*"

The warrior woman did not pause in her ablutions. "I cannot."

He flung his cloak on the floor. "You sent me on that mysterious trek, knowing she would be there, and ordered me to remain pure knowing it would be nigh upon impossible and now we are returned and you will still not lift the *gessa?*"

Calmly, Scathach took a sip of water from a wooden cup. "I cannot," she repeated.

"You sent me on a fool's errand!"

"Naisi, sit!"

Her voice brooked no argument. He flung himself in a chair made of yew. It rocked dangerously under his fury, but held him. He glowered at his teacher. "I know not why this has come on my head!"

"Nor do I," she said at last. "I knew not of your involvement until I dreamed her dreams and saw you. I did what I could to protect you, Naisi, but I fear the gods mean to use you to teach Conchobar a lesson of his vanity—and I know not what I can do to save you."

"So I am to die, too?" he spat out. "At least let me love her first!"

Scathach chuckled, not unkindly. "When it is time, it will be my joy to give her to you, Naisi."

"When?" he asked raggedly.

She touched his hair gently. "Soon," she promised. "Very soon."

chapter 8

Just past dawn the next morning, Scathach led Deirdre to a meadow some distance from the dun. Deirdre was nervous, but she admired Scathach very much, striding along with the arrogance of a queen and the strong grace of a warrior. She was beautiful and strong and wise—all the things Deirdre hoped one day to be herself.

The meadow lay on the top of a hill, overlooking the sea. A cluster of snowy sheep grazed in a pen. Beyond, the sea moved in undulating calm.

Scathach breathed deeply. "Wonderful," she commented.

Deirdre only looked toward the sea, wondering what the Scathach would want of her.

The warrior woman's words were a surprise. "I dream your dreams, Deirdre of the Sorrows. With you I dreamed of Naisi, before you ever saw him. With you I dreamed the three ravens bloodied on the beach." Her mouth tight, she turned her head to look at Deirdre. "With you I dreamed of Conchobar holding your love's severed head in his hand."

Deirdre closed her eyes, suddenly sure Scathach would tell her she had been wrong to follow after him this way. "Not for the world would I cause his death," she said.

"And yet, you followed him when he would have left you to the king."

"Aye."

"What made you risk all, to do that?"

Deirdre took a slow breath, thinking of the night she had dreamed Naisi the first time. "He is my fate, and I am his. Else why did the gods give me a vision of him before we met?"

"So it is, with fate. One must do what one must do. And yet, you give yourself much sorrow by this path."

"Do you mean to say there is naught I can do to save my love from the fate I dreamed for him?"

Scathach looked away. "Magic is, like all things, bound by natural law, Deirdre." She sighed. "Often I have pondered this coil and cannot see an end to it. It seems written you are to be a sacrifice, you and your love."

"But to what purpose, my lady?" Deirdre cried. "What good will our deaths serve?"

"To that there seems to be no answer. You are the lambs the bards will use to teach lessons of obedience, no doubt."

Deirdre felt bold and whirled to meet the warrior's eyes. "No! I'll not go easily to that fate. By our joining, something rare and true might be given the world." She took Scathach's hands. "Can you not help us?"

"The laws binding this magic are very strong," Scathach said slowly, peering at Deirdre's face as if for an answer. "The beauty is a punishment for your father's greed, who was not content with a healthy babe, but longed for the power he could seek through you."

"Aye, that much was explained to me by Leborcham." Deirdre shook her head. "But my father is dead—what purpose can it serve to kill my love and I?"

Again Scathach shook her head. "I know not the answer, Deirdre, only that magic is governed by rules. No magic I make can interfere with the first enchantment."

Urgently, she tightened her grip on the girl's fingers. "I need you for that."

"Anything!"

Scathach let her go. "First, there are tests. Close your eyes."

Deirdre did so.

"Scent the grove, tell me what there is here."

With a smile, Deirdre breathed in the salty wind. On it she smelled salt and brine, the coppery blood-scent of water, but hidden in those notes was a lighter, sweeter scent of fresh water. "A brook," she said. "Filled with trout that have fed on the sweet eggs of salmon. They are fat, healthy fish, ready for plucking."

"Well done. Now tell me what you hear."

Deirdre listened and spoke again, telling Scathach of the bees drinking from the lips of trumpet flowers, and the boar snoring in a muddy, shady spot. She smiled as she spoke, confident in the game she and Lebrocham had played endlessly.

But as she quieted herself, reaching beyond the grove, out to the softly undulating waves, she heard the faintest reverberation of evil . . . on the water. Her eyes flew open.

Scathach regarded her sadly. "They come already to take him from you," she said. "Two days, perhaps a little more. Do you love him enough, Deirdre?"

"I love him more than my life, and gladly would I give it to save him."

"It might not be your life you are asked to give."

"What greater sacrifice could there be?" Deirdre asked, bewildered.

"Oh," said Scathach, "there are far worse things than dying. Far worse."

A sharp quiver touched Deirdre at the knowledge in Scathach's words, but she grabbed her arms eagerly. "Tell me how I may save my love," she cried. "No price is too high."

"I wonder," said Scathach, but began to lead the way back to the dun. "But we will speak no more of it now. Come, I know me a warrior who longs to the point of murder for his lady."

At evening, as the shadows grew long and the birds twittered their last whistling songs, a small party gathered in a grove of oak trees. A tent, decorated by the young girls in the camp with blossoms and ribbons and tiny bells, sat below the sheltering arms of the most massive tree. In front of it were Scathach, flanked by two of her warriors; Deirdre and Naisi; Naisi's brothers. There were others, too, watching as a purple gloaming moved through the grove.

Deirdre stared at Naisi as if she'd never seen him. And in truth, she had not. His black hair gleamed down his back. His tunic was richly decorated with red gold, and a red-gold torque glowed around his neck, and bands circled his muscled arms.

The moment was sacred, as they knelt together, hands linked as rowan arms waved over their heads on the sea wind, and Scathach said the ancient words that would join them. Deirdre felt a pounding anticipation in her chest, and she was suddenly frightened.

Naisi nudged her. She glanced up from under her hair. He smiled mischievously, his cheeks ruddy, his bright blue eyes dancing, and winked.

Deirdre smiled.

Then Naisi was bending his head to let Scathach take the necklace from him and Deirdre allowed her own to be taken.

Deirdre had often removed the necklace when she lived in the forest, but the importance of keeping it on had been emphasized when she went to the king's court. As it was ceremoniously removed now, she glanced at

Naisi and felt something new well up in her, something thick and hot, hitherto unknown to her, even when he kissed her.

And in his face, she saw the same heat and need. With laced fingers and locked gazes, they rose as one being and moved to the tent, no longer aware of anyone around them. Deirdre saw nothing but Naisi. His eyes and mouth, his long brown throat and glossy black hair. He cupped her face—his fingers were fierce—and pressed his mouth to hers, then to her nose, and reverently to each eye and eyebrow. "Deirdre," he breathed between kisses, "ever will I love you."

Deirdre trembled and put her hands over his, unsure of whether she could stand upright. The passion in her did not let her speak, nor scarce breathe. She opened her lips to his.

They disrobed each other urgently, and knelt together upon the furs and silks, smelling of violets, that had been prepared for them. Naisi laid her upon the luxurious bed and kissed her breasts and belly, and then moved over her, touching his mouth to hers with the same exquisite reverence of moments before. "I love you," he whispered.

And she was ready for what came then, for the bold feel of his strong, furred thighs against her own, and the joining he made, and the swelling sense of rightness that they should be there together in the lowering light, making love.

But she was not prepared—nothing could have made her ready—for the strange thing that happened when they nestled together as close as two humans could be. From beyond or from within, she couldn't tell, but a wild song began to play, and it seemed to circle and color them with light, a glow of purple and green, soft as the muted colors of the meadow in a fog. Deirdre opened her eyes just as Naisi opened his.

"I love you," she whispered, and let their spirits blend as they would, knowing there would be no parting them, not here or in the Otherworld. Now, for all eternity they would together walk.

Wild crabapple cider in a jug and a cold plate of cooked grouse waited outside the tent when Naisi, pleasantly spent, roused himself. He brought the food inside and looked it over by the light of a candle.

Deirdre still slept. Naisi left her undisturbed as he poured the intoxicating cider into a cup and nibbled at a plate of berries, nuts and cold meat. There was to his very bones a sense of perfect contentment, an emotion of well-being as vast as the sky. The food tasted a thousand times better than ordinary; the crisp cider tart and sweet.

As he nibbled, he watched his love. Her hair trailed in waterfalls over her flesh, cascading over a breast, an elbow, and eddied into pools of silken color on the furs below. She stirred a little as if she felt his gaze, and with a teasing smile he extended a foot and brushed his toes over her knee and calf.

She curled up and scratched at her knees. Taking pity, he tossed a fur over her shoulders against the chill. There was time enough for her to wake. The night was young. With an agreeable sigh, he tossed another fur over himself and dug his teeth into the cold meat.

Only moments passed before he heard a dark moan from Deirdre's throat. And a rustling vision stirred his mind. As her distress increased, the vision came clearer in his head, a vision of Deirdre broken and bleeding under the heel of a triumphant Conchobar.

Unable to see anything but the bloody vision, Naisi reached for Deirdre, and his hand closed on her arm as the nightmare unfurled in his mind—her gaze, as if from below, moving up and up and up the king's powerful body, to the prize he held in his hand—

Deirdre's cry rent the night, shattering the dream. She sat bolt upright and Naisi hauled her next to him. Her body trembled like a birch in a storm, and he held her tight, close, his hands smoothing her back, her hair. "Sssh," he said, though she said nothing. "It's all right. It's all right.

"I will kill him before I let him near you, Deirdre."

She lifted her hand and urgently covered his lips. "You must go nowhere near him, Naisi. Nowhere close. If he comes you must flee."

"A warrior does not run from his enemies, my love."

"Then you and I will die at his hands, but it will be long years before he frees me to death."

Grimly, Naisi shook his head. "Better we both die by our own hands than let him kill us that way."

Her eyes were dry and tragic. "Is there no hope for us?" She moved a lock of hair from his face. "None?"

All at once, he could not bear the sweetness of this night to be so marred. He bent his head and kissed her tenderly, gently. "Aye, my love, we'll find a way," he said, even though he knew it to be a lie. "And I'll kiss you thus till we are white-haired and bent." As they sank again to the silks and furs, he kissed her, again and again and again. "Forever, Deirdre, I swear it."

part three

pierced hearts

The way it is written, I am a hero. But I know better. Every man has a weakness. Deirdre was mine.

You must understand how long I had waited for her, hearing snippets of news here and there that she was indeed growing into an unrivaled flower of a woman.

And, too, I was growing older. A vain man I'd been, but not without reason. In my day, I pleased many a maiden, and not only because I was king. They flocked to me when I was young.

A man can only ever become truly a fool over a woman, and I proved it so with Deirdre. Another time in my life, I might have let her go when I saw what bloomed so fast and hot between her and the good Naisi. At other times I might have been wise enough to know love cannot be cut down with a sword, no matter how fiercely it is wielded.

But in truth, my lust was engaged and I could not think. 'Tis the curse of men that the one cancels the other.

You must understand, too, I loved Naisi. He had been like a son to me, not a young god like Cuchulain, who always belonged more to his mother than me, but a youth who shared with me a pleasure in ribald jokes and much dancing and drink, a lusty youth with deep intelligence and great courage. I did not think to lose the girl to him.

Another time in my life, I might have let them go. But, you see, I had begun to grow old, and only the head of that traitor would soothe my injury. To get it, I would use the same treachery he had given me.

chapter 9

A girl came to the tent in the morning. "Scathach will see you, one at a time. Deirdre first."

"Perhaps she has some answer to our trouble."

Naisi did not look hopeful. "Perhaps."

The grass was still wet with dew as Deirdre hurried to Scathach's chambers. The warrior woman was dressed in softer clothes than Deirdre had seen, and her hair was laced with ribbon to keep it from her face. The flesh about her eyes was drawn, as if she had not slept, and yet she was still as beautiful as a honeysuckle blossom at first light, and she awed Deirdre.

"You called for me?" she asked.

"I think I have found a weapon you might use to thwart the king's desire to possess you."

Deirdre moved forward. "Tell me!"

"I have thought of a spell for you to use." From the table she took a tiny bag tied with ribbon that she put in Deirdre's palm. "Toss the herbs toward the sky and let them fall upon you." She told her the secret words to say, simple words, but powerful.

Deirdre closed her fingers over the bag. "What will it do?"

Scathach covered Deirdre's fingers, and there was a terrible gravity in her face. "It will depend upon your

heart, Deirdre. If you are vain, you will be forever deformed. If you are willing to forego beauty for love, I
think the spell will work."

"In what way?"

"No more will men war for your beauty, for only those
with true vision will be able to see it. The rest will see
something else."

"Something horrible," Deirdre said, a thick dread in
her chest. "What of Naisi?"

"I do not know."

Grief touched her—this is what Scathach had meant
when she had said there were things worse than dying:
she might be a repulsive thing to her love. How could she
bear it?

"This is between us, only," Scathach warned. "You
must not tell him."

Deirdre nodded. Holding the soft deerskin bag in her
hand, she took a breath. "And if I do not use it?"

"Then you will live to see Conchobar hold your love's
head in his hand."

A pain stung her heart. "Very well."

Scathach kissed her cheek. "You are brave and fine,
Deirdre. I would that I could give you better."

Deirdre roused herself from her foolish self-pity. "You
have given much, and I thank you."

When Naisi came to Scathach, he knelt with a flourish
and kissed her hand. "May the gods grant you all you
desire," he said. "I am ever grateful for the night you
gave."

Scathach smiled, and bade him rise. He saw the smile
did not reach her face, but only sat like an uncomfortable
crown upon her lips. The thick dread of Deirdre's dream
came back to him and settled in his chest. "We will die for
this love," he said with certainty.

Scathach lifted a shoulder. "It seems I have been trying to avert this tragedy since the child was born. Despite all, I fear I will fail her."

"I will kill her before I let the king take her—for he'll punish her as long as she lives."

"Yes." From the table, Scathach lifted a small bag tied with ribbon. She held in her hand, musingly.

Naisi had never seen her so distracted. "My lady are you well?"

"No," she said. "I am sick at heart, and my head aches with sorrow." Into his hand she put the bag. "Take this spell. When the king comes, you must cast it into the air and speak these words." Gravely, she repeated them to him.

Naisi held the bag with dread, knowing magic always carried a price. "Will it kill her?"

"No. But it depends upon the purity of your love. If your love is not true, she will be horribly deformed."

"Deformed?"

"It is an unstable spell—I cannot control it." She took a breath. "It grieves me to mar so beautiful a flower, but it is the only way."

"It seems a cruel answer."

"Less cruel than death." She raised her eyes. "If you love her truly, Naisi, it will only transform her in the eyes of other men."

"How can I know if my love is pure?" He thought of the near-painful joy of loving her in the night, when there was no light with which to gaze upon her beauty. "I have been ever afraid since this began that I am pawn, that we are both pawns, in the game of gods and druids and sorcery." Urgently, he asked again, "How can I know?"

"Search your heart, Naisi." Heavily, she leaned forward. "For this, too, you shall know: if you do not truly love, you are bound to a long life of deepest misery—for both of you."

"Scathach—can you not divine the workings of my heart and tell me if I am the subject of some lust?"

She only shook her head.

"I have been smitten before," he said quietly, holding the bag now in his fist, as if he would crush it. "But never like this. I feel, when I am with her, that all the world pulls into a settled harmony it has not known before—that by our loving, we are bringing something good and true to the world that will be forever lacking if we do not love."

Scathach gazed at him steadily.

For a moment, he gazed back. Then he bowed his head. "If I do not truly love her, I am a heinous traitor."

"Yes."

He left her.

Deeply troubled, Naisi did not seek out Deirdre or his brothers, but went to the edge of the island, where sometimes the curtain of Scathach's magic parted and the true sea could be seen.

Across the blue-gray waters lay Erin, that land of his home, of his heart, and Deirdre too. He settled on a rock and tossed pebbles down the slope, watching them tumble faster and faster to their drowning under the crush of waves that sent spray, cold and salty, over his face.

Did he love her enough?

The question still troubled him when he sat later in the hall where the warrior students and visitors gathered. Tonight, a strained air of anticipation hung in the air. Naisi, sitting close to Deirdre, noted well the alert pacing of the guards at the door and along the bridge to the main island. Uneasiness moved in the room.

None had seen Scathach all day, nor did she come for supper. When questioned, a girl told Deirdre and Naisi that the warrior woman would see no one. The girl confided, "She has a terrible pain in her head. She says she cannot think for it."

Deirdre stood. "I should go to her," she said. "I know the healing arts. Did I not heal my own broken arm?"

"No." The girl was firm. "This is not a pain of the body, but one of the soul. She battles evil forces."

Deirdre looked at Naisi with sorrow. "We have done that to her."

"She chose the quest for herself, Deirdre, long ago." With a gentle smile, he brushed her smooth, peach-colored cheek. "When she looked upon you as a babe."

She smiled at him, gratefully, and the expression gave a shimmer to her deep eyes. Naisi marveled at the play of color in the irises, at the fringe of her dark lashes. With the pad of his thumb, he touched her fragile eyelid. "So beautiful," he whispered, and kissed her.

Guiltily, for it had been in that moment her *beauty* he admired, he lifted his head—and for one fleeting instant, caught a fury of sorrow in her face before she hid it.

"What marks you so, my love?" he whispered, moving his fingers on her jaw.

Her smile was strained. " 'Tis nothing."

"What did Scathach tell you this morning?"

"I am not free to say."

"Nor am I." He glanced around the room. "I fear we have not long to wait until we know what our fates will be."

"Then we should not waste our time," she said. Standing, she tugged him to his feet and pressed his hand to her belly. "Come plant me a babe."

He halted her. "Wait, my love."

She turned to look up at him, and even so small a gesture held uncommon grace. "What is it?"

Naisi touched the curve of her neck with one finger. "How am I to know?" he muttered under his breath.

"Know what?" Playfully, as if there were no warriors on

their way, as if there were no strain in the room, as if they were only newly wed and hungry, she smiled and pressed her pliant, strong body into his. "Know that I love you? That I long to please you?"

A heat rushed through his loins at the touch of her mouth and hands. What part of her he loved, he did not know—only that he did love, and deeply. "Come," he said, and swept her into his arms. "A babe you want planted, a babe I will plant."

She laughed softly and buried her face against his neck and Naisi thought that whatever happened on the morrow, or had gone before now, mattered not. Urgently, he kissed her.

Back to the tent they retreated, and there made love again, and again, until they slept, limbs entwined.

In Deirdre's dream, three gray hawks bloodied the throats of three ravens, and left them for dead on the pebbled beach. Restlessly, she stirred, trying to warn the brothers, but they would not listen, and flew away to meet the hawks in the air as Deirdre stood behind, crying out after them.

Naisi dreamed of Fergus, his oldest and most beloved friend. "I come in peace," Fergus said. Naisi embraced him. Overhead, a raven screamed and flew at the head of Fergus. Naisi shook his head. "Bold creature."

Scathach tossed and turned in her bed. Pain filled her whole head, every crook and cavity, and yet still she saw the breaches in her magic fortress. She cried out, but could do nothing.

Conchobar had come.

chapter 10

At daybreak, Arden and Ainnle came to the tent. Deirdre awakened to their attempts to rouse their brother. "Naisi!" they cried, pulling on his toes to awaken him. "Wake up!"

"Is there some trouble?" Deirdre asked, rubbing the narcotic sleepiness from her eyes.

"I don't know. There is a messenger here from the king, but the guards won't let him into the camp." Arden said, and slapped his brother's feet again. "Naisi!"

At last Naisi stirred, and blinked. All at once, he sat up. "What is it?"

He touched his head, as if it pained him, and Deirdre raised a hand to his smooth, hot back, taking comfort from the feel of his flesh. "Are you ill, Naisi?"

"No." But he swayed as he tugged his tunic on. "I must have drunk overmuch."

Alarmed, Deirdre looked at his brothers and shook her head. "He drank nothing last night."

Ainnle frowned. "Fergus is at the gate. He'll speak to you alone."

"Who is Fergus?"

"My oldest friend," Naisi said, and for a moment, he looked befuddled, and touched his head again. "I dreamed he would come."

Her own dream tumbled into Deirdre's mind, and she grabbed Naisi urgently. "You must not go! I dreamed again of the hawks and ravens. I fear there is some trick here."

"Fergus would not betray us," Arden said, and Deirdre saw the ruffled male pride in his expression. For all that he had accepted his brother's love of her, he had not come to full acceptance of Deirdre.

She sighed and looked to Naisi, buckling his sword belt. "I'll return in a little, my sweet," he said.

"Naisi, no!" Clasping the bedding around her, she struggled to stand as the brothers ducked out of the tent. "I tell you, there is mortal danger if you go."

His mouth tightened, and he turned, waving at his brothers to go on without him. He took her arms. "You are growing so fearful it muddles your brain, Deirdre. Fergus will not hurt me, and I am only going to the bridge to speak with him, not across the sea to battle the king." He smiled and brushed a lock of hair from her face. " 'Tis only woman's fancy that makes you think I am in danger, and while I am glad to see your love, I swear I will be back in a trice to make love to you again."

Deirdre narrowed her eyes and shoved his hands from her arms. "Go then if you are so wise and manly."

"I do not wish to bicker with you, my love."

Bitterly, she shrugged. "I thought you a different sort of man," she said. "I see that like all men, you discount the words of women."

A frown darkened his brow. "We will talk more of this later."

In silence, Deirdre watched as he tucked a dagger in his sleeve and tied a small bag around his neck below his shirt. When he bent to kiss her, she turned her face from him and he caught only her cheek. For a moment, he paused, as if he would say something, but then turned and ducked out of the tent.

Aching with terror, she moved. "Naisi!" she cried after him. "Do not go, I beg of you!"

He glanced over his shoulder, but kept walking, flanked by his brothers, until the morning mist swallowed him up.

Deirdre flung on her shift and tunic, and ran out into the mist to find Scathach. Barefoot in the silent forest, she ran.

It was only as she neared the dun that she began to wonder at the strangeness of the morning. The first day she and Naisi and his brothers had come here, there had been deep fog on the beach beyond, but when Scathach lifted the barriers to their entrance, the island had been sheathed in sunshine. And it had ever been so, in every moment, since they came.

She halted as the knowledge penetrated. Going still, she closed her eyes and listened. In the hall were snores and shufflings; not far away she heard a deer drinking from a lake—a good omen!—and she sent out a prayer: *Flidhais, guide me!*

But there was silence elsewise. Too much silence for a morning. Where were the sounds of pots? Firewood? Chuckling girls? Dogs?

An enchantment!

With a soft cry, she turned, ready to rush back to the tent and some manner of safety, since it was hidden. The king's guard could not find her there as quickly.

But as she turned, she ran into a hard chest, and a pair of arms snared her. Deirdre screamed in her terror, but then bit the flesh in front of her, and kicked as hard as she could.

A man slapped her. The blow stunned her for a moment, and she found herself flung over the enormous back of a warrior in full dress. "Behave, my lady, and I'll not need to do that again."

The arms held her fast. The warrior's name was Eaghan, and he was a friend to the king. In fury, Deirdre slammed her fists into his great muscled back, but her fists might have been gnats for all the discomfort she seemed to cause him.

He carried her to a high hill, and put her down, though still he held her firmly in his bearlike grasp. "Now watch the destruction of the sons of Uisnech," he said.

And only then did Deirdre see that the fog had parted, that the hill overlooked the beach of her dream, and that there were warriors on eager battle-hardened horses.

From this vantage point, she could see three figures winding downward, one black head sandwiched between two fiery ones, into the waiting trap.

"No!" she screamed.

In her bed, Scathach tossed and turned, her head burning with fever. A worried servant girl bathed her face once more and Scathach opened her eyes. "Go!" she cried, slapping the girl's hands away. "Wake all the soldiers. Send them to the beach now!"

The terrified girl ran to do as she was bid.

As they walked down the hill toward the bridge, the brothers were silent. Naisi frowned. "Why has Scathach let it all go so gray?"

"Her servant says she is ill."

Uneasily, Naisi glanced over his shoulder. "Ill? I've never known her to be ill."

Ainnle shrugged. "For all that she appears young, it is said her years equal that of the great tree at Lough Ravel. Soon or late such age carries a price."

"Perhaps," Naisi agreed, but his uneasiness trebled. "Beware. It may be Deirdre knew something we did not."

But when they rounded the bend toward the bridge,

he forgot his worry, for there, dear to him as his own heart, was Fergus, as fair as Naisi was dark. When Fergus spied Naisi, he jumped to his feet and the two men embraced. "I missed you at Emain Macha by only a day," said Fergus. "By then already the king was crying for your head."

"Aye," Naisi said heavily. He glanced over his shoulder to his brothers. "It was not my wish to raise his ire."

"She must be a great beauty indeed," Fergus said.

Naisi nodded, but the warning knot of tension in his chest tightened all at once, as if the gods had given the rope of worry a sharp tug. "She is my own true love, Fergus."

"And the king believes her to belong to him."

"She belongs to herself, and only graces me with her heart as she chooses," Naisi said, bristling.

From the woods came a sharp, bleating cry, like a raven screaming warning. Naisi lifted his head to seek out the creature, but saw nothing.

"What will you do?" Fergus asked, more gently. "You cannot run forever."

"I expect we will die for this—that will be our punishment."

Fergus lowered his head. Red crept over his cheeks and nose, a mottling Naisi knew only came to the warrior at moments of great emotion. "What grieves you, Fergus?"

He grasped Naisi's arm and leaned close. "It is a trick, Naisi. Conchobar bade me come within so Cathbadh could breach Scathach's magic. There are warriors all around us."

"Draw your swords!" Naisi cried over his shoulder, shoving Fergus from him so he might draw his own.

And from out of the mist came a great army, and from behind, Scathach's warriors emerged. And then there was battle and nothing else.

* * *

In fixed horror, Deirdre watched the battle rage below. Between her breasts hung the small bag of magic herbs, but her arms were caught fast at her sides by the brutish strength of the guard.

Below raged a battle of great proportions—Scathach's army against King Conchobar's men, swords leaping, horses crying, the sea roaring. Deirdre had not thought battle would be such a noisy thing, but it was.

Until it came nigh that the king and Naisi stood face to face, and it was as if all the battle ceased. The king came down from his horse and faced the youthful warrior. Deirdre covered her mouth with her hands, yanking away from her guard.

It was then she saw that it was only in her mind that the battle had ceased, for it had not. Around the mortally bound pair raged soldiers and the screams of wounded and the furious and the grim. But Naisi and the king circled each other. One parried, then the other, and then there was a fierce and terrible contest alive between them.

Deirdre fingered the bag of herbs against her breasts, wondering if she might be spared the use of the spell. Naisi was stronger; with her own two eyes she had seen him best the king at contests at Emain Macha.

That day seemed very long ago.

From one side came Cathbadh, and Deirdre caught her breath. The druid would not cease in his quest to vanquish her and remove the threat against Erin's warriors that was in the prophecy by killing her.

A thick oily smoke choked her. A magic smoke, Deirdre knew. It choked her and the warrior behind her. "Curse him," the man growled. "I am to stay here with you no matter how the battle goes, but Cathbadh wants you in the battle so you'll die."

"Think you I'd rather live?" Deirdre asked.

"Aye, I do." He lifted a cynical brow. " 'Tis not so bad a thing to be queen."

The smoke thickened, and roughly the warrior lifted her. "We'll smother here," he said, and nimbly descended the hill.

The noise rose and rose as they were enveloped in the smoke and sounds. Deirdre smelled blood and saw warriors dead on the beach, saw blood staining the pebbles, and all was just as it had been in her dream.

"No!" she cried aloud, beating at the immovable wall of Eaghan's chest. "Take me to Conchobar! I go to him willingly, to save the lives of my love and his brothers!" She beat at him. "Take me!"

The thick oily smoke cleared, and there was the king, and Naisi, deep in the throes of mortal combat. Both bled from small wounds, and staggered with exhaustion. Ferocity made masks of their features.

"Stop!" Deirdre cried, but her voice was lost in the mad music of battle. Cathbadh alone heard her, and emerged from the noise like a ghostly owl, his lean handsome face glowing with a queer satisfaction. "They must battle this way," the druid said. "For lust and greed."

He grabbed her, and at the moment, Naisi spied them. "Halt!" he cried, and turned from Conchobar to raise his sword at Deirdre. With his other hand, he grabbed the small bag from around his neck.

Enraged, Conchobar lifted his sword high above his head.

"No!" Deirdre cried. "Wait!"

The king brought down the sword, but it skimmed Naisi, who now ran toward Deirdre with a bleak expression.

Deirdre took the bag of herbs from her breast and tore it with her teeth, pouring a fine white powder into her hands. With a triumphant cry, she tossed the powder into the sky.

And in a strange, slow scene, she saw Naisi, too, throw the contents of his pouch into the air, so it was together their voices rang out the magical words, her voice and the voice of her love, ringing as one.

As the dust drifted over all of them, a wide deep hush fell on the battlefield. All eyes turned toward Deirdre, as if drawn by some beacon. Deirdre wanted to hide herself, as she had so often at Emain Macha.

Instead, she lifted her head proudly and straightened her shoulders and tilted her chin upward. Proudly she would meet their gazes. Proudly she would bear herself, beauty or not, even deformed.

She felt no difference in herself. Still her same bones in their covering of skin and her hair lifting on a breeze and her breast, still hungry for the touch of her love, who stared around him but did not look at her.

The silence went on and on and on. Then Cathbadh, beside her, began to laugh. The sound was bold and deep and filled with delight. "Scathach is a wise one, she is!" he cried, and all his animosity toward Deirdre seemed gone. Not even a trace of it lingered in his gray eyes.

"What has it done to me?" she asked in some fear.

"It has done nothing to you," he said, and pointed. "It is to them it was done."

Now there came a strange, rippling murmur from the too-quiet crowd. Not the high whining hunger that so frightened her at Emain Macha, but a groan here, a gasp there, a soft sigh still there. Deirdre clutched her skirts in her hands and looked from face to face of the warriors. Some smiled gently in return, some grimaced and glanced hurriedly away, and yet others wore expressions of such stricken horror they cried out.

"What do they see?" she asked Cathbadh.

"Scathach has made of your beauty a mirror," he said. "Henceforth, men will see what is in their hearts when they gaze upon you. Those running from you are seeing their own lust, twisted to parody."

Deirdre closed her eyes, afraid to seek out the one face that might now wear that loathing. And then she took a breath to look—but Naisi he still did not look at her.

At last she looked to Conchobar. His sword hung forgotten at his side, and misery cloaked his face. "I am old," he said, as if apology. "And a fool."

He turned away.

Deirdre touched her chest and spoke the name of her beloved. He stood stonily where he'd been when he flung up the powder. His black hair shone in the brightening day, and the high plane of his cheekbones wore a flush.

"Naisi," she repeated. "Look at me."

Naisi heard Cathbadh's words with dread: *a mirror of men's hearts.*

In his throat he felt a pulse beating, almost strangling him with the power of the blood below, and he thought of Deirdre's dream. Touching his neck, he looked at the king. "I regret the sorrow I caused you, my lord. In truth, I loved you long."

"You are dead," said the king, and turned heavily away.

"Naisi!" Deirdre spoke his name. And again, "Naisi."

For one brief moment, he closed his eyes and thought of the way she had looked last night in his arms, her skin white and pure, her hair a rippling glossy fall, her body a tender morsel.

Then slowly, he lifted his head and turned, and opened his eyes.

And there stood Deirdre, unchanged, unless she was even more beautiful. Her lavender shift clung with sweetness to the curve of her high, full breasts, to the length of her waist and legs; her magnificent knee length hair rippled around her like the mane of fine mare. She was so bright and beautiful it almost hurt him to look upon her.

Her mouth quirked suddenly, and a smile as bright as dawn burst on her face. She laughed and opened her arms to him. "Come, my love."

With a gasp of relief, he dropped his sword and stumbled to her. He kissed her plainly on the mouth, and on her neck and on the sweet swell of her breasts.

As they clung to each other, the king motioned his warriors to come away. In a weary tangle, they trailed after him, leaving a few to gather the bodies slain on a rocky beach, just as they had been in Deirdre's dream.

In fierce joy, Naisi lifted her and carried her back up the hill to do more planting.

Cathbadh gathered his robes about him and followed after the king. Scathach rose from her bed and ate a piece of fruit. Arden and Ainnle found willing women and had their lusts slated.

And in a small hut in a great forest, an old sorcerer sighed, and turned over, and breathed his last breath, for his last spell had met its end. The harper's daughter had been saved.

epilogue

I am old now. My flesh has fallen loose on my limbs, and my hair is thin, and the breasts that so inspired a king have gone flat.

But my Naisi still kisses them, and wants to hold me in the night, and tells me his stories in an old man's craggy voice. And therein lies more truth than my story can tell.

Together we have had seven children, and they all favor their father but one, my youngest daughter, who all say is the very image of her mother. It is for her I have told the truth of Naisi and me, for her and for the girls who will feel responsible for the way men react to them.

Remember when you hear of the tragic end of Deirdre that sometimes men would rather kill beauty than see it fade. Remember, too, it was a woman who saved me.

To live and fade.

the trysting hour

BY

Susan Wiggs

The Trysting Hour is dedicated to Sharyn Cerniglia, first a devoted reader, then a treasured friend. Her exquisite collection of books, her generosity of spirit, and her unquestionable martini-making skills all contributed to the inspiration for this story.

Author's Note

"The Trysting Hour" is based on the myth, "The Wooing of Etain," as translated by Jeffrey Gantz and retold by Moyra Caldecott.

PROLOGUE

The dark pulse of the night penetrated the silence. The whispered cadence was sung by wavelets hushing on the pebbled banks of the river, by breezes soughing through the wind holes of the shelter, by the harsh, tandem breathing of two wakeful lovers.

The man, long-limbed and powerful, might have appeared rough and formidable to one who did not know him.

Ah, but she knew him, and knew him well. She knew the caress of his lips on her throat, the deft skimming of his hands over her breasts and belly, the delicious lick of heat she felt when his loving fingers found her soft, hidden parts.

She touched him wantonly, welcoming his strength when he groaned low in his throat and rose above her, hovering, waiting, gazing down at her. The moment felt curiously disparate; the rhythm of the night quickened and carried a thought that had never occurred to her before . . . *hurry, hurry, hurry.*

She did not know why she felt an urgency tonight, of all nights. Tonight they were safe in a thatched dun, far from any who would do them harm.

"Our hearts are joined," he whispered as his long bright hair went tumbling over his noble brow.

"Then let it be so with our bodies," she said, rising to meet him, to guide him. They touched, melded, and inside her, something burst like a flame set to a pitch torch.

A searing sense of completion seized them both, lifted them and swirled them about like petals in a storm. Pleasure was pain and pain was pleasure, and for one ecstatic heartbeat of time, the night quiet was shattered by wordless cries of abandon.

They drifted, settling back to earth, shaken by the fervor of their joining.

When she dared at last to move, she turned and propped her hands on his chest so that she could gaze upon him.

Her lover was more noble than the windswept crags of the western shores. His hair, the color of winter sunshine, tumbled in profusion around a face that was so dear to her she nearly wept each time she saw it. Sometimes she had to look away, for it was like staring too long into the sun—intense, painful, irresistible.

His hands, cupping her face, were as gentle as mist on the moors. "You felt it, too," he whispered, his hands dropping to her shoulders, pulling her up so that her eyes were level with his.

"Yes, my beloved. Such joy. And such pain. Why? Why must loving you hurt so?"

"There is no joy without pain."

The catch in his voice made her look at him sharply. Though night dimmed her vision and a gathering storm outside obscured the moon, she saw the eyes of her beloved. Clear and deep as a lake they were, and within them dwelt a grief beyond mending. A knowledge she did not want to share.

Suddenly frightened, she drew away.

Outside the dun, thunder trumpeted like the blast of a war horn.

She jumped up and ran to the wind hole, clutching the edge to steady herself. "What is happening?"

"Turn around," he whispered.

She forced herself to obey, even as fear made her throat go tight.

He had donned his bleached tunic, and for her, he held out a robe.

She had never seen the garment before. It was made of red silk. Red, the color of anger, the color of death.

"What is this?" she asked. "I don't understand."

The wind screamed across meadows and moors, ripping hanks of thatch from the roof of the dun. Though aware of the tempest clawing at the walls of the shelter, she saw only her lover, his huge, sad eyes telling her what he could not bring himself to say: There is a magic more powerful than our love.

Even now, that dark magic tugged at her, compelled her to obey. She took a step forward, toward the inevitable. Toward her destiny. She pressed her fingers to her trembling lips, then touched them to his mouth.

He closed his eyes, a sort of ecstasy transforming his features into a visage of agony. He was as beautiful as midsummer dawn, and his pain shimmered like the rising sun on the moors. Then he looked at her. "Remember what I have said. There is no joy without pain. My love, this is all I can give you now. It is the only way I know to save you."

Deep in her woman's heart, she understood. Pain and joy, forever inseparable. Two sides of the same coin.

She slid her arms into the sleeves of the red robe. The rich silk rippled like fire over her nakedness.

As the storm took wing, the wind came bellowing up from the dales. The wild river boiled over its banks like the sea, with swells rising into waves and biting with frothy white teeth at the shore. The roaring tempest ripped the roof from the dun, wrenched the door from its thick leather hinges, sheared the walls to dust and rubble. Wind and water lashed the lovers and swirled around them, brutal, merciless, cleaving them apart.

She became one with the storm, helpless, a victim of its hungry fury, swept up by a power far greater than her own. She was changing, splintering, fading from her lover's embrace. Borne on fragile wings, she circled and swirled, an offering to the earth and the storm, no longer a creature of free will.

Seconds before the tempest hurled her away entirely, she called out to him in terror and panic and grief. "How will I remember how much I loved you?"

"Aideen," he said, raising his fist to the lightning-veined sky. The flash lit him from behind, outlining his perfect masculine form, his broad shoulders and flowing hair, his feet planted as if in a battle stance. "I will make you remember!"

chapter 1

"I had the most extraordinary dream." Even before she arose from her bed box, Aideen felt the need to give shape to her dream with words. If she failed, she would lose the vision, the bright images, the terror and the hope.

Shelagh, her handmaid, knelt down and took both her hands. "Let it go. Dreams come from the dark places inside us. It's best to banish them with the night." Shelagh's face lit with a broad smile. "Especially on such a day as this."

For a moment, Aideen ignored the portentous words. She stared out through the wind hole of her chamber, watched the clouds rolling in the summer sky, and clung to her dream. A princely lover holding her in his arms. A face too comely for words. A voice calling to her through the clamor of a storm. And a love so powerful that the feeling reached beyond time and space and embraced her in gentle, all-consuming folds.

"Aideen?" Shelagh flipped back the wolfskins and woven blankets.

"My wedding day!" In one motion, Aideen jumped up.

"Dearling." Shelagh hugged her close. "It's a grand day indeed. The feast of Lugnaid. The day a princess weds the High King. Deep magic is at work."

Aideen felt a chill waft over her skin. She decided it was caused by the morning air striking her unclad form, and she shivered.

Clucking like a ruffled hen, Shelagh wrapped her in a robe of soft lamb's wool. "A pity your parents never lived to see this day."

The sadness, as familiar as the morning mist that rose from the river, crept over Aideen. She was alone now. She would go to her husband alone. If the marriage did not please her, she had nowhere else to go.

Shelagh bustled about the chamber, calling for Aideen's other women to bring herbs and blackthorn combs, fragrant oils and artifices and jewels.

Almost before Aideen knew what was happening, her maids arrived, chattering and giggling with excitement. Full of stories of the crowds surging up the roads to Tara to see the High King wed, the women accompanied Aideen outside. They were all young that day, flushed with their youth and with the knowledge that they would never be as lovely, as fleet of foot, as carefree, again.

In a ripple of bleached tunics and flowing hair, the women crossed the grassy bawn and raced down a summer-green slope to the river Boyne.

The women had come with her from afar, from her father's kingdom on the wild western shores. On this day of all days, Aideen found comfort in their presence, in the familiar, winking dimple in Sibheal's cheek, the solemn dignity of Riona, the shy glow that emanated from Nainsi. Their knees pressed into the fine sand as they settled down on the riverbank, to ready Aideen for her husband.

"Are you nervous?" asked Nainsi, using a deerhide cloth to buff Aideen's nails.

"Unbearably." Aideen leaned forward, dropping her voice. "What know I about being a queen? Why was I, of all women in Eriu, chosen to wed the High King?"

Shelagh stirred a willow wand in a vat of deliciously scented water, steeped in sweet bergamot. "King Echu's druids advised him to seek out the perfect bride. And who could be more perfect than yourself, I ask you?"

Aideen blushed and ducked her head. "Shelagh—"

"Mannerly, that's what you are, and skilled at the hearth as if your poor mother hadn't passed to the Land of Promise all those years ago. And quick of mind, that's thanks to your kin on her side as well." Shelagh winked at Nainsi. "By her seventh summer, she was beating her father at games of fidchell. And of course, there's not a lovelier face in the five kingdoms. . . ."

Embarrassed, Aideen broke away, shed her robe, and slid into the crystal waters. Sinking into the cold river, she blocked out Shelagh's speech, for her praise sprang from years of loyal service to the family.

A terrible lie festered within Aideen. She knew she was deeply flawed inside, wholly unworthy of Shelagh's praise. All her life, Aideen had suffered from a feeling of separateness, of not belonging. She felt more alive in her dreams than she did awake. Why was it not apparent to the woman who knew her best?

"They believe you'll restore prosperity to the land," Riona was saying just as Aideen broke the surface.

"That is much to ask of one woman." Aideen shook her head, scattering spray over the water. It was odd, too, to think that Echu would marry her for such a purpose. She had always thought that a man—even a king—would wed for more personal reasons.

She arched her neck and dropped her head back. Sibheal waded in and poured the herbal water through Aideen's hair. "Perfection is no more than men generally ask of women," the maid said with a laugh.

Nainsi and Riona, who were readying Aideen's gown, called out in agreement. Like their good-natured teasing,

the rich green silk, embellished with red carbuncle gar-
nets and gold thread, floated on the summer breeze.

"So men have done since the world was young," Sibheal said stoutly.

Shelagh chuckled. "Take pride, dearling. Echu sent his
ambassadors far and wide, instructed them to find the
most flawless beauty in the land. No surprise that the
search led to you."

Aideen's cheeks heated as she remembered the events
of a fortnight earlier. It was an ordinary day of high summer. A too-familiar restless melancholy drove her from
her bed.

She had always been ashamed of the yearnings inside
her. Even after the death of her parents, she had everything a woman could want—wealth and safety, high good
health, and a loving *tuath* comprised of many aunts, un-
cles, and foster parents who cared for her.

Yet always, from earliest memory, she had the unset-
tling sense that something was . . . *missing*. She knew not
what. It was like lacking a piece to a shattered vase and
not knowing the shape of the piece. Like waking up at
night to a terrible sense of loss yet not knowing just *what*
she had lost.

And the worst of it was, she dared not speak of her
formless fears to anyone lest she be regarded as insane.

The same day the ambassadors had chosen her for
Echu, they had bought a horse from her uncle's marshal.
And paid more for the horse.

Aideen took in breath on a gasp and sank again into the
river, into the clean, healing waters where the ancient
spirits ran deep. She had always loved the water, swimming and bathing more often than her elders deemed
healthy. As a child, she had flung simple offerings into the
mere by her father's hall—a broken antler, a string of
beads, and once, a circlet of beaten bronze.

But the river gods had not listened. They had not

heard her dreams and her yearnings, had not healed the ache in her heart.

Other women in her *tuath* knew better than to question her good fortune in being elected to wed the High King. Why couldn't Aideen simply thank the goddess for her favor and settle down in contentment at Tara, the magnificent seat of kings?

Shaken by her doubts, Aideen planted her feet on the sandy river bottom and stood, wringing out her hair, shivering when the wind caressed her. Shelagh took her hand and brought her out of the water.

Her women gathered round, drying her and anointing her with scented oil. The oil, stored in precious glass bowls, had been warming in the sun. Aideen let out a soft sigh and felt the soothing women's hands gliding over her, comforting her. She loved her women; she trusted them. For now, she would not think of the rough touch of a man, the crude embrace wives had endured for generations.

Aideen allowed herself to be lulled by the sweet murmur of voices, the burble of the river slipping past, the heat of the high summer sun, the fragrance of the oils. She succumbed to a sweet languor and remembered that not all men's embraces were rough. The lover in her dream had held her gently, revered her with his body, lifted her spirits to a realm of impossible splendor.

Bidden by her thoughts, his voice whispered to her. *Aideen, I will make you remember....*

Her eyes flew open. He seemed so real to her. *Too* real. She had no right to think of him on the day she was to marry Echu.

"It will be all right, won't it, Shelagh?" she asked.

Shelagh's round face glowed like a harvest moon. "By the wind and fire, why wouldn't it be? Echu has chosen you to be his queen." She gave a broad wink and nudged

Nainsi. "And if Echu's warriors happen to cast their eyes on such as us, so much the better, eh?"

The women laughed together, and Aideen felt her anxiety ease a notch. It was only a case of nerves, due to the coming changes in her life.

She stood still as they added the crimson of rowan berries to her lips, the tips of her breasts, the ends of her fingers. They draped her in a chainse of sheer, undyed silk bought from traders of the far seas. The gossamer fabric caressed her skin with each movement as she waited for Riona to fetch the green gown from where it hung on a branch.

"I will do honor to my station," Aideen declared. Her vow rang through the forest glade, lilting across the waters of the stream and filling the sunlit silence. "I will make Echu a good wife."

At that very moment, the wind picked up. This was no soft summer breeze, but the angry breath of a tempest. The wind took the women by surprise, ripping at Aideen's silken garments, oversetting a glass bowl or two, tearing green leaves from the branches and whipping up crests on the surface of the river.

Shelagh, Nainsi, and Sibheal went racing after the blowing emerald gown while Aideen stood there, shivering, fearful, barely covered by the silken undershift. The air seemed curiously heavy, and it was tinged an angry yellow. Aideen reached her hand toward Riona, who stood frozen and wide-eyed, but the distance between the girls seemed as vast as the sea. Aideen's feet were on the ground; she could feel the springy grass, cool against her bare soles, yet she felt detached, melancholy, and strange, as if she was not part of this world.

The wind tangled her hair with furious fingers and whipped the strands against her back and neck and breasts.

And beneath its throaty howl, Aideen sensed something extraordinary. Suddenly forgetting her fear, she cocked her head.

Hear me, Aideen. Hear me. . . .

"What is it?" she asked. "Who are you? What do you want?"

"Did you say something, my lady?" Shelagh hurried over with the silken gown she had caught just before it had blown into the river.

"No." Aideen glanced at Riona. The girl, still goggling and speechless, shook her head. With an effort of will, Aideen threw off her disquiet. "Nothing, Shelagh. Nothing at all."

She did not hear me, he thought. His sight was devouring the woman he had loved since time began. Aideen. His lover.

His *wife.*

When he had heard her proclaim herself Echu's bride he had emitted such a roar of anguish and rage that the wind had run in fear before his wrath.

How could it be? he wondered. How could there be a force more powerful than the love they had shared? Their love had been made before time, before giants walked the earth, and it had promised to endure deep into the twilight of eternity. Yet something had happened, a deeper poison than he ever could have imagined had sunk into him, and he had lost her.

He touched the corner of his eye. He had lost more than that, but the blindness had been passed to a mortal. He'd had to sacrifice a child's eye; one day that child would find rewards beyond his wildest dreams.

If the curse could be lifted. The enchantment was powerful indeed. The spell had been whipped up by one whose hate was stronger than love.

Straining against the delicate veil between their two

worlds, he slung the tempest one more time, ripping a sapling from its roots, watching Aideen's wild, red-gold hair blow like a flame from a torch.

But she did not hear. Still she did not hear.

His heart splintered as he watched, helpless, powerless to halt her preparations. Her staggering beauty had made her vulnerable to the desires of a powerful king. She was to marry a man who was mighty yet weak, virtuous yet venial, a man who would, if not stopped, bind her forever to the sad, limited world of mortals.

He must make her remember. Time was running out.

chapteR 2

·

Echu had given Aideen many gifts, and her women insisted that she display them all for the wedding ceremony. The tempest in the river glade had quieted as quickly as it had come upon them, and she had almost succeeded in dismissing it from her mind.

Only moments before the ceremony and feasting began, she stood in her sunny *grianan* high in the dun of Tara.

The lofty chamber gave her a view of the twisting, stony roads leading to the High King's hill fort. The byways were crowded with freedmen and nobles from the neighboring kingdoms of Ulster, Leinster, Munster, and Connaught. It was Lugnaid, a festival held at the pinnacle of the sun season, and the wedding day only added to the air of excitement.

"What think you?" Shelagh asked Nainsi, stroking the shimmery silk of Aideen's gown. "Does she look like a queen?"

Riona and Sibheal drew near, crowding round. Their sharp, appraising eyes took in her green dress, fastened at one shoulder by an enameled brooch. Echu had employed the best goldsmiths in the kingdom to create hammered armlets and anklets, an openwork diadem to hold the veil over her hair. The ornaments were dazzling, with

lines that swirled and had no beginning and no end.
Flowers became leaves became feathers became fish, the
images changing, finally melding and winding at last into
the restless middle of a single eye. Echu's taste in ornaments favored the clever, the dark, the complex.

Shelagh stroked Aideen's red-gold hair. "It is like a veil
of silk. You *do* look like a queen."

"I don't feel like one," Aideen burst out in a sudden,
nervous blaze of honesty. "Tell me, what does a queen
do?"

The women giggled until they saw her expression.
"Why, she gives life to princes," said Sibheal.

"Thus does a brood mare come to foal." Aideen twisted
a strand of polished silver beads that adorned her chain-
work girdle. "That does not make her any better than
other horses."

"A queen leads armies into battle," Riona said with
great hope. Beneath her timid surface, she was as blood-
thirsty and warlike as the champions who boasted around
Echu's feast table.

"A queen consults on great matters with oracles and
lawgivers," Nainsi suggested.

"To what purpose?" Aideen asked. When no one answered, she said, "I suppose it will be my lot to spin and
weave and grow sons in my belly." She winced at her own
prediction. She was not one to shun hard work, and she
did cherish the thought of becoming a mother. But the
world Echu offered was a different place than the sunlit
world in her dreams.

Shelagh held out a torque made of bronze, hammered
thin and clad in brilliant enamels. The neck ornament
was beautiful, coldly so—its perfect symmetry of knots
and fitful whorls giving it a sharp-edged look.

As Aideen lifted her hair so Shelagh could place it
around her neck, she felt a faint shiver of revulsion. The
ornament resembled the collar of a hunting hound.

She dismissed the shiver with a bold, clear laugh. "There are worse fates than giving sons to Echu!" she declared.

Something happened. Neither Aideen nor any of her women could see clearly how the mishap occurred, but somehow, by some mischance, the delicate torque slipped and fell to the stone-paved floor.

The shattering sound froze them all. It was like strange, discordant music that left them disturbed and vaguely fearful. The torque lay ruined. The enameling scattered across the floor in tiny colored shards. The bronze form was bent and colorless now. Denuded of ornament, it was but an obscene twist of metal.

Even as the women emitted horrified gasps, Aideen felt a curious lifting in her heart. She knew she should regret the destruction of a gift from the high king, and yet as she stared down at the torque she felt only relief.

Shelagh turned pale. "It's my fault. He'll have me flogged for certain."

"He will not." Aideen surprised herself with the ring of certainty in her voice. "It was but one of many baubles. She spread her arms. Her voluminous red undersleeves were belling out like a set of wings. "Look, I am all but in shackles from Echu's gifts."

"The torque was the most important of all. It—"

"My lady?" A small, hesitant voice called from the doorway.

She turned toward the voice and smiled. "Come in, Kieran. What is it?"

The boy peeked shyly through the locks of dark hair that fell over his brow. He stepped into the *grianan*, holding out a small, carved casket.

Under her breath, Shelagh whispered the words of a charm. Aideen sent her a venomous look, and Shelagh stopped, though she continued to regard the lad with suspicion.

Kieran had been born with one blind eye, the iris eerily milky. Why his family had not set him out for the wolves while the birth blood still clung to him was a mystery, for that was the usual fate of a deformed babe.

When Aideen had come to Tara, Kieran had been a pig boy, working in the filth alongside miserable, tongue-cut slaves. Something in the way the boy had held himself, with innate dignity stiffening his frail form, and the staunch quiet with which he endured the taunts of others, had touched Aideen. She had persuaded Echu's chief houseman to allow the boy to work as her servant.

She bent and touched his shoulder, feeling his delicate bones. He was like a fawn, timid and fey, liable to shy away, unused to a kind human touch. But he did not shy now.

He looked at the broken torque and something flashed in his good eye. Something secretive and glad.

"I've brought you two gifts." He set the box on the floor and handed her a soft leather pouch. "This is from me. It's a charm to fasten to your girdle."

"Thank you, Kieran." She took it out of the pouch. It was a simple thing, dry little bird bones and a feather strung together with twine. Holding it gave her a curious wistful feeling. Her spirits rose as if the remnants of the long-dead bird had raised them.

"It's a swan feather," said Kieran.

She bent and kissed the lad's cheek. "This is very special. I'll treasure it always." She knew why Kieran's simple child's offering meant more to her than all the riches from Echu. Kieran's gift had not been fashioned by skilled artisans and paid for with cold metal and stones; instead, it was fashioned with love.

The bashful grin of the boy touched her heart. If being queen meant bringing that look of joy to a child's face, then perhaps being queen would not be such a trial after all.

He indicated the box. "That is from Niall of Brí Leith."
And then, like the silent shadow he had become, Kieran
slipped from the sunroom.

"Odd little waif," Shelagh said briskly, picking up the
box. "You show him too much favor. Who is Niall of Brí
Leith, and why does he send you a gift?"

Aideen stared at the box. "I don't know." The words
caught in her throat as if the honest admission were some
sort of betrayal. "Open it, Shelagh."

The box was carven of honey-hued oak and fitted with
bronze hinges and clasp. Shelagh tipped up the lid.

A collective gasp sucked the air from the sunny chamber. There, nestled upon a pillow of violet silk, lay a
torque so exquisitely wrought that it dazzled the eye.

"Oh!" With unsteady hands, Aideen lifted the ornament from the box. It was made of beaten gold. Without
enamel or jewels to compromise its purity, the neck ring
shone like a slice of sunlight. Its surface was smooth as
glass, the only decoration the two swan heads at the ends
of the fastenings. Aideen had never seen anything so elegant.

Even the feel of it in her hands was unique. As if, like
the bird charm, it had been fashioned with love. An un-
canny feeling rippled through her. Surprise. Recognition. The shock of meeting someone she had thought lost
to her.

"Put it on me."

Aideen was not even aware that she had spoken until
Shelagh scowled and said, "You cannot be serious."

"Put it on me." Aideen's voice grew strong and commanding.

"You cannot wear a gift from a strange man to your
wedding."

Aideen caught her breath, and her throat felt warm.
"There is a *gessa* on this ornament. I am compelled to
wear it, forbidden to ever take it off."

"And how would you be knowing that?"

Aideen fixed the woman with an imperious stare. "I just know. It's a *gessa*, Shelagh. These things happen. It's not for mortals to question why."

"Ah, there you go, getting queenly on me." Blowing out a sigh, Shelagh took the torque and fastened it around Aideen's slim, white neck. When she had finished, she brushed her lips across Aideen's brow.

"It is done. And it's on your head, not mine, if Echu gets the rage on him when he sees it."

Far in the distance a swan trumpeted. The sound raised a prickle on Aideen's skin. She returned Shelagh's kiss.

"Come. We must hurry." She raised her voice as if to fix her mind on the events to come. "The High King waits."

He had failed again. The gift had not brought back her memory. There had been a moment, when she had first touched the torque, that a bright joy had lit her eyes.

Those incomparable eyes.

The thought of them stung like poison. Soon those eyes would be gazing up at Echu.

Her failure to remember wasn't Kieran's fault. Though the boy did not know it, he had suffered much for the sake of his master. Someday Kieran would be repaid.

If there *was* a someday.

Discontent and worry sifted through him. He had to make her remember. Make her see him, let him hold her in his arms once again, let his love flow into her, before it was too late. There was only one way to do so. It was painful. Dangerous. Fatal, sometimes.

He would become human.

chapter 3

Great branches of yew and rowan arched over the High King and Aideen. They stood together on the broad lawn outside the banqueting hall while legions of wedding guests gathered round.

On a hill above them loomed the Stone of Destiny, its oblong shadow falling cool and black over the bridal couple. According to the bards, the stone used to roar when a king sat upon it, but no one in living memory had seen the miracle happen.

White-robed druids stood in a row before the couple. The bearded faces of the holy men were intent, solemnly approving. Dallan, the chief druid, was powerfully built and skilled in his arts. His waist-length hair gleamed blue-black in the sunlight, and his hawklike face was spare and bony, yet not without a certain kindness. Aideen liked him almost as much as she feared him.

The druids had decreed that Echu should take a wife. It was they who had chosen Aideen.

She could hear her handmaids whispering behind her, commenting on the splendor of the wedding guests and the comeliness of the High King.

She ducked her head, peeked at Echu, and found him looking down at her. With one sweeping gaze, he drew her in, possessed her. She felt a small, quiet death inside her. The look was not that of a man whose heart was filled with love, but that of ownership. His big, many-ringed hand covered hers.

"I am content with my choice," he said, smiling.

He was a dark, handsome man. He had a meaty face with a full beard parted down the middle and decked with tiny bronze bells. A thick moustache shadowed his lip. His eyes were black and merry, lacking guile, yet hard with male, territorial possessiveness.

Aideen scorned herself for doubting him. His arrogance must not sit amiss with her. He was High King and a great warrior. His dominion was the very center of Eriu, like the great heart of the land from which pulsed its life-blood.

He was splendidly arrayed in a crimson cloak girdled around his waist with a broad, jeweled belt. Looking at him, Aideen felt a flush of pride, though her stomach churned with nervousness.

At an imperious nod from Echu, the ceremony began. Druids lifted wands of alder and oak, calling down blessings from the four winds, from the stars, from the sun and from the sea. Maidens brought forth sheaves of wheat, and warriors offered racks of antlers and a huge boar carcass borne on a shield. Dallan, the druid, crowned Echu and Aideen with circlets of hawthorn.

Pipes and drums and reed flutes struck up a wild, breezy melody, concluding the rite. Cheers rose from the wedding guests. The music and the shouting grew louder, more insistent, a heavy, gut-felt rhythm no listener could escape. Only through sheer force of will did Aideen keep herself from running away, from hiding.

This is not supposed to happen to me, she wanted to scream. Indeed, a wise, unfamiliar part of her seemed to be watching from afar, aloof and cynically amused. How earnest they were in their ceremonies and celebrations. How little they knew of the vast mysteries of life and eternity.

But she knew no better.

Echu's kiss was hard and grinding, taking Aideen unawares. His arms bound her fast against him. The polished stones on his tunic pressed into her. His mouth was damp yet firm. His coarse beard abraded her tender skin. His kiss was one of mastery, of possession. Once again she felt that sense of loss, as if he had stolen something from her.

The wind blew hard, skirling up the valley of the Boyne to the heights of Tara.

Aideen! Hear me!

The voice blew on the wings of the wind. Echu made a strangled sound and pulled back. Just for a moment, she saw pain and surprise flare in his face.

"I am burned." He touched his throat. His gaze fixed on her golden torque.

A terrible guilt assailed Aideen. She should not have accepted a gift from a stranger, should not have worn it to her wedding with the High King.

I am not a stranger, roared the wind.

"I'm sorry, my lord," she said. But she was not. She had wanted to escape his embrace. "I am sorry," she repeated. It was the first lie she told him. She had a sick feeling that it would not be the last.

The formal feast took place in the Mi Cuarta, a hall erected many years before. The bridal couple sat in the middle. To Echu's right was the king of Ulster, to his left the king of Connaught, and across from him sat the kings of Leinster and Munster.

The hall teemed with great princes and sages, silent druids, bards and acrobats and musicians. A cupbearer brought forth a jeweled chalice filled with mead, and the druid Dallan called for a salute.

Aideen took the cup and held it out to Echu. "To you, my lord husband," she said loudly. Echu sipped from the chalice she held, and in that moment, looking at him over the rim of the glass, she felt a subtle sting of excitement. She was a wife now; she was a queen. After the feast would come the ritual abduction.

Then Echu would take her to bed.

She wanted that, wanted the bedding. Her body was as ripe and full as one of the apricots in the bowls being passed around. Her women had kept her up late the night before, speaking of the lusty mysteries of sex. Yes, she was a woman grown, and she knew what wanting was.

She had felt it in her dreams.

Echu held out the cup to her. "To my queen, my wife. To Aideen. It has been foretold that, by marrying you I shall bring prosperity to the land. Your body will increase with my seed, and so shall the land yield a bountiful harvest."

Aideen looked at her great, handsome husband, and she knew what wanting was.

She bent her head to drink from the cup. The chalice was wide and deep, and the mead was golden. Just before she touched her lips to the rim of the cup, she caught a glimpse of eyes reflected in the honeyed wine, eyes looking out at her. Clear blue eyes full of pain and pleading, thick-lashed eyes, beautiful eyes.

Aideen knew it was but a vision, a fanciful moment, but she closed her eyes to blind herself to the image in the cup.

She felt afraid, for she knew those eyes. She had seen them in her dream.

She drank deeply of the mead Echu offered. It should have tasted sweet—of summer honey and autumn wine. Instead it was bitter, scalding her throat as she swallowed.

She had to force herself to smile at Echu when she finished. He did not seem to notice her discomfiture, no more than he had noticed that the torque she wore was a gift from another.

After the wine, the entertainments began. Aideen watched, enchanted, the dancers and musicians, the bards and poets, the sword dancers and fire eaters. She began to shed her discomfiture over the vision in the cup. Her cheeks glowed with wine and excitement. After a singular demonstration by a troupe of supple tumblers from Ulster, the boisterous crowd in the hall went wild with appreciative clapping and stomping. Echu lounged upon his tasseled cushions, beaming at the spectacle.

A hush descended, and at the same moment, the torches ensconced on the walls flared. In the center of the hall appeared a man in a pale green cloak lined with silver.

At first Aideen paid him no more mind than she had the other performers. The hour was growing late, and fatigue tugged at her spirits.

Then her gaze fell on the singer, and time stood still.

You.

Her mouth shaped the word, though no sound came out.

He strode to the center of the hall and swung off his cloak. The garment dropped like mist to the ground. Beneath it he wore a green tunic and tight leather leggings. His hair, so pale it was almost white, flowed long and loose, and his face was beardless.

He was splendid. His skin was the warm gold of polished oak, as if he lived constantly in sunlight. His eyes were the deep, shifting blue of a mountain lake, and his mouth was soft, tender, unsmiling. The extraordinary hair, the color of sea foam, gave him an otherworldly look. There was about him some indefinable air of wistful sadness, the look of someone who bore, uncomplainingly, a burden of ancient tragedy.

He was the man from her dream.

Aideen tried to flee from the thought, tried to tear her

gaze from the man, but she could only sit, spellbound with enchantment, and watch him.

In his strong, long-fingered hands he held a harp carved of ashwood. Aideen felt a stab of terror and awe when she saw, carved in the harp, a pair of swans.

"I am Niall of Brí Leith," he said. His voice was strong and musical, rich and deeply pleasing to the ear.

Aideen stole a glance at Echu. The High King waited politely, giving Niall the same cordial, distant favor he had shown the other performers.

Thank the gods, Aideen thought weakly. Echu does not know. And with that thought came a nauseating wave of guilt. Already she hid secrets from her husband.

She glared at the beautiful, mysterious man. How dare he send her presents, disrupt her wedding day?

He looked back at her. His eyes, placid as mountain pools, were fixed on the torque that adorned her neck.

She lifted her chin. She wanted to be imperious. Queenly. Cold as ice. Yet even as she struggled to keep her cool composure, her heart took fire.

Niall stroked his harp. The instrument sang with a shimmer of sound. Immediately, people froze, cups poised in midair, joints of meat forgotten on trenchers. They all heard it in that first stroke of sound. They were in the presence of a master.

He began to sing, and his voice rang clear and true. It was a vibrant sound, full of emotion. At first, Aideen was so enthralled with the voice that she did not heed the words of the song itself. Then, gradually, the verses he sang penetrated her terrified stupor.

It was a tribute to a woman of surpassing beauty, a woman who dared to dream. He sang of sunlit groves and bowers garlanded with wildflowers. Of a place free of hunger and want, a land where no one grew old, and all lived in a state of perfect contentment.

As she listened, her heart filled with yearning and a

sharp, bittersweet melancholy. When, after seven verses, the song finished, she found herself on the verge of tears.

As the last plaint of the harp died, Aideen realized that others, too, had been moved. Echu tossed the musician an arm ring. Others added their gifts to Echu's— brooches and coins, knives and polished stones.

Niall ignored the tributes. He sank to one knee before Echu and said, "I am grateful for these gifts. But there is only one thing I want from you."

"And what is that, Niall of Brí Leith?"

"Aideen. I want Aideen."

She pressed her hands to her throat, touching the golden torque. Her teeth sank into her lower lip. She thought Echu would have Niall killed.

Everyone present in the hall stared in horror and amazement at the brazen stranger.

Echu surprised them all by roaring with laughter. "That's a fine jest, Niall of Brí Leith. A fine jest indeed." He clasped Niall's hand in his.

Only Aideen sat close enough to see what passed between the two men. The handclasp was brutal, whitening their knuckles. A brilliant blue-white bolt of light flashed in Niall's eyes. It was as sudden and powerful as a stroke of lightning, and it made Echu blink.

The moment passed in a heartbeat. Niall withdrew as quickly and gracefully as a breeze. A troupe of dancers began to perform to a wild, discordant tune.

Dallan, who stood near the entrance of the hall, made a subtle sign with his long, elegant hands, a sign against enchantment. Aideen shivered. Dallan *knew*.

Echu seemed somehow diminished by the encounter. He was as bluff and hearty as ever, and yet his laughter rang hollow; his jollity was forced. The feast went on and on. Aideen ate and drank but little. Like Echu, she worked hard to appear laughing and content when in sooth she was deeply troubled.

It was almost a relief when Echu grasped her around the waist and bent close so that his wine-sweetened breath touched her face. "Call for your women," he said.

Aideen knew what that meant. The time had come for the bedding.

chapter 4

It had been a day for traditions, for customs centuries old, swathed in the mists of the ancients. One such custom was the ritual abduction of the bride.

Aideen and her women retired to the *grianan* to prepare.

"Are you afraid?" asked Sibheal, running a comb through Aideen's long, wavy hair.

"Of course she's not afraid," Shelagh said before Aideen could answer. "Tonight is the night all her dreams come true."

"Is it?" Aideen fingered the thin white fabric of her gown. "Must a woman's dream always center around a man?"

"No," Riona said with a wink. "But they always involve true love."

The *other* dream tiptoed in through a back door of Aideen's mind. She caught her breath and closed her eyes. Her lover was so close she could smell him, and it was the scent of greenwood groves and freshets and wildness. . . .

"Aideen?"

She snapped her eyes open. Scarlet heat rushed to her throat, her cheeks.

Shelagh lifted her eyebrow. "Are you quite well? You look feverish."

"I never dreamed of marrying the High King," Aideen hedged. "I never dreamed of marrying at all. I only wanted . . ."

"Wanted what?" Shelagh prompted.

Wanted him. Wanted the world he promised in his song.

"I don't know." She tried to shake her mind free of the thought. "I'm a bit nervous, that's all. But not afraid."

Shelagh winked. "He's a stallion, is Echu, or so the gossip goes. But you've a woman's strength, which is the strength of a tree blowing in a storm, bending but never breaking, renewing itself each sun season." Shelagh kissed her. "Remember that, Aideen."

The women left, and she stood alone in the darkened room. The chamber had many wind holes, all in a row looking east. Aideen walked over and leaned against the timber embrasure. She gazed out at the hills plunging to the moonlit valley and the black sky pierced by stars without number. The moon cast soft blue light over the landscape. The faint sounds of revelry haunted the breeze.

Below, not far from the dun, a grove of hawthorn trees swayed like dancers. The cool green scent of summer filled the air. Shadows moved, live things in the grove. Aideen shivered and hugged herself.

Soon, her husband would come.

Then, high above the soughing of the wind and the noise and laughter from the hall, came the glistening plaint of a harp. The piercingly sweet notes came from the hawthorn grove by the river.

Aideen leaned out the window, and let her long hair swing free.

The singing began in that rich male voice, the voice that called across time for her. The song was different from the one she had heard in the hall; this one was brief

Take 4 FREE Books!

Zebra created its convenient Home Subscription Service so you'll be sure to get the hottest new romances delivered each month right to your doorstep — usually before they are available in book stores. Just to show you how convenient Zebra Home Subscription Service is, we would like to send you 4 Zebra Historical Romances as a FREE gift. You receive a gift worth up to $24.96 — absolutely FREE. There's no extra charge for shipping and handling. There's no obligation to buy anything - ever!

Save Even More with Free Home Delivery!

Accept your FREE gift and each month we'll deliver 4 brand new titles as soon as they are published. They'll be yours to examine FREE for 10 days. Then if you decide to keep the books, you'll pay the preferred subscriber's price of just $4.20 per title. That's $16.80 for all 4 books for a savings of up to 32% off the publisher's price! What's more...$16.80 is your total price...there is no additional charge for the convenience of home delivery. Remember, you are under no obligation to buy any of these books at any time! If you are not delighted with them, simply return them and owe nothing. But if you enjoy Zebra Historical Romances as much as we think you will, pay the special preferred subscriber rate of only $16.80 each month and save over $8.00 off the bookstore price!

We have 4 FREE BOOKS for you as your introduction to KENSINGTON CHOICE!

To get your FREE BOOKS,
worth up to $24.96, mail the card below.
or call TOLL-FREE 1-888-345-BOOK

Take 4 Zebra Historical Romances FREE!

MAIL TO: ZEBRA HOME SUBSCRIPTION SERVICE, INC.
120 BRIGHTON ROAD, P.O. BOX 5214,
CLIFTON, NEW JERSEY 07015-5214

YES! Please send me my 4 FREE ZEBRA HISTORICAL ROMANCES (without obligation to purchase other books). Unless you hear from me after I receive my 4 FREE BOOKS, you may send me 4 new novels - as soon as they are published - to preview each month FREE for 10 days. If I am not satisfied, I may return them and owe nothing. Otherwise, I will pay the money-saving preferred subscriber's price of just $4.20 each... a total of $16.80. That's a savings of over $8.00 each month and there is no additional charge for shipping and handling. I may return any shipment within 10 days and owe nothing, and I may cancel any time I wish. In any case the 4 FREE books will be mine to keep.

Name _____

Address _____ Apt No _____

City _____ State _____ Zip _____

Telephone ( ) _____ Signature _____

(If under 18, parent or guardian must sign)

Terms, offer, and price subject to change. Orders subject to acceptance.

KR0699

4 FREE
Zebra
Historical
Romances
are waiting
for you to
claim them!

(worth up
to $24.96)

See details
inside....

KENSINGTON CHOICE
Zebra Home Subscription Service, Inc.
120 Brighton Road
P.O. Box 5214
Clifton, NJ 07015-5214

and even more spellbinding than the other. The words
caught at her heart.

Come back to me, if my true love you be,
Come back to me at the trysting hour.

Aideen knew, in some still-thinking part of her mind,
that she was supposed to stay here and wait for her husband. Yet the voice beckoned her, compelled her, drew
her like a lodestone.

On feet that had no regard for her thoughts, she
climbed to the ledge. Her body welcomed the caress of
the summer breeze as it lifted her hair and the hem of her
gown. She left through the wind hole, dropping silently
to the dewy carpet of grass and wildflowers. The dampness chilled her bare feet and she ran, swift and instinctively as a doe, down and down to the swaying,
shadow-hung trees beside the water.

He waited for her there, leaning against the trunk of a
tree. The last note shimmered from his harp, and then he
set it down.

"Aideen," he said, and on his tongue her name
sounded as sweet as birdsong.

She stared at his broad-shouldered form, swathed in
the pale fabric of his cloak. "Who are you?" she whispered. "You say you are Niall of Brí Leith, but that does
not explain why you call me with your song from my wedding chamber. Who *are* you?"

He held out both hands, palms up, supplicating, com-
pelling. "That is for you to remember, Aideen. Come. Let
me help you remember."

"Remember what?"

"Remember *me*, beloved."

"But I . . ."

"Come, Aideen. Come to me."

The moonlight glistened like mist around him, flecking
his hair with silver. He did not move, and yet somehow
he drew her. She found herself moving toward him,

lured by the the sadness and the secrets in his eyes. His attraction was powerful. She could not resist it. Nor did she wish to.

She placed her hands in his. A fount of joy welled up in her, filling her chest like a deep breath of summer-scented air. Touching him, she felt such a shock of recognition that she gasped.

"*You.*"

He smiled, and his smile warmed her to her toes. "Yes, Aideen."

She was not certain what that familiar accord between them meant, but it felt right to be with him. His arms went around her and drew her close. In his embrace, she was safe. She was fulfilled. She was *home*.

She lifted her face and awaited the kiss she knew would come. Ah, she wanted this, she ached with wanting it, wanted their breath to mingle, their tongues to mate, their bodies to meld.

His hands clasped her shoulders. Mystery and tenderness glinted in his sea-silver eyes as he bent his head. His mouth descended slowly, as if he wanted to be certain of her, to give her a chance to pull away. But she could no more draw back than the tides could resist the tug of the moon.

Their lips were almost touching now. She could feel the warmth of him mingling with her own heat. She could hear the swish and hiss of the blood pounding in her ears. She came alive, burning and tingling in her breasts and loins. She knew there would be magic in his kiss, powerful magic that would change her life splendidly, irrevocably.

He held her close; his mouth hovered, opening slightly with a quiet, age-old hunger. Soon, she would be his . . .

The throaty baying of hounds and the thump of hoofbeats shattered the spell.

With a cry of anguish ripping from her throat, Aideen

stumbled back. Lightning flashed in Niall's eyes. Aideen covered her face with her hands.

When she removed them, she saw only a swirl of mist where Niall had been standing.

"Ye gods," she said, lifting the hem of her gown. "He is a ghost." She began to shiver uncontrollably. "I have touched a ghost."

She stumbled back up the hill to the dun, bruising her feet and shins in her frantic scramble to enter the *grianan* through the wind hole. She was panting with panic and exertion.

She had almost kissed a ghost. If she had allowed it, he would have sucked the very life from her.

She had not a moment to recover her composure before Echu arrived.

Laughing lustily, he burst into the room. Aideen had no time to feel fear. He swept her into his arms and carried her outside, slinging her over the bare back of his warhorse. Together, they galloped three times around the dun.

It was all a blur to Aideen, whirling images of torchlight and laughing faces, the thatch of the buildings bristling in the moonlight, dancers swirling to the rhythm of drums, warriors leaping a bonfire and hooting with drunken glee.

Echu took her into the hall, partitioned by ornate screens, and brought her to the bed box they would share.

"You are home, my queen," he said. "This is where we will make sons for Tara and daughters for all the kings of the provinces."

"Yes, my lord," she said quietly, still unrecovered from her encounter with Niall in the grove.

Remember me.

How could she remember a man she had never known? Or *had* she? The recognition she had felt when they touched still tingled through her, tugged at her mind, refused to be thrust aside.

Echu reclined on the heap of woven blankets and wolf-skins. "Come here, Aideen."

Her soul cried out in denial. She looked around wildly, her gaze snared by a movement of the trees outside the window. The wind tore at the branches and bowed them. The moon seemed to catch fire. It lost its silver-blue glow and burned a hot, angry red.

Echu was High King and her husband. She had pledged herself to him today. Summoning a flinty inner strength, she went to the bed.

He lay with his eyes closed, his mouth slightly open, his beard a tangle on his massive chest.

"Echu?" she whispered.

He made no response. Then he loosed a loud snore.

Aideen exhaled the breath she had been holding. She crept into the bed and slept fitfully, as untouched and maidenly as she had been the night before.

Outside, high in the sky, the fiery moon subsided to a cool, soulless blue.

The days and nights at Tara took on a rhythm. The summer sun burned lower and lower, the days shrinking toward harvest time. Echu was pleased by an unusually abundant harvest, and credited his marriage to Aideen with the bounty. He held court and received visitors and settled disputes. Aideen worked at her embroidery and music, sitting for hours with her women or receiving guests in the hall.

Echu seemed wholly pleased with her.

She passed the days in a state of quiet bewilderment. How could such a proud, fierce man be pleased when he did not cleave to his wife?

She plied her needle endlessly, creating great long

robes worked with gold and silver thread. She wondered
. . . and she waited.

Part of her was secretly relieved. Nothing about Echu
called to her. Nothing about him moved her. She could
admire his strength, his firmness with his subjects, but
there was a slyness about him she did not trust, and her
woman's heart lay cold as a stone in her chest.

In unguarded moments her mind wandered, traveling
invisible paths, pausing to relive the magical dream of her
lover. She heard his voice on the wind, she saw his eyes
reflected in a cup of mead, she imagined his melodious
voice beckoning her to a perfect world. She remembered
his touch, the warmth of him, and her own yearning for
his kiss.

She caught herself daydreaming about him one hot
day in late summer, and she grew angry with herself. She
looked down at the rack that stretched out her needlework, and was shocked by what she saw.

Her hands, with wills not her own, had embroidered a
pair of golden swans in flight.

"No!" she said under her breath. Rising, she yanked
the work from the frame, wadded up the fabric, and went
to the central hearth. She fed the work to the flames. The
cloth bloomed with orange fire, then turned to black,
crisp flakes of nothingness.

Yet even as she watched, the swans she had sewn did
not burn. They shifted and changed, became weightless
as air, rising on a mist of smoke and disappearing out the
smoke hole in the roof.

"I did not see that," she muttered.

"Is something amiss?" Shelagh asked. She was cracking
hazelnuts and feeding the shells to the fire.

"The design displeased me." Aideen brushed ashes
from the hem of her tunic. "I must go and see Dallan."

She found Echu's chief druid working in the shade of a
great oak tree. As always, she felt a tug of reluctance to

approach him. He bent over the stump of a tree, which he used as a table. He was totally absorbed in his task, his dark head bent, his long hair slick and glossy in the sun.

Dallan had quite a collection of skulls, old and new. The magic of the relics was powerful; Aideen had enormous respect for them, but she could never look at the skulls without remembering that they had once been men.

Men with wives and daughters and sons. Men who had been slain by her husband and his warriors.

Dallan was busy crushing herbs with a mortar and pestle. The pungent spice of vervain filled the air, and the druid muttered soft phrases as he worked.

Aideen pressed her hands together, twining her fingers. She shifted back her shoulders, hoping she appeared queenly, and cleared her throat.

"Yes, lass, what is it?" Dallan had a kindly face lined with quiet wisdom, and busy, capable hands. He was learned, having studied the magic arts and the old stories for years with a master. He was known to show great love and gentleness—even when he was up to his elbows in sacrificial blood.

Aideen studied Dallan's stark, bony face and could think of no way to broach the subject. So she took a deep breath and blurted out, "Is it customary for the High King to avoid his wife?"

Dallan's hands, twisting the pestle with a steady, grinding motion, never faltered. "What are you asking me, child?"

She looked from side to side to make certain no one was about. Cows browsed in the bawn, and in the distance, reapers worked a sloping field. "In the bedchamber."

"You don't share a bed?"

"Yes, but Dallan, I am a maid!"

Still he worked, his hands grinding away, but his eyes

flared wide, betraying shock. "Tell me," he said, his voice tight and strained.

Feeling relieved, she sank onto a cut stump. "I thought you might not believe me."

He set aside the mortar and took out a sifter made from a bronze dish pierced by tiny holes. "Why would anyone lie about such a thing?"

She smiled thinly. "Why indeed?"

"So tell me," he urged her.

"Each night, when it is time to retire, Echu gets into the bed. He usually calls for me and sometimes holds out his arms. But by the time I reach the bed, he's sound asleep. I can't awaken him. In the morning, he arises refreshed and content." She knotted her fingers together in her lap. "We never speak of this . . . problem. Indeed, I'm not certain he's even aware of it."

A look of irony crossed Dallan's face.

She lifted her chin, her inborn pride surging, unbidden, from a hidden well of dignity inside her. "You'll not judge me inadequate, Dallan."

He held up both hands, palms out. "I never said that."

"Then what is the cause?"

"Echu is clearly under an enchantment. Or a curse."

She felt a little catch in her chest. Echu was, after all, her wedded husband. "Why would anyone call a curse upon the High King?" Then a dizzying thought struck her. "Could it be that *I* am the one who is cursed?"

Dallan said nothing. He fell as still as the oak tree that shaded him. She heard the swish of the river rushing past, the hush of rustling leaves. "Niall of Brí Leith," she whispered, touching the golden torque around her neck.

Dallan's gaze fixed on the magnificent ornament. She knew he could see himself reflected in its curving surface. Everyone could. That was what was so entrancing about the torque.

"He gave you that?"

She nodded. "I received one as a gift from Echu. Yet on our wedding day, it broke. When this one arrived moments later, I knew I was bound by *gessa* never to remove it."

Aideen tilted back her head and closed her eyes, letting the sun warm her face. She saw a field of orange red, the blood feeding her eyelids. Then the field began to change into a shifting shadow, and the wind picked up and she heard his voice.

Come back to me, if my true love you be,
Come back to me at the trysting hour.

She blinked fast, feeling as if she should run away, yet knowing she could never escape what was part of her, in her head and in her heart. "At the wedding feast, he told Echu he wanted me."

"Everyone heard that." Dallan emptied the bowl into a clay jar and added some amber liquid from a flask. When Dallan worked, a mystical significance enhanced even the most commonplace of actions. Aideen wondered what he was making—a cure for blindness, or one to conciliate the heart?

"It's a common enough way to compliment a man on his wife," Dallan continued. "Everyone thought it was only that."

Aideen gazed off into the distance, where the gray-blue sky melded with the soft green of the hills. "You didn't see the way Niall looked at me. His eyes were strange, and I—" She broke off. Of late, often found herself faltering, groping for the right word and feeling unsure of herself.

"You what?"

"For a moment, I felt that I knew him. It's silly, actually. I had never seen him before except"—she stood and began to pace in agitation—"except in a dream."

Dallan uttered a foul word. He took a slim rod and began to stir the mixture in the clay jar. "You should have consulted me before."

She told him then, about the dream of two lovers torn apart in a storm. About the wind in the woods, the voice that had called to her. About the eyes, the mystical blue eyes, reflected in her cup of mead.

"This Niall of Brí Leith," Dallan said with quiet certainty, "is a prince of the Sidh."

"No!" Aideen's voice rose with anguish. "He cannot be an immortal. I saw him—we all saw him—at the wedding feast."

"Men of the Otherworld have the power to appear human. It does not happen often. It's very costly, sometimes fatal. He must be very determined if he came to walk among us."

"Fatal," she whispered. A cold wind blew across her soul.

"Did you touch him, Aideen?"

She paced more quickly, the hem of her gown twitching in agitation. "I can't lie to you, Dallan. On our wedding night, he sang to me from the grove by the river. I went to him." Her hand came up to touch the torque. "We embraced."

Dallan hissed in a breath. "He wants you."

Aideen's hands clenched into fists at her sides. Nothing had ever been simple for her. Even as a child, she had lived in a state of dreamy discontent. She had dared to think that, once she became a wife and mother, her restless soul would settle. Instead, the sorrow pulsed heavier than ever in her veins.

"He said he wanted me," she agreed. "But for what purpose? He is not mortal. I am. I'm bound in this world. I must live and die here. I can't be with Niall."

Dallan poured his mixture from the clay jar into a precious glass vial. He held the vessel up to the sunlight and squinted at the amber fluid. "The first way to prove something possible is to deny that it can be done."

She stopped pacing and touched his sleeve. "Can it be done, then? *Can* I cross into the Otherworld?"

"Only when the most powerful magic is present." He pulled his sleeve away and bent his head to sniff his concoction.

Annoyed at his mysterious air, Aideen said, "What is this potion you're so intent on mixing?"

Dallan grinned, lifted the vial, and took a long drink. "It's very potent."

She shrank back, expecting him to turn into a crow or a toad. "What *is* it?"

He held out the vessel. "A remedy for flatulence. Would you like to try it?"

She glared at him. "You are a most difficult man, Dallan. You give me no solution to my problem."

"I cannot, my queen. The answer has to come from you."

"I possess no powers save those of an ordinary woman. There is no magic in me, Dallan."

"So long as you think so, you will be right."

"All I want," she said, raising her clenched fist to the sky, "is to be like other women. To cleave to my husband, to bear his children."

"Is it, my queen?" asked Dallan.

"Yes!"

But even as she struck out across the sunlit bawn, she heard again the seductive melody of Niall of Brí Leith. *Come back to me at the trysting hour.*

The yearning pierced her. She kept hearing the words like the song of a bird at sunset, its voice lamenting the dying day. She was struck by such a sadness that she had to stop walking, to catch her arms around her middle, and squeeze her eyes shut. She threw back her head, clenching her jaw against the pain while tears ran down her face.

chapter 5

Autumn came on the wings of a storm, leeching the green from the hills and the groves. The torch of Lug, the god of light, set the trees aflame with crimson and gold.

Through sheer force of will, Aideen thought no more of her conversation with Dallan or of her strange and seductive encounter with Niall of Brí Leith.

She found much to do around the dun, much to occupy her. It was with unexpected delight that she discovered fulfillment in her role as queen. Echu was gone frequently, making a last progress around his dominion before the winter closed in. Aideen found that her status gave her the means to make a difference in people's lives. She could mediate disputes, nurse the infirm, succor the poor, coax a smile out of a child's tears.

That, she thought with a warmth in her heart, was true power. To ease suffering, to heal a hurt or mend a rift.

Little Kieran became her constant shadow, trotting at her heels like a loyal hound. He observed her with a curiously adult solemnity as she consulted with the lawgivers and druids and battle chiefs, acting in Echu's stead. She welcomed Kieran, even though his presence reminded her of the one thing she lacked—a child.

As Echu's wife, she had a duty to produce sons and daughters for Tara. But she was not increasing and her women knew it. Sometimes she would enter the *grianan* to find them talking in low tones. Spying her, they would break apart, ducking guilty heads to their weaving or needlework.

She knew what they were saying. Her union with Echu was cursed.

And so it was, but not in the way the women thought. It was cursed because Echu never touched her.

She shook her head, surveying her work. Now that the high summer was past and the harvest was in, she turned to other pursuits, the preserving of foods and laying in of supplies for winter, rendering oil for lamps and supervising the spinning and weaving.

But no matter how busy she kept her hands, her mind wandered. Always to the same dark, misty place, to the hawthorn grove by the river, where, just for a moment, she had looked into a stranger's eyes and glimpsed eternity.

"He was a ghost," she told herself stubbornly. "You are well away from him and the things you don't understand."

But her heart ached, just as if it had been pierced by a war spear, only deeper. This injury was more grave than a wound of the flesh. This one would never, ever heal.

He had failed. Taking on the shape of a mortal had sapped his powers. And his sacrifice had gotten him nowhere.

She was still Echu's wife. She still clung to the role foisted upon her, for that role was all she knew.

Sometimes, at odd moments, she would slip into a dreamy state and he would draw close, in secret, to feel her yearning. At such moments, they melded in spirit if not in flesh. They touched each other in the most profound and unearthly way, almost as if they were together again as they had once been.

But just as she began to hear—to truly hear—his voice in her mind, she would shake free of the bond, confused by it, frightened by it, and slip back into her sad, mortal existence.

She was a woman torn between two worlds. It was not for him to claim her, only to wait and see which world she would choose. But if she did not make her choice soon, he would lose her forever.

He howled at the injustice, the frustration. He and Aideen had shared a perfect love. She had been snatched from him like leaves from a branch in an autumn storm.

How could he make her understand? How could he get her to see? She believed she was not of the Otherworld. She had no idea that she possessed the power to cross that threshold.

It was not so simple as telling her. She had to find out for herself, to come to him of her own free will, and to rediscover the strength of her powers.

He was a man who knew what made the shadows live, and yet he, too, hung suspended between two worlds. He could not rejoin his world without her.

He had a choice to make. He could give himself completely to her world. He could do battle for her heart, could fight Echu, mortal to mortal, until one of them died.

And then what?

He thought of the river, and the seasons slipping past, the years unfolding, time without end.

As a mortal, he would find the end.

There had to be a better way. He must possess her. First her body. Then her soul.

* * *

The days passed, and Aideen dreamed. She no longer fought the haunting, seductive visions, for they were as much a part of her as the green of her eyes, the timbre of her voice, the way she walked and laughed.

She let him come to her, because Echu would not. Each night the beautiful lover slid into her mind, into her soul. He touched her in the hungry places of her body, bringing her to fiery life with deft hands. His tongue did homage to her breasts; his mouth shaped itself to hers and they shared breath and life itself. His long, strong body parted her legs and she clasped him hard as he joined with her and moved, swallowing her cries of joy with his own mouth, and leaving her warm and replete.

Each morning she woke sated, slightly dazed, damp between her legs as if her body wept with wanting him.

Her women would notice her sleepy, heavy-lidded eyes and nod and whisper.

They thought they knew.

At first, Aideen had wished with all her heart that the marriage would come right for her and Echu. She had wanted to do her duty, to be a proper wife. Now she no longer held that wish. Now she wanted only *him*.

The man who called himself Niall of Brí Leith. The man who sang to her while she slept, and who loved her in her dreams.

The man she could not have, because he was not a man at all.

Dallan said he was a prince of the Sidh. A member of a race so ancient and noble that mere mortals could not touch them.

Then what did he want with her? With Aideen, a mere woman?

She went to the sentry walk of the dun and began to pace. The wind rushing up from the river held the dry cold of winter, and the chill pierced her woolen mantle.

As she surveyed Echu's kingdom, she was struck by the

harsh, rugged beauty of it. The green of the hills had died with the sun season. The Stone of Tara, the great seat of kings, sat like a lone sentinel on a hill. The bog was brown and black, yet endlessly fascinating to her, its edges bristling with pine and oak and alive with birds and darting, secretive badgers and hedgehogs.

"I hate the bog," said Echu.

Startled, Aideen turned to him. "My lord. I did not hear you approach." Seeing him, she felt a familiar tumble of emotions. Pride in his kingly aspect. Shame at his lack of desire for her. Guilt, because she no longer cared.

"Lost in your dream world again, Aideen?" One dark, bushy eyebrow pushed upward. "I do know," he said, and his cryptic words unsettled her. "And I do hate the bog," he repeated. "Worthless piece of the world."

"Is it?" she asked quietly, staring out at the dark smudge of bog with its tar pits steaming in the late autumn air.

"Worthless," he stated. "I can't graze cattle there. Can't plant a crop. Can't ride my horse across it."

"So the bog is worthless to *you*, not simply worthless," she said.

He scowled. "What other sort of value is there, if not the value of the land to a king?"

"There is its value to the birds and the trees and all the creatures of the earth."

Echu snorted. "You're beginning to sound like that know-all, Dallan."

Ye gods. Had Dallan spoken to Echu of the curse she had confessed?

Echu's hands shot out so fast that her wrists were caught before she realized his intent.

"My lord!"

He peered with dead black eyes into her face. "You think I don't know."

"Know what?" She forced herself not to flinch at the strength of his grip.

"That you are yet a maid!"

"Echu." It would not do to show him fear now. Fear was weakness. Besides, she was surprised to realize he did not—could not—frighten her. Whatever threat he posed could not touch the dreams inside her. "I tried each night to be a true wife to you. I swear by the sun and stars, I did try."

"Indeed. Then you won't mind"—he backed her against the high plastered wall—"my attentions now."

A denial leaped to her throat, but he stifled it with his hungry, possessive kiss. She felt his weight pressing at her, his rough hands yanking up her robes, his muscled legs forcing her knees apart.

Niall!

Her mind silently screamed his name. At the same instant, Echu stumbled back, doubled over as if in pain, and collapsed onto the walkway.

Aideen stood frozen, watching him, afraid to touch him, afraid to turn her back on him. He was a brute, she told herself. If he lay here and died like a dog, it would be no more than he deserved.

"Aideen," he gasped. "Aideen, help me. I beg you." He was weak and withered now, his pale face twisted with pain. "Fetch Dallan."

She hesitated, then stepped back. One step. Another step. He was her husband. She refused to accept his blood on her hands.

"I'll get Dallan." She turned with a flurry of her mantle and rushed to the end of the sentry walk. As she descended the ladder, the past moments played through her mind. She had been lamenting her ability to cross to the enchanted realm of Niall of Brí Leith.

Yet she had, for the first time, spoken to him. With a

single, focused thought, she had called his name, and Echu's crude caresses had ceased.

The first way to prove something possible is to deny that it can be done.

Could it be that she had crossed the invisible boundary to the Otherworld?

As she ran across the inner yard and out the gate, she felt the cool, solid earth beneath her feet and the wind on her face. She thought of the long, barren years slipping past. She was neither wife nor maiden, but a woman who found love only in dreams.

The old ache flared to life. She could not soothe it with thoughts that she was queen, free from want and hardship.

She stood atop a hill crowned by sere grass. Flinging out her arms, she threw back her head so that her hair blew and lifted like a banner on the wind. Again and again she called to Niall, not with her voice but with her mind. She called to him of the wanting inside her, of the terrible restless heart that beat in her breast, of the shining love that came over her only as she slept.

Then she waited.

But the wind was only the wind, rattling through the branches, clacking them together. And the river was only the river, clear and lifegiving, yet wholly silent on matters of the spirit.

He was not there. She could not reach him, for she was mortal. She could not live where Niall was. She had no magic in her.

The magic in her was powerful, if she would but acknowledge it. For the first time, she had reached out to him with her own free will.

His love for her burned like the sun. He had once

made the ultimate sacrifice for her. He knew he would do so again and again till the end of time, if need be.

He wondered if he should have killed Echu. The sight of the High King pawing at her had certainly warranted it. But no. She was still too far away, still too unsure, and his own powers had been compromised by his appearance at her wedding.

Until she made her final choice, he could only wait and see.

But ah, the waiting, the watching, hurt more than he had ever dreamed possible.

"This malady is not curable by ordinary means," said Dallan, standing at Echu's bedside.

The king lay half conscious, rolling his head from side to side and shivering beneath a mound of furs and blankets.

"How do you know that?" Aideen asked.

"Never ask a druid to explain," Dallan snapped.

"Is he . . . going to be all right?"

"That is up to you, my queen."

Her heart felt like a knot in her chest. "Why must *I* be responsible?"

"Because you are his wife, woman. Even if he does not mate with you, you're bound to him." The druid fixed her with a clear-eyed stare. His eyes were gray and wintry and commanding. "Make your choice, Aideen. Will he live or will he die?"

"He will live." She did not hesitate the slightest before answering. "It is not for me to call death down on a man's head."

Dallan reached out, cupped her cheek with his cool, soft hand. As always, he smelled faintly of herbs and mystery. "So be it," he said. "I shall see what must be done."

* * *

She sat by Echu's side and nursed him while the hours tiptoed by. She kept the brazier filled with hot coals, kept Echu's drinking horn filled with warm mead and his bowl filled with broth. Whenever he awoke, she cradled his head in her hand and urged him to drink.

He was High King and he was her husband. She would do her duty.

Despite the encounter on the rampart, she felt no fear of him. It was hard to imagine him as he had been only hours before, roughly demanding, forcing her to accept his crude embrace.

He was almost childlike now, grateful for the comfort she offered.

"Where did Dallan go?" he asked weakly.

"He went to the sacred grove to divine a way to heal you."

"Aideen." Echu squeezed his eyes shut, then dragged them open. "I am sorry."

"I know." She stroked his brow until the frown lines relaxed and he slept.

As she sat with her husband, the visions assailed her once again.

Hear me, Aideen . . .

Go away.

Hear me.

She stared at the earthen floor, at the dusty hem of her mantle, at the soft, creased leather of her boots. Even so, she saw him again, his sea-foam hair, his eyes of blue.

Go away.

Hear me . . .

You are not of my world, nor I of yours. Go away.

Aideen . . .

His song shimmered through her, as if she were a harp string and his the hand that plucked it.

Go away. Your time is not my time. You are not real to me, Niall of Brí Leith!

Haunting laughter flowed like the wind over her. *I am as real as you are, Aideen. You cannot make it otherwise.*

"Dallan!" she shouted, leaping up, going to the wind hole and leaning out. "Dallan!" She would ask him to make a charm to purge her mind of dark thoughts. She had to get free of the visions. They had tainted her marriage. They were killing the High King.

Dallan hurried into the sleeping chamber. "I think I found a way to make things right between you and your husband."

"Husband," she whispered. The word bothered her. "Tell me," she forced herself to say.

"You must meet him on a holy hill far removed from the dun," said Dallan.

"Meet him? But the man can scarcely move."

"Your true husband will be there," Dallan said, and he spoke with his usual ringing certainty.

"Very well. We meet on the holy hill. And then what?"

"And then it is up to you, Aideen."

So much weighed upon her shoulders. Sometimes she felt like the axle between the wheels of a chariot, her strength was taxed to its limit. Everything turned on the choices she made.

She knelt at the bed box and touched Echu's hand. "Did you hear, my lord?"

"Yes."

"And you agree?"

"Yes."

"Then there is nothing else for it." She stood and threw back her shoulders and lifted her chin. Her stony pride and sense of duty kept doubt and despair at bay. "I am ready, Dallan. Tell me what I must do."

* * *

The druid showed promise. It had been dangerous, using Dallan, yet the risk seemed to have borne fruit. Interfering with a druid's divining process was perilous, but sometimes necessary.

Like a blossom in the sun, Dallan's mind had opened. A true master of the ancient arts, he had been uncritical, unquestioning, capable of receiving knowledge from beyond the world of mortals.

The druid had drunk in the plans, the hopes, the thoughts, and made them his own.

Aideen trusted Dallan.

Echu trusted Dallan.

Neither would know that the druid had surrendered his will. Now, Dallan served the purpose to which he had been working all his life. He served the gods.

At the darkest hour of the night, when the autumn wind howled down the corries, Aideen wrapped herself in a mantle and laced her boots snugly up to her knees.

Dallan had said she must go alone.

He said she must go at night.

She passed the long bawn, smelling the cattle and imagining the comfort of their sleeping warmth. She walked on, fording the river over a rope bridge and striking out due west.

The moon came up cold as snow, and lit the swollen underbellies of the clouds.

She walked quickly—her haste due both to the cold and to the urgency of her mission. Her long strides carried her up the grassy slope.

At the top stood a ring of stones, slender and erect, spaced evenly apart. They shone like white marble in the pale light. A faint, misty glow washed the landscape. The moon hung over the stone circle, shedding white light like a benediction.

"This is a holy place," Aideen whispered, transfixed. She knew it was not always so. During the day it was as ordinary as any place. Sometimes children played here, and badgers burrowed into the soft, loamy earth.

But tonight, with the moon hovering in perfect alignment with the circle, it was a place of deep magic.

"It is the trysting hour," said a rich, masculine voice.

"Ye gods!" Aideen covered her eyes with her hands.

"I knew you would come." Niall stepped toward her, took her hands away from her face, and folded her into his arms. "I knew you would come back to me, Aideen."

chapter 6

Startlement and a sharp, sweet longing held her immobile and speechless in his embrace. He felt as sturdy as the oaks that stood like sentinels in the distance. He smelled of fresh water and clean air, and she could feel the steady, welcome thud of his heart against her cheek.

The sensations that coursed through her were those she had felt only in her dreams—a perfect aura of peace, of belonging, all threaded through with the finely spun silk of a woman's desire.

His large hand slid up her back. His fingers caught in her hair as he cradled her head in his palm. "Aideen," he whispered, his mouth hovering very close to hers, "at last it is our time."

Ah, those lips, soft, offering promises. Aideen swayed closer, reaching . . . and then she felt the cold wind at her back, and she remembered. This was not a man, but a spirit, a danger to her and her world.

"No," she forced herself to say, edging away from him. "This cannot be. You are no lover for a mortal woman who is another man's wife."

He made no move to catch hold of her. She knew instinctively he would never force her, never hurt her. He brought her fingers to his face, his beautiful face carved of shadows and moonlight, and let her trace his clean-shaven cheeks, his mouth, the bridge of his nose, the ridge of his brow.

"Am I not a man, Aideen?" he asked. "Am I not as real to you as these ancient stones?"

She ran her fingers down over his throat. "I don't know. You have the look of a man. You seem made of flesh and bone and muscle." She snatched her hand away, for touching him filled her with bittersweet, forbidden yearning.

"I came here because of Echu," she forced herself to say. "My husband."

The word had a curious effect on Niall. His face did not change, but a cold white fire sparked in his eyes, then died.

"I am not easily moved to anger," he said. "But when I am, my rage is a perilous thing."

"You have no right to become angry because of Echu," she stated. "He is High King, a man who is dying. I came here to cure him."

"You came here to meet your husband, Aideen."

"Instead, I encounter a stranger." She tightened her fists in frustration, planted her feet, and glared at him.

There was an odd stillness about Niall; she had noticed it before, the other times she had seen him. He had the most singular way of holding himself immobile, almost aloof, while at the same time using his eyes to bind her in a state of near-enchantment.

"Aideen, listen to me," he said at last.

"I am listening. I have been."

"With your ears, you have been." He sank to one knee before her and took her hand in his. "Now you must listen with your heart."

At first she did not understand. Then she looked into his blue-misted eyes and nodded. "Yes. Go on."

Even on bended knee, he was huge, nearly as tall as she so he barely had to look up as he spoke.

"Beloved Aideen, in the time before time, *I* was your husband."

Though her lips shaped a horrified *no*, her heart said *yes*.

"I love you still," he said, rising to his feet.

His words burned like bright stars in her mind. But she was too much a woman, a creature of the here and now, to accept what he was saying.

"That cannot be," she said. "We are strangers, you and I. I have never seen you, except at my wedding to Echu."

"Have you not?" he said, and now she detected the blade-sharp edge of anger in his voice. "Are you certain you never saw me, Aideen, never heard my voice, never felt my caresses on your breasts and your belly, never tasted my lips?"

A soft moan escaped her. "In dreams only, Niall. *In dreams only*. Dreams are not real. *You* are not real." She swept her arm at the black gulf of emptiness that lay on the hill between them. "You are a shadow man. A creature of air and darkness."

"Watch, Aideen." He took a step toward her. His long shadow, outlined by pale moon-silver, contracted. "If I stand close enough to you, there won't be any shadows between us."

The moonlight broke like a crashing wave over him, gilding him in silver so that he appeared more extraordinary, more godlike than ever.

In that moment, memories came rushing back at her, things she knew she had never dreamed. She felt the feathers and silk of a bed, heard a storm hissing in her ears. She felt him sink into her, and she cried out, seeing herself catch his head to her bosom and hold it there to suckle while she soared to the stars and beyond. They loved with passion and lust and sheer exultation, and together they found a perfect joy.

As abruptly as the vision came, it faded with a last cruel

twist. The roaring wind tore them apart, and she was hurled like a breeze-borne petal, far away from him.

Despite the chill night air, sweat trickled down between her breasts. She pressed a hand to her heart. Listening and aware, she felt a pain beyond enduring.

"Niall," she whispered, hoarse and horrified. "What happened to us?"

A faint, heartsore smile curved his beautiful mouth. "At last you begin to understand." A cloud cloaked the moon, and, looking up, he sucked in a breath. "And none too soon."

"What do you mean?"

"My time is running out." He spread his magnificent cloak on the ground and sat, pulling her down beside him.

She sensed a curious lethargy in him. He moved laboriously, as if he were in pain. Before she could question him, he cupped her chin in his hand, gazed deeply into her eyes, and began to speak.

"Aideen, our story has no beginning, and if we choose wisely, it will have no end. What can be the beginning of such a love as we shared? It burned brighter than the midsummer sun."

"How can a love like that fail?" she asked, pierced by random, flickering images of a different Niall, a younger Niall, a Niall who laughed with his eyes.

"Because I grew complacent. Careless," he said. "There was a sorceress called Fúamnach who took it into her head that she desired me."

An ironic smile tugged at Aideen's mouth. "This surprises you?"

"I never wanted her," he said harshly. "But I should have found some way to tell her so without hurting her pride."

"Such words do not exist in this world or the next,"

Aideen said with certainty. "For a woman's affections to be spurned is the deepest and least forgivable of blows."

"So it would seem. She sought to destroy us both. She would have, had it not been for the extraordinary power of our love. Yet she did do damage to us, Aideen. And perhaps she will destroy us yet. This is a thing I cannot foresee."

"She tore us asunder," Aideen said, her head filled with memories or dreams, she knew not which. Scarlet. A scarlet robe, scarlet wings . . .

"She changed my shape!" Aideen said in horror.

"You became a butterfly, beloved. A creature of sunlight and soft air. But even so, our love endured. Each night of the moon, at the trysting hour, you became Aideen again, and we cleaved to one another and loved more fiercely than ever.

"Fúamnach became even more furiously jealous. One midsummer's night, she summoned a storm. . . ."

"The wind ripped the thatch from the roof," Aideen recited as if the words had been given to her by a higher force. "It wrenched the door from its hinges and tore me from your arms." She pressed the back of her hand to her mouth. "Niall! It is all true."

"Yes, my beloved. Fúamnach meant for you to drown in the storm. But even she, deft mistress of the black arts, still did not understand the force of our love. I found one last way to save you."

"Yes?"

"With the power of my love, I made you mortal."

"Made me mor—" Aideen could barely choke out her question. "What was I before?"

He smiled. "A goddess, beloved. And wife to me, whose true name is Midir, a prince of the Sidh."

She hugged her knees up to her chest. While he had spoken, she had forgotten the cold, but suddenly the chill and the darkness pierced her to the bone.

"My parents were simply a man and a woman," she insisted.

"Your mother drank from a cup one day, swallowing a red butterfly. In that way, she bore you, a mortal child."

It explained much. Explained why she had always felt different from other children. Even when playing at her favorite games or lying beside her mother in the dark heart of the night, she had felt that persistent dreamy melancholy, that separateness, that yearning.

She looked at Niall. "You paid a high price to do this for me," she said.

"By making you human, I lost you to the world of mortals. You grew up like any other girl, a creature of the earth. You were memoryless. You had forgotten our previous life and our love."

She looked away, for it was painful to gaze into his beautiful face, into his ancient eyes. "How can I be certain?" she made herself ask. "How can I know beyond doubt that you and your magical events are more than just visions in my head?"

"Look at me, Aideen."

She looked. She saw a man who was more than a man. The silent agony in his soul reached out to her.

"You must give me your absolute, unquestioning trust," he said. "The slightest doubt will defeat us."

"But whatever we once were together, you're still a stranger to me."

"Open your heart to me, beloved. Deep within you lie the memories, if only you know where to find them. You tapped into that well before. They are all there. *I* am there. In your mind, in your heart. Waiting for you."

He held her hands lightly in his. "We are both from a world where there is no time. Our story will have no end. Come away with me, Aideen!"

"Niall—"

"Come away to the realm where our love was born. It is

a place of sun and splendor, a place where the shadow of mortal pain will never fall on us. I sang to you of this place. I felt your yearning, saw it in your beautiful green eyes."

"Curse you, Niall!" She ripped her hands from his. "You make me love you and want you—"

"Then why do you fight me, Aideen?"

"Because you are too late!" She was fierce in her anger, sitting up on her heels, her hair swirling like fire around her shoulders. "You revealed yourself to me too late. I married Echu. Why did you let me?"

"I tried to stop you." His voice was quiet, as if he spoke from some distance away. "I gave you the torque and placed you under *gessa* never to remove it. I thought it would make you see."

"I am a mortal. You made me one. A mortal cannot see what a god sees. And a woman is bound by mortal laws." She made herself look into his face. He was paler than ever in the moonlight.

"I am bound to Echu," she said. "I cannot dishonor him."

Niall went whiter yet, and to her horror she realized his vibrance was fading. "Aideen," he said, whispering now, "would you leave Echu if he willingly gave you up?"

"Echu would never willingly—"

"Would you?" His harsh, urgent voice cut like a knife.

"Yes," she said, as obstinate as he, "but only if Echu is truly willing, and only if you will lift the spell that is sapping his life."

Niall caught his breath. The darkness made pools of sadness in his eyes. "Very well, Aideen."

At his words, love poured through her. She swayed toward him, suddenly afraid.

Afraid she had asked too much.

Afraid she wanted too much.

Afraid she was willing to forswear all that she was in order to be with Niall.

She closed her eyes, reached out, and her heart whispered, "I love you."

But her arms, her aching arms, grasped at empty air.

chapteR 7

Echu sprang from his bed, hale as any island stallion, and threw himself into the business of being High King once again.

His subjects lit bonfires and made offerings to celebrate the king's recovery. They thanked the god of light and the spirits of the woods and the river, and while the revelry went on, Aideen stood alone in the shadows.

Dallan found her there, with her mantle wrapped close around her and her gaze fixed on the burning heart of the fire.

She narrowed accusing eyes at him. "You *knew,* Dallan."

"I did not. I suspected. And I was right. It was a true husband you met that night, met him at the trysting hour. I had to take that chance, or Echu would have died."

"Now Echu lives," she said, watching her husband lift a jug of mead. "He lives, and Niall pays the price."

"Does he?" Dallan looked intently into her shining torque.

"He paid with his own life for Echu to live." Aideen put her hand to her throat, where a sob gathered. "He did so because I asked it." She turned away. "And now he is gone, and because I know of him, I feel that absence. I grieve for him. I grieve for myself."

"Would he want that, my queen?" Dallan asked archly. "Would he want you to despair?"

The druid's words touched her. Gave her strength. She looked across the fire and saw that Kieran had dropped the joint of meat he had been eating. The little lad watched in dismay as two hounds snapped and growled over the prize.

Aideen went to him, dried his tears and placed a special kiss over his blind eye, then led him off to the banqueting table to get more food.

His hand in hers trembled like a baby bird. Warmth surged through her, and she smiled and waved at Dallan.

"You spoil the boy," Shelagh scolded as Aideen cut meat for Kieran.

She smiled. "I should hope so."

"Now that Echu is hale again, you'll be getting babes of your own."

Fear and uncertainty leaped up inside Aideen. She kept her face impassive, but she could not help thinking of Niall. He was with her always, yet he lay remote as the stars—cold, mysterious, unreachable.

And she knew beyond doubt that no man save Niall would ever touch her.

Winter came, bitterly cold and sere. The cattle grew shaggy coats and huddled in clumps around the mounds of hay. Ice gave lacy edges to the river Boyne, and frost rimed the bogs with brittle crystal patterns.

The inhabitants of Tara kept close to the hearth. Men sharpened their hunting spears and oiled their shields. Women kept busy with their spinning and weaving. Bards and songsters filled the silent spaces with their stories. The warriors tried to best one another with their boasting, and each night the fidchell board and pegs were brought. They played for stakes high and low—a bauble, a pebble, sometimes a handsome enameled bridle.

Echu sought comfort with other women. He did not bring them to his bed, but neither did he take pains to hide the liaisons. Aideen could summon no feeling save a hollow bleakness. She never confronted him, not even when she saw him returning with Sibheal to the dun, both of them flushed and full of the secret delight of love-making.

There was little sun to light the *grianan*. The days were short, the air pale and watery through the thick winter clouds. For Aideen, the hours ran together in the endless march of time. She felt it often, the yearning, the knowing, and sometimes at night when she slept, Niall called to her in her dreams.

But she never saw him again. He had made her choose between him and Echu. She had, out of fear and duty and a very human compassion, chosen Echu. She had failed to give Niall the one thing he asked—her absolute trust. She should have known her doubts would take him from her.

Dallan had warned that for an immortal to take on human form was risky business. It sapped one's power, surrendered it in bits to the known world.

Niall had twice given of himself for the sake of Aideen. She wondered what he was now, where he was. With a twist of anguish, she imagined him suspended between her world and his, buffeted unmercifully by the two disparate forces of the Seen and the Unseen.

Aideen began to wonder how long a woman could survive with such discontent eating at her soul. Her only happy moments were spent with Kieran. She had managed to convince Dallan that the lad should begin to learn the magic arts. Perhaps one day, after decades of study, he would become a druid or lawgiver.

Dallan had been dubious. It was not done for a boy of unknown *tuath* to learn such things. Particularly not a boy with a physical deformity.

But Kieran had a curious effect on those who troubled themselves to look at him and truly see him. He had the appearance of a child, but deep within him dwelt an ancient, uncomfortable wisdom.

And sometimes, foreknowledge.

One day, Aideen left the *grianan*, drawn to the pole barn where the bronze smiths worked at their forge. Kieran sat in a corner. A thick woolen blanket covered his legs and a scrying bowl was held in his lap.

"Kieran?" A chill unrelated to the winter slipped down her spine.

The child looked up. His blind eye remained as blank as an uncarved stone. Yet in his other eye glinted the knowledge of the ages.

"My queen," said Kieran, "he will come with the springtime."

She was unprepared for the torrent of joy the words gave her.

Kieran held up a thin hand. "He will be changed, my queen. More I cannot say."

The sound of a sentry's welcome horn awakened Aideen. She jumped up, not even bothering to call for her women. She was barefoot and belting on her tunic even as she crossed the main hall, crowded with sleeping men, and stepped out into the yard.

He will come with the springtime.

She stood still, alone, slender as a willow in the middle of the yard. The morning was cool but not cold. Beneath the dry yellow-brown grass, tender green shoots pushed up. She could smell the new growth she bruised under her bare feet.

The apple trees that shaded the apiary bore the tightly folded buds of blossoms. High in one of the trees, a lark trilled.

The main picket gate to the dun swung outward.

A lone rider entered.

Aideen blinked. It was like watching the sun rise. He was too beautiful to look away from, yet looking at him burned her eyes.

The morning light gave him the golden glow of a returning hero. His silvery mantle shimmered like mist with the slow movements of the horse. The animal itself was magnificent, its white coat the same hue as Niall's pale hair, its mane a darker shade of ivory, its hooves polished to a high gleam.

Aideen strode across the yard, closing the distance between them.

"I bid you welcome, Niall of Brí Leith." She used the formal greeting as she caught the reins of his horse. But since there was no one about, she lifted her gaze to him and said, "Your enchantment is fierce, my beloved. I have thought of little but you since last we met."

She stayed there, feeling the warmth emanate from his horse. She expected to see Niall's heart-catching smile, composed equally of joy and melancholy. She expected him to touch her, to cradle her cheek in his palm, to caress the side of her throat with his thumb. To kiss her the way he used to kiss her in her dreams.

Instead, he looked straight ahead, at the round hall with the door she had left gaping open.

"I have come to see the High King on a matter of business," he said.

It was odd, hearing the silky, melodious voice from the mouth of a cold stranger.

"Have you no greeting for me, Niall?" she asked. Even as she forced out the question, dread curled in her stomach, knotted there, and pulled taut. It was all she could

do not to fling herself to her knees, to plead with him to
see her, to remember who she was.

"Niall, please!" she said.

"I bid you fair greetings, my queen."

He said no more. She understood then how he must
have felt, the frustration and hurt, when she had not recognized *him*.

A groom, yawning and scratching himself and plucking
bits of straw from his hair, came to take charge of the
horse. Niall dismounted, slung his mantle over one
shoulder, and strode toward the hall.

Aideen stood alone again, only now the tingle of anticipation had turned to a terrible chill.

He will be changed.

Kieran had been right about the springtime. He was
right about Niall being changed.

Aideen's hand came up to press at the torque she always wore around her neck.

She did not need Kieran to tell her more. Now she
knew. Niall had forgotten the love they had shared.

This time, it was up to her to make him remember.

Midir . . .

He came awake in the middle of the night, blinking as
his eyes adjusted to the dimness.

Someone was calling to him. Calling him by his true
name, calling him Midir.

But he did not hear the voice again, not with his ears,
nor with his mind, nor with his heart.

She could not help herself. Like a shameless wanton,
she followed him down the path to the river, where he
had gone to wash.

With his long, sure strides, he passed through the hawthorn grove where he had once called to her, sung to her of the trysting hour.

She hoped he would pause and remember, but his graceful, long-limbed pace never faltered.

He knelt on the bank of the river and scooped up water in his hands.

Aideen joined him there. "Good morn, Niall."

He nodded at her, cordial and distant.

Aideen blew out a sigh. She had attempted to reach him last night, calling his true name with her heart. Once before, when she had felt threatened by Echu on the ramparts, she had summoned a power from beyond. She had dared to hope that she possessed, even slightly, the power of the immortals.

Last night her plea had not worked. And the effort had left her exhausted.

Despite what she might have been in another world, another time, in the here and now she was a woman. She had naught but her woman's heart to guide her.

"Niall," she said, trying not to flinch as he lifted his cold regard to her. "You do not remember who I am, do you?"

"Of course I do." He spoke plainly, as if she were a child. "You are queen, wife of Echu the High King."

"Is that all you remember, Niall?"

"What more could there be?"

She took a chance. She took his hand in hers. His was chill and wet with river water. She saw the merest flicker in his expression. The spark quickly died, but she had seen enough to give her hope.

Hope.

"Niall, in the time before time, I was your wife. It was you who told me this."

He snatched his hand away. "You are the king's wife."

"That was not my choice. And you told me, too, that I did have a choice. Was that a lie?"

"I never lie."

"Do you remember now, Niall?" She sat forward. "Do you?" She peered at his face, a face too comely to be real, his eyes like jewels that reflected images of the places she had seen only in her dreams—crystal walls and sunlit gardens and time without end.

"Say that you remember, Niall!" she whispered.

He turned away and glared down at the placid water. "I do not."

chapter 8

After Aideen had stalked away through the hawthorn grove, he stared for a long time into the shady pool of water. The river ran deep here, and slowly, and he could see clear to the bottom where the brown, rounded rocks lay, and secretive fishes darted in and out.

Say that you remember . . .

What an extraordinary woman, was Aideen. What an extraordinary thing she had said to him.

Aideen!

He blinked, and the reflections in the water began to move with lives and wills of their own. As if borne by the swirling currents, half-formed memories surged up from the depths. He saw himself, only he was younger, smiling, his eyes soft with love as he gazed upon a woman of surpassing beauty. He joined her on a bed of silk and feathers.

Aideen!

The ivory mounds of her breasts were like the hills after the first fall of snow. Perfect and white and pure. There was a sweet berry flush upon her lips and cheeks and the crests of her breasts. He tasted each blushing spot, first with his hands and then with his hungering mouth.

Aideen!

He treasured her, this woman who owned his soul. When he sheathed his body within her, she cried out and clutched at him. He dug his fingers into her dawn-hued hair and held her close, speaking words of love into her ear.

The image of the lovers clouded, then transformed into a rippling stream of other memories. He saw Aideen in a summer-green field. The wind was playing with her red-gold hair as she bent and straightened, gathering flowers. She paused to bring them to her face to inhale their scent, and her eyes danced with mirth. Then he saw her lit by orange fire, swathed in her tunic of vivid green, her head slightly cocked as she listened to him play a love song on his harp. She held out her hand to him, reaching, reaching . . .

She was his wife for all eternity. There was nothing he would not do for her. Nothing he would not give to her.

And yet he had lost her. Try as he might, he could not find the love inside him, the love he knew he had once felt for her.

The image on the water broke into a thousand pieces.

Niall blinked. All he saw now were red petals littering the pool, blown there by the spring wind.

"Some call this the game of life," said Niall.

Aideen had been reclining on her cushion beside Echu in the hall. She did so each night. He never touched her. Nor did he ever wish to. For that, she knew she should be grateful.

Niall set the playing board on the floor in front of Echu. "Do you play *fidchell*?" he asked.

"Of course," Echu said amiably. "It is, as you say, the game of life. Set out the pegs, and I shall play you. But I warn you, I am very skilled."

"Then I am forewarned." With a polite smile, Niall

began to set out the little carved pegs and polished stones. "I take it you will not object to a high stake in this game."

Aideen caught her breath. Clearly, Niall was up to something. But she did not know him anymore. She could not guess his plan.

Still, the faint glimmer of hope she had felt in the grove flickered again. Perhaps he was beginning to remember, though she still didn't see the love in his eyes; she saw only determination to possess her.

"High stakes?" Echu fingered his bristly beard.

"My horse," said Niall. "If you best me, I forfeit my horse. If you lose, you forfeit something of your choosing."

"Indeed!" Echu crossed his legs and sat up straight upon his cushion. "Did you hear that, wife? I shall win a horse tonight."

"If you win," Aideen said, knowing she should not voice a doubt about the High King. It did not matter. He was not listening. He never did.

His eyes glowed with the light of avarice. The greed in her husband's regard was so bright and piercing that she looked away.

"I have admired that horse for all the days of your visit, Niall," Echu said. "Truly, it is a magical beast. Never have I known one to have a swifter, smoother gait. Aideen! Pour the mead. The play is about to begin!"

She wanted to tell Echu he should not play games with Niall, but how could she? She had no right to order him about. Silently she poured mead. The men-at-arms gathered round to watch.

The game pieces went back and forth. Luck first favored Echu, then Niall, then Echu again. So it went, for an hour and then two. Someone restoked the central hearth fire. Aideen brought more mead.

Echu at last saw an opening and moved in on Niall with devastating certainty.

Niall watched his final peg fall. He showed no anger. No resentment.

"To you, my king," he said. "The horse is yours."

With a *whoop* of triumph, Echu jumped up. He called for the horse to be brought, and he rode it bareback, seven times around the dun. The horse, no doubt unused to such a hard, aggressive rider, snorted and pawed the air.

Aideen stood in the yard and watched. Niall stood beside her.

"How could you!" she whispered. "You let him win that horse so it will throw him and break his neck."

"He won it on his own," Niall stated. "And if he kills himself, it is none of my fault."

She saw then that their love was brutal. Fierce. Brooking no obstacles, not even the life of a man. It frightened her. She wanted to turn away. She was afraid to look such a love in the face and lay claim to it.

But neither could she deny it.

"Our love will be the death of Echu," she whispered.

"Our love?" Niall regarded her archly. "I think you mistake simple desire for love."

She pressed her hands to her middle as if he had thrust a lance into her. "Niall—"

"Neither of us has the power to cause his death," he said. "If he suffers misfortune, it will be because of his own greed."

"You are making him greedy! He had nothing but admiration for your horse—until you offered it up as stakes in your game."

"It is not my game," said Niall. "Nor is it Echu's. *Fidchell* is the game of life. It is the struggle between Echu and me. Between light and dark, between two opposites.

Neither of us chose the struggle, but we are both entrenched in it."

"And the real stake in the game . . ." Aideen shivered and looked away.

"Is you," said Niall.

The next night, Echu brimmed with laughter and goodwill. Despite Aideen's fears, he had not fallen from the beautiful horse. His delight in the prize was like that of a child, and like a child, he craved more.

Niall did not even have to offer the game of *fidchell*. Echu insisted.

"There's no shame in losing to the High King," Echu said when Niall appeared reluctant to play. "It is right that I should win. I excel at the game."

Niall caught Aideen's eye. They shared a long glance, and what passed between them was a message of bewilderment and hope. She did not wish to hurt anyone. Nor did he. But they both understood that Echu was making his own destiny.

But what of theirs? Would his heart remember her? Would they be together as before?

"What shall the stakes be this time?" the High King asked.

"What would you like?" asked Niall.

Aideen held her breath. It was Echu's choice, then. He could choose worldly goods, never knowing the cost was his soul. Or he could choose her.

She opened her mouth to speak, but Dallan's hand on her arm stopped her. The druid said nothing, yet she knew what he was thinking. Echu could ask that the curse on his marriage to Aideen be lifted. He could take her as a true wife, if he so chose.

"I would have your sword, Niall of Brí Leith," Echu said.

Dallan's hand relinquished Aideen's. She slowly ex-
pelled her breath. She was beginning to understand
Echu very well. He was all too mortal. Though he was
High King, he was too much a subject of other men's
minds.

Even in choosing Aideen as his wife, he had not chosen
freely. He had taken her because his druids had advised
it. And so when he had the opportunity to mend the rift
between them, he had forsaken it—for a sword.

"My king," Niall said, kneeling with the board before
Echu, "I am at your service." His hands were sure and
steady as he set up the pegs. He played with dispassionate
skill, his face betraying no emotion.

In contrast, Echu grew florid, his black eyes shiny as
beetle shells. He stormed his opponent's game pieces,
captured them, and caused the last to fall.

The men-at-arms exchanged sidewise, lidded glances.
To lose one's horse to the High King was unfortunate
indeed. To lose his sword in addition to that was a blow to
his very manhood.

Niall betrayed nothing. He merely stood and took his
sword from its sheath and held the blade flat upon his two
hands, an offering to the king who had bested him. It was
a magnificent weapon, with an enameled hilt and a winking cabochon garnet in the weighted pommel.

Echu took the sword. He threw back his head and
roared with delight, calling for mead, bidding his men-at-
arms to gather close to admire the singular weapon.

"Niall," Echu said, "there is something about you that
intrigues me."

Niall said nothing. Everyone in the hall seemed to wait
with breath held.

Echu turned to his chief druid. "What say you, Dallan?" The king held the sword up to the light and
squinted at the endless swirling designs etched into the
blade. "This is not the sword of an ordinary man."

"It is not."

"You are of the Sidh, then, are you not, Niall?" Echu rested his elbow on one knee and leaned forward, grinning with expectation.

Aideen squeezed her eyes shut. Niall could not lie.

He said, "I am."

"And I bested you!" Echu's hands shook with excitement as he set up the pegs again. "I have bested an immortal. We must play again. And again, I shall name the stakes."

"As you wish, my king."

Echu finished setting up the board. He stood and went to the door of the hall and flung it open. Through the opening, Aideen could see the greening hills all folded into each other, and far beyond, the secret, shadowy bog.

"I want my fields cleared of stones," Echu said, "and the marsh drained, and a causeway laid across the bog so that my subjects might come to me by that way." Echu spun around to face Niall. The High King's face was ruddy now with excitement. "Those are my terms."

Aideen watched as the familiar stillness claimed Niall. She had seen him like this before—remote, unreachable. With naught save the icy gleam in his eyes to distinguish him from a carven image.

Frightened, she rushed to Echu and dropped to her knees before him. "Husband, you ask too much! I beg you, drop your demands, for you make them at a cost to your soul."

Echu gripped her shoulders and pulled her up so that she was standing. He gazed deep into her eyes. Just for a moment, she saw a shrinking, frightened creature inside him. Then his eyes crinkled with amusement or torment, she knew not which. "My dear," he murmured, "I lost my soul long ago."

He *knew*. He had probably known all along. She had always wanted Niall, and only Niall. Despite what she had said to Echu on the rampart, despite her part in healing him, she could not force herself to desire him.

But, surprisingly, he looked past her, and the pain in his face deepened as he gazed upon the boy, Kieran. "Long ago," he whispered, half to himself. He explained no further, but set Aideen aside.

Like a man on a runaway horse, he had been hurtling toward his destiny, and nothing she could say or do could stop him.

"I agree to the terms," Niall called across the hall.

As if she no longer existed, Echu brushed past Aideen and hurried over to the *fidchell* board.

"But I have a request of my own," Niall added.

"And what is that?" Echu asked.

"When we are done with this game, you will play one more with me."

"I should hope it would be more than one," Echu declared, slapping his knees.

"One will suffice. And *I* shall name the winner's prize."

"It is done," Echu said.

The hall quieted, and they played with intent, concentrated skill, and as before, Echu won.

His shout of triumph caused the timbers of the dun to shake.

At sunset, Niall quietly left the hall. Aideen followed, knowing no one would notice them. They were as nothing to Echu and his jubilant court. The king and his subjects were so easily pleased by magic tricks.

She and Niall climbed the high hill to where the Stone of Destiny stood stark and ancient against the fiery sky. They could see the fields and the marsh and the layers of hills all ablaze with flaming clouds.

Niall turned to face her. He was still the stranger, still remote, yet deep in his eyes she saw a familiar flicker of

. . . feeling. It came and went so quickly she could not name it.

"Niall?" She spoke his name softly, a whisper on the wind. He did not respond. Something odd took hold inside her, and it was warm and bright, as if she had swallowed a star. "Midir?"

She saw the knowledge break over him then. His eyes lit and his lips smiled and it was like a miracle, like the sun coming up after endless darkness.

He held out both hands and she took them, speechless with joy.

The wind blew his long, pale hair around his shoulders. "In another time," he said, "in another world, our love was so simple. So pure. Now it is not so easy, is it, Aideen?"

"No." She swallowed hard. "It . . . hurts. We are both wounded. Echu is wounded. I carry a feeling of guilt with me. Can I ever be free of that?"

"Yes, my beloved. But you think you know what it feels like to hurt. I'm afraid you do not. I'm afraid you have barely brushed the surface of what you will have to endure if you want to love me."

"I want to love you," she vowed. "No questions. No conditions. I want us to love as we did before."

"We'll never love as we did before," Niall said. What a beautiful picture he made, his shoulders so broad, his mantle green and flashing in the lowering sunlight. "It will be much, much better, Aideen."

She threw her arms around his neck and clung there, savoring his scent of woods and water, loving the solidness of his form.

With a look of depthless regret, he set her away from him. "Not yet, Aideen," he said. "First, I must do Echu's bidding. What he wants will not be easy. It could sap my strength. My powers."

"Then let me help."

"That's not possible. Your own powers can only serve your will. You cannot do what has been commanded of me."

Dread closed in around her. "Niall, what if I lose you again?"

"That is what I meant about the hurt." He touched the gleaming torque. "There is also hope. You know that, don't you?"

She took his face between her hands. "You are the sun, Niall, and I am the dawn. But the dawn does not grow stronger with the sun."

"Aideen—"

"In order for the sun to live and light the day," she said brokenly, "the dawn has to die."

He made her leave the lofty hill. He made her promise not to look back. She trusted him now. She knew better than to disregard his instructions.

Ah, but it took all of her will to keep walking, to hold her gaze straight ahead, once the noise started. Behind her, she heard the roar of wind and thunder, heard his hoarse, ragged voice calling her name.

Clapping her hands over her ears, she ran down the hill to the river, swollen now with the spring thaw. The hawthorns had not yet begun to bloom, but they were budding, green and tender and fragrant.

She stood there with her back against the solid trunk of a tree, and she drew strength from it. She felt a tingling warmth seeping into her as if she herself were the tree, and the sun was bringing her to life.

A blaze of ecstasy flared in her, and she caught her breath, stunned and seduced by the intensity of the feeling. She knew then that it was the power of the immortals flowing through her, bubbling and seething inside her.

"Yes!" she cried out, flinging back her head. Closing

her eyes, she let the fading glow of the setting sun bathe her face.

The cold wind swept over her then, and darkened the world.

Aideen opened her eyes to see the river stippled by sharp white crests, the trees bending in the high, shivery wind. A huge, dark-winged creature alit on the opposite bank of the river. Aideen could not see it clearly, but the burning, malevolent eyes and the shadowy beating of the wings told her all she needed to know.

"Fúamnach!" The name of the sorceress burst from Aideen on a wave of shock.

The sorceress spoke, not with a voice but with a shout of thunder. An invisible fist seemed to hurl Aideen back against a tree. She slumped there, breathless and dazed by the blow. She tried to summon Niall, but her mind could not reach him. He was spending his powers to do Echu's bidding.

Another blow came, slapping her down with the force of a storm-driven wave. Aideen lay on her side, unable to drag herself up. When she finally managed to prop herself on a shaky elbow, the third blow crushed her down again.

Darkness flickered at the edge of her vision. She would die here, she knew, at the hand of one whose hate was more powerful than love.

The thought awakened the dreamer inside her, and the dreamer said *no*.

She remembered Kieran, how he loved her, trusted in her. And Niall, how he had crossed time and space to be with her, no matter what the cost. And behind her, where her shoulder touched the greening hawthorn tree, she felt that warm tingling again.

The power. The burst of strength.

Aideen was on her feet in an instant. With every shred of energy in her, she fought back. Her weapons were invisible, like those of the sorceress. They were shapeless masses of raw, potent emotion. She absorbed more blows from Fúamnach, but each one seemed to strengthen her own powers. The wind screamed and the river roared, and she fought on and on, relentless and unforgiving, brutal to this threat to her love.

When at last she collapsed, exhausted, on the riverbank, she was surprised to see that the sun was rising. She had fought through the night. Panting through clenched teeth, she dared to look across the river.

Rather than the black-winged beast, she saw a thorn tree growing there, scraggly and black, its spines long and barren of new growth.

It took all of his powers to weave the spell. He had thought he was prepared for the agony, but when the pain pierced his chest like a lance, he cried out and doubled over, crumpling to the ground.

"Aideen!" he called, but she was gone. He had banished her from the hill, hoping to protect her from the swirling sorcery that snapped like heat lightning around the Stone of Tara.

He lost consciousness, and when he woke, his head throbbed as if it had been stomped by wild horses. He blinked, and for a moment he thought the sun had still not set. Then he realized the pink light came from the east. It was dawn.

In order for the sun to live and light the day, the dawn has to die.

Aideen had spoken with the wisdom of the ancients.

Pushing the heels of his hands against the grass on the hill, he levered himself up. The spell had taken him to the very limits of his strength, and his mortal self was weak, dazed.

He squinted off into the distance, and there he saw it.

The fields, smooth and green, no stone or rubble to mar the land. The marsh, moist and fertile, waiting like a lush woman to be planted with seed. The bog, its sacred mystery now compromised by a causeway spanning it.

He collapsed back on the grass and stared up at the brightening sky.

chapter 9

"I can't watch," Aideen said to Dallan and Kieran. The druid and the boy stood with her just outside the hall. Within, the people of the household were gathering to observe the final match of fidchell between Echu and Niall.

"You must watch," Kieran said, hopping from one leg to the other in agitation. "You must."

"Why?" she demanded. "So I can see Niall further weakened, sacrificed to Echu's greed?"

"You must"—Kieran fixed her with a fierce, unboylike glare—"because I command it."

She almost laughed. He was so solemn, so—Aideen gasped and lifted the lad up. "Kieran! Your eye!"

Dallan clasped his hands together. "Is it not wonderful? He can see with that eye."

"But what . . . how?"

Dallan's gaze strayed to the hall.

"Niall," she whispered. Her battle by the river had taught her that power could be used to destroy or to heal. She shivered and held the lad tighter.

Kieran squirmed out of her arms. "He did not simply do Echu's bidding. He heard my wish as well. Now." The child folded his arms across his chest. "Will you go and support him, or will you hang back in the shadows?"

Her heart full of wonderment at Kieran's miracle, Aideen felt a glimmer of true happiness and hope. "You give me no choice."

She threw back her shoulders and entered the hall. The spectators made way for her, moving aside, clearing a path to Echu. She followed the path, but she did not stand behind the High King as they all expected. She stood beside Niall.

He played without relish; Echu played without skill.

The High King lost.

Aideen watched the rage rise in him like a fount, the heat and redness of anger lighting his neck, his face, his eyes. "You tricked me!" he shouted at Niall.

"My king, you knew from the start that you were not playing the game of life with an ordinary man. I have won. Now it is for me to claim the prize."

Echu was wearing the priceless sword. His meaty hands closed around the hilt. He seemed certain Niall would demand the return of his prizes.

Niall didn't even glance at the sword. "I want only one thing," he said. "A kiss from the queen."

Every listener in the hall drew audible breath. Echu stood stock still, for he, like everyone else, knew it would be no ordinary kiss. "From Aideen? From my wife?"

"Yes."

Aideen felt a thrill of longing mixed with fear. She knew that the kiss would have a mystical, irrevocable significance. The moment Niall kissed her, she would be his forever. He was a stranger, and yet he was not. She gazed at him, as she had so many times before, and the light in his eyes offered her the world.

But she was not certain it was a world she could live in.

"I concede the match," Echu snapped churlishly. "You'll have your prize, but . . ." His gaze darted away, and Aideen detected a sly glint in his black eyes. "But later. We'll hold a special feast in your honor upon the hill of Tara. Is that agreeable to you, Niall?"

"Of course," said Niall.

"You mean to trick him, don't you?" Aideen asked as soon as she and Echu stood alone in the partitioned chamber off the great hall.

"He has made me the wealthiest of men. He has powers that will serve me as no other king as ever been served."

"You'll make a slave of him," Aideen said in a horrified whisper. "Echu, no. I beg you to honor your word."

"My word!" he roared, so loudly that she flinched. "My word! *You* are the faithless one, Aideen. You came to this marriage knowing you would never truly belong to me."

"That is not so," she said. She feared his anger, but she feared even more what would happen if she did not try to stop him. "I had every intention of being a good and true wife to you. But it was not to be. I think, Echu, that neither you nor I could have done anything differently."

"You've been faithless," he repeated, thrusting out his bearded chin.

"I have not," she said, and a sense of wonder and certainty broke over her. "I have not. I realize that now. I have been faithful—both to the memories hidden deep inside me, and to the husband I willingly served. Because of those memories, I have stayed chaste. Yet when you were dying, I surrendered my will to stay by your side and to serve you until you recovered. It is you who have been faithless, Echu. You gambled me away like a chattel."

He laughed then, a coarse, ugly sound. "Do you think you are any more than that, Aideen? Any more than a chattel?"

* * *

Night fell, and a bonfire raked the black sky with talons of gold. On the Hill of Tara, Echu had set up a banqueting table beside the fire. He had draped the table with a length of bright purple cloth, and the dancing flames reflected off the shiny fabric.

With defiance burning in her chest, Aideen stood beside the table and waited. The images on the hill wheeled about her—laughing faces, men and women lifting their cups, musicians singing, servants rushing about, carrying food and drink up the hill to the guests. Smells assaulted her too, smells of warming mead and roasting meat, of herbs and smoke and, oddly, the hot tang of tar, as if someone had brought in a bucket from the bog pits.

Niall strode up the hill on long, muscled legs, his silver-green mantle sailing out behind him, his hair like mist around his bold, handsome face. He went directly to Echu and showed no special deference to the High King.

"I have come to claim my prize," he said. "I have wooed Aideen with gifts beyond price—"

"Those were not gifts, but forfeits rightly won by me," Echu stated.

"No." Dallan stepped forward. "With all due respect, my king, you knew from the start that Niall could have bested you at any time."

"Surrender, Echu," Niall said. Although he spoke to the king, his gaze clung to Aideen, and it was overflowing with adoration. "I have earned the right to her love. She was mine before the world was made. She will be mine forever."

A terrible roar split the air—once, twice, three times.

"The Stone of Tara speaks!" Dallan shouted.

As one, everyone turned to the ancient monument. Upon it sat Kieran, looking small yet supremely self-assured. The noise was deafening, echoing across the land like the bellow of a giant. When at last it quieted, men fell to their knees before the boy.

All knew that, when a true king sat upon the stone, it roared three times.

Echu's cheeks paled behind his beard. "By the moon and stars," he whispered. "This cannot be."

Aideen regarded him suspiciously. It was a well-known fact that Echu had never attempted to sit upon the Stone of Destiny. *I lost my soul long ago.* So Echu had confessed to her. Now she wondered if he meant this—that he had, by treachery, kept a rightful king from the throne.

Kieran was so small that he had to hop down from the great rock. Very solemnly, he walked to where Echu and Niall and Aideen stood.

"Echu and Niall are forgetting one thing," he said. He smiled shyly at Aideen. "Are they not?"

Gratitude flowed through her. All along, she had suspected her own part in this, but until now she had not dared to voice it.

"I claim the right to choose." She looked from Echu to Niall. "I am a woman with a will of my own. It is not for either of you to command me." She turned to the man she had loved forever. "I choose Niall."

Murmurs spread like wildfire through the spectators. Echu regarded her archly; then his glance slid to the cloth-covered table. "Niall gets a kiss, as he requested. And it must take place atop this banqueting table. I want all to see that I fulfill my promise."

Niall leaped upon the table. Bending, he held out his hand.

Aideen hesitated. Not because she doubted Niall, but because she suspected treachery from Echu. Yet the love shining from Niall's eyes compelled her to reach for him, to take his hand, to climb up to his side.

For a breathless moment, they stared at each other. He

was all that he had promised and more. He was eternal contentment and bliss. He was summer without end.

She reached around behind her neck and unfastened the torque. The *gessa* had no meaning anymore, not now that she was about to find her destiny.

The golden ornament flashed as she tossed it to Kieran, once a slave child, soon to be a king.

And something else flashed.

A torch.

Plunging into the tarred kindling Echu had secreted under the table.

The fear nearly destroyed her. In panic, she started to look away from Niall, to doubt him, to withdraw her trust and forfeit their love once again.

But he caught her against him and the fear dissolved. She felt no heat from the fire. His lips descended slowly, so slowly, and it was the moment she had been waiting for since before she was born. Their breath mingled. Their mouths brushed together, then opened. She tasted his sweetness, sighing with the splendor of it.

Behind her closed eyes, she saw crystal palaces and green fields with the sunlight shimmering over them. She saw gardens ablaze with flowers and butterflies, a golden world where the very air pulsed with the joyous love she felt for Niall, for Midir, for the mate of her soul. It was exactly as he had described it to her, exactly as he had promised.

So long ago, Dallan had spoken the truth. She *could* cross over to a higher world. She just needed to learn to listen to her heart, as she was doing now, as she would do forever after. The only magic she needed was the only magic she possessed—the magic of love.

Standing atop the hill, the people of Tara could see nothing but a cloud of smoke billowing up from the draped table. Echu emitted a bellow of fury, racing around the bonfire. Dallan, his ancient face full of sympathy, stopped him and pointed upward.

Echu looked into the sky. His vision started to fade, just as his right to be High King was fading. But his last sight, the last glimpse of light before the darkness fell, showed a pair of white swans aimed in flight at the moon, winging their way to eternity.

RARER than a WHITE CROW

BY

ROBERTA GELLIS

*To Elizabeth Lee, my dear little granddaughter, whose
imminent arrival seriously hampered the early stages of
this book . . . and gave me intense joy.*

chapter 1

Vaguely uneasy, Angus Óg set his horn drinking cup into the beautifully wrought stand and looked down the long hall and out the open doors. He could see to the bottom of the low hill on which his hall stood, all the way to the trees that bordered the river because, unlike the villages and manors, the raths and duns of the Milesians, no walls surrounded Bruigh na Boinne. There was no need for such defensive structures; his blood was in the earth, the earth was in his blood, and only those of good will—or of very mighty magic—could walk up that hill and in his doors.

The hall was very quiet. The manservant who had poured his ale was waiting silently behind his chair and the woman who had offered food had gone out. On this late spring day with the sun shining, the household folk were all out of doors doing such tasks as would be marred by rain. He had only come in himself a little while ago, heated with the joyful work of breaking a young horse and needing a drink and the cool of the house. When he had stepped inside the door, that was when the feeling he was doing something wrong had come over him.

Angus looked over his shoulder at the *sencleithe*, but the servingman seemed perfectly at ease, smiling and coming forward to refill Angus's drinking horn as soon as Angus looked at him. Although he was no longer thirsty, Angus did not stop him but waved him away when the horn was full. When the man was gone, he looked along each side of the hall, letting his eye rest in each alcove formed by the supporting columns where the men of the household slept. However, the trouble was not from any sleeping place nor anything stored within each place, nor up among the lofty rafters, with their fine carving blackened by ages of smoke from the two great central hearths.

Once again Angus's eyes went to the open door and gazed down the slope to the wooded area along the river. There was nothing wrong in the hall, yet he had become uneasy when he entered it. He was needed outside? And not on his own *lios* but down by the river? Was he, then?

Half-smiling Angus rose, unhooked his sword belt from the back of the chair, clasped it around his waist, and drew his scarlet cloak over his shoulders. His blue eyes were bright as sapphires with curiosity as he strode out of the hall, past the enclosure where the young horses were penned, and down the graveled path toward the river. As soon as he left the hall, the uneasy feeling had lifted, but now he felt an odd desire to swim in the pond near the river. Twice he shook his head as friends called out to ask if he wanted company, but when Fraoch caught him by the arm, a flicker of caution woke in him.

Not that Angus felt any threat in the faint summoning, only that he was called at all was strange. Although he had his own Gifts, he was not one of the great ones, like Lugh, who could work magic. Thus, he was not greatly feared and anyone who wanted him usually just walked in his door and spoke. Fraoch might be too suspicious, but his man's look of surprise implied he was acting out of his normal pattern.

"I am going down to the pool," he said. "I will not be long—but if the sun is westerly and I am not back, come and look for me."

"Will that not be too late to be looking, Angus-Righ?"

Angus laughed. "Well, now, if you hear the clang of swords or me shouting for help, it would be well if you came sooner. I am thinking someone wishes to speak with me in private, and I would not want that person to be interrupted by you coming too soon."

"It would not be good if I came too late, either. Better a short conference than a long death or captivity."

"But Fraoch, what could anyone gain by taking me captive or killing me? Do you know any who wish me harm?"

Fraoch shrugged. It was true enough that Angus was the darling of the entire Tuatha de Danaan and that his easy good nature made no enemies even among the common folk.

"I still think I should walk down to the pond with you," he said. "It is not your way to go alone; you are a man who likes company."

"And I am going to seek it, but the one waiting does not desire company other than mine or he . . . ah . . . or she would have walked up to the hall."

"A woman?"

"Women seek me sometimes." Angus smiled.

"Just be careful," Fraoch urged, frowning. "Women can carry long, sharp knives."

Angus laughed aloud. "Not when they come seeking me."

Fraoch laughed too, then, and Angus turned away and continued down the hill. It was cool under the trees, and he smiled again, pulling his cloak closer about him and thinking that it was early in the year to be swimming but that it was unlikely that was the purpose of whoever was calling him.

He stopped suddenly on the path through the thick growth of brush and saplings that bordered the pond when he caught, through the misty green of spring

leaves, a flash of white skin in a patch of sunlight near the
water. The saplings and brush had been planted to give
privacy to those who wished to use the pond and he hesitated to intrude. In that moment, a woman rose to her
feet and looked toward him.

"Glad I am for your coming, Angus Óg," she said.

Her hair, which only partially veiled her white body,
was so black and silky that an iridescent shimmer played
over it. Angus stepped past the last curtain of brush and
saplings and saw that her eyes were black too, bright and
beady as a bird's. He came a few steps closer, and she held
out her hand to him, but he did not take it.

"And what is it that you want with me?" he asked.

"What does a woman who has laid aside her garments
usually want of you, Angus Óg?" she asked in turn,
laughing.

Her voice was shockingly harsh and her laugh held a
cackle, ill fitting with her smooth, young body and her
lovely face. Angus shook his head. "It is not so common in
my experience as you seem to think that a woman as
lovely as you seeks me out for so simple a purpose as you
imply. Tell me first what favor you will ask in return for
the favor you offer me."

She laughed again, the grating cackle more apparent.
"Why are you so suspicious? And you so toothsome a
morsel. I like big men with red hair and such bright blue
eyes. And those freckles over your nose are quite delicious. That is enough for me. Come." She walked closer
and lifted her hand toward him again. "I will not bind
you to me in any way, I promise."

Angus laughed in reply. "No, you would not bind me
because you would not want me. I have been known to
give an hour's love to comfort a woman hurt or scorned
or to wake a glow in a plain maiden that will bring her a
longer, truer love, but you do not want or need comfort

or assurance. I will not couple with you only to satisfy your lust."

"Oh, will you not?" she muttered, coming right up against him and placing both arms around his neck.

Angus raised his own arms as if to embrace her, looking deep into the bright, beady eyes, so inhuman in the soft female face. He did not embrace her, however; instead he caught her wrists and forced her arms down between them. Now he was certain who held him: The Morrigan, who was called by the common folk the goddess of war. She was no goddess to him, only one of his own people, and the Tuatha de Danaan worshipped only the goddess Dana, the Great Mother. But The Morrigan had great power, and she was as capricious in the use of it as the weather in the spring. She was a fomenter of war because nothing amused her so much as a misunderstanding that led to violence. She was the twister of good into evil—and sometimes of evil into good; it was the twisting she loved, not the evil. Angus sighed.

"Morrigan," he said, "I know you. Old Crow, you cannot beguile me by drawing on the seeming of a lovely body. You did not come to me for love. A woman of war who truly desires love from a man is rarer than a white crow. Now, what do you want of me? Show me the truth."

Her red lips drew back from her teeth. "You need to be shown the truth, indeed, for a man who scorns honest lust is a fool! The truth?" Her head turned over her shoulder, impossibly far, the way a bird's head turns. "Look there," she cried.

Shocked by the inhuman twist of The Morrigan's neck, Angus obeyed involuntarily, his eyes following the line hers had taken to the water of the pond. His breath drew in and his grip on her wrists tightened. A woman was looking back at him from the quiet water—not The Morrigan. He could not say the face was beautiful; it was too strong, too austere for beauty, but he knew he would never forget it. Gold-brown hair in thick plaits was coiled atop her head, and gold-brown eyes stared back at him from under thick straight brows. The lips were full, but firmly held, the chin strong under cheeks that were slightly hollowed by high cheekbones. The Morrigan's cackle filled his ears, but Angus was caught by the level gaze of the gold-brown eyes.

"That is the truth!" The Morrigan's voice was now more like the caw of a crow than human speech. "I set this *geis* upon you, Angus Óg. Seek love there! You will love that woman and no other all the days of her life, and you will find no peace, ever, until you win her, Milesian though she is, for your wife."

A pain as sharp as a spear pierced his chest. Angus gasped but instead of releasing his hold on The Morrigan's wrists as he knew she expected, he gripped so hard, the bones ground together. The Morrigan cried out and the pain in his chest ended, but when it was gone Angus could still feel something, as if his heart was caught in a fisherman's net. It did not hurt or impede the beating, but Angus knew that if he did not fulfill the *geis*, those knotted threads, like a fisherman's net, would draw tighter and tighter until he could not breathe or move.

"Let me go!" The Morrigan shrieked, her voice breaking between rage and laughter, as she struggled to wrench her arms free. "Let me go or worse will befall you. The *geis* is upon you and you cannot undo it no matter if you break me and rend me. You cannot kill me, and no matter what you do, I will heal. Let me go!"

"I cannot kill you, but I can hold you caged, Old Crow, and break you again and again."

"That will not save you," she cackled, twisting and kicking at him, "and soon you will be beyond breaking so much as a straw."

"I may be, but my father will not be, and I swear I will

cage you and summon him if you do not answer me true."

"Oh, answers." She stopped fighting him and smiled. "I am willing to give answers—and you know I never lie."

It was true. The Morrigan never lied, but, Angus Óg reminded himself, she often spoke the truth in such a way that those who heard her were able to lie to themselves and twist her words so that they caused great harm.

"If I find this woman and bind her to me, what harm will come of it? To me? To her? To the Tuatha de Danaan?"

The Morrigan laughed long and loud—and the laugh was the most human she had uttered. "*If* you can find her and win her—no harm at all. No harm to you. No harm to the woman. And good to the Tuatha de Danaan. *If* you can find her and win her." She was silent a moment, then shook her head and added, smiling, "If you had not been such a self-righteous fool and insulted my honest desire, I would have told you who she was and explained my purpose to you in pillow talk. Likely you would have thought it good and agreed."

Feeling somewhat ashamed of himself and beguiled by The Morrigan's relaxed, passive stance, Angus eased his grip. He was trying to think of a way to apologize without either lying or further insulting her. The truth was that he had felt no flicker of desire's heat even when she pressed her body against him. The beauty she displayed was too clearly a cover on a false core. And when he recognized her, her reputation precluded an assumption of honesty about any of her purposes.

"I—" he began uncertainly, his grip weakening further, whereupon The Morrigan wrenched herself free, leapt back, and shimmered into the form of a huge crow, which flew up and perched out of reach on a sapling that bent and quivered under the weight.

"Now I will watch you wither with pleasure," the crow

cawed. "And I will find another to fulfill my purpose with the woman."

"No!" Angus cried, and then bit his lip as the crow flapped away cawing laughter.

He knew quite well that his protest only increased The Morrigan's amusement, but an unreasoning rage had overcome him—not when she spoke of his withering but when she said she would find another man for the woman he had seen in the water. Knowing he would see nothing, he still turned and looked at the pond, but no image formed on the still water in answer to his desire. It did not matter, her face was clear enough in his mind's eye. Slowly his lips curved as he recalled the words of the Morrigan's *geis:* that he would love only that woman all the days of her life.

He looked away from the water, smiling. That was no curse to him. Many loved him, too many. And he loved in return, but on both sides it was a gentle warmth. He knew he had never been touched by the searing flames of a binding passion. Just as he stepped into the cool of the saplings' shade, he looked back over his shoulder at the pond once more. The still water reflected only the sky, but he saw the gleaming bronze of the woman's hair and the glitter of gold in her level brown eyes.

When he found her, the heat of his love would sear away the net holding his heart. When he found her! Angus turned away from the water and started back toward the dun with swift strides. Find her he must, and soon, before The Morrigan could bind her to another man. But the Old Crow could not overtly interfere with a *geis* she had herself set. The worst she could do was to send other suitors. Angus Óg frowned as he recalled the level stare of the woman's eyes. If she gave her word, she was not likely to break it—not for him or for any man. Then he took a deep breath and began to walk even faster. Nor, he thought, was she likely to give a promise in haste. But he must find her soon.

Cáer Ibormeith stared at her father with a mingling of dislike and distrust tinged with wary contempt. She was aware of the lesser lords of her father's princedom watching. Not one was laughing, nor had any laughed at her for years. All of them were grudgingly pleased with the prosperity they enjoyed, but most of them still resented her and the troop of warrior women called the White Swans that provided the peace for that prosperity.

"No, I will not," she said.

Her hand rested on the hilt of her sword, which was belted on over a man's *lena* of striped yellow and brown cloth. Below the hem of the knee-length tunic, brown trews were bound to her legs with yellow wrappings, the lower edges of which were hidden in ankle-high boots of soft leather.

"Why should I start a war over a herd of cows you say strayed onto our lands?" Cáer continued. "We have the cows. If the fools who lost them attack us, I will fight, of course. But to attack them for their loss . . . No."

"That is woman's thinking," Ethal Anubhail snarled. "A *man* would know that it is better to strike first."

Cáer's lips tightened over what she thought of men. It would not be politic to speak her opinion to the half circle of liegemen sitting on the benches to her father's right. Respect and resentment mingled in them now and insult could only tip the balance against her. She smiled and shrugged.

"A man who attacked a neighbor for a gift of twenty cows would not have sense enough to *know* anything. That one is like a rutting bull who roars and gores until the cow is taken to a safer pasture to graze."

"I am still Rígh of Uaman," Ethal bellowed. "You are

my airechta, *my* champion and avenger. It is for me to say who must be challenged and on whom vengeance is to be taken."

"At such times as you are sober and not in a senseless rage." Cáer's voice was so calm, her expression so unmoved, that Ethal's roaring became apparent as useless bluster. "Father, let us leave this talk now. I tell you I *know* how those twenty cows came onto our land and I *know* there will be no attack to take them back."

Her purposeful stare made her father swallow and look away, but before his eyes dropped the flash of fury in them gave an unneeded confirmation to the news a herdsman had brought her. The "strayed" cows had been secretly paid for by Ethal in the expectation he could induce her to launch a preemptive raid. If she won, he would be the richer by another lord's property; if she lost, he would be rid of her.

Cáer should have been only mildly annoyed. The antagonism between herself and Ethal went back a long way, to before her birth, in fact to before her mother's marriage to him.

Hearing the tale was Cáer's earliest memory and as much a part of her as her blood and bones. Macha had not desired that marriage, had not desired any marriage; she had wished to be what her daughter was, so Macha had refused Ethal. To force her into marriage—for her rich dowry and to salve his hurt pride—Ethal had set a band of his men on her and had her hamstrung. Pretending horror over the "accident," Ethal had again offered marriage—in restitution, because lame she could not train as a warrior and no other man would take her to wife as she was.

Crippled and with her dreams shattered, Macha had agreed to the marriage so she could kill Ethal in their wedding bed. She had prayed to The Morrigan for help, and the Old Crow had come—but with a better plan. Let

Ethal get a daughter on her, The Morrigan had urged Macha, offering in exchange two prizes: The first was a spell that would cause such cramps in a man's legs as to make him a worse cripple than Macha was. The second was that the daughter Macha bore would be a greater warrior than her mother could ever have been and that daughter would bear another, who would be called Macha, and would be a great queen.

So Ethal had had his way. He had married Macha—and had regretted it bitterly every day since Cáer was born. On that day, Macha threw off the disguise of a cowed victim and used her spell on Ethal when he blamed her for bearing a girl child instead of a son. She laughed when he screamed and writhed until she released him, and had continued to use the spell ruthlessly to protect herself and her daughter until Cáer was trained to the sword and could use the spell as well as her mother.

Content, Macha died, but well as she knew her daughter, carefully as she had molded Cáer, she had overlooked one fact: Cáer might dislike and distrust her father, but she loved Uaman. She loved the hills and the rich river valley, the flocks and herds that provided a livelihood for the people, and the common people themselves, who offered to her a warmth she had found only from her mother in the rath.

She knew when her mother died that she was too young to rule, that the lords would not yet accept her. If she wished to protect Uaman, she must not destroy her father but support and control him. And so she would have done had he not tried to subdue her by force again and again. In the end, he had defeated himself by making her wield both spell and sword against his hirelings until no man would serve him. As the male mercenaries sought other employment, Cáer hired women to replace them until she had formed the White Swans.

Thus her father's attempts to be rid of her were an old tale and Cáer should have been no more than irritated by this latest device. It was, in fact, more harmless than usual—twenty cows purchased at a fair price—and she was sure many of the liegemen approved her restraint, knowing that a challenge to An Fhairche might end in disaster, and that some probably guessed what Ethal had done. Nonetheless, she found herself furious, certain she would say more than she should if she were challenged again. So she did not sit down in her place in the half-circle of benches on the left of the fire, all occupied by her armswomen. She walked past the bench and past the rows of couches to the nearest of the seven door openings in the round wall of the ale hall and out into the afternoon sunlight.

What she really needed, Cáer thought, was some strong exercise to sweat the bile out of her belly, but there was no one to fence with her. Those of the Swans who were not on guard or on patrol or busy with some other duty were inside the Hall eating their dinners and, incidentally, making sure that no quarrels arose among the men and that they did not drink themselves into the bravado necessary to concoct any unhealthy schemes. She looked toward the horse pens. She could hunt. No, she would not! There was sufficient meat, and the beasts were still thin this time of year. Why should a stag or boar die because Ethal had annoyed her?

The question made her realize that her fury was unnatural. Something was arousing in her a rage beyond the cause. Cáer had lived a life balanced on a knife edge for too long either to dismiss the anger as irrelevant, a result of many cumulative slights, or to take a chance it would drive her into some foolish act. And a practice bout was an even worse idea than a hunt. In her present mood, she would surely end up paying for a healer's attention or a funeral for a friend. She did not need to fight or hunt; she needed to be alone.

Cáer set out afoot to walk off her unreasonable rage, passing swiftly through two of the three gates in the three great earthen walls of the rath. As she came to the last gate, she heard the harsh cawing of a crow and she looked up and hesitated, aware of a chill that raised the fine hairs at her nape.

The unreasoning fury crested in her, a crazy urge to fight, to kill. But Cáer had survived and triumphed by controlling her impulses, not by yielding to them. She set her teeth into her lower lip and walked on, out onto the road that led east. The crow cawed again, a sound almost like harsh human laughter, and a shadow flashed by her right shoulder and then her left. Although she could feel her heart racing at twice its normal speed and the chill was spreading down her back, Cáer walked on. The shadow passed a second time, and the harsh call sounded. And a third pass. Then the bird was visible just ahead of her, a huge black crow flying down the road.

Every instinct Cáer had bade her stop and go back into the rath, to run away and hide in the darkest corner. Pride and the knowledge that she could not hide from her mother's bargain kept her to a steady pace. She could not even tell herself that it was no bargain of hers. She had used the laming spell, more than once. Had she not in the early years after Macha's death, she would have been broken or killed. But somehow, despite the efficacy of the words she could not understand, she had never really believed that her mother had seen and spoken with The Morrigan.

In all the years Macha had cared for her and in the ten years she had lived since her mother's death, not a sign had Cáer ever seen that The Morrigan was not a figment of Macha's imagination. Deep within, Cáer had been convinced that her mother had exaggerated to make herself important, to make up for her helpless, crippled state. Although she never challenged her mother's claim, she had believed that Macha had obtained the spell from an ordinary witchwoman and that the Old Crow was only part of a magical tale.

When the bird did not return, Cáer laughed at herself for her uneasiness. Maybe her moon days were coming early, she thought. Sometimes before her bleeding started she was very quick to anger. Smiling a little, she told herself that she was *not* going to start imagining legends were real at that time in addition to feeling as if she were ready to jump out of her skin. She felt better already, she insisted, ignoring the fluttering just under her breastbone; if she walked herself into a good sweat . . . And then she saw the hunched black figure seated on a rock by the side of the road. Cáer was proud that her step did not falter. Straight as she could stand, she stopped before the bent woman in dusty black.

"Good day, mother," she said politely. "Why are you here all alone? Is there something I can do for you?"

The bent head lifted. Eyes as bright and shiny as polished obsidian met hers. Dry wrinkled lips drew back from long, yellow teeth. "Mother you call me rightly, Cáer Ibormeith," she cackled, "for if not for me you would never have been born."

"So my blood mother told me," Cáer replied calmly, although every short hair on her body was standing erect, "but I am not sure whether I should be thanking you for it. My life has not been so sweet and easy that I am very grateful."

The old woman cawed laughter. "Gratitude is a cheap thing and you may keep yours. And why I am here? I have fulfilled my part of the bargain. Macha was safe from her husband and bore a daughter who is a greater warrior than she could ever have been. Now you must fulfill your mother's part of the bargain. I want from you a daughter, to be named Macha."

"No!" Cáer exclaimed.

"You cannot say no to me," The Morrigan said, her voice soft for once and human sounding.

Cáer had to set her teeth for a moment to keep them from chattering, but she held the black eyes with hers and when she could speak, replied steadily. "I have done so."

"I will strip away your magic," The Morrigan snapped.

If that was the worst the Old Crow could do . . . Cáer raised her thick, straight brows. "You are welcome to take the spell back," she said. "I have not used it in years."

"But use it you did." The Morrigan's head lifted higher, the bent neck straightened, the chin dropped and thrust forward so that her great hooked nose seemed like a beak about to peck. "By that use you confirmed your mother's bargain. Macha was neither a cheat nor a coward. Will you shame her memory?"

"Give me a task within reason," Cáer cried, "and I will do it or die, but I will not bear a child and hand her to you—"

A crow of laughter stopped her. "Oh, is that your trouble? I do not want your child. You may keep her and raise her and tell her anything you like about me." The Morrigan began to laugh again. "Warn her as you like, what she will be she will be and what she will do she will do to my purpose without my prodding."

"No," Cáer repeated, but more quietly, almost regretfully. The idea of having a child, a daughter, someone who would love her as she had loved her mother was as sweet in her mind as honey in her mouth. "I must not conceive a child knowing she will be tangled in an ill fate."

The Morrigan cocked her head in an oddly birdlike

way. "Who said her fate would be ill? She will be a greater warrior than you and a great queen."

"A great warrior and a great queen does not make for a happy life."

"Do not be stupider than your mother," The Morrigan remarked contemptuously. "Do you think being a slave or a bodach woman ensures happiness? Every life includes grief and misery."

Cáer blinked. Was she being too suspicious just because The Morrigan was involved? She had always suppressed her desire for a child, just to avoid the slim chance that it would be a daughter who might be claimed by the Old Crow. But here was The Morrigan and she had said she would not take the child away. The old legends said that The Morrigan never lied.

"I know no life can be totally free of pain," Cáer said even less certainly. "I am not asking you to promise that my child will always be perfectly happy—I would not trust you if you did. I am asking you—it is said you never lie—to tell me that you will not make my daughter's life one of extraordinary pain and hardship."

The Morrigan shrugged. "I can say that fulfilling my purpose will not cause her death nor cause her any other future ill. I can say that what she does suffer will be of her own will and desiring, not of my doing." She cackled laughter once more. "Will you forbid your daughter life altogether or make her a mindless, will-less thing to protect her? Is this a better fate than to live to wield great power and be a queen whose name will be remembered long, long into the future?"

"Very well," Cáer said, her heart suddenly leaping in her breast with joy, although her voice and face showed nothing. "I will bear a daughter whom I will name Macha, and you will leave her utterly to me to raise and train. Nor will you come to her and impose your will on her at any time. Do you agree?"

"As to the child, yes," The Morrigan nodded in a quick jerk of movement. "But I will choose the father. He is, like your father, of the Tuatha de Danaan and his name is Angus Óg."

"A daughter I will bear for your purpose," Cáer said, color rising in her face, "but the father was no part of the agreement. I want no more to do with the Tuatha de Danaan."

"Your father was your mother's burden, and you will bear Angus Óg," The Morrigan said, showing her long, yellow teeth again. "You can lie in the ditches with every man in Eiru and you will not conceive. To fulfill your mother's bargain, you must couple with Angus Óg."

Red fury drowned the gold in Cáer's eyes and her hand flashed to the sword at her side, but the old woman was no longer there. Only a black crow flapped above her head, cawing derision before it flew away.

chapter 2

Before the sun set, Angus Óg was at his father's sidhe. He paused before the great dark doorway to look westward at the glory of orange and purple sunset. He hated to go under the earth. Rich and beautiful the sidhe might be, but the sun did not rise and set there nor did birds sing or cattle low. Fraoch brought his own horse up to take the reins of Angus's dappled gray stallion.

"I will go down to the hostel and stable the horses," Fraoch said. "Will you be coming down to sleep there, or will you be wanting me to come up into the sidhe?"

"Whichever is most pleasing to you, Fraoch," Angus replied, smiling. "I will be safe enough in my father's house."

Fraoch snorted cynically. "You said you would be safe with the woman," he remarked, "but I suspect something far from good happened at the pond."

Angus laughed. He had told no one that the woman by the pond had been The Morrigan, nor hinted to any of his companions of the *geis* set on him. "I said no woman wished to stick a long, sharp knife into me. And that was true enough. Nor am I sure that no good will come of that meeting."

Even as he spoke, however, he could feel the binding on his heart, and he slipped off the horse's back and walked through the dark doorway more eagerly than usual. He and the Dagda had had their differences, and he had never agreed with his father's choice of stepping back into the shadows and leaving the bright earth to the younger race, no matter how beautiful, comfortable, and secure the life inside the sidhe. However, he did not fear he would be bound to the sidhe—he was bound already to Bruigh na Boinne—nor that any help he asked for would be withheld.

Light blossomed from the the ceiling as he walked forward, banishing the seeming of a shallow, empty cave to show a gorgeous corridor with painted walls. Ahead, the corridor opened out into a huge circular chamber from which led many doors. In the center of the room, a fire burned on a polished hearth without a breath of smoke, only heat waves quivering above the clear red and blue tongues of flame. Beyond the fire was a high chair, against which leaned a huge club, and there were benches, all as empty as the chair, set in two semicircles with an opening opposite the chair.

Angus came forward and seated himself at the end of the bench on the left side, in the place of least importance. Almost immediately one of the doors opened and a very large man dressed in a coarse tunic shambled in, climbed the two steps, and seated himself in the high chair. He laid his hand on the club, and then looked at Angus.

"What trouble are you in now?" he asked. "And why should I help you, who will not obey me?"

"Because this trouble was not of my making nor of my mingling with the Milesians. The Morrigan has laid a *geis* upon me."

The irritation in the Dagda's coarse face faded into concern. "I cannot lift a *geis*, Angus."

"I know that, nor do I wish it lifted. This *geis* I wish to fulfill. It is that I find a woman and love her all the days of her life."

A look of mingled amusement and disgust preceded a harsh laugh. "I think The Morrigan has lost what few wits she ever had. Putting a *geis* of love on you is like giving a fish water to drink. Since when has any woman been able to say you nay? And what woman, married or not, would refuse a life bond with you?"

"This one, I think, might, but that is not my first problem. You are not listening, father. I said I must find her. I do not know who the woman is."

The Dagda grinned and caressed the handle of his club. "Careless of you to forget to ask. You will have a hard time of it, futtering every woman in Eriu in the hope one will satisfy the *geis*."

"I need not work as hard as that. I know the looks of the woman, but I do not think I will have time to look at every one. The binding on me will stop my heart and breath long before that."

"What?" The Dagda jerked upright in his chair, letting go of the club. "What did you do to make your time so short? Why should the *geis* take hold if you are truly searching for the woman—"

"I did not give The Morrigan the satisfaction you once did give her," Angus said. "Looking back, I see it was foolish, but at the time . . . It did not suit me to swive a bitch in heat."

Disgust again was the main component of the Dagda's expression as he leaned back and took hold of the club once more. "You have been a fool from the day you were born," he said. The harshness of his voice did not quite cover a slight unevenness generated by fear for his son. "How can I help you find one woman—unless she is of the Tuatha de Danaan?"

"No, that much the Old Crow told me, that she was Milesian . . ." But Angus's voice drifted away uncertainly and then he smiled. "But she was too fair to be pure Milesian. She must be of mixed blood. Her hair was the color of bronze and her eyes more gold than brown."

"A big help that is." The Dagda shook his heavy head. "You know I have nothing to do with those of the outer world. Those of the Danaan who refused the shelter of the sidhe, taking instead wives or husbands from among the Milesians, I know no longer—" He shrugged. "Except you, the thief who stole my house, the house in which I got you on your mother." He laughed so heartily that the huge club began to slip, and he caught it and hauled it back to where its weight and movement had worked a hollow in the thick boards of the dais.

"Well," Angus stood up, "it did no harm to ask. I will ask my mother, too. And then—"

"Wait. Do not go yet. Bodb is here. He knows more about The Morrigan than any other of us."

He lifted the club, seemingly without effort and banged it on the floor, which elicited a hollow booming. A lovely girl came into the room from the same door the Dagda had used. She laughed when she saw Angus and ran forward to embrace him. He returned the hug and kiss with open affection until the Dagda hit the floor again.

"Enough," he said, trying to look sour. "Cesair, I did not call you here to cuddle Angus. Go find Bodb and tell him we need him." And when she had released his son— smiling and without the smallest look of regret—and had gone, he shook his head. "What is it about you?" he said to Angus. "Mother Dana knows you are no beauty with that red hair and those freckles."

Angus did not answer the question. It had been asked many, many times, and he knew no better what to say now than the first time he had been asked. Most women were drawn to him, but like Cesair their open affection was light-hearted. Some might offer more than the kiss she had given him, but the coupling was equally light-hearted, and just as Cesair had run off to do the Dagda's bidding without regret, so would the others go on with their lives without him.

For a very long time he had been content, even grateful, that the women who were all eager to love him were also willing to let him go and never be jealous. Suddenly it was not enough. He saw again the level gold-brown eyes under the piled gold-brown hair and he was less sure he could win her even if he could find her. She did nothing lightly, he suspected, and would not lightly love and lightly leave.

Quick footsteps broke into Angus's thoughts and he looked across the chamber toward the sound with renewed hope. Although Bodb had obeyed his father and retreated to a sidhe near Loch Dearg, he took a great interest in the doings of the new race. Men of his sidhe wandered among the Milesian courts, sometimes as fighting men but more often as bards, offering advice and sometimes altering the progress of events; the women as frequently enticed noble wanderers into the sidhe from which they sometimes emerged with different intentions than they had when they entered.

"Angus," Bodb said, smiling as he came across the floor, but then he stopped suddenly, and the smile turned grim. "Mother Dana, you stink of the Old Crow. What have you been doing?"

"Refusing her and having a *geis* set on me."

Angus grinned at his half-brother, who was as tall as the Dagda but much more slender. His large eyes, the broad brow under curling golden hair, and the sensitive mouth bespoke his kindness and intelligence—that was in the Dagda too, but hidden behind a gross appearance. The Dagda was far more direct, far less subtle in his dealings, than Bodb too.

"Oh, Angus!" Bodb groaned. "You have less sense

than you had when you were three. Then you knew
enough to avoid her."

Angus laughed. "Then she did not seek me out. But I
do not think she meant harm at first. After she set the *geis*
on me, she said if I had not angered her she would have
told me in pillow talk what she desired and the purpose
she had and that she thought I would agree. You know
she does not lie."

"She does not, but you did anger her and her cursings
are strong." He sighed and came forward again to give
Angus a rough embrace. "But I am strong too, and I will
try to break the craving."

"I do not want it broken," Angus said, twisting his neck
to look up at his brother. "To me the *geis* is no curse. It is
that I find a woman and love her until she dies."

"Great Goddess," Bodb released his grip on Angus and
pushed him lightly away as he sputtered into laughter.
"Why involve me? All you have to do is pick the one you
want or if none you know suits you, stand at a
crossroad—"

"No, no," the Dagda put in, "it is a particular woman
he must find, and the curse is that there is no long time
spared him for the finding. She has netted his heart to
this woman and he feels the binding already."

Bodb's laughter stopped abruptly. "Netted your heart?
That is why you smell of her. Angus, I have power and I
know magic, but to tamper with such bindings is very,
very dangerous. One wrong touch might cause the net to
draw tight—"

"I tell you I do not want the binding removed," Angus
said. "I want to find the woman. I have seen her. She is
beautiful . . . No, not beautiful, not as our women are
beautiful, but she is not light of heart as they are either
and will not yield lightly to me and as lightly turn to the
next man." He looked up at his brother, who had come
closer again and placed a hand on his shoulder. "I have

never in my life felt more than fondness, Bodb, but I know when I win this woman the net will burn away in the heat of my passion."

"Such passion is not always a good thing, not for the man or the woman," Bodb said gravely. "You might be better off to take your chance with my working to undo the binding on you."

"But the sorrow that might come to me . . . and to her . . . will not be of The Morrigan's planning. I held her hard and asked if ill would come of this love to the woman or to myself and she said *if* I could find the woman and *if* I could win her, no harm would come to me or to her and good would come to the Tuatha de Danaan."

"If and if," Bodb said musingly. "I see. To find one woman among the thousands of thousands in Eriu . . . I do not know a magic that will do that."

"No, but you know the plays of power among the Milesian kings and you know The Morrigan," the Dagda said to Bodb, although he was looking rather curiously at his youngest son. "Between the two you may guess at the Old Crow's plans and by that path come to knowledge of a woman who could forward those plans by bonding to Angus. Remember, she said she had a purpose to which Angus might agree concerning this woman."

Bodb bit his lip thoughtfully. After a moment, he released Angus's shoulder and sat down on the right-hand edge of the bench. He began to shake his head, and then straightened, looking intent.

"I cannot think of any great kingdom where there is a wife or a daughter of such importance that her lying with Angus or going away with him could cause any more than a momentary excitement. And the lesser realms do not seem to provide large enough opportunities to create a disaster to draw The Morrigan's attention." He shrugged and went on, "Still, I seem to remember it was said The

Morrigan gave a spell to Macha, wife of Ethal Anubhail, that would defeat any man who wished to master her."

"If she were married to Ethal Anubhail," the Dagda said, his mouth turned down as if he had bitten something rotten, "she would need such a spell. He was of the Tuatha de Danaan, and glad I was when he chose to stay in the outer world and I did not need to put a sidhe into his hands."

Angus had not once looked at the Dagda, although he waited politely for him to finish; his attention was fixed on Bodb. "Is this Macha a young woman of stern face with gold-brown hair—like twisted bronze her braids were—and gold-brown eyes?" he asked eagerly.

"I do not know," Bodb replied, frowning into space as he strove to remember all he had heard, "but I doubt it. Likely she was dark eyed and dark haired. I know Macha was Milesian and her father desired a bond with a prince of the Tuatha—" He paused and wrinkled his nose, clearly in agreement with his father about Ethal's character. "He offered gold and herds with her—no . . ." Bodb hesitated again. "No, it was her elder sister that Ethal was bound to, but she died, and he said he would take the younger, Macha, in her stead for the sake of the dowry. Ethal is a greedy beast." Then he lifted his head sharply to stare at Angus. "A young woman?" he repeated, as if suddenly recalling what Angus had said. "No, then Macha is not the one you seek. For a moment I forgot that time passes much more swiftly for the Milesians than for us. By now Macha would be old, surely more than forty years of age."

Angus, who had been perched on the edge of the bench, stiff with eager tension, slumped in disappointment, but the Dagda cocked his heavy head to the side and said, "Wait now. Angus, you said the woman you sought might be of mixed blood when we first spoke of her."

Angus sat up straighter again, but it was Bodb who spoke. "There could have been a daughter. Ethal is of the fair de Danaan. The mixing with a Milesian could give the hair and eyes Angus described. And there is this to consider, I have heard of no great events, no war, nothing that embroiled Ethal with his neighbors or with the rulers of Connacht since his marriage. So, for what did The Morrigan give Ethal's wife such a spell? Woman though she is, the Old Crow is not one to offer something so potent out of kindness or without hope of creating some mischief that would amuse her."

"True, but she is not impatient either," the Dagda said thoughtfully. "She might well be willing to wait for a generation or two of those short-lived folk to garner the crop of mischief she had earlier seeded. Yes, because she would take real delight in hugging to her bosom secret knowledge of some truly great disaster that might take place years in the future."

Bodb let out a long, low whistle. "Ethal's rath is Uaman, which is in Connacht, although he does no homage to Medb or Ailill—"

"And Medb leaves him in peace?" the Dagda remarked with a harsh laugh.

"But if Macha is not the woman I seek—" Angus began.

He stopped abruptly as both his father and halfbrother looked at him with reproving expressions, but their attention did not remain on him long. Bodb looked back at the Dagda, his lips curved in a half smile.

"For one who swears he has shut himself off from the outer world," Bodb said, "you have a good knowledge of one woman's character."

"Because she is, as much as anyone can be, a favorite of The Morri—" He stopped, then smiled broadly at Angus. "My son, the woman you seek might well be Ethal's daughter. Not for certain, but it seems her mother owes the Old Crow an unpaid debt and to add to that debt someone—and I do not doubt it will be found to be The Morrigan—has kept Medb from swallowing Ethal. Is it too much to think both of these debts might be settled on the head of the daughter and connected with the *geis*—"

"But she said no harm would come to the woman if I found her and won her," Angus put in.

"So she did." The Dagda nodded, but turned his eyes from Angus to look at Bodb.

Bodb also nodded and said, "No harm to her or to you so the price of the spell will be paid by someone else." He shrugged. "Perhaps by everyone else. No, she also said the Danaan would benefit." He hesitated, then shrugged again. "If we are right in our guesses, the finding seems too easy. Still this has the true 'smell' of the Old Crow's work, something that starts out as a broad, smooth road and turns into a tangled, overgrown maze once you are so far along you cannot turn back."

"Yes," Angus said. "I am not really surprised the finding may be easy. Somehow I never felt The Morrigan did not intend that I find the woman. She showed me her face and told me she was Milesian, which saved me looking among the Danaan, whom she more resembled. And even when the Old Crow threatened me, she was laughing." He laughed too, remembering. "I am strong enough, but now I think back on it, it was too easy to hold her. She answered my questions gladly, too. Yes, all the time she was laughing at me."

"So likely the woman is Ethal's daughter." The Dagda made a sour mouth. "That may be trouble enough. Do not trust him, Angus. He is treacherous."

"So he is," Bodb said, pursed his lips thoughtfully and then smiled. "But there will be help not too far distant. If Ethal gives you trouble, go to Medb and Ailill at Cruach. They might—" Bodb's speech checked and his brows lifted. "Could that be the Old Crow's purpose? To give Medb a good cause to swallow up Ethal's lands?"

He looked at the Dagda and they both looked at Angus.

"That seems too simple," Angus said, but he looked back at each of them hopefully.

"Unless The Morrigan wishes to lay an obligation upon Medb?" The Dagda smiled.

"It would be like her to use the most complicated way and to involve as many innocent bystanders as possible," Bodb said, also smiling. "Well, Angus, do not cast any obstacles in the path of events if that is what The Morrigan wants. Go to Medb and ask for help if Ethal stands in your way."

"Very well, I will," Angus agreed and stood up.

"Where are you going?" the Dagda asked. "It is too late to start for Uaman today. I will call for a bath for you."

"I thank you, but no," Angus answered. "I will go down to the hostel. Fraoch is there and I want to get an early start." He grinned. "If I stay here, I will have a very unquiet sleep—if I sleep at all. Your ladies like to make merry, so it is too noisy all night and too quiet in the early morning."

Both his father and his brother looked at him in dumbfound amazement. Angus had never been the last or the least in making merry nor one to discourage the attentions of the women. But before either could think of a sufficiently quelling rejoinder, Angus laughed and went out the door into the painted corridor. As he stepped out of the sidhe into the dark, he heard the girl Cesair call his name but he did not turn back as he would have only the day before. In fact, he might have done so anyway, out of good nature and kindness, but down at the base of the low hill a hidden fire was reflected from two smooth surfaces on the side of a building and from the roof thatch—and Angus saw two golden eyes and a heap of gleaming bronze hair.

He started down the hill toward that lodestone of his desire, but the change in position also changed the light so he lost the image that had caught his eye. Then he stopped and shook his head and began to laugh as he turned back toward the sidhe. His eagerness and his righteousness had turned him into an idiot. He had never heard of Ethal Anubhail or Uaman before Bodb mentioned them. Getting an early start would make better sense if he found out from either Bodb or his father in which direction to go.

Cáer was so enraged at the idea she would be forced to mate with one of her father's ilk, that she ran after the crow for miles. Only when she fell, her muscles no longer able to operate, and the crow, cawing derisive laughter, circled her again three times and again from right to left, did she come to her senses enough to realize that The Morrigan was baiting her. The bird could have outflown her at any time; the Old Crow had been deliberately keeping just far enough ahead so that she would run herself into exhaustion.

She turned on her back then and closed her eyes, calling herself ten times a fool as the rage drained out of her for allowing herself to fall into the trap. Senseless rage was The Morrigan's favorite device, and Cáer, who thought she had conquered that particular weakness, could have wept over how easily she had lost control. Her one consolation was that no one in Uaman had seen her shame. Later, when she got painfully to her feet and began limping back to the rath, she did weep a little. How could she explain the state she was in? No one would believe her—any more than she had believed her mother—if she said she had met The Morrigan.

Before she was in sight of the walls of the rath, Cáer had come to the conclusion that she must never admit what had happened—at least not unless The Morrigan chose to expose the bargain and herself to all in the rath.

No one, Cáer resolved, would wonder whether she were mad or, on the other hand, whether her ability in arms was not a result of her own hard work but gifted to her by the Old Crow. The resolution was comforting only for a few minutes. Then she saw landmarks that told her she would soon be in sight from the rath, and she must now pretend she had only walked off her bad temper.

The pain of pulling herself into her usual long stride gave her a shock and presented a new problem. She was so stiff and sore, she would be easy prey to any man who wished to issue a challenge to her just now. Not that she feared any man in the rath, but she was certain The Morrigan's tool would have been told she would be vulnerable and be waiting for her. However, all was quiet at the rath, and the guard at the outer gate told her that no guest had come while she had been gone.

Cáer ate her evening meal and went to bed, cursing The Morrigan and her own stupidity with equal fervor. She would feel worse the next day, she suspected, and surely this Angus Óg—her mouth watered to spit on his name—would arrive and claim her then. Well, she would not lose her temper again, Cáer promised herself. She would find reasons for not answering him whether he issued a claim or a challenge. She had promised The Morrigan she would bear a daughter and she would fulfill her promise . . . but in her own good time, not when The Morrigan chose to force a man of the Danaan on her.

Cáer leashed her rage, but it struggled within her to such an effect that several of her father's men left the rath some days before they intended and a path cleared before her when she walked. But Angus Óg did not appear the next day, nor the next. By the third day after her meeting with The Morrigan most of the aftereffects of chasing the Old Crow had worn off. Cáer no longer had to be conscious of every step to conceal the twinges in her overworked muscles nor think about the process of lifting a goblet to make sure her hand would not tremble.

As her physical well-being was restored, Cáer's violent antipathy toward the mate selected for her began to mix with curiosity—although not about the man himself. She was sure she knew what a Danaan chosen by The Morrigan would be like—beautiful as a sunlit summer morning to look upon, and rotten at the core. For the first time she looked beyond her instinctive recoil from mating with a man like her father and began to consider and analyze what had happened without being torn apart by a mingling of rage and fear.

The first question she asked herself was why she had reacted so violently? She had known from childhood that she was destined to bear a daughter who would serve The Morrigan's purpose. Even admitting that she had never really believed what her mother told her and that the Old Crow's reality had been something of a shock, she should have been able to accept what she saw with her eyes and heard with her ears. Moreover, having been warned of The Morrigan's delight in creating trouble, she should have been able to hide her distaste for the father chosen. No matter what his race, the man would be gone long before the babe was born and would not be able to influence her character and training.

The anger had come first, Cáer realized. She had been unreasonably angry when she was refusing to provoke the Lord of An Fhairche, bristling with aggression toward the liegemen, whom she now realized had been more horrified than she at the notion. An Fhairche, though small and weak of itself, controlled the narrow pass between the great lakes, which was used freely by Uaman and by Leenane, Sraith Salach, and all the smaller raths and duns to the west. That weakness and free usage was An Fhairche's security. No matter what their personal quarrels, every lord in the area would join together to prevent that dun from being taken by a stronger holder. Had she been in her proper senses instead of half crazed with rage, she would have laughed in her father's face instead of refusing, as if his proposal could be taken seriously.

That rage must have been the work of The Morrigan, but twist and turn the fact as she would, Cáer could make no sense of it. She had to accept that it was The Morrigan's way to make trouble, seemingly for the pure mischief of it. Now going over the entire incident calmly, that delight in infuriating her victims and driving them to stupid actions seemed to cover Cáer's entire experience. She recalled suddenly that although The Morrigan had circled her three times, as if to fix a spell, she had *not* flown widdershins but deasil, the direction of good will. And although she had run herself nearly to death in a senseless effort to catch the crow and wring its neck, no harm had come from her foolishness.

So although she had not asked about herself, likely The Morrigan meant no ill to her, and the Old Crow had promised no harm to her daughter. To Angus Óg? Cáer shrugged. That was his business, not hers. She was not obliged to protect one of the Tuatha de Danaan from another of the accursed breed.

chapter 3

Six days later, when Cáer was totally restored to her normal strength and fitness and almost beginning to doubt her memory of The Morrigan's appearance, Angus Óg finally arrived at the rath of Uaman. Watching the visitors ride in from the top of the innermost wall, Cáer assumed Angus Óg to be the breathtakingly handsome man riding behind his guard or servant, who was red-haired, freckled, and broad-faced. She snorted gently with contempt. He was certainly a lot more beautiful than she was; not many women could compete with those gleaming golden curls or those lustrous, long-lashed eyes.

As they rode past her through the last gate and into the bailey of the rath, where Ethal or the steward would greet them, Cáer laughed softly. No wonder The Morrigan had introduced the subject of fathering her daughter in so infuriating a way. Doubtless the Old Crow assumed that any woman would fall on her back and spread her legs the moment she saw Angus Óg's face, which would not be at all amusing for that maker of mischief. The thought made Cáer wonder whether inviting the man to her bed that very night or delaying their coupling for years would work a greater spite on The Morrigan, who had clearly intended to set her against him.

With that choice in mind, Cáer did not disappear as she had considered doing—to delay meeting Angus Óg—but made her way into the ale hall. Ethal gestured her forward and said, with a sly smile that invited the male guests to take his words as a jest and possibly say something offensive, "This is my airechta, my champion and avenger, also my daughter, Cáer Ibormeith."

Cáer barely stopped her hand from going to her sword in warning. However, neither man seemed surprised or seemed to think a female airechta was to be scorned. Both rose from the bench on which they were sitting, an unnecessary but pleasant courtesy.

Ethal Anubhail shrugged at the strangers' politeness and added, "These are my own people, airechta, Tuatha de Danaan. See that you attend their wants closely and guard them well from insult."

Cáer met her father's eyes and said with a half smile, "I hear and obey, Righ."

She smiled a little more broadly at the flicker of rage that lit his eyes. He knew what she thought of the Danaan and he knew how she ordinarily reacted to a peremptory order from him. He had expected her to disgrace herself with rudeness to guests, who, whatever their race, were sacred. Soothed by having frustrated Ethal's little ploy, she turned to the guests. The redhead she decided, taking in his fixed stare and partly open mouth, was probably too stupid to recognize her father's subtle prodding and the handsome one might have already taken Ethal's measure—he looked clever enough. Oddly, she realized, he looked uneasy too, glancing at his companion and frowning as if a little troubled.

He brought his eyes back to her, quickly dipped his head in salute, and said, "I am Fraoch, and this is Angus Óg, to whom I am liegeman. I give you greeting, airechta." He turned his head. "Angus?" he added sharply. The redhead shook himself slightly, as if he had been lost in his own thoughts, and smiled. His eyes were now as bright as sunlit water, and his broad face was transformed by a look of joy. Almost the freckles across his nose seemed to be dancing with delight. Still, there was nothing possessive in the look, nothing that hinted he knew of her meeting with The Morrigan—or that he had had a similar encounter.

"I give you greeting, Cáer Ibormeith," he said and his voice was as sunnily friendly as the smile he had given her.

Cáer was so surprised at the strange mixture of delight and neutrality in his expression that she merely nodded in return and said, "You are both well come to Uaman."

"And what brings you out of your dark sidhe?" Ethal asked, just a hint of a sneer in his voice.

"Father!" Cáer exclaimed, shocked at the bad manners of questioning guests about anything, except what form of hospitality they desired.

"Oh, they are my own folk," Ethal said. "I do not need to conform to your petty conventions with them."

"You did not much conform to our conventions either, my father says," Angus remarked with a laugh. "But I am willing to answer. I do not live in a sidhe." At that moment, servingmen hurried in, carrying tables and cups and flagons and dishes of eggs and cheese. "Will you not join us, Cáer Ibormeith?" he asked as he sat down again.

Still undecided as to what she intended to do, Cáer sat down also. "So you, like my father, took a wife among our people, Angus Óg," she said. Her voice was merely pleasant and conversational and gave no sign that she was not sure whether she was relieved that he had ties that would surely rid her of him or further outraged by the fact that The Morrigan had chosen a married man to father her daughter.

"No," he replied, somewhat indistinctly around a mouthful of cheese. When he had swallowed he said, "I simply like the sun and rain—and perhaps the uncertainties of life in the outer world too much—"

"If you are not married already, you doubtless travel to seek a wife who will bring you a livelihood," Ethal said, looking at Cáer and laughing.

"A livelihood, no," Angus replied. "I have that and more. A wife?" He looked down, smiling. "Perhaps. What I seek is a woman I will love all the days of her life."

"I do not think you will find such a woman here," Cáer snapped. "We are all warrior women in this rath. And I did not think bonding with one woman was the way of the Tuatha de Danaan."

Angus nodded, still smiling. "You say it is true, then, that a warrior woman who desires a man's true love is rarer than a white crow? But a rare thing is very precious. And why do you believe that a long loving is not the way of the Tuatha de Danaan? The Danaan are no more cut from one piece of cloth than any other people. Each has different desires from the others."

"Every man, Danaan or Milesian desires more," Ethal remarked before Cáer could speak. "Perhaps you have come to the right place. My daughter is all the blood kin I have, and my successor has not yet been chosen."

Cáer stood up abruptly, her hand on her sword hilt. "Your daughter is not within your disposing, nor that of any man, so do not raise hopes you cannot fulfill."

As she turned away, she caught sight of Fraoch's handsome face, eyes wide with amazement. She did not see whether his expression mirrored that of Angus Óg because Angus had been closer to her and her turn had hidden him from her. She took a long stride toward the door, stiffening in the expectation of hearing a scornful voice call her back and remind her of her promise to accept him, but only her father's laugh followed her.

As soon as she was away from the ale hall, Cáer became annoyed with herself for moving so quickly. She should have watched to see whether Angus Óg had looked as surprised as Fraoch. If he had, even though he had not demanded her return, she would have known for certain he was aware of The Morrigan's plan and that she could not refuse him in the end no matter how proud her words.

Or would an expression of surprise be proof? The Morrigan had not said she was to marry Angus Óg, only that he would father her child. Even if he knew that, he might have been surprised when her father brought up the subject of marriage. But if he knew he must lie with her, why wrap up a stinking clod in a crimson cloth? Why talk about seeking a woman to love all the days of her life? Why say each of the Danaan was different from all others, thus separating himself from her father? Why make a point that the love of a warrior woman was rare and thus precious?

All the moves were those of a man who wished to win a woman, not a man who believed she was his for the taking. Then likely, Cáer thought, staring blindly into the pen where the visitors' horses were, The Morrigan had not told him I was fated to conceive only by him and bound by oath to bear a daughter he had fathered. But why? If The Morrigan wants a daughter from me, why not simply tell him to get me pregnant?

Cáer shook her head disgustedly. The Danaan were enamored of slyness and trickery. Despite what Angus Óg said, they all seemed incapable of doing anything directly. If the path to any end was not slippery and tortuous, the end lost half its value. It must be that The Morrigan did not tell him of my promise to her so that he would court me to win me. As the thought came, Cáer frowned and shook her head again. That made no sense. If she were fated to yield to him, being courted would make that process more pleasant and the Old Crow was not likely to have chosen a path that gave pleasure to others.

Unless the pleasure turned to pain. Was she supposed to give her love to Angus Óg, who would then leave her? That made no sense either. If The Morrigan had wanted her to love and lose, why try to set her against the man in the beginning? To make winning her harder? Yes, at last something made sense. The mischief had little to do with her, Cáer thought. To The Morrigan she was only a tool, unimportant except as mother to Macha and, yes, of course, as lover to Angus Óg. It was Angus who had somehow won the Old Crow's spite.

Remembering his joy in seeing her—he might have been fooled by The Morrigan into believing her a monster of some kind—and the guilelessness of his blue eyes, Cáer gave some thought to warning him that The Morrigan might wish him ill. Two things made her decide to hold her tongue: The first was purely selfish—if she told him, he might refuse to get her with child, assuming he would be safe from The Morrigan until he had done so, and by now Cáer was very eager to have a daughter to love. The second was somewhat more nebulous—she did not really think either of them could escape the fate The Morrigan had set on them; she felt they could give in easily and perhaps enjoy their union, or they could resist and make that union painful, but unite they would in the end.

So the only question remaining was how to yield. If, as Cáer now believed, The Morrigan had not told him she was fated to lie with him, he might be disgusted if she simply invited him to her bed. Cáer found that idea unpleasant. Fate or no fate, she had no intention of giving any man the impression she was simply a harlot. She could, of course tell him of her mother's oath. A sharp feeling of doubt stabbed Cáer, a sensation of portending disaster. That was too direct and easy a solution. The Morrigan's mischief was never easy to circumvent.

A shadow fell across the fence, and the handsome gray horse Angus Óg had ridden whinnied and started forward. Cáer stiffened and stepped sideways.

"I wish you had not so ill an opinion of the Tuatha de Danaan," Angus Óg said, coming up beside her and stretching a hand toward the horse, who blew into it softly. "Dare I say to you that you are unfair to blacken all of us because of your experience with one?"

Cáer had been about to move away, less because of any distaste for being in Angus Óg's company than because, knowing what she knew and uncertain of how much he knew, she felt oddly shy. Now she leaned one hip against the fence again, watching him stroke the horse's soft muzzle and then take something from his pouch, which the beast lipped up and chewed with relish.

"Do you know my father?" she asked.

"No, but my father did, and did not like him. He warned me that Ethal Anubhail was greedy and could be deceitful." He hesitated and then added quickly, "Fraoch would be horrified if he heard me say that. I am sorry if I offend you, but I have few social graces and tend to say what I think."

Cáer laughed. "That, if true, would be a pleasant change. There are few enough among the lords in Uaman who speak their minds honestly."

"And you are among those few?"

He sounded as if he were smiling, and when Cáer looked up, she saw his blue eyes were bright with amusement although his face was still. "No, indeed," she said, laughing harder. "If I said what I thought honestly, I would have more enemies than cow's dung has flies. Men are quick to feel slighted by even well-intended words from a woman who can fight better than they can."

"Ah," Angus Óg said, with an air of being suddenly enlightened, "I can understand that. But you need not much fear my sensibilities on that subject."

"Because you are so sure of your ability to master a woman?" Cáer asked mildly.

"Great Goddess, no." Angus laughed aloud. "Scáthach nUanaind could peel both the ears off my head with her blade before I could lift my sword. I can fight, but it is not my favorite occupation and I do not value my fighting skills very highly. If you said you could break a horse better than I, I might challenge you to a contest."

Smiling Cáer shook her head. The gray had come even closer while they talked, first nibbling at Angus's hair and, when he pushed its head away, nuzzling his breast and finally resting its chin on his shoulder. Meanwhile the fine chestnut Fraoch had bestrode had come to the fence too, also trying to get to Angus.

"No, I thank you," she said. "I can break a horse so that it does not hate me, but just looking at those beasts of yours tells me who would win." Then she cocked her head at him and asked provocatively, "Do you never propose a contest except those you know you will win?"

"What I said was a jest." Angus turned away from the horses for a moment to look at her. "Forgive me. Everyone at home knows I never would propose a contest. I am of a peaceable nature and such a fool that I think well enough of myself as I am without having to prove I am better than another."

"No fool for that." Cáer felt a twinge of nervousness, as if he had issued a warning, but there was only friendliness in his face and he had already turned back to the horses. "But do you not find that others will not leave you to your quiet good opinion but must try to take it from you?"

"Not among the Danaan. I am younger than most of my people, you see, and the pet. I have met a few challenges from your mother's people—"

"And?"

Angus shrugged, smiling. "Let us say I won my point, but not at sword's point, and made no enemies."

"I would like to know how you did that!"

He turned to look at her again, his expression totally serious for once. "I do not know. I would tell you if I could, but I suspect it is something born in me."

"You are fortunate in your inborn gifts then."

"Yes," he agreed, but there was a kind of sadness dimming the cheerfulness that seemed a part of him. "But every Gift has its price. To be beloved by all makes you special to none."

"And you wish to be special to someone?" Cáer frowned, surprised by the feeling of sympathy that made her want to touch him comfortingly. That was surely a trap for her. She needed to conceive a daughter out of this man not to develop any affection for him. She made herself laugh. "Then you are greedy. To be a favorite among your own, so that they do not challenge and torment you, and able to conciliate those of another race, who might be expected to hate and fear you, should surely be enough."

Angus's red brows lifted suddenly almost into the red curls that tumbled down his forehead. "Then your father is right, is he not?" he asked, sounding troubled. "Every man, Danaan or Milesian, wants more."

"He is too often right," Cáer said, her lips twisting with distaste. "We all have a black spot or two on our souls."

"So we do." Angus laughed suddenly, joyously. "Come, I do not like to have the black spots on my soul pointed out to me. Let us forget your father—and Fraoch, too, who is himself the soul of honor but persists in seeing much ill in others. They will keep company admirably. Will you not allow me to restore my good opinion of myself? Ride out with me and show me what is very beautiful, but what I am 'noble' enough not to want."

"What you are noble enough not to want?" Cáer repeated, her slightly puzzled tone and lowered eyes hiding a sudden fury because she thought he meant herself as the thing he did not want although it was very beautiful.

"Your lands," Angus said, his head cocked in question as if he felt something wrong in her despite seeing no sign of it. "This country is nothing like my own, which is all flat fertile fields and very low hills. We have only a river, not great lakes, and your mountains . . . After we passed the dun of An Fhairche and climbed the high hills, they took my breath away." Angus grinned and shook his head. "Not Fraoch's though. He comes from the south, where the hills are even higher and he laughed at me for gawking."

"You expect me to ride out with you?" Cáer said. "With no escort?"

"What better escort could I have than you alone? Surely you will not laugh at me for admiring your countryside. You will show me what is most beautiful and what is also safe for a stranger to see without betraying the secrets of your defense." Angus opened his eyes wide. "This is not done? But surely the airechta, male or female, must have freedom of movement."

For a moment Cáer was stiff with indignation. So that was what Angus Óg's sweet words of loving a woman all the days of her life were worth. They were a gilded wash over the rotten desire to tumble her in a hidden place, on the ground, like the veriest drab. Even as the idea formed, she realized the secrecy would suit her as well as him. She did not really want to lie with him openly. Her women would snicker over the fact that she had at last taken a lover, and the men of the rath would again begin to lick their lips and try to seize her and draw her into dark corners so she would have to lesson them anew . . . and wake their resentment of her anew.

"Yes, we can ride out if you wish," she said. "I will get my horse."

She turned away before he could answer to hide the sick disappointment she felt. Stupid, she chided herself as she walked into the adjoining enclosure and whistled sharply for her horse. *It is better to get this mating over with at once and give him plenty of chance to set seed in me as soon as possible. That way, I can be rid of him the sooner. And it is better, too, that he should show his true foulness. I know what the Danaan are. I will not be fooled again by that look of innocence or his fine words.*

Only Cáer found no foulness in Angus Óg. He was the pleasantest of companions. He made no sly sexual suggestions nor did he challenge her subtly to ride better, skirt more dangers, test more dares as most men did. His entire attention was fixed on the countryside through which they rode, and he exclaimed with such delight over each new vista that she could not doubt the sincerity of his appreciation. Cáer was responding with pleasure to his comments and questions when they arrived at a headland that looked down into a narrow inlet of the Lake of the Dragon's Mouth. Here Angus stopped and dismounted, looking about as if he could not believe his eyes.

Cáer's familiarity with the place had dulled her appreciation of its beauty and his joy in it gifted her with the power to see it afresh. Her lips parted to thank him for renewing her sense of wonder and delight, but she did not speak. She saw that his eyes had turned away from the lake to the headland itself and fixed on a dip, lush with grass and sheltered by a rise of bare rock.

"I cannot go from here yet," he said. "Let me stay and fix this for always in my memory."

The bright gift had been tarnished. It was all false, all a pretense for choosing a comfortable site for futtering. Cáer set her teeth and dismounted too. *The men of Danaan,* she reminded herself, *did the most exquisite metalwork and their women wove fabrics that dazzled the eyes, but the men were all liars and the women all whores. An* appreciation of what was beautiful did not imply a fine character. Cáer told herself she needed Angus Óg to be virile, not moral, but her lips were tight with disgust as she watched him explore the little cup and finally lay his cloak upon the ground.

Nonetheless, she joined him when he invited her to share the cloak. But when she had sat down beside him with bile rising in her throat, Angus Óg surprised her yet again. He did not reach for her. He only looked out over the water and spoke first of the beauty of the stark cliffs and after a while of the green mistiness of the distant shore.

"That has the look of Bruigh na Boinne in the early morning when the mist is still lying on the river. I am glad to be here, glad to have seen so much of Eriu that I had not seen before, but even after this short absence, I ache for my own place. I am bound and cannot be away from that land for long. When the time comes, I will build my sidhe there."

Tense with expectation, Cáer did not answer, but Angus did not seem to mind. He fell silent himself, seemingly content to stare out over the water, until his eyes were caught by movement. Then he smiled and seemed to wake from the trance of beauty that had held him. He remarked cheerfully on the fishing boats on the lake and asked what their catch would be. By that time, Cáer's conviction that he had asked her to ride out only as an excuse to couple was badly shaken; she answered the question, heard a comparison of lake fish and river fish, shared some nuts which he drew from his pouch, and found herself laughing heartily over a tale of young Angus's falling into the pond near his *lios* because he would not believe he could not catch the boy that looked back at him from the water.

She was startled when his voice faltered over those

words and asked more gently than usual, "Did you lose someone by drowning?"

"No," he said softly, turning his head to look at her, his eyes clear and deep, "I found you. I saw your face in that pond a week since, and set out to seek you that same day."

"How very fortunate you were to find me so quickly," Cáer remarked, her voice dry.

Angus laughed. "I am not so trusting of my good fortune as to set out aimlessly. I knew from your looks that you probably had one parent who was Danaan, and my uncle Bodb remembered that your father had married a Milesian woman—but it was still likely his guess would be wrong. Since it was the best hope I had, I came here first, but I was overjoyed to see you—you might have noticed that I acted even more like an idiot than usual."

"Ohhh . . . I would not call your act idiotic," Cáer remarked sarcastically. "I would call it quite accomplished. And you have gained your objective, have you not? We are here . . . alone . . ."

The sarcasm seemed to go right over Angus's head, nor did he seem to recognize her final words as an invitation. He looked as innocent and happy as a child as he said, "Yes, I did, didn't I? I was afraid it would be very hard to court you in your father's presence. He has a way of turning the most innocent words into insults. And I am not such a fool—although I am often called simple—as to believe you must be stricken with me just because I am stricken with you."

"You are a likeable man," Cáer said neutrally.

She felt strangely neutral. She was now certain that her early guess had been correct: The Morrigan had driven him to seek her out while concealing her manipulation; Angus did not know that she was already committed to bearing a daughter he would father. Cáer could no longer dislike him; she was, in fact, quite willing to lie down and couple, but her suspicion of The Morrigan's intentions was increasing every moment.

She knew the Old Crow had laid a trap for her—or for Angus Óg—but she could not guess where it was laid nor how it would be sprung, and she was no longer totally indifferent to The Morrigan's plans for Angus. He seemed a good, kind person, too good to be sacrificed on a whim of the mischief-making Old Crow. Then she became aware of how long a silence had followed her words, and she looked questioningly at Angus. He was staring down into his empty hands and lifted his eyes to her reluctantly when he felt her gaze.

"It is not enough," he said. All the laughter was gone from his face. "I will love you all the days of your life, Cáer. That should be enough for me, to love you, to feel for once a real passion rather than only a gentle fondness, but there is that black spot on my soul that your father showed us both. It is true; I want more. It is not enough for me to love you. I need you to love me."

She shook her head. "I am not willing to give you that, Angus Óg." She hesitated, then added, "I would consider giving you my body, if that would ease you, but I do not love you and do not *wish* to love you."

At that he laughed aloud. "Of course not," he said. "You do not know me. And believing what you do of the Tuatha de Danaan, how could you love, or wish to love, me? I am simple, but not really an idiot. I know it will take time."

chapter 4

By the end of the next week Cáer was torn between the conviction that Angus Óg had told the literal truth when he said he was simple (in which case some deity was surely watching over him and guiding him) or he was the cleverest, most subtle snake living. She had tried very hard to believe him a deceiving snake, but she could not discover any purpose for a deception, no matter how high and wide she let her imagination soar. The only reason for his behavior that made any sense was his openly stated desire to win her love. And she needed to find some foul purpose, something, anything, to blacken him—because he was succeeding.

Cáer turned restlessly in bed to lie flat on her back and stare upward into the black shadowed roof. She could see Angus's face—broad, with the freckled nose and bright eyes that gave him the look of an eager child. But he was no child; he had none of the deceits and insecurities of childhood. He valued himself enough neither to need nor to care for praise or admiration of others—except, possibly, hers.

Uneasily, Cáer shifted again. Angus was the most admirable man she had ever met, combining a perfectly calm disposition—which kept him out of the stupid, petty fights that destroyed most men and their property—with more than enough battle skill to prove his refusal to leap at an insult was not cowardice. The fighting skills he said he set little store by had been amply demonstrated on the third day when she and Angus had returned from another long ride together. One of the men who still believed she would take him as consort accosted them and, with clear deliberation, insulted Angus—who blinked his eyes as if he could not believe what he heard and then smiled gently and asked how he had offended a stranger.

"By laying hand on my woman," Stariat Sebach snarled.

Cáer had been startled by the swiftness with which Angus's head snapped around to her, but when he saw her expression he laughed aloud and replied equably, "Cáer Ibormeith is no one's woman but her own, and since she has given me no leave to touch her, I have not."

Cáer flopped over onto her stomach and ground her teeth when she remembered those words. Technically they had been true; she had not said in plain words that Angus had her leave to couple with her or openly asked him to do so, but she knew he was wilfully ignoring her hints. No one, not even a true idiot, could have failed to understand, and Angus Óg was not at all stupid despite his transparent honesty and simplistic approach to any problem. Stariat, who was only looking for a quarrel and *was* too stupid to realize that only curiosity about what Angus would do had so far prevented her from calling insult herself and whipping him soundly, had sneered when he heard Angus's mild answer.

"Her father did not deny my suit," he said flourishing his hand at Angus as if to brush off a small bug. "Give me your promise that you will not ever touch her and will not even be in her company in private in the future, and I will let you escape me."

"Why should I wish to escape you?" Angus asked, with

such gentle amazement that the whole crowd that had gathered roared with laughter.

Fraoch, who had come out to meet them and was standing near Cáer, shook his head. "He means it," he muttered to her in a disgusted voice. "He did not intend to make a jest of the man."

Cáer shrugged. "It does not matter what he meant. Stariat Sebach is like an ox: stubborn and stupid. He has decided, for reasons best known to himself, that if he drives away Angus it will improve his chances with me."

With a short bark of laughter, which Cáer still did not understand, Fraoch stepped up to Angus, who was looking around at the laughing crowd and at Stariat Sebach, who was purple with fury. Complete bewilderment was all that showed on Angus's face. Fraoch sighed.

"Angus, the man was threatening you."

"Threatening *me?*" Angus exclaimed, eyes wide with disbelief. "Poor thing, he must be mad with love for Cáer. What can we do—"

"You have done enough," Fraoch growled. "No one knows you here so your answer has made Stariat Sebach a laughingstock. You have mortally insulted him by implying he is of no account compared with you."

"But that is very likely so, Fraoch." Angus pointed out with earnest anxiety. "Is it not plain to all he is not my match? Can the truth be an insult?" He then turned his head and looked briefly at Stariat, who was bellowing incoherent threats, before looking back at Fraoch. "Truly, I do not wish—"

"Never mind what you wish," Fraoch shouted. "He is about to charge you! Draw, you fool!"

Although Fraoch already had his bare sword in hand he did not need to defend his leige lord. Before Stariat had parted the laughing crowd with dangerous swings of his weapon and covered the short distance between himself and Angus, Angus had put Fraoch gently aside and caught Stariat's first wild blow with the flat of his blade. He then proceeded to fight a purely defensive battle, countering every furious thrust and slash with a parry or a sidestep, all the while wearing an expression of deep concern and trying to calm his opponent. Having immediately sheathed his sword, Fraoch stood by with his arms crossed across his chest, looking completely exasperated.

Cáer pulled up her knees so she was on her side and bit her lip, recalling that even four days past she had probably been lost. When Stariat attacked, she had found her own sword half drawn, her muscles tense to rush forward and rescue her gentle lover from a raging onslaught she feared he could not long withstand.

It was the irritation expressed on Fraoch's face that stripped from her eyes the distortion of anxiety bred of . . . desire? love? . . . and let her see how easy and relaxed was Angus's defense, how soft and even his breathing, how steady his voice. She had had to put her hand across her mouth then to hold back a contemptuous giggle over Stariat's ineffectual fury. Angus was like a father fending off the hysterical blows of a very young child using his very first sword.

The crowd of onlookers was only a little slower than she to comprehend what was happening. For a few minutes, they had been silent, expecting that so violent an attack must soon either break through Angus's guard or generate an equally violent counterattack. When they realized that Angus was not only fending off Stariat with ease, but trying to reason with him and then, incredibly, giving him advice on how to fight, first a snicker, then a gust of chuckles, and finally howls of laughter swept back and forth across the bailey.

In the relative quiet that occurred between new shouts of laughter, Fraoch suddenly bellowed, "That is enough! Angus! End this."

It was Cáer who had ended it, however. She curled up

a little tighter as she recalled the look of distress on Angus's face when he realized he had let Stariat struggle too long. What he had meant as a kindness had turned into cruelty and to stop it by one contemptuous blow now would only add to that cruelty. Understanding had forced action on her before she even realized what she was about to do. She had drawn her own sword, stepped up behind Stariat, who was by now breathing like a bellows needing mending, staggering, and hardly able to lift his sword, and tapped him firmly with the flat on the top of the head. He fell unconscious, and she stepped over him and bowed gravely to Angus.

"I am sorry to have made you hold him off so long. And I wish to thank you, here before my people, for not defeating him and forcing him to yield or killing him. I understand now you did not wish to raise even the shadow of a doubt that you intended to win his claim to me. He has none. My father denies no man the right to address me because that right is mine alone to confirm or deny. But Stariat Sebach did not admit the truth. I denied him that right long ago."

Angus had bowed in turn and sheathed his sword. Later, when the crowd had dispersed, he had found her and offered thanks in turn. "That was very clever," he said. "You have saved me the enmity of many here, who would soon have stopped laughing and been angry at my cruelty." He shook his head sadly. "I have now a much larger blotch of black on my soul. I am ashamed of myself. I saw at once that he had neither the strength nor the calm of temper nor the cleverness that could match me. I wanted you to see how strong I am. That is shameful."

"Silly, not shameful." Cáer remembered saying. "A man courting a maid does many silly things."

Unfortunately, Cáer now thought curling up even tighter, she had been more concerned with soothing him than with the truth. She should have realized then that

Angus did nothing silly—simple, yes, but never silly. He told the plain truth in plain words, and she was so used to half-truths, evasions, and bald-faced lies that she had deceived herself.

Cáer sighed and straightened her body. Behaving like a hedgehog could not protect her. If anyone was silly it was she for not sooner acknowledging that Angus was as quick-minded as he was direct. He had seen an opportunity and seized it. The fight that had gone on too long was no boy's silly attempt to impress his sweetheart, nor was the confession that he had wanted her to see his strength silly. She realized now that he had not been ashamed about showing off his prowess against a weaker man—it would never have occurred to him to do so. He was ashamed because he had used Stariat Sebach to demonstrate his abilities so that Cáer could judge whether he was worthy of her without needing to match him herself.

Relaxing somewhat, Cáer started to smile indulgently. Now that was silly; that was a man's way of thinking . . . ah, no, it was not. That was Angus being simple again. He had remembered when they first met that she had all but told him she was accustomed to testing and being tested. Cáer lost the point she was following as she thought tenderly that he remembered everything she said. His first intention, always, was to please her. She slipped over on her back again, her gaze lost in the shadows above while she savored Angus's true desire to please *her*—not his own idea of what should please his image of a woman. That could only be the result of serious thought—or, Cáer warned herself, a perfect hunter's instinct—about the living woman with whom he was dealing.

Vignettes from their expeditions for hunting and exploring flickered through her mind. Angus picking his way across a raging stream without even a glance over his shoulder at her—perhaps because he knew it would be more offensive to her to offer unsolicited help than to let her fall in, but equally because he did not expect her to fall in any more than he would expect Fraoch to do so. Then she burst into giggles and had to smother them. It had been Angus who had fallen in, right at the bank which had given way under his weight. He had not been ashamed to yell for help in hauling himself out. And she had yelled just as freely and just as loud up on the mountain a day later when her foot slipped and caught in a crack. He had helped her with no more comment than he would make over assisting Fraoch. What was more, yesterday he had complimented her no more when they fought and killed a boar together than he would have a male companion, merely laughing and seizing her in a bloody embrace of mutual congratulation.

Cáer's mind caught on the memory of that brief moment in Angus's arms. It had certainly made clear that he did not regard her as sexless or undesirable. Touching her had immediately changed the powerful excitement generated by killing the boar into violent sexual arousal for both of them. She would have achieved her objective of lying with him had she not been so surprised by her own reaction, so slow to recognize what she felt, that she had become paralyzed and failed to seize the advantage.

Cáer sighed. She had wanted him, but even when the momentary paralysis had passed she had done nothing. Like a fool, she had suddenly turned shy and failed to act as simply as he and say so in plain words. He would have taken her gladly. She felt how slowly his hands dropped away from her, the lingering of his eyes on her face as he stepped back. He had been waiting for a sign—and after all the suggestive touches and remarks she had made when she did not desire him at all, at this moment when she wanted nothing so much as to devour him with both mouths, she had been stricken mute and motionless by shyness.

It was the accursed knowledge that she *had* to lie with

him that was spoiling everything. Except for that, she would not have turned shy. They were perfect companions. Why could he not have been a Danaan cast out of the sidhe—doubtless because he was too kind and honest—needing a clan that would take him in? How wonderful it would have been to share her body and her burdens with someone she could trust. What a pleasure it would have been to take as consort a man like Angus Óg.

Cáer drew a deep breath and then let it out in a slow sigh of hopelessness. Of all the hunters for lands and power that had come to Uaman in hopes of marriage with Ethal Anubhail's daughter and heir, the one man she had ever wanted could not be tempted by the offer. Angus had his own lands and people and loved them dearly; from his fond descriptions she could almost find her way over every foot of land in and around Bruigh na Boinne. She thought again of those loving descriptions and came to a new realization: His purpose was not only to win her love but to take her home with him—and she could not go.

It would be a joy to see Bruigh na Boinne, to see any part of Eriu other than this place, beautiful as it was, where she had been confined all her life. Confined? Cáer stiffened slightly and drew a sharp breath. She was not a prisoner! She was free! These were very strange thoughts. The Morrigan! Could the Old Crow's purpose be to induce her to leave Uaman?

Her father would destroy it. Uaman had been a hollow shell by the time Cáer seized control of it. Ethal Anubhail had eaten up her mother's inheritance and beggared the people to make himself great by flamboyant entertainments and buying mercenaries to attack his neighbors. Loosed from the fear of the spell that could cripple him and any man he bought to side with him, he would drive away the White Swans who kept the land at peace as soon as she was gone. Angus might praise the beauty of moun-

tain and ravine, but it was that very beauty that made
Uaman poor. Uaman had to be carefully managed to
provide a living for its people. Could the destruction of
Uaman be what The Morrigan wanted?

Cáer bit her lip. Such a small purpose? Could it be
worth planning and waiting for so many years? Why
bother? As much as she loved Uaman, Cáer could not
pretend that it had any importance in the great scheme of
things. Besides, there were myriad far less chancy ways
The Morrigan could use to bring about the destruction of
Uaman.

Closing her eyes, Cáer tried to bring to memory her
meeting with The Morrigan. She saw the old woman
hunched by the roadside, remembered the stab of disbelief and panic she had suffered and her pride in concealing it. But they had talked only about the daughter she
would bear. Certainly Macha's birth was The Morrigan's
main objective . . . and her second one had been to set
Cáer against Angus.

Cáer's eyes snapped open again. Angus was Danaan.
Likely The Morrigan's quarrel was with Angus. Somehow
The Morrigan had made him love her before he even
came to Uaman. But he could not stay in Uaman and she
could not leave it. Then likely it was Angus's pain The
Morrigan planned to enjoy. Well, she could spite the Old
Crow—and keep her promise to bear a daughter by
Angus Óg at the same time. Tomorrow, in the most lacivi-
ous way she could, she would seduce him. She would
make him despise her. Tears leaked down Cáer's cheeks,
but she stared resolutely ahead, refusing to close her eyes
on her pain. If she could save Angus from the Old Crow,
she would, whatever it cost her.

Although Cáer's resolution held firm, she did not find
it easy to accomplish. No way could she bring herself to
act seductively within the dun; aside from the damage it
might do her ability to control her father's men, it could

not accomplish its purpose. The effect of making herself
seem lewd would be entirely spoiled by the surprise and
laughter of those who knew her, which would show too
plainly that her behavior was unusual. That would only
flatter Angus by showing him he was special to her. The
best she could manage was to lay her hand on his arm and
say, "Ride out with me. I have something I wish to say to
you in private."

His happy agreement was a knife in her breast, but she
was prepared for that. She would have led him to where
they had fought the boar, but that was by a fallen tree on
a hillside where the ground was all patches of grass too
rough for grazing between sticks and sharp stones. Perhaps it would have been possible to couple after they had
killed the boar, either standing or ignoring discomfort,
but that was no place to take a man and prove lewd intent.

She led him instead to that cup in the headland overlooking Dragon's Mouth Lake where she had suspected
he meant to have her. Her conversation while they rode
was somewhat disjointed because she was trying to think
of a way to display a brazen desire. All her concentration
accomplished was to make Angus look at her strangely
and produce the firm conviction that it is very difficult to
make sexually suggestive gestures while riding a horse.
Recalling the failure of her past efforts, Cáer thought
with chagrin that she seemed to have no idea how to en-
tice a man even when not on horseback. She had spent
her whole life trying to discourage men.

As they came out of the trees on to the barren headland, it occurred to Cáer that no matter how she behaved,
Angus would know she was not a practiced whore because she was a virgin. She still had to couple with him,
still had to get with child—she looked away from him out
over the water and her spirit lifted on wings of relief and
delight. The wings folded, the flight of joy ended when

she remembered she still had to find a way to save him from The Morrigan—but the coming loss did not seem so dreadful if she did not need to make him despise her.

The realization stripped away a black pall that had hung over everything and the beauty of the place struck her anew. She slipped from her horse, dropped the reins to make it stand, and moved toward the grassy dip. Angus followed, but Cáer was aware that this time his eyes were on her rather than on the view. And this time it was she who spread her cloak.

"Sit," she said, doing so herself. "I must tell you that I have had a hunger for you since we embraced after killing the boar. I know you have desired me since you came. I do not understand why you did not accept my earlier hints, but now I will say in plain words that it is stupid for us to deny ourselves this pleasure."

She sighed a little when, instead of reaching for her and drawing her to him, Angus knelt down beside her and took her hands into his. Although he was direct as a knife in the breast, nothing that involved him was ever simple.

"I did not know you were inviting me, because I knew you had no desire for me," he said. "When we killed the boar, we both hungered, yes. It is common that danger rouses desire. But you are not hungering now, Cáer, and I am simple as a beast. Men may force women, but bull or stallion, fox or he-wolf, a beast takes only a willing mate."

"I may not be aroused right now," Cáer said, quite exasperated at this moment with a thoughtfulness that she would have considered admirable at any other, "but I remember what I felt and wish to feel it again."

For a long moment Angus looked into her face. Then he dropped his eyes to their hands. Finally he looked up again and asked, "Are you sure?"

"Yes," Cáer said, smiling.

He leaned forward and kissed her, touching his mouth

to hers only lightly, slowly letting go of her hands while his lips lingered on hers, leaving her free to draw him closer or push him away. She did neither, only let her eyes close, and after another moment he asked again—his lips moving against hers, "Are you sure?"

The faintly ticklish sensation, the warm, sweet breath on her mouth caused an odd flutter just below Cáer's breastbone and made her want to squeeze her legs together or rub herself against the ground. She ran her hands up his arms, held his face against hers for a moment, but that only made her want to pull him close so she released him—but she only drew back far enough to murmur, "Yes, but you will have to sit or lie down or something. Your knees will begin to hurt very soon."

He laughed aloud, a hearty peal, as he straightened his legs and sat. "That is the Cáer I know," he said pulling her onto his lap. "Practical even in loving. What other woman would reason out the need to be in the right position so as not to be interrupted at a delicate moment."

"Possibly a woman who has considerable experience," Cáer snapped.

"No, love," Angus said, shaking his head and pulling her close against him so his words brushed her ear like fingers. "That I know also. You are as innocent as a yearling doe."

She did not answer, could not because his mouth had closed on hers again, not gently this time but with a warmth and insistence that stirred to life the fading sensations she had felt earlier. But even as her breasts swelled against the band that confined them and she became aware of a fullness and moistness in the lips of her lower mouth, somewhere in the back of her mind she knew his words had provided the answer to why, if she were no whore, she had yielded to him without love.

She could not pick out the reason just then; her power of thought was slipping away into a rosy warmth of sensa-

tion in which each movement—Angus's unpinning and
dropping of his cloak, his arm tight around her back
stroking her breast with extended fingers while his other
hand slid up along her belly to the tie of her trews and
then down her legs to loosen the leg wrappings—somehow intensified the response of her body. Even when he
tipped her backward, he did not jolt her out of the trance
of feeling. He held her tight against him and leaned with
her, lifting her hips upward by supporting her back on
his thigh so that he could draw off her trews.

He kissed her still, smoothing a hand along her thighs
and between her legs while he slid out from under her so
she was lying flat on her cloak—but not for long. When
his fingers reached her nether mouth and he teased the
lips, she heaved upward, wanting them inside to still a
craving she did not know she felt. He lifted away when
she pressed upward, and Cáer clutched him tighter and
tighter again as she felt him twist and writhe. Somehow
she associated his contortions with imminent satisfaction
of her need, although it was only later that she understood he had been taking off his own clothing.

Through it all, his mouth never left hers, his lips first
soft then harder, his tongue sliding out and in, touching
her lips, tempting them to part, withdrawing in invitation. Below, his fingers touched and stroked, finding the
tiny tongue in that mouth. Muted by his lips, Cáer still
could not help opening her mouth to cry out with pleasure; his tongue slipped in, caressing her tongue and the
back of the roof of her mouth, withdrawing, giving her
room to invade his mouth—but that only made worse the
tumult in her loins.

Somehow he had loosened her breastband. He
brushed his hand across her upstanding nipples and a
lance of fire ran down her belly making the mouth below
ooze moisture. She struggled against him, lifting her legs
around him, trying to draw him into her. She could feel

his rod, hard and hot, atop her mount of Venus and she squirmed to drive it down and in, all in vain. Angus stirred and tried to pull away; she held him tighter. He was trembling, and she could hear his panting breath and between the gasps murmured words that made no sense until at last he got a knee up between hers so he could lift himself.

In the next instant the hand that had been trapped between them with just enough freedom for his fingers to rub and rub the burning little tongue, left it. Cáer moaned a protest, but Angus found a deeper satisfaction for her. He grasped his shaft, and set it between the gaping lips of her nether mouth. Cáer shrieked with triumph and relief. Angus thrust. Cáer gasped with pain, but pain was an old familiar friend to her and could not distract her. And mingled with this pain was a pleasure so fierce that her legs tightened harder pushing him deeper.

She heard him utter a single sharp cry, but could not wonder why. An instinct old as the first coupling between male and female drove her. She held him hard only an instant then relaxed her grip so he could draw to thrust again. The pain diminished; she drove him faster, harder, twisting and writhing so that her little tongue could lick the hot shaft that filled her with each stroke. The pleasure increased until it, too, was pain, and Cáer wailed aloud as pang after pang of joyful torment passed from the place their bodies linked through her . . . and trailed away with little shudders of pure delight that soared up into joy again when she felt Angus convulsing in an equally violent satisfaction in which he cried, "Cáer! Cáer! Cáer!" as if her name filled his whole being.

After, they lay entwined for some time, trying to steady their breathing and gather their wits. Angus being somewhat less shaken, although in all his lovings he had never had a similar experience, finally lifted his head, levered himself up on one trembling elbow, and drew his cloak over their bare lower bodies.

"That was a little like killing the boar," he murmured, then sighed. "A first loving should be slow and gentle, particularly the first loving of a maiden."

"I am not a gentle person," Cáer said, smiling. "You need not fear to be rough with me."

"It was not you I was concerned about." Angus's voice held a faint note of indignation. "My poor shaft is not of steel like my sword, you know."

"Well . . ." Cáer drew out the word, her grin broadening. "It was warmer, of course, but I have no complaint to make of its sturdiness."

He chuckled ruefully, lifted himself off her and dropped to his back, sliding an arm under her neck and drawing her close. "Thank you. I am glad to have given satisfaction, but for a moment or two I feared it would be bent into folds. Cáer, it is much easier for *me* as well as for the maiden if she be broached gently."

Cáer blinked but managed to prevent herself from stiffening or pushing him away. If she did not plan to continue as his lover she had no right to be jealous. And she had always praised his honesty—when it had not touched her. She knew she should not react, but she could not help saying, "You sound as if the broaching of maidens is a very familiar task to you." To make herself sound indifferent, she uttered a cross between a snort and a laugh.

Angus drew a deep breath. "Alas, yes. The halt, the ugly, the painfully shy—they all came to Bruigh na Boinne for comfort." He turned his head to her and smiled like the sun rising. "No more, beloved Cáer. I will have a wife and good reason to offer them no more than words."

Although an ache had come into her throat that made it hard to speak, and though she knew she should say nothing and let him hope until she was sure he had got a daughter on her, Cáer said, "I never promised that, Angus Óg. This coupling was no pledge to marry."

He sighed. "I know. I wondered when you asked me to lie with you whether I should deny you and say I would not until you agreed to take me as your husband, but . . ." Cáer saw him look away into the distance. "I wanted you too much to deny you. I was not happy when I first saw your garb and weapons. A warrior woman uses a man the way she uses a rag to clean a sword, and cares for him about as much."

Cáer sat up. "You mean the way most men use most women? You fool. The reason a warrior woman bonds with a man as rarely as a crow is white is because she has no need to gain anything from that bonding, not house, nor herd, nor food, nor protection. Such a bond is truly for love and only for love, and that is as rare as a white crow."

Angus looked up at her and smiled. "Yes. I understood that later, when I came to know you as well as love you. And so I came to know also that you must come to me and with me of your own will, not as a stubborn ass is driven with a carrot ahead and a stick behind."

He held out his hand and, stricken with a revelation, Cáer put her hand in his, and as he closed his eyes, still smiling, let him pull her down beside him again.

chapter 5

With the words "stubborn ass," Cáer's smoldering jealousy was doused in the chilly water of guilt. She suddenly
remembered—Angus was always making comparisons
with animals—how he had said she was innocent as a doe
just before he began to make love, and that moment the
reason she would give him for sending him away had
come to her. A doe has her season, she would say, and in
it she bawls for her stag, as the veriest bawd bawls for custom, and abides with him and urges coupling upon him.
I warned you, she would say, that I did not seek love nor
wish to find it. Now my time of heat is over, I do not want
you any more.

She looked sidelong at Angus, whose arm had relaxed
away from her. He was asleep; Cáer's lips quivered into a
smile. Everything about Angus was different. Often with
their hard or cruel or knowing eyes closed, men looked
more childlike in sleep. Not Angus. With his eyes closed
and the innocent look of wonder in them hidden, he was
all man.

Tears prickled behind her eyes, but she blinked them
away. He would be angry, very angry, if she said, with the
right tone of kindly contempt that her heat was over and
she wished to be rid of him. Perhaps he would be angry
enough to hate her and that would surely break whatever

subtle enchantment The Morrigan had set on him. At least he would not couple her with things unclean ... only accursed. That would free him—and free her too.

Cáer bit her lips to strangle a sob, and then her breath eased out. She would have her daughter, her Macha, and in the child a precious bit of Angus. And the parting was not yet, not yet. She sighed softly and let her own eyes close. It was not so easy for some women to get with child, particularly warrior women whose blood times were often not regular because of hard work and hard living. It might be many months before Angus's seed took root and until then she would have him.

Only, of course, it was not many months. If she had hated the man, Cáer thought bitterly, if she had been desperate to conceive, no doubt it would have taken years. Because each day in Angus's company was a precious jewel, all sparkling with laughter and set in a golden glow of shared satisfaction, it was scarcely three weeks before her moontime came and went without a drop of blood. At first she paid the time of the month no mind; she was often late or even skipped a month if there were heavy fighting. Of course that was not true at present, and, in fact, she knew, somewhere in the back of her mind, that she felt different, but she shook off the knowledge as a wolf shakes off water—as she shook off the pain of bruises and half-healed wounds or the discomforts of her bleeding.

Then she began to dream, always of Angus—and of crows. She and Angus were always bound together, but the crows only attacked him. They pecked his eyes, tore strips of his flesh, and he cried out for her to help him, but she could not nor could she explain why she only stood and watched his torment. And that was to Cáer,

who was a doer, a torment worse than what was being
inflicted on him.

Cáer told herself the dreams were sent by The Morrigan to bedevil her because she had judged for herself and
found Angus fine and taken pleasure in their joining instead of hating it and him as the Old Crow desired. But
there was a chance she was being warned; the Mother
sent true dreams, she knew that, and she had never
heard The Morrigan could send dreams at all, true or
false.

She held out until Midsummer Night, until she and
Angus had leapt the fire together—playfully, she was not
so lost to everything that she would have leapt a Beltain
fire with him—and had run into the wood like all the
other leapers to play Midsummer Night games. Above
them as they joined, a crow cawed. Cáer gasped with
fear—crows did not fly by night—but Angus, mounted
and already riding hard, seemed unaware or indifferent.
He laughed, teasing her breasts and kissing her lips and
ears and throat until the fear was swallowed up into passion and mingled with it and made the bursting of fulfillment even more violent.

The dreams were worse that night, much worse; Cáer
woke with tears drying on her cheeks, too terrified to lie
to herself any longer. But although she had accepted the
necessity of their parting, she found could not herself tell
Angus to go. Because his eyes looked into hers with such
open honesty, Cáer choked on the scornful words, "You
have played bull to my heifer long enough. I am freshened, and need you no longer."

She woke screaming the next night and had much ado
to calm her women without explaining the cause. But she
could delay no longer and told her father to bid Angus
leave, to tell him that Cáer did not wish to speak to him
again, having decided she would never marry him or

leave Uaman; thus, his presence was painful to her and he must go.

Ethal Anubhail had stared at her, judging, she guessed, between the pleasure of saying, "Tell him yourself," and the pleasure of telling him in the way that would make her most despicable. At last he nodded his head, once, and smiled a slow smile.

"I will tell him . . . daughter."

Cáer's mouth opened to cry that she had changed her mind, that she would not permit her intentions to be swallowed, changed in Ethal's bowels to something foul, and then voided on her lover. But a vision of her dream rose up before her waking eyes and she gritted her teeth over the pain of knowing Ethal would make Angus hate her and despise her if he could. She would not be completely alone; she would have Macha to love. She had no right to deprive Angus of the chance to be free of her, and her father's filthy bile should be disgusting enough to cure any obsession. She could not bear to see it, though, so she took a strong troop and rode out on patrol.

When Angus did not see Cáer in any of her accustomed places from morning until evening, he was clearly worried but asked no questions. The next morning, when she did not join her women to break her fast, he found the captain of the White Swans and asked where was the airechta. Grian looked at him steadily with an expression all too familiar to Angus from seeing it on Fraoch's face, a compound of exasperation and resignation.

"Gone," she said. "And will not soon return. You should be gone too. It is a black and crying shame to be inhospitable, but Uaman is not in my keeping so I can say what Cáer could not. It is time and long past time that you were going from here to wherever else you wish to go."

Angus stared at Grian's broad, weathered face, but she looked back unflinchingly, taking back nothing she had said. His eyes dropped, and the net about his heart, which he had not felt at all after he had found Cáer, tightened so that it was hard to breathe. Fraoch, who had been close on his heels since seeing his face when Cáer had not broken her fast with the others, caught at his arm and drew him away. Angus went without protest—he had no breath for speaking.

The only thought in Angus's head was that Cáer had not even bothered to bid him go herself. He had known for many days that all was not well with her. He had felt the desperation in her lovemaking, heard it in her laughter, seen it in the way her eyes fixed on him when she thought he was asleep or his attention was elsewhere. And he, who had never hesitated to open his mouth and ask for what he wanted no matter what the threatened consequences, became so terrified by the signs of her discomfort that, equally desperately, he pretended he did not see it. The only reason he could think of for Cáer to go without warning was that she knew what she had to say—go, I have had enough of you—would hurt him.

"Angus, enough," Fraoch said. "There are thousands on thousands of women in Eriu and every one would pluck out her eyes if that would life-bond you to her. Are you such a fool as to want this one only because she does *not* want you?"

"I love *her*. I must have her."

"That is not love, Angus." Fraoch stepped back and his hand dropped from Angus's arm. "Love cares for the other more than the self. Let her be."

Beneath his flesh and bone the net had become a mesh of metal loops that cut and squeezed. "I cannot. I *must* win her. The Old Crow has netted my heart and hooked it to Cáer's soul."

Fraoch stood staring, then swallowed. "You must tell

Cáer. She is a fine woman and will wed with you if she
knows your life is at stake."

Angus shook his head impatiently. "Can you imagine
The Morrigan leaving so easy an out for me? Surely to tell
Cáer would violate The Morrigan's condition that I win
her. Find her and win her, the Old Crow laid that *geis*
upon me."

"Curse her!" Fraoch exclaimed without raising his
voice. "The woman at the pond. We have been running
ever since that morning. I knew the trouble started with
the woman, but never thought the woman was The Morrigan." Then Fraoch frowned. "Angus, if The Morrigan
bade you find Cáer and win her, there *must* be a way to do
it. Are you sure Grian spoke the truth?"

The reminder and hint of a hope eased the pain in
Angus's chest, but he was not fooled. It would come back
tenfold if he gave up or despaired. He said thoughtfully,
"Grian is no liar, but I see what you mean. You think
Cáer is playing a woman's game?"

Fraoch shrugged. "*Some* game. I do not explain women
to you, Angus, for you know them better than any other
man—all but this woman. Because your heart is netted to
her, can it be that you do not read her clearly? I would
have sworn that she was more besotted of you than any I
have ever seen. Most come and sup of you but are willing
to go. To me it seemed as if she would not willingly part
from you for the time it took to blink her eyes. Why
should she suddenly ride out, without saying farewell,
without telling you herself that she did not want you?
Lady Cáer is too strong and proud simply to run away or
hide behind her captain's shield."

"I thought because she did not want to see me hurt."

"Spared herself? Knowing what she did would hurt
you more? A strange way to avoid giving hurt," Fraoch
said.

After a moment Angus nodded agreement. Although

he was still aware of the weight on his heart, speaking to Fraoch was pointing out so many inconsistencies in what Cáer had done that he no longer felt he would choke and die. He began to think. One hopeful possibility remained: Cáer had told him several times she would not marry him; if she had changed her mind she might be too proud to admit it and would rather send him away than ask him to repeat his proposal. Angus did not think that likely. In fact, although it was the first notion that had come into his mind when he first saw Cáer concealing unhappiness from him, he dared not say, "We are mated and well mated. It is time we were married."

He had not spoken because he feared she would laugh and send him away—no, not laugh; he was sure her heart ached for him—because she had tried and could find no deeper feeling for him than pleasure in coupling. Little and faint as the possibility that she had ridden off without a farewell in the hope it would prod him into renewing his proposal, acting upon it was simple and the response might suggest the next step to take if the hope did fail.

"It is easy enough to prove her intentions one way or the other," Angus said to Fraoch. "Let us find Ethal Anubhail and I will make a formal proposal for his daughter. When we have his leave, we can go after Cáer and I can ask."

"You think Ethal's permission will constrain obedience in Lady Cáer?" Fraoch asked with open disblief.

"No, of course not," Angus replied, "but it will be excuse enough to follow her. If she does want me but did not wish to say so . . ." His voice faltered. It was impossible; Cáer was not that kind. "Well, likely that is not true, but then getting her father's permission to marry her will make her so angry she will explain in plain words what she did."

So they went to seek Ethal Anubhail. He was easy enough to find, having just seated himself in his high chair on the dais as if to give judgement. However, there was no assembly of pleaders or captives and Ethal gestured them toward him immediately.

As soon as Angus reached the dais, he said, "Ethal Anubhail, I have loved your daughter and we are well suited. I wish to marry her."

Ethal leaned back in his chair. "But I do not wish it," he said, and laughed. "I was just about to send a servant to summon you so I could tell you that. I thought when you came, being Danaan and with enough spirit not to creep away into a sidhe, that you were one who could deal with Cáer, but you are a weakling and will let her go her own way in everything. Barely have I kept her from yielding all to any challenger in the name of peace. You will make it worse. I need a husband for Cáer who will teach her who is master and lead my liegemen to war, not sit on the wall and admire how the rising sun gilds the hills."

"*You* do not wish it?" Angus repeated, as if he had heard nothing after that statement.

"No, I do not. And Cáer, who has been known to cross my will, will not cross me in this for two reasons. First because you have a living of your own and she will not leave Uaman and the women she has gathered to her. Second because she does not desire any man, even a weakling, to have a claim on her. You have wasted your time here."

"If you knew this," Angus said, "why did you encourage me when I first came."

Ethal shrugged. "I told you. I thought you were a man. I thought you would ask for her at once and challenge her when she refused you. If you had defeated her in arms so that she was forced to obey you, you could have had her. Sweet words will win no warrior woman to wife."

That was not true, Angus knew. Not that what Ethal said was actually a lie—doubtless he would have enjoyed seeing Angus challenge Cáer and defeat her, if he could—but there was something false . . . The sense of falsity woke memory. "Do not trust him," the Dagda had said of Ethal. "He is treacherous."

"Are you urging me to ride after her and challenge her now? And if I conquer, will you then give your permission for me to take her to Bruigh na Boinne?"

"Oh, certainly," Ethal said with a snicker. "If you can beat her, you can have her."

Angus nodded. Behind him he heard Fraoch draw a sharp breath and he turned quickly, his eyes commanding Fraoch to silence. Then, without speaking, he bowed to Ethal Anubhail, and gestured to his liegeman to follow him.

Outside Fraoch said softly but urgently, "That is not the way, Angus—"

Angus laughed without mirth and answered, "I know. My father warned me that Ethal was treacherous. First I thought he was encouraging me because he wished to be rid of his dominating daughter. Now I believe that he has been working on Cáer from the beginning to make her refuse me."

After a heartbeat of silence, Fraoch uttered a wordless sound of mingled surprise and anger. "I think you have hit the truth again, Angus," he said. "The way he spoke of the Tuatha marrying for a livelihood and offered her as an afterthought to the property was enough to breed resentment in the most obedient of daughters—which it was plain already Cáer was not. And why I was such a fool as not to see it, I do not know. Why should he wish to be rid of her? She manages this whole rath and protects him too, so he does not have to risk his silly neck in battle."

There was the reason for The Morrigan's laughter when she challenged him to win Cáer. Angus shivered a little as the metal mesh cut tighter into his heart. He could not leave Bruigh na Boinne for very long—when he had taken the place from the Dagda, his blood had gone into the earth; there he must live, and there go down into a sidhe in the end—and Cáer would not leave Uaman because she felt it her duty to manage the rath and care for the people. Nor was she self-deceived about her importance. In their travels around the countryside Angus had seen how all welcomed her and depended on her.

Ethal did not need to say much to her to make her refuse to marry me, Angus thought; he did not need to say anything. In fact, Ethal's simple presence was the root of the problem Angus realized, remembering what some of the people had said and how Cáer had assured them that her father could not do as he had threatened.

Fraoch had fallen silent, clearly trying to think of a way around the problem. Fraoch was clever, but—Angus unconsciously rubbed his chest in a hopeless effort to loosen the band that constricted his breathing—he did not think Fraoch would find an answer. He had begun to put aside his recent vision of Cáer's gold-brown eyes full of tenderness and recall the image of those eyes in the pool of Bruigh na Boinne, staring into his so seriously, so sadly. He was recalling her face, hard with purpose. He had thought then that Cáer would do her duty regardless of the cost and saw the trap into which he had fallen. The more she loved and desired him, the more adamant she would be in her refusal to leave Uaman to be destroyed by her father.

If he walked back into the house and killed Ethal . . .Angus sighed. That was a little too simple and direct. It would be murder, which Cáer as airechta would be obligated to avenge. And even if they could somehow get around that, Ethal's death would leave Uaman without any leader, which would make it even more impossible for Cáer to marry him. If she did, the rath would be torn apart while first one and then another of the liegemen tried to seize power. If only Ethal could be trusted to

. . . but the Dagda said he could not be trusted. And that memory brought back another: Bodb telling him that help against Ethal would not be far away, that he should go to Medb and Ailill at Cruach if Ethal should stand in the way of his fulfillment of the *geis*.

With the thought came a slacking of the tightness in his chest. Angus took an experimental breath and found it easier. Was that what The Morrigan wanted? To involve Ethal in some way with the rulers of Connacht? Medb and Ailill could certainly control Ethal, but would Cáer trust them any more than she trusted Ethal? Angus raised his brows and cocked his head. Not Ailill perhaps, but Medb was a woman. Cáer trusted women. Suddenly Angus laughed aloud. With Medb as ruler, not only would Ethal's liegemen be obedient but no neighbor would be likely to attack Uaman either.

"You have an answer?" Fraoch asked eagerly when he heard Angus laugh.

"Bodb gave me the answer before we set off on this journey, but I had forgotten it," Angus said, smiling. "Come, let us ask for supplies for traveling. I will explain on the way."

They came to Cruach in the afternoon of their third day of traveling and stared across the narrow neck of the lake—or the wide river that flowed out of the lake—at the three great ringing walls. Each could be seen because the *lios* had been built atop a hill that rose high above the lake, and each wall of the dun was built into the hill with the next wall towering over it. Looking down on all was the huge circular main house of the *lios*.

"I would not wish to try to take that dun," Fraoch said.

"I suppose that was the intention of building it as it was built," Angus answered somewhat absently, his eyes on a large raft that had set out from the opposite shore. "They keep good watch," he remarked.

"And are swift to welcome guests," Fraoch said, as one of the two men on the raft waved and shouted for them to go to the landing, pointing a little south of where they stood.

Turning their horses' heads in that direction, they came almost at once to a sturdy but narrow dock. "And they are not foolishly trusting." Angus smiled as he dismounted. A silly thing to say. He was not practiced in war, but whoever built that rath was not likely to be other than cautious, even in hospitality. Only one man and one horse at a time could approach the raft.

"Be welcome to Cruach," one of the men called as he directed the raft in to nestle against the dock. "If your horses will come aboard you are welcome to bring them. If you would like to leave them, Grec will see that they are stabled down below."

"They will come," Angus said, leading his horse forward.

The gray did not like the unstable footing and the chestnut liked it even less, but though they shivered and snorted and spraddled their legs a little, their training held and they stood like rocks until led ashore on the opposite side.

"Those are well-broken horses," Grec said, looking hard from Fraoch's golden head to Angus's red.

"They love Angus," Fraoch said, "and will follow him anywhere."

"Are King Ailill and Queen Medb here?" Angus asked. "I have a—"

His voice checked as a loud caw preceded a black shadow that flapped past the two men. Grec, who had started to nod an affirmative, stiffened a trifle and led the way to the gate in the first wall without completing the gesture. The crow screeched and circled as they passed through, and again when they went through the second gate, and a third time as they entered the grounds of the *lios*. No one had spoken a word after the crow appeared—and then it was gone, as suddenly as it had arrived.

"If you will come to the guest house," Grec said, "you can take your ease while I stable the horses and ask where are the king and queen."

Angus and Fraoch released the horses and entered the guest house where Fraoch caught Angus's arm and said, "She circled deasil—and she never lies."

Angus nodded. "She means well to our coming here and she always intended for Medb to have Uaman, I think. Bodb said that might be her purpose and that she only used me because I angered her. I suppose once Medb is acknowledged Ard Righ by Ethal, The Morrigan does not care whether I get Cáer or not—or perhaps she wants Cáer out of Uaman." He shrugged. "In any case, I expect my favor will be granted without any great trouble."

His assumption was soon proven true. Hardly had they opened their blanket rolls to take out clean garments when a servant came to lead them to the bath and, when they were clean and decently dressed, to show them into the great mead hall, past the rows of couches, past the drinking benches, right to the dais where Medb and Ailill sat. Those in the hall, having a cup of ale or mead before the evening meal was served, hushed as they passed; and then broke into talk again.

The chairs of the king and queen were exactly the same height and of exactly the same richness of decoration, and the queen was as tall as her husband—and breathtakingly beautiful. Medb's hair was a darker, richer red than Angus's carroty curls and tumbled down her back and over her shoulders in glowing waves, a startling contrast to her gown, which was all white, intricately woven with patterns of gold. Her eyes were green and dark as a fine emerald, her mouth full, the lips very red against the tanned skin.

Ailill was less spectacular, but when he spoke formal words of welcome and drew Angus's eyes, Angus saw he was a good match for his lady. Broad bare shoulders were exposed by a *lena* of the same dazzling whiteness as the queen's and interwoven with the same pattern in gold thread, but his garment was additionally fringed with gold. His hair was black, his eyes dark enough to be called black, his skin swarthy but with a rosy glow that spoke of good health and good spirits, and his features regular enough and strong enough to be called handsome. Best of all, there was a look of calm confidence about him that made Angus draw a deep breath of relief.

"You are well come to our house for as long as you desire, but if there is more we can do for you, saving our honor and our own necessity, we would be glad to hear of your need," Ailill finished.

"My name is Angus Óg," Angus replied, giving the identification that Ailill, politely, had not requested. "My *lios* is Bruigh na Boinne."

Ailill's brows went up and Medb, who had been looking at Fraoch rather as if he were a side of beef she was thinking of eating, turned her eyes to Angus. He made a tiny nod of the head, acknowledging that both knew who he was; without much change of expression, both now looked wary.

"This is my liegeman and friend, Fraoch," Angus continued, "and I do, indeed, have a need, which I hope will cross neither the honor nor the necessity of Cruach. I left my *lios* to seek a woman whom I was told I would love all the days of her life—"

Angus hesitated, having noticed Medb stiffen and glance swiftly to her side, where a very young maiden sat on a little stool by her chair. She was lovely, Angus noticed, with a softer, gentler version of her mother's spectacular beauty, her hair more brown than red, her eyes a lighter, mistier green. But he gave the girl no more than the single glance and smiled reassuringly at Medb.

"I do not seek her here," he went on. "I have found her in Uaman. She is Cáer Ibormeith, daughter of Ethal Anubhail. She found me also to her liking and came willingly to lie with me more than the three times required for wedding. But when I went to her father to ask approval of our handfasting, he said he would not accept me as husband for his daughter."

"Ethal Anubhail?" Medb said, cocking her head in a birdlike way that sent a shiver down Angus's spine. "But he is not under our authority."

On the last word, her voice turned hard and a slight tone of resentment colored it. Rustles and whispers from the folk in the hall gave evidence of their awareness that Medb was not satisfied with Ethal's independence.

Ailill put a hand on her wrist and she turned her head sharply. Their eyes met. Her lips drew tight against her teeth, making her mouth bitter, as if she were about to spit venom, but Ailill met her ferocity with half-smiling understanding, and in another moment she nodded and turned back to Angus with a slight shrug.

"I had heard that," Angus said, "and I am sorry to know it is true, but is it not possible—as a favor to a guest—that you would ask Ethal Anubhail to send Cáer here to answer for herself whether she would be willing to have me?"

"As a favor to a guest?" Medb repeated very softly and turned her head to meet her husband's eyes again.

Ailill bit his lip. He looked like a man who had been offered a bite of the Salmon of Knowledge, eagerness heavily overlaid with awareness that what he desired was wrong. Angus understood what Ailill desired: If he sent a message to Ethal asking him to send his daughter Cáer to

Cruach and Ethal refused, Ailill would have cause to take offense and march on Uaman. But why was it wrong? What had kept Ailill and Medb from bringing Ethal to heel? A powerful oath or *geis*, Angus thought as he watched Ailill set his teeth and shake his head slightly. Medb drew an angry breath. Angus held his; if Medb would not oppose her husband's decision, he was in far worse trouble than he had believed. And an ear-shattering cawing preceded a huge crow through the easternmost of the seven doorways of Cruach's hall.

The room fell as silent as if every person in it had been stricken dead. No whisper of breath or flicker of movement gave a sign of life—except for Angus and the crow. Angus had leapt at the creature as it flapped past him, crying out with rage and anguish, but it eluded him easily and perched on a rafter cackling with almost human laughter. Angus stared up at it, his face white as bone. The crow stretched one wing then the other, settled them neatly, and leaned down to look at Medb, making a low, chuckling noise.

Medb rose to her feet and, staring upward at the crow all the time, said, "It does not seem fair to me that Cáer Ibormeith should not have a chance to answer for herself whether she will or will not take Angus Óg as her husband. Is that not a woman's right?"

Rare it was that when Medb spoke all eyes should not be fixed upon her, but this time every pair was raised aloft. The crow chuckled softly again, sidling a few steps along the rafter and back again.

"Surely," Medb went on, her voice stronger, her eyes, gleaming more brightly, now turned toward her husband, "it would be no more than a common courtesy to fulfill so modest a request? Only to invite a woman to a neutral place where she can speak her mind? Ethal Anubhail should know that I would permit no forcing of any woman against her will, but I would be willing to offer safe conduct to Cáer to come and go at her own desire."

"I would be grateful beyond measure for the favor," Angus said, his eyes wide with surprise as he, and everyone else, saw the crow bob its head and heard another low, satisfied chuckle.

He had, in fact, barely got the words out, being faint with relief. Death had fastened iron fingers around his heart when he saw The Morrigan fly into Cruach's hall. He had been certain in that moment that all his guesses and Bodb's were no more than false hopes, that the Old Crow had been so angered by his rejection that she had set at naught the fury of the entire Tuatha de Danaan so long as he perished in pain. And in the next moment that fear had flown out of the westernmost doorway with the black crow that had wakened it.

Medb stood watching the doorway, her head tilted slightly as she listened for the cawing that might signal the bird's return. Everyone else listened too, breath held or passing silently through parted lips. Angus was as frozen as any other, his heart aching with the expectation that this was only another cruel trick, but no bird sounds at all drifted into the hall and nothing at all moved. A slow smile curved Medb's lips and she looked down at her husband.

"Well, my lord," she murmured, "it seems that Ethal Anubhail will come under our authority after all."

"Under yours, my love," Ailill said, smiling back at her. "This must be your doing, yours alone. Remember, I am oath-bound never to seek a quarrel with any of the Tuatha de Danaan." He rose and touched her glowing face, his dark eyes bright and hot. "But I do not doubt that you can manage without any help or advice from me."

chapter 6

Angus found Ailill's remark to be nearly a miracle of understatement. By the time the sun rose the next day, Medb's messenger was on his way to Uaman, bearing a demand that Ethal Anubhail send his daughter Cáer to Cruach with sureties that Cáer would be unharmed during the time she stayed and free to leave whenever she desired. That was all well and good. Even if Cáer came only to say she could not marry him for the sake of Uaman, Angus could put forward the idea of asking Medb to ensure the safety of the White Swans and the good governing of Uaman.

What Angus liked much less was that the messenger had three days to ride and three days to return; on the seventh day Medb bade him say, she would come with her army to fetch back either Cáer or the messenger. He had the feeling that he had loosed a wild mare with no way to control her, and before the sun had risen to noon knew he was right. By then Medb's liegemen were riding in to Cruach, and by evening their armsmen were gathering into an army in the fields across the lake.

The army set out for Uaman on the morning of the third day, meeting the messenger on his return journey before they had traveled far. Medb's man was much incensed by his treatment. He was accustomed to being greeted with courtesy, sometimes fawning, and to being attended with great interest—and often with considerable anxiety—by the lords to whom Medb's message was directed.

At Uaman neither Ethal nor Cáer had deigned to see him even after he said he carried a message from Medb. A servant—not even a liegeman—had been sent to listen to his message and in hardly time to understand it had delivered to him an arrogant refusal of Medb's request. Adding injury to insult, the servant had sent him back on his way without the offer of so much as a drink of water or a crust of bread. Medb's jaws shut with a snap and her eyes shot sparks.

Fraoch was astonished. "That is not like Ethal," he said to Angus when Medb had ridden back to harry more speed from her men. "I had expected him to say the airechta was away and that he would send her as soon as she returned or to make some other excuse."

"He did not really have that choice," Angus pointed out with a lopsided grin. "Medb never had any intention of allowing him to do anything except submit—one way or another. She gave him no chance to use any excuse. She said she would be there on the seventh day if Cáer did not arrive sooner. And if he sent Cáer, he had submitted already, acknowledging that Medb had a right to make demands of him."

"But he could not know what the message was before the man spoke it. Why not be courteous? What could he gain by offending the messenger? What would it have cost him to speak to the man himself, to feed him well, to say that he was sorry he could not comply? And to say to *Medb* he would not answer to a woman? It is insane deliberately to infuriate a ruler much more powerful than yourself."

Angus shrugged. "None of this makes sense to me. I thought he would yield. I thought he would send Cáer. I thought that, seeing himself in a cleft stick, he would take the easy way out." He shook his head, mouth grim. "Perhaps The Morrigan stirred him to a senseless rage—but why? If The Morrigan's first purpose was to punish me, she only needed to forbid this enterprise rather than further it. Medb would have bowed to The Morrigan's will, if to no other. If her purpose is to put Uaman into Medb's hands, why involve me at all?"

"I think you allow The Morrigan's purpose too much weight," Fraoch said slowly. "For all we know her purpose was that I come into Cruach and lay eyes on Findbhair—"

"Who?" Angus said.

"Medb's daughter," Fraoch replied.

"The little maid? But she is only a child, Fraoch!"

"I know it. Nonetheless, there is my fate." He laughed uneasily. "My heart is not netted to her so time is no danger to me, but have her I will, however long it takes. So how do we know that The Morrigan has not that distant courtship in mind?"

"But that is—"

"Ridiculous? So are some of your guesses and doubts. It will be safer for you, Angus, if you do not count on a senseless rage in your enemy. To account a foe cleverer than he is seldom has a bad effect; to put him down in your mind as less than he is will certainly bring you to ruin. So let us assume Ethal has some purpose for pricking Medb."

"Yes, I am very willing," Angus said, with a small shiver. "But what purpose?"

To that Fraoch had no answer, and none had occurred to either of them, or to Medb, who had recovered her temper enough to realize that when Ethal had addressed his insult to her he might not be counting on Ailill's oath never to challenge one of the Tuatha de Danaan to keep him safe. Ethal certainly knew she fought her own wars, so enraging her might be an attempt to make her rush headlong into a trap.

Thus, with great caution they approached the narrow neck of land commanded by An Fhairche broadening the front of the army until it stretched nearly from one shore to another of the great lakes. No ambush was set for them, however; the land was empty. And when Medb sent a messenger to the dun saying she wished to pass through An Fhairche into Uaman, she received an obsequious reply.

So they wheeled the right wing to the south and took the easiest road, but still with caution, with scouts ahead and a good rearguard behind. There were birds and little beasts along the way, but for all they saw of man or woman, cow or sheep, it might have been a dead land. Ethal Anubhail had gathered in his people and was prepared to resist.

Angus felt sicker and sicker. If Ethal fought back, Cáer would be in the forefront of the battle and might be hurt. Had his first suspicion been right, that Ethal would risk anything to be rid of his daughter? Did Ethal hope that resistance would so infuriate Medb that she would demand Cáer as a prisoner if she escaped death? But Medb was not in the least angry at the preparations for war; her eyes glinted like jewels and her teeth flashed in smiles. Medb liked a good fight.

Midmorning of the seventh day, as she had promised, Medb rode toward the closed gate of Uaman dun, stopping just out of javelin range, and called for Ethal Anubhail to send out his daughter. Angus rode beside her, shield ready to ward off any missile of unexpected power that might threaten the queen. At the challenge, a bright helm rose above the rim of the wall followed by a body in burnished bronze mail. The warrior walked across the depth of the wall, then stood and looked out at them. A shield rested by the warrior's left leg, rising as high as the shoulder, and a sword was belted around the armed body but no bow or javelin was in hand. The warrior was armed only for defense.

"I am Cáer Ibormeith, daughter to Ethal Anubhail, airechta of Uaman," the armed figure called. "Why have you come into Uaman demanding that my father send me forth, Queen Medb?"

Angus gasped, his netted heart leaping against the restraints around it. Medb cast a single glance at him, which said: I will settle with you later, for not mentioning that Cáer was a warrior, who need have no fear of her father. But the glare faded almost as it formed and Medb smiled.

"Because," she shouted, grinning, "I bade him send you to Cruach to answer free from fear whether you were willing to take Angus Óg as your husband. Ethal Anubhail was discourteous to my messenger and through his servant insulted me."

There was a brief silence, then Cáer called, "I am here. I am free from fear. I will not marry Angus Óg. You have your answer. I beg you to leave us in peace."

Medb laughed long and loud. "It is too late for that. If Ethal had sent you to Cruach, you could have given your answer and returned to Uaman without let or hindrance. Since the Righ of Uaman has seen fit to insult me, the rath must bow down to avenge my hurt. I will give you until noon to send out Ethal Anubhail. Perhaps I will have his head; perhaps I will ask no more than that he do me homage and arrange the tribute he will pay. If he does not come out, at midday I will come in to seek my own satisfaction."

There was another silence, then Cáer answered steadily. "I am airechta. It is my duty to fight for Uaman, not to yield it. I will give your message to my father. He is righ and has the right of decision."

She turned to leave. Medb, still laughing, wheeled her horse and trotted off. Angus sat staring at the place where

Cáer's helmet had disappeared behind the wall. What had he done? He had fallen into every trap The Morrigan had laid. It was as if he had been enscorcelled and could follow only a single path, oblivious to all others. Now that he had gone too far, brought about utter disaster, the bindings were removed from his eyes and he was allowed to perceive the full extent of the Old Crow's victory.

Cáer would fight; Cáer would die. The net would release his heart because the *geis* would end with the days of Cáer's life. He would not die. The Tuatha de Danaan would not avenge him on The Morrigan. But he would be punished. Oh, how he would be punished. He would mourn Cáer all the days of *his* life, and that would be a long, long time.

"Angus!"

He turned his head slowly at Fraoch's call, then lifted his rein and touched his horse's ribs with his heel.

"Angus!" Fraoch repeated, horror thinning his voice.

"When this battle is over," Angus said, "I will build my sidhe and go down under the earth. I will never see the sun rise again."

"Why? What has happened, Angus?" Fraoch whispered.

For a moment Angus could not find his voice, but then he explained the full measure of The Morrigan's revenge on him.

"No!" Fraoch exclaimed indignantly. "Why should the Old Crow win? There is always a way to cleanse her foul purposes and between us we will find it. Only do not despair. Despair hands her a victory without even a struggle."

Meanwhile Cáer had turned and gone down the steps along the inner side of the wall. "Noon," she said to

Grian, who was waiting with a group of armswomen to rush up and defend the wall if necessary. "Set a watch against any surprise, although I do not expect it. I must speak to my father."

She hardly knew what she said. She was so stunned by seeing Angus beside the queen of Connacht and then by what she had heard that she felt nothing at all. She had only come back the previous night from the border between Uaman and Sraith Salach, where one of her father's men had started a nasty fracas, and Ethal had told her nothing about the queen's messenger.

Had her father really been discourteous to Medb's messenger? That seemed unlikely. And deliberately to insult Queen Medb? That was insane. Surely it was more likely that the queen had chosen to take offense at some imagined slight. Then she remembered what Medb's messenger had demanded. How could Medb know what had passed between herself and Angus if that traitor Angus had not told her? Why should the queen of Connacht interest herself in who Cáer of Uaman married unless that foul, crawling worm had sought her help to avenge himself for the refusal he had received?

Those two questions—to which the answers were all too obvious—sent such a shaft of pain through Cáer's heart that she put them out of her mind and hastened her steps past the two inner walls and into the courtyard of the *lios* where her father was watching his men make ready to fight.

"Medb says you were discourteous to her messenger and insulted her," Cáer said to Ethal. "What do you say?"

"That the man came while I was in my bath. I told the servant to bid him wait or if he were in great haste to listen to his message and tell me what it was. He chose to take offense because I did not come at once from my bath. And when I heard the message . . . What could I say? You were not here, so I could not send you even if I wished."

Her father's defense was perfectly reasonable but Cáer had known him a long time and there was a note in his voice that roused her doubts. Very likely the words might be true but did not convey the truth. "You could have told the messenger you would send for me," she said. "You could have asked the messenger to wait. Even if he would not wait, he could not have said that you insulted the queen."

"I did not send for you because you would have followed him and gone to Medb to keep the peace," Ethal snarled, looking around at his liegemen. "What good would that do? If you appeared at Medb's order, it would be the same as agreeing that Medb had a right to make demands of me. Next would be a demand for tribute. If she desires to rule Uaman, let her shed her blood."

"Our blood will flow also," Cáer remarked dryly.

Ethal laughed. "Why should it? All you need do is stand on the wall and lay your curse on Medb's army. Her men will be crippled, rolling screaming on the ground. That will teach her to leave me and Uaman alone."

Cáer stared at him. "Are you mad? *Did* you deliberately affront Medb's servant because you thought you could end any threat from her for all time? *It is not true!* My spell will not affect a whole army! It was given to my mother as a defense against such men as took her in an ambush and cut her hamstrings and it will protect me—no one will be able to touch *me* without being afflicted—but what good will that do anyone else? And in any case you know I will not use that spell. I have never used it, except against your men who wished to toy with me before I was able to defend myself with my own weapons."

To Cáer's amazement, Ethal ignored the sudden tenseness of the men around him who had just had the floor pulled from under their feet. He did not roar with the rage he often used as a cover for panic. In fact, after a flash of surprise, she could have sworn she detected a flicker of satisfaction in his eyes.

"Then you will have to rid Uaman of Medb by force of arms," Ethal remarked calmly. "That is the duty of the airechta and the fighting band the airechta leads. It is your duty to go out and drive away the invaders."

Cáer fought to keep her face expressionless and to suppress a gasp of understanding. Ethal apparently had two strings for his bow. His first had been the glory that would accrue to any man who defeated Queen Medb, and if Medb's army could not fight, and withdrew, he would claim a victory. The second was to be rid of her once and for all. If she were killed and the White Swans decimated in a hopeless defense, he could yield and agree to pay tribute. He would not care; it was a few more cows or sheep that he would wring from the people. She would not be there to say him nay nor her troop to keep him from seizing anything he wanted. And he would benefit all around, since he could blame Medb's exactations for any excess he committed.

Cáer's jaw set and her lips pulled tight over them in a smile without mirth. Turnabout was fair play. "Why no, dear father," she said. "You are wrong about my duty. It is the airechta's duty to avenge any insult to you or any assault on this rath. But it is you who was careless in courtesy and gave insult to the queen, so I have nothing to avenge."

"You call your righ a liar?" Ethal bellowed.

"You are a liar," Cáer muttered, but not loud enough for the men behind Ethal to hear. Louder, she said, "It does not matter because I am sure even if you had been courteous that she would have found a reason to come. She has desired for years to bring you to heel."

"Do you think blaming me will convince Medb to leave? Or do you intend to send me out without any defense in the hope she will kill me and favor you with rule of Uaman because you are a woman? Coward! Woman-heart!"

"I have already told the queen I would not drive you out. If the rath is assaulted, I and the White Swans will defend the walls and the *lios*. Let us see if you and your liegemen are equally brave before you call us cowards. If you feel we are not daring enough, I will not stand in your way if you wish to attack. When you are prepared to charge, let me know. You will find me by the outermost gate. I will open it for you, and the White Swans will stand by to guard it against any rush by Medb if you are over-whelmed."

She turned away without waiting for an answer, and walked quickly through the first gate. Instead of making the left turn, which would bring her to the gate in the second wall to join her women at once, she turned right into the passage between the walls. It was very quiet, the high mounds of earth obstructing sound both from out-side and from the inner courtyards. As soon as she was sure the curve would hide her from a casual glance from someone passing through the gate, Cáer sat down on the rough grass and let her body sag with despair.

This was utter and complete disaster. Even with the support of her father's men, there was no way she could hold the walls for long. She was prepared to fight her neighbors, small kingdoms like Uaman. Medb's army was already three or four times the size of her own—includ-ing the men, and there was no assurance they would fight—and the queen could summon more forces, and from close by too. Sraith Salach, An Gort Mór, and Lee-nane had always envied her father's independence from the rulers of Connacht. They would be happy to help Medb make Ethal bow to her.

Cáer bit her lip to repress a sob. She had never cared. Several times when quarrels arose between Uaman and

other holdings she had wished they could bring their differences before an Ard Righ who could mediate. But that
was not possible as long as her father held to his stupid
independence. When in the past she had suggested he
would be warmly welcomed and highly valued if he himself offered to do homage to the rulers of Connacht, he
had been furious.

"I am of the Tuatha de Danaan" he had roared. "I acknowledge no Milesian ruler. And why should I send to
Ailill and Medb the tribute I can use to draw liegemen
and power to me? You have no spirit," he had added,
sneering. "You are not fit to be airechta."

Perhaps she was not, Cáer thought. Certainly she did
not spend her days strutting and boasting, pricking men
to fight just so she could have another victory song and
crow over her conquest like the old airechta. She loved
the fighting, the skill and art of battle and the excitement.
But she took no pleasure at all in the maiming and death
her ability could produce. Immediately memory brought
up images of Stariat Sebach being fended off with easy
grace, with an almost contemptuous defense that beat
him back without anger, without lust. That fight had
made Angus so desirable to her . . . Angus, whose mean
spite had taken him to Medb to complain and bring disaster upon her.

She would die for Angus's spite, Cáer thought, because
her father wanted her to die, because Ethal Anubhail
would refuse to yield, would insist she go on fighting until
she was dead and most of the White Swans with her.
Then he would yield. Then he would buy his life from
Medb by offering rich tribute and be free to destroy
Uaman and its people.

There was no escape. She could not yield without her
father's permission. To do so would only make everyone
believe she was a coward and a traitor, even the White
Swans. She would have violated her oath as airechta to

defend the righ and the realm and by that violation prove herself unfit to remain in her position or to be acceptable as a human being anywhere. She bit back another sob. All she had struggled for, all she had torn her own heart for in denying Angus, all was lost.

Lost because Angus was not what she had believed. He was true Tuatha de Danaan, evil and selfish. She had explained why she could not go with him to Bruigh na Boinne; she had grieved with him that he was bound to his land—differently but just as inexorably—as she was bound to hers. He cared nothing for her or for Uaman. He would not accept a little loneliness, a little longing, but would take her by force—if he still wanted her, if rejection had not turned him so mean and petty that he wanted her dead too.

She uttered a little hiccup, half laugh, half sob. At least she would be at peace—and she would have her revenge on The Morrigan who had forced her to lie with one of the accursed Tuatha de Danaan. Her mouth shook when she thought the babe must die with her, but she steadied it. Without a mother, with Ethal Anubhail as grandfather and no other kin, her little Macha, barely alive now, would be better off dead.

The White Swans too? The vicious feeling of satisfaction over The Morrigan's loss of a tool she seemed to desire very much disappeared in a wave of remorse. Her armswomen did not deserve to die nor would they be better off dead. And if they did not die, they could go off as a troop—Medb herself might be glad to have them. But they, too, would have to die because if she could not yield they could not either—all because of that stinking, selfish, arrogant Danaan. It was *Angus Óg* who should die!

The thought of that joyful warmth, that merry heart stilled by death and entombed in a cold mound, wrung a little spate of sobs from Cáer. But even when she had swallowed down the tears, reminding herself that the merry heart was also selfish and traitorous, the thought of Angus's death remained, twisting together with the knowledge that she too must die. And the joining—as had the joining of her body to Angus's—bore fruit.

If she offered to settle the conflict by single combat, herself against the man who had complained against her, she might save the White Swans . . . Cáer blinked as a new idea came to her. She might save more than the White Swans; she might save Uaman too!

First, although Angus was mighty in defense, that was no warrant that he would defeat her. She had seen his style. She was no stupid, arrogant boar like Stariat Sebach to attack wildly until she was exhausted. She had her own tricks, the tricks of a woman warrior who was shorter of reach, lighter of weight, than the bulls she faced, and Angus Óg might not be so practiced in the avoidance of those tricks.

Second, and far more important, perhaps she could make terms for her defeat. If she went down to death, Uaman would have to become subject to Medb, just as it would if Medb's army conquered, but it was Ethal who had offended the queen. Would Medb demand his death? Cáer frowned; she was not sure she could agree to that. Perhaps she could convince the queen that the cruelest punishment that could be visited on Ethal was for Medb to appoint a warden over him. Anxious as she was, a choke of laughter escaped her. Perhaps Medb would be willing to appoint Grian, and leave the White Swans, whom Ethal hated, in control. The faint smile lingered on Cáer's lips. That would be a most satisfying knowledge to take down to the grave with her, that her father would be bound by Grian's will and, instead of her spell, have Medb's power behind that will if Ethal did not conform.

Cáer rose lithely to her feet and turned back the way she had come, hearing the voices of the men raised in disagreement as she entered the courtyard. She snorted softly to herself as she made out some of the shouts. Her father had managed to foment discord again, setting the overbold young men, who wanted to charge into Medb's army and turn them back by pure daring, against those who wished to support the women armsmen to make a solid defense. That was no lack of adroitness but deliberate, she thought. The longer they argued, the less likely they would be in time either to divert some of Medb's force with a charge or give any support to the White Swans.

As she came closer she saw men in groups on the outer edge of the crowd of liegemen. Those voices were lower, but she heard them ask each other what need there was for war on their own land, which could lead only to the ravaging of their own crops and herds. Better take terms, those muttered to each other—a fine to pay for Ethal's insult and then a fair tribute. Cáer stopped by one group.

"I agree," she said, "there is no need for war, but the righ will not agree, and Queen Medb, who is the stronger here, may not agree either. I will offer a settlement by single combat against the man who started this quarrel by his unfair complaint and ask such terms if I am defeated that will protect the liegemen of Uaman. Pass the word among the like-minded of you and support me."

She smiled as she pushed her way through the shouting crowd closest around her father. He had outsmarted himself this time. Cáer drew her sword and clashed it against the central metal boss of her shield.

"My lords," she shouted, "there is no need to quarrel among yourselves. If courage alone will be sufficient to protect Uaman, it is the airechta's place to supply that courage. I intend to offer to settle this quarrel by single combat against Angus Óg, who caused this trouble by being unwilling to accept my father's refusal of his suit. But I fear that Medb will not wish to give reasonable terms to cover my defeat, if I should be defeated, until she has seen that it will cost her high to overrun Uaman. Thus, we will need to withstand her first attack and do her men all the hurt we can."

Naturally, the statement that there was no need to quarrel only started more vociferous argument. Cáer listened and replied, when that was necessary, with one eye on the sun, which was climbing higher. When the shadows had shortened enough so that noon could not be more than a quarter candlemark, she clashed her sword over the boss of her shield again.

"The attack will come very soon now," she called. "I go now to lead my armswomen. Those who wish to see us throw back this first assault, come with me and lend your strength. You will be welcome among us or as a separate party."

On the words she stepped away from her father, just in time to avoid the hand he put out to catch her. Only his low snarl of "bitch" touched her as she pushed her way through the men, many of whom were casting startled glances at the sun. Cáer did not smile, but a little thread of satisfaction lightened her heart as the exclamations of surprise and the movement of the crowd proved that most, absorbed in their arguments, had not noted the passage of time. Her father had intended to hold them there, arguing, until the attack began and they were too late to be of any help.

She had foiled that ploy, she thought, as she ran quickly through the gate and turned left into the passage that would lead to the second gate. In fact, she realized with a spurt of bitter amusement, she had even dragged her reluctant father with her. She heard him shouting at her to stop, and she laughed as she sprinted through the second gate and turned right to double back to where the steps went up the first wall. Now that he was at the last gate, he would have to join the fight himself or lose the respect of his men. They would not follow and obey a creature they considered too great a coward to protect his rath.

She was well ahead, but gasping when she reached the outer gate. "Let me out," she said to Grian, "then close the gate and go up on the wall to call for a parley. If Medb agrees, send out the chief of my father's liegemen to hold my weapons—and do not let my father up on the wall until I am finished."

chapter 7

Medb was chuckling when she returned from her parley with Cáer to the area she had chosen as her central command post. "I can see clearly why you want her," she said to Angus as he came up to ask anxiously whether Ethal had thought better of fighting. "She has good brains and high spirit, that one. She proposed, since her quarrel is with you, that you settle the matter by single combat."

"Yes!" Angus exclaimed, light coming back into the blue eyes that had been dull, grayed over like a winter sky.

Medb laughed. "Oh, you are too eager. I do not think the fight would last ten minutes before you yielded."

"No," Angus said. "I will swear by whatever you like not to yield to her, she will have to kill me to win."

"Then you do not think she can win? Are you so angry because she refused you, that you wish to see her dead?" Medb asked.

Angus smiled. "No. I do not wish her dead. I love her. I think I can make her yield without hurting her."

Medb hesitated but then shook her head. "I like her, but it would not do. The conditions she set are beyond what I could grant—not that they would not satisfy me. I said I might take Ethal Anubhail's head, but that is really out of the question. Ailill is oath-bound never to harm one of the Tuatha de Danaan. A small bending of that oath, such as my coming here and bringing Uaman under the rule of Connacht, is safe enough, but if real harm came to Ethal and more especially were I to order his death—I fear that evil would soak through my bond to Ailill to bring evil on him."

"Then why—" Angus began.

"You heard my men," Medb answered. "They think they will push open the gate and walk in waving their swords to ward off the women as they would use horsehair switches to ward off flies."

"Not these women," Angus said. "I have watched them practice and fought alongside them when a patrol turned back a raiding party."

"So?" Medb stood looking past Angus toward her liegemen, the older sitting or leaning in relaxed readiness, their eyes on Uaman where armed groups had begun to come out of the gate and form before the walls, while the younger men talked to each other, moved about restlessly, or gave useless orders to their armsmen. After a moment she said, "It makes no difference. I cannot accept any terms except total surrender before my men discover those flies can sting. If Cáer and her women can hold off an attack, then we can parley again. Besides," she glanced over her shoulder at the formation before the wall and turned a feral smile on Angus, "I want to see what they can do."

She walked past him toward her men, who all sprang to attention. "I have been offered a settlement by single combat," she told them. "The airechta challenges Angus Óg, who, she claims, has brought this trouble upon Uaman unjustly." She then described the terms Cáer had proposed and ended, "Let me hear your counsel."

The oldest liegeman shrugged his shoulders. "It is for your saying, Queen Medb. If you are content that Ethal Anubhail should bow to you and pay tribute rather than

lose his head, then let the quarrel be settled by Cáer Ibormeith and Angus Óg. We will have a cheap victory—"

"A cheap victory it will be," one of the younger men
cried. "We will have among us barely the cost of our coming from the fine offered. Why should we take so little?
We can sweep aside those dear little White Swans and
take it all. Look at the silly things in their pretty burnished feathers strutting about to overawe us."

"They are not all women," Medb said, smiling a little.
"And the ones doing the strutting are the men." She
paused, then added, "Not all women are silly."

The young man stiffened and drew a quick breath. He
was foolish enough to have spoken without thinking
when he was angered by the chance of loot slipping away,
but he was not foolish enough to try to hide or excuse
himself—or say he did not think of Medb as a woman.

Her glance flicked him like a lash, but she only smiled a
little more broadly and continued, looking around at all
the men, "Those are the choices, fairly stated. How do
you divide on them?"

The groups of men began to shift, some toward the
older liegeman, some toward the younger. Some consulted with others before they moved, but it took no long
time before they had divided into rather even parties.

"I have no strong feeling either way myself," Medb
said, then laughed. "You know that. If I preferred either
path I would have said so and we would have walked that
path. If I saw a strong leaning to one way or the other
among you, I would go that way, but you are almost
evenly divided. Thus I propose that the party that desires
to attack do so. If the defense of the gate fails, we will all
join in the taking of the walls, which will be the bitterest
work. If the defense of the gate does not fail, the second
party will stand ready to cover the retreat of the first, and
I will think again of the terms proposed."

Medb held up a hand to forestall any reaction, looking

at the men and smiling now with a warmth that made each feel important and cherished. "You are all dear to me, and I would not wish you to be hurt for nothing. This is a poor land. You will find little enough in the dun to make a heavy bloodletting worth while. Ethal Anubhail *must* be lessoned, and Uaman *must* join the rest of you in doing homage to Connacht. However, I can see no reason why you need bleed for those purposes if Cáer Ibormeith offers an easy path to them. Now," she beckoned closer the young man who had protested the loss of loot, "let me hear how you propose to attack and what support you desire from the rest of us."

When Cáer had been setting forth her proposals to Medb, for a while she had almost hoped the queen would accept them immediately. Medb showed a flicker of relief and then open amusement when Cáer suggested that a warden, supported by Grian and the White Swans, would be more satisfying a revenge on Ethal Anubhail than execution. Cáer could almost see the name of the warden—she had soon realized that Medb would not appoint Grian, who after long residence might favor Uaman too much—forming in the queen's mind. Nonetheless, she was not much disappointed when, after a glance at the men massed around her banner, Medb shook her head and said she would have to insist on total submission if Cáer was beaten.

This Cáer refused, saying she did not distrust her own ability to defeat so treacherous a beast as Angus Óg but that her father had not the same faith in her skill and would rather risk his fighters' lives than stake all without sureties. Medb had shrugged and said that if Uaman was not overrun, they might parley again. Cáer smiled and remarked with a nod that she would look forward to their next meeting. Medb looked just a trifle surprised but then smiled back before she turned away.

When they parted, Cáer slipped back through the gate and told those within the result of the parley. "Hold them off and bloody them well in this first rush," she urged, "and you have little to lose. If they come through the gate or over the wall, I think we will all die. Medb will set a new righ over Uaman, and he will swear liegemen of his own choice."

Her father's eyes met hers and, if looks could kill, Cáer knew she would not have had to wait to die in battle or in single combat. Nonetheless, he had apparently realized he could no longer hope to force the White Swans to bear the brunt of the attack alone. He nodded acceptance. Cáer turned to the captain of the armswomen.

"Grian, you know what I expect from my White Swans."

"Airechta, we will stand until we die."

Cáer smiled. "Hold them off and you will not need to die."

Grian nodded brusquely and gave orders for the women to start out and form up before the gate. When they were moving, shields on their arms, javelins lifted in salute, Cáer turned toward her father's men.

"Lords, I will not presume to tell you how to fight. You will be welcome to thicken the lines of the White Swans, but if you decide to charge to beat back Medb's men before they reach us, be assured there will be a refuge if a retreat should be necessary. The White Swans will open ranks for you."

It was a pledge she saw the men welcomed. There had been friction enough between Ethal's liegemen and Cáer's armswomen to raise a suspicion that a shield wall might be closed against them, trapping them between their enemies and allies who would not help them. Now they converged on her father with greater eagerness.

Cáer looked over their heads and beckoned to a man who stood a little apart. He came forward slowly. Cáer's lips thinned; she had no time to cosset her father's steward just now.

"Luchtar," she called, "Send all the hunters, herds-men, farmers, and other common folk up every wall stair-way. When the command is shouted from the watchplace in the outer wall, they are to rush out onto the wall and use their bows and slings to take out as many of Medb's men as they can."

The steward stared at her for a moment with open ag-gression, but an instant later he nodded and began to transmit the orders. Cáer was relieved to see that the common folk were already prepared to fight in their own style, the bowmen with full quivers, the slingers with their leather sacks of stones, the huntsmen with javelins to repel any armsman who got up the wall. Apparently Luchtar resented that she had given him an order but was not fool enough to weaken the defense of the dun.

It would be pleasant to give an order to a household officer and see the man smile, Cáer thought, as she picked up the javelins and shield she had left in the sentry room and went through the outer gate herself. The thought made her choke on a breath that was half laugh and half sob. It was not a problem she needed to worry about any more.

She found Grian where she expected, in the center of the front line. Subcaptains held the far right and left ends. A third subcaptain, just as hard and experienced as Grian, was placed off-center in the second line where she could take command if Grian fell. Cáer squeezed her arm as she went past to tell Grian that she would be in the watchplace to signal the bowmen and slingers on the wall and to warn with horn blasts—she touched the curved ram's horn at her belt—against any movements of Medb's men meant to trick or surprise the defenders. Unless the fight went badly; if it did, she would join the battle to hold the gate.

The chief armswoman nodded, her face grim. Cáer would not lead the troop as usual as long as she hoped she could fight Angus. She would need to be as fresh as possible for that trial. They clasped wrists briefly and turned to look across the open space to where Medb stood surrounded by the leaders of her army. The men moved, shifted, separated into two groups. Then Medb walked aside, her crimson cloak brilliant against the duller striped and checkered wear of her liegemen. One of the groups began to shout to the massed armsmen. Companies came forward to follow the men who had called to them; others formed up but held their ground behind Medb.

"They will come at us in two waves," Cáer said. "Do not be tempted to follow the first when they retreat."

Grian laughed and Cáer clasped her arm briefly again before she turned aside to climb up to the watchplace in the outside of the wall. Since the moments of panic and agony when she learned of Angus's betrayal and understood she was unlikely to survive it, she had been too busy, too intent on salvaging something from the treachery of her father and her lover to feel much. Now she was so torn between hope and fear that she had to set her teeth and clench her hands on the handhold of her shield and her weapons until metal and wood cut into the flesh. She stared at the opposing force as if the power of her will could move them—and then they did move, shouting threats and waving their shields and weapons.

Cáer blinked, her anxiety banished by astonishment. Shouting battle cries, yes, that was normal, but the waving must surely expose vulnerable parts and interfere with the aim of the javelins. She watched the yelling, gesticulating men come closer with starting eyes. What did they think they were doing, flushing a covey of ducks?

driving a herd of sheep? She shook herself hard. Who knew? Perhaps they were trying to stun the defending force!

They had come near to doing that, Cáer realized, shaking off her surprise and shouting, "Bowmen! Slingers! Make ready! Ready! Ready! . . ."

She heard the scrape of boots on stone as the men ran up the stairs and along the wall. Her lips parted to draw breath to shout a final order. Suddenly her throat closed, her eyes blurred with tears. Loping easily along right in the fore near the center of the group with his red hair streaming out from under his helmet—but with his shield held steady and his mouth closed—was Angus. Cáer drew a forceful, agonizing breath.

"Now!" she screamed. "Now! Shoot!"

Men's voices transmitted the order right and left along the wall and moments later a cloud of arrows and a hail of stones flew outward. In the oncoming force some of the yells changed to shrieks of pain. Here and there men stumbled, others fell. A few cast their javelins—a stupid, angry reaction, which could not endanger those on the wall.

"Shoot! Shoot!" Cáer shouted, unable to tear her eyes from that graceful runner with flaming hair.

Another volley of stones and arrows. The attackers were closer and the missiles took a greater toll, but not nearly so great a one as to discourage them. However, more cast their javelins at the more sensible target of the massed defenders. They did little damage and a return shower of weapons also took a lesser toll because shields and weapons were being held ready for defense and attack; also the herding and hunting halloos had changed to the threats and taunts showered on a worthy enemy.

Angus was still running. "Shoot!" Cáer shouted.

She tore her eyes away just as the first missiles of that volley struck to look outward toward Medb's reserve. In a moment, her father's men should move forward to engage the first wave of attackers. As the thought came, Cáer heard the roar of men's voices close by and Ethal's liegemen began their charge, but she did not watch them, she watched the reserve. She would give no order to shoot again unless a second wave of Medb's men came at them. For now, the bowmen and slingers would have to hold their fire or they would be as likely to hit friend as foe.

Cáer did not believe Ethal's men could turn Medb's force; she did not even believe they could divert them for long. Cáer was not worried about that nor about the impact of this charge on the White Swans. They would move forward next, not as an undisciplined band of egoists but as a double line which could cut down each attacker as he came while protecting each other's sides and backs. The danger was that the second part of Medb's army might try to charge around the ends of the battle to get between the White Swans and the gate when they moved forward or that there were hidden forces that with sheer numbers could overwhelm her armswomen.

She heard the men crash together, heard the shouts of satisfaction at coming to grips with an enemy, the clash and thud of sword and javelin against shield, heard bellows of rage and shrieks of pain that rose above the general roar of battle. Still she watched the lines of men beyond the field and Medb's brilliant red cloak, her eyes shifting from the male leaders to the queen, hoping to see a gesture that would warn of new action on the part of Medb's fighters. There was no movement there. The men were formed into groups and all were watching the fight, but there was no tension, no inching forward, that might indicate a charge was imminent.

There was no need yet for Medb's reserve to move, Cáer knew. She heard the change of tone that meant her father and his men were falling back. Very shortly thereafter the shriller shouts of triumph coming from Medb's men changed to lower curses and bellows as they met the wall of White Swans. In no time, more and louder shrieks of pain and furious yells of frustration told Cáer that her women were holding their own and pushing back the attackers. Cáer set down her javelins and loosened the horn from her belt.

The noise diminished somewhat and rose in pitch as fewer men had breath for shouting and more of the calls came from the White Swans. Cáer longed to look, to see her women beat back the attack, but she dared not turn her eyes away from the lines of men across the field. She lifted the horn to her lips, expecting any moment that Medb would signal them to start to move, and she wanted to blow the warning to her women as early as possible so they would be prepared for the new onslaught.

Suddenly the sound changed. Not far from the watch-place there was a crescendo of noise, men shouting her father's name, and a doubling and redoubling of shouts for aid—all men's voices. An ugly flash of hope that her father had been cut down, that she was rid of him and the need both to protect him and to stand buffer between him and the people, pulled her eyes from Medb's reserve. She saw at once a knot of struggling forms that made a dent in the White Swan's line. Two women were down, others trying to close the space behind the fighting men.

At first Cáer did not see her father's gilded armor and helmet because she was looking at the ground. The moment her brain reluctantly accepted the fact the Ethal had not fallen, she spied him, weaponless, his arms caught behind him, thumbs held in his captor's iron grip. And the captor—Cáer had to swallow back a cry of surprise—was Angus Óg!

The fighting around them had been bitter before her eyes were drawn to them, Cáer realized. Medb's men had been determined to keep this precious prisoner and had converged on Ethal's men from other places in the field. The White Swans had fought them as well as Ethal's men. Cáer suspected that was to thrust them out of the dip created in their line and to protect their fallen companions, not to rescue Ethal, but the men might not realize that, so the action might serve to better relations between the two groups.

By the time Cáer took in the situation, however, she saw with relief that any hope of rescue was ended and she did not need to order her armswomen to try. Medb's men had already formed a wall around Angus and his prize and were beyond the fighting, retreating swiftly and gathering more men as they ran back toward the protection of their reserve. Those of Medb's men who had been too busy with their own battles to notice what had happened were being struck down and forced back under the women's onslaught. And in another moment the attack was broken off completely. The remainder of the men were running away as swiftly as they could while protecting their backs from the javelins the White Swans caught up from the ground and cast after them.

"Shoot!" Cáer screamed at the bowmen and slingers. "Shoot!"

A few more targets fell to the volleys that followed, but not many. As they had been ordered, the White Swans did not pursue; alternate women scavenged the ground for loose arrows and javelins, some wrenching them out of bodies that lay unresisting or shrieked with pain. When they had cleared the area, they backed slowly, still scavenging, until they were in their original position. There they stood, resting on their shields, waiting for the next wave to rush at them.

With every woman's attention on the opposing force, Cáer felt free to watch Medb, knowing that her father would appear before the queen soon and from her would come the orders for the next attack—or, a call for a parley. Cáer's heart was beating fast and hard. If Medb could force Ethal to yield, she would give Cáer a victory, a victory she was still alive to taste, snatched from the jaws of defeat.

Such a victory had been Angus's purpose when he struck unconscious two of the White Swans—quite unfairly, for Fraoch had been engaging one and Ferdia the other, according to his plan—slid through the line, with Ferdia and Fraoch keeping his retreat open, and seized Ethal, who had been so sure another Danaan would not attack him that he had not even been watching Angus. What Ethal had said when Angus struck his sword from his hand, tore away his shield, and grasped his thumbs behind his back might have been cause for a lifelong feud—except that Angus was laughing too hard to listen.

There had been a lively few minutes for Fraoch and Ferdia until a group of Medb's men had reached them. Angus discovered that it was very difficult to assist his friends; hitting an enemy or parrying a stroke was nearly impossible when someone wrenched and pulled at his shield arm. Nonetheless he managed to hold his prisoner and ward off most of the blows directed at him while a wall of men formed between him and Ethal's rescuers. Once he knew he could not get away, Ethal stopped struggling.

"You are a fool, Angus Óg," he said, his lips turned down in contempt. "You should have taken Cáer prisoner. She and the women will fight until they die, unless I yield—and I will not yield."

So much vicious satisfaction rang in Ethal's voice that Angus stopped dead for a moment. Suddenly he understood that Ethal had not acted out of stupidity and pride when he rejected Medb's message or even out of overconfidence in Ailill's *geis* not to attack any of the Tuatha de Danaan. His own first assumption—that Ethal wanted to be rid of his daughter—was correct, and if he could not be rid of her by marriage, even to a man she clearly loved, then he would be rid of her by death. Ethal had seen that Medb's trap would close on him no matter what he did, and had coldly decided to use the trap to rid himself of Cáer and her women.

For a moment such rage rose in Angus that he almost broke Ethal's thumbs. Then he remembered the terms Cáer had proposed to cover her defeat in her offer of single combat and began to laugh. Cáer was a match for Ethal Anubhail any day. They were close enough to their own lines by then for Angus to stop and yell for Fraoch to tie the prisoner's arms, and when he reached Medb, he pushed the bound man down on his knees in front of her.

"I will not yield," Ethal snarled, his head twisted so he could see the queen, "and you cannot kill me or even force me to it or a foulness you cannot dream will fall on that fancy-man you call husband. You cannot fool a *geis*, Red Medb, by coming here instead of Ailill."

Medb's eyes flickered. "Holy Bridget," she muttered, casting an angry glance at Angus, "for what did you bring me that?"

"I thought it would be a good idea before I learned that it is not merely proud and stupid but vicious." He shrugged. "I did not know that his purpose in mistreating your messenger and insulting you was to bring about the death of his daughter and destroy the White Swans."

Medb's beautiful skin flushed red with fury when Angus stated baldly how she had been used. Ethal spat obscenity and kicked at Angus with a force that could have broken his shin had the blow landed. Angus hopped aside, smiling, and Ethal overbalanced and fell flat.

Angus looked down at him as he struggled to come upright again and his smile broadened. "It does not matter," he went on. "I was too stupid to see it until he told me himself, but Cáer knew. Remember, he has already agreed before his liegemen to abide by the result of single combat between myself and Cáer. You have only to accept her offer—unless you wish to further his purpose by another assault on that line of 'dear little White Swans'?"

The flush of frustrated rage had died out of Medb's face when Angus reminded her that Ethal was bound to the terms of Cáer's challenge. She laughed at his remark about the dear little White Swans. There was almost pride in her face when she looked out over the field at the bodies, most of them of her own men. Some lay still but many others were stirring. The women were a formidable force, but fought clean. No further hurt was done or threatened against the wounded. The lines of women merely stood watching, resting on their arms. Ethal's men stood in groups behind them.

"We have the worse so far," Medb said. "Will the airechta still be willing to fight?"

"I am sure she will," Angus said, a shadow dimming his blue eyes. "She is surely very angry at me and will wish to be sure her punishment will fall on the right person."

Medb snorted. "Yes, but after what I have seen, I am not so sure you will win. If she has trained and leads those women, she is likely a better warrior than I."

"What if I do not?" Angus said. "You need make no terms for Ethal's release. He is my prisoner, and I will cede him to you in case of my death. Take him back to Cruach with you and demand as ransom what you would have taken as a fine." He paused and laughed. "Cáer is very honorable and will probably pay the fine, although there is a chance she will be so glad to be rid of him . . . No, she will pay."

"I did not come here only to avenge an insult," Medb said, frowning. "I do not like an independent rath in Connacht. It gives other righs ideas."

"I do not think I will be beaten," Angus said, "but I also think you will find Cáer much more reasonable to deal with than this." He looked down at Ethal.

Medb looked out over the field again and the men who were now straggling, limping, crawling, helping others worse hurt, back to her lines. She turned her head toward where her own household troops were waiting and shouted, "Aoife!"

A woman almost as tall as Angus came forward. "Take charge of that," she said, prodding Ethal with her foot so that he fell over. "Do it no hurt, but keep it close and see that it does not get away. It is not a nice thing, but study it closely, for you may be its warden if Cáer Ibormeith is defeated."

Ethal roared with rage, but Aoife merely hooked a hand in the collar of his armor and lifted him off his feet as if he had been a puppy. Medb smiled as the pressure choked off his roars, whereupon Aoife shook him twice before she set him on his feet and led him away. Then Medb gestured to Angus to follow and began to walk out onto the field toward Uaman.

chapter 8

When Cáer saw Angus drag her father away, she could have sung with joy. He had brought the trouble on her, but that was because he did not understand how devious and vicious Ethal Anubhail was. His own goodness and innocence had befooled him. When he realized what he had done, he had acted—she uttered a half hysterical giggle and had to smother it—just like Angus, in the most direct way, to correct his error. It had not occurred to her that once Ethal was a prisoner he would have to yield, but Angus would not have overlooked that answer to the problem because it was so simple.

Then Medb started out toward the open space between the armies, which meant she wished to parley rather than launch another attack. Cáer thought her heart would burst with happiness—and then a shadow flew past her and a harsh cackle turned all joy to ash.

The crow flapped heavily toward a tree in the field, cawing, and Cáer saw Medb look up, hesitate, and finally alter her path in that direction. Behind her a man, a man who had removed his helmet so that his red hair stirred with his movement, looked toward the tree and then toward the White Swans. Cáer could not see his face, but she saw his body stiffen. For a moment she considered sending Grian to demand another meeting place than under the tree on which The Morrigan perched, but she knew there was no way to avoid the Old Crow's presence if she wished to be there.

Cáer came down from the watchplace with no need to fear she would betray an unseemly joy over a need to surrender. With a face set like stone, she bade Grian carry her javelins and shield to the parley, then turned to the group of Ethal's liegemen—smaller than it had been—and asked if one of them wished to come also and hear Queen Medb's demands. However, the man who had accompanied her to the first parley was hurt and one of the others said, "We will trust you to make the best terms you can, airechta."

That should have cheered her as should the knowledge that the White Swans were not glancing suspiciously over their shoulders at the men behind them. The men, too, were clearly more at ease, comfortable with the knowledge that they had done their part and were welcome to the shelter of the shield wall. Now that both had fought together and saw how the two styles complemented each other they would have more respect for each other and find fewer reasons to quarrel. She felt some satisfaction, but nothing could lift her spirits. The crow, perching hunched and silent now, could only be an omen of evil.

As she covered the last few spearlengths, Cáer permitted herself a single glance at Angus. To her horror, he was staring at the crow in the tree with bright eyes and a half smile pulling up the corners of his lips. How could he be glad of The Morrigan's presence? But then his eyes turned to her, blue as the sky—and his smile grew tender and full of love. Cáer could not understand his expression; what she did understand was that there was blood on his armor, some still bright and red and he looked very tired.

A flicker of bright red and Medb's voice: "Airechta?" drew her eyes away. Cáer stood as erect and as proud as she could before she bowed only her head to Queen Medb.

"Since the righ of Uaman is captured, great queen," Cáer said, "we are ready to fulfill the terms of his yielding."

"Ethal Anubhail has not yielded," Medb replied.

Cáer caught her breath. She had felt momentary gladness when she thought Ethal had been killed, but now she knew that was foolish. Although the men might now accept her as queen—she glanced quickly at the mess of black feathers in the tree—she knew she would not be available, and without Ethal or herself, there would be a battle for supremacy in which the White Swans had no right to interfere and Uaman might be destroyed. If Medb had had him killed and meant to appoint her own man to rule—

"For my own reasons," Medb continued, breaking into Cáer's scurrying thoughts, "I will not kill him or force him. Thus, you must, as you earlier offered, settle this conflict by single combat against Angus Óg, or I must wage this war until Uaman is conquered."

Cáer wanted to close her eyes, but the vision that had flashed before them could not be shut out by physical means. From the beginning she had known that The Morrigan wished ill to Angus, perhaps to her also for resisting and bargaining. She had believed that ill was only in bringing heartbreak upon them, but it was worse, much worse than that. Her flash of vision had shown her what The Morrigan wanted—Angus lying dead by the red-stained sword in her hand.

At another time and place, Cáer would not have doubted Angus's ability to protect himself, even to overcome her. He was larger and stronger and almost as quick and graceful. But today he had already fought a hard battle, he was already wounded and tired, while she had not struck a single blow and was fresh and strong.

Then her heart clenched because she knew why Angus was able to smile so tenderly at her. He intended to die to restore everything to what it was before he came.

Cáer flashed a single bitter glance toward the huddle of feathers in the tree. Vicious, stupid creature, drawing her joy out of agony and tears! Well, the Old Crow would get no satisfaction out of this game she had played. Angus would *not* die, and the babe for whom the Old Crow had such special plans would never come to life.

"So long as the terms I offered in our first parley are acceptable," Cáer said to Medb, "I will fight."

"And you, Angus?" Medb asked, turning to him.

He was looking at the ground, his usually mobile face rigid. "Yes," he said. "I will fight."

Medb frowned, but all she said was, "The choice of weapons is for the defender."

"Swords only," Angus stated promptly.

"Accepted," Cáer said, feeling a flicker of relief. She was very good with a javelin, but a throw to just miss might easily hit instead if the target guarded against where the shaft should strike rather than where it was actually aimed.

"The choice of time and place is for the challenger," Medb said, her voice not quite so sure and her eyes flickering to the crow in the tree.

"I cede the choice of time to your champion," Cáer said. "He has fought a battle already, and should have rest and food before he engages." She also looked at the crow but with a clear challenge in her eyes; however, the bird did not stir. She knows she has pushed me as far as she can, Cáer thought, and she went on, "As to the place . . . here is as good as any other." She wanted the Old Crow to have a good view of the failure of her cruel plans.

A brief bob of the head showed Medb's approval of Cáer's offer. "You have the naming of the time, Angus."

"Now," Angus said.

Cáer turned toward Grian to conceal the little shudder that went through her. She knew she had to die, but she had expected to have a little time to prepare. Nonetheless, she reached for her shield, and Grian handed it to her, retaining her hold on the javelins. When she faced Angus and the queen again, she saw that Medb was looking at him, with lifted brows.

"You swore," she reminded him.

Swore what? Cáer wondered. Whatever it was, the reminder did not trouble Angus because he had lifted his gaze from the ground at his feet and smiled faintly at the suspicious queen.

"I remember," he said and stepped away from her, turning toward Cáer.

Medb caught his arm and shook her head at Cáer, who had lifted her shield. "Now cannot mean this moment," she said to the combatants. "We must have adequate witnesses. I require that Ethal's liegemen be present so that they cannot later cry treachery, and I wish my own to see that the fight is fair. However," she said, looking at Cáer, "I do not mean to cheat you of any advantage you might gain from my . . . ah . . . champion's lack of wits. I will make no long delay. You and Angus will meet as soon as our witnesses can gather."

Having said that, she cast another cynical and annoyed glance at Angus and turned away to walk back toward her men.

Angus stood one moment longer, looking at Cáer. "I tried," he said.

"I know," she answered. "You never really understood what Ethal was."

Then quickly, before she could burst into tears and throw herself into his arms, she walked away. By the time she reached her own people, the fierce pain tears had caused in her throat had subsided a little and she was able to report the results of the parley to Ethal's liegemen.

Even the brash young ones made no objection. They
knew that half, and likely the better half, of Medb's army
had never engaged at all. Those men were fresh and
ready to attack while the ones they had fought rested,
and when the second group were driven back—if they
could be driven back—the first group would be rested
and ready to come at them in turn. For them there would
be no rest, and even to the boldest it was clear they could
not win. All agreed with relief to stand as witness and to
accept the outcome of the battle, although from their expressions Cáer was certain they did not expect her to win.

It did not matter, she told herself, as she also chose ten
of the White Swans to stand as witnesses and set out to the
tree in the field. Had she intended to return from this
conflict and rule the men, she would have been disappointed in their low expectations, but as it was, it did not
matter. Uaman was safe and the White Swans were safe;
Angus would live and the Old Crow would have nothing.
That must be victory enough, even though she would not
live to enjoy it.

Medb's party was approaching at the same time, Angus
walking beside the queen. He was looking at the ground
again, a faint furrow of worry between his brows. Cáer
longed to smooth the frown away and tell him that she
did not blame him, that she was content with what must
be the outcome of this battle. And then, fearful that her
father's men would see where her eyes dwelt and watch
for any failure in her attack or defense, she deliberately
looked at the others accompanying the queen—only to
gasp with surprise when her eyes met her father's.

Ethal looked somewhat more battered than Cáer remembered from her last sight of him, but he was not
bound, walking free beside a woman as tall as he and
broader of shoulder. He stared at Cáer, his eyes fixed
with purpose, but she could not give her mind to what it
could be. She was too full of a sense of shock and betrayal.

She had not considered that her father would be a witness. It was bad enough to go down to defeat before her father's liegemen, but having him there was too much.

She had just drawn breath to speak when the woman beside Ethal said, "You stop that, little man. It is too late for you to be laying plans and giving signals. The champions will fight their battle, and I will see that you accept the outcome." The voice held a kindly contempt that was utterly withering.

Cáer choked, feeling much better. Her father would not enjoy her downfall at all. She turned briskly to Medb. "I am content with the witnesses."

Medb was smiling. "I am content with the witnesses also. Let the field be cleared."

The two parties withdrew, forming two rough semicircles with the tree on which The Morrigan sat at one edge. Cáer came forward, her shield held well before her and her sword bare. Angus walked toward her and stopped a little less than a double sword length away. Cáer lifted her sword. He lifted his. She touched the tip of his weapon, a gentle tap. He twisted his blade, driving hers down, and she sprang forward so that the lowered point of her weapon slid along his and drove toward his chest.

He continued the twisting motion. Cáer's blade was forced to the side and Angus's shield swung toward her. She turned slightly left, sliding her sword out from under his and bringing it up and over in a strong slashing blow aimed at his head. His shield rose to catch the blade and his own sword thrust forward. Cáer leapt backward, bringing her shield forward, tilted at an angle that caught his sword and thrust it upward. She came down with knees bent and slashed at his legs, but he had jumped back too and she missed, staggering forward a step.

Making an advantage of being unbalanced, she used the stagger to rush forward, slashing backhand as she came, but Angus's shield was there and he was driving

forward also. With a muscle-wrenching effort, Cáer
dragged her sword from between the shields as they met.
Angus pushed hard. Cáer had expected that and was well
aware that he had the advantage in strength. She did not
fall, but gave way as suddenly and completely as she
could, causing Angus to stagger toward her in turn bent
slightly forward. She used the opportunity to strike at his
head again.

He parried the blow, but barely, her blade coming so
close that it caught on the ridge of his helmet. As if that
had annoyed him and made him lose his temper, Angus
slashed and hacked at her in a wild flurry of blows. It was
a spectacular but singularly useless display. Cáer had no
trouble parrying the wild swings and thrusts with either
her sword or her shield. The only danger to her was the
enormous strength of each stroke. To diminish the impact, she gave back a little with each blow.

As soon as the first ardor of the attack flagged, she
struck at him, high, low, little rushes and thrusts that
made him jump and bend. Then he slipped and went
down on his knee. Cáer rushed forward, sword raised as
if to chop at his neck, only to be met—as she expected—
with an upward leap and a thrust of his shield that drove
her backward once more. Again the apparent near suc-
cess of Cáer's assault seemed to incite a crazy rage in
Angus and unleash another all-out onslaught in which
sheer force was substituted for skill.

Oddly, Cáer's consciousness was less fixed during these
violent barrages of blows. Her body was well able to react
by long training, which made her responses almost instinctive and left a corner of her mind free for thinking.
She knew such attacks were not Angus's normal style. She
knew he did not believe he could win by using such a
brutal technique. She was tiring, yes, but the effort he was
making was much greater than hers, so he was tiring even
more. She could hear him breathing in gasps, see his

chest working like a bellows. It seemed clear to her that Angus was putting on a show for the witnesses, for Queen Medb, which proved to her that he intended to let her kill him.

How could she tell him that was wrong? That his death would solve nothing, only give a cruel victory to The Morrigan and put her back in the same hopeless struggle with her father. But she could think of no way to communicate, and even as she watched for some unexpected move on Angus's part that would endanger him, she was aware that something else had changed.

She was conscious, as she parried and backed, backed again as she caught blows on her shield that could have hammered her into the earth if she had not known how to dissipate the force, of the yelling and cheering of the witnesses. She wished they would be still. Something was bothering her, something she had seen from the corner of her eyes but could not call to mind. She needed a moment to think, and she could not because of the other demands on her: the need to protect herself, her fear that Angus was setting the scene for allowing one of her parries to kill him, even the distraction of hearing her name called by proud supporters and having to remember that she must not listen. With all that, she could not concentrate on that oddity she knew was important.

The harsh screech almost above her head revealed what had been worrying her. Her eyes had seen a wide open space of field lay behind Angus's back and the ring of watchers without her brain taking in the meaning. All the time he had been hammering at her with such ferocity that she had to back away from the impact of his blows, he had been driving her back toward the tree in which The Morrigan was perched.

Why? Cáer wondered, but at that moment Angus's attack began to falter. In instantaneous and unthinking response, Cáer caught his sword on her raised shield and launched a slashing blow at his exposed side. The slash was too successful. It slid under Angus's arm and struck with sufficient force against his burnie to break a link or two. A thin trickle of red showed as Cáer retracted her weapon as if to strike again.

Actually that streak of blood frightened her so much that her fighting instincts were momentarily stilled. She leapt backward—in time to avoid Angus's counterstroke but not because she knew it was coming, only out of horror at what she had done to him. But instead of the flat surface she expected, the side of her foot landed on the edge of a tree root, her other foot found nothing at all because behind the root the ground was hollowed out.

She began to fall. Even then her training held. As her ankle turned, she twisted her body so she would land on her back and be ready to thrust upward, keeping Angus away until she could get to her feet. Unfortunately, she had had no chance to judge how close she was to the tree. Her elbow jarred against the trunk with such force that her fingers sprang open and her sword slipped from her grasp. Even as it fell, Angus's shield had caught it and tossed it far beyond her reach.

Before he could have known she had lost her weapon, as soon as he saw her slip, Ethal's voice rang out: "The spell! Use the spell!"

The breath beaten out of her by her fall, Cáer could not reply. Angus stood over her, sword poised above her throat.

"Angus, your promise," Medb's voice came, sharp and hard as steel.

And atop it, her father's bellow, "Use the spell, you idiotic bitch! Use the spell and we are all free and clear."

"I will not!" Cáer cried, regaining her breath. "Swords only was the weapon named and I accepted."

"You . . ." Ethal screamed; then his voice cut off suddenly.

"Quiet, little man," Aoife said. "Your daughter knows the meaning of honor. You need schooling!"

"Yield, beloved," Angus said, leaning forward.

Cáer heard words, but they had no meaning for her. She was half dazed by the shock of her fall, and her father's command had fixed into her confused thoughts the bargain with The Morrigan and the conviction that she had to die or The Morrigan would win and Angus would suffer.

"Kill me," Cáer gasped. "The days of my life will be ended and your love with them. You will be safe from The Morrigan."

Angus went down on one knee beside her. His sword lay against her throat, but he said, "My love will never end, all the days of your life or all the days of mine."

"No, you fool," she cried. "You must kill me or you will come to dreadful harm. I carry your child—that is what The Morrigan desired, the child. If you kill me, you will spoil her plan."

Blue eyes opened wide, the sword was lifted and flung away. "My child," Angus whispered. Then his face twisted in pain and he flung up his head to stare at the crow. "No," he shouted, "You will not have Cáer's child and mine."

Sense was returning to Cáer. "She does not want the child." She shook her head as well as she could with her helmet half buried in the churned-up soil. "She swore she would not take the child nor harm her nor interfere with her in any way, but she and—and I, too—must be part of a design to bring you to grief."

For one moment more Angus stared at the crow, which flicked open and resettled its wings and strutted along the branch and back. Then he burst out laughing and lifted Cáer into his arms. "Sacred Dana," he gasped between chuckles, "that Old Crow is truly fuller of mischief than most crows are of lice."

"Maybe so," Medb said, standing above them with her own drawn sword in her hand, "but this is a strange end to a trial by combat. Do you refuse to yield, airechta? Have you forgotten your oath, Angus Óg?"

Angus laughed up at Medb, still hugging Cáer tight. "Yield, love, yield," he urged. "Do not fear. Medb will not allow your father to despoil Uaman, and as for The Morrigan, she has had her fun with us already. When she set the *geis* on me she swore that if I could find you and win you no harm would come to me nor to you and good would come to the Tuatha de Danaan. To you she swore no harm to our child. She never lies, so we are all safe."

Cáer pushed free of Angus and struggled to her feet. "I yield," she cried. "By the terms of my yielding, Uaman will be subject to Queen Medb and she will set a warden over Ethal Anubhail, who will keep his place as righ, and pay a reasonable fine to assuage the insult to the queen. Is this acceptable to you, Queen Medb?"

"It is acceptable to me and to my witnesses." Medb did not bother to look at her men. What she accepted they would accept. "Is it acceptable to your witnesses?"

"It is acceptable to the White Swans," Grian replied. Ethal Anubhail's men were less pleased, but they had known the terms and a glance at the army waiting Medb's orders beyond the field of combat was a strong encouragement to comply. The eldest of them came forward and accepted the terms. Aoife brought Ethal over to his men and smiled at them. The men drew somewhat together. Grian stepped forward to stand beside Aoife.

Cáer blinked back tears. Uaman was lost to her. The tears dissipated when a warm hand fell on her shoulder and drew her back, away from those of Uaman. An arm encircled her shoulders and a sense of being wanted desperately filled her. No one in Uaman wanted her; possibly the White Swans had some affection for her, but they would soon be as attached to Aoife and the men would prefer Medb's deputy to someone they had known from childhood and were ashamed to acknowledge as superior.

Despite her bumps and bruises, the growing ache of muscles tested to the uttermost by Angus's attacks, Cáer felt herself growing lighter with each step that divided her from her past, from the animosities and petty slights, from duties and burdens that were made more onerous by her father's spite. She looked up at Angus.

"Can I believe this?" she asked, turning her head a little so that her range of vision also took in The Morrigan chuckling and nodding on her branch. "Can it be true that there is only good for all in this—and that is the mischief the Old Crow intended?"

"Yes." Angus shook his head slowly from side to side and sighed. "How The Morrigan must have laughed to see us hurt each other by concealment, nearly kill each other, only because we expected evil from her and she has done only good."

"Only good." Cáer looked up and chuckled. "No, she is still black. I really expected to see her turned white."

Above them the crow cackled again. Then suddenly it rose and flapped away, flying straight, not circling. In eight swift months Macha would be born and a whole new cycle would begin, a cycle that would start with contempt for a woman and end in the humbling of the proud men of Ulster. Only good? Cackling harshly The Morrigan flew to her sidhe.

Angus watched the bird disappear in the distance. The net around his heart was gone. The Morrigan was no longer interested in him or Cáer—yet his love remained. He had the deepest wish of his heart, a woman who truly loved him, loved him enough to offer up her life for his good. And Cáer would have the love she craved all her life, and work enough among the people of Bruigh na Boinne. Still . . .

Only good? Angus's brow lifted. He shrugged and held Cáer closer. Rarer than a white crow, rarer than the true love of a warrior woman, rarer than all was a deed of The Morrigan that brought only good. He would watch carefully over his daughter Macha.

Glossary

airechta: champion and avenger.
banshee: female spirit who cries out a warning in the night.
Beltain fire/Beltaine fire: May Day bonfire.
bodach woman: mischievous sprite/a serf; a bound servant.
chainse: kind of garment.
corrie: hollow in a hillside.
druid: Celtic priest.
dun: fort.
fidchell: a chesslike medieval game.
geis: a spell.
gessa: a spell.
grianan: sun room.
lena/leine: a shirt.
leprechaun: one of the fairylike "little people."
lios: fairy fort/property under the direct rule of a lord.
Lugnaid/Lughnasa: Celtic festival of Midsummer for the fertility god Lugh.
mead: mildly alcoholic drink made from honey.
pooka: a mischievous spirit.
rath: a chieftain's fort.
righ: a king.
Ron: seal-people.
scry: predict the future.
sencleithe: a servant.

Sidh/Sidhe: Celtic spirits, or the underground dwelling where they live.

swive: have sexual intercourse with.

trews: an undergarment.

tuath: family, clan, tribe.

Tuatha de Danaan: the Magic People.

About the Authors

Roberta Gellis is the critically acclaimed author of dozens of novels, including such national bestsellers as *Bond of Blood* and *Dazzling Brightness*. *Romantic Times Magazine* has given her novels, *Roselynde* and *Alinor,* five stars (classic), the first such ratings given to historical romance. Roberta Gellis has received numerous awards, including the Lifetime Achievement Award from the Romance Writers of America.

Gifted storyteller Barbara Samuel is the author of *A Bed of Spices* and *A Winter Ballad,* medieval romances of unusual sensitivity and lyricism. Under the pen name Ruth Wind, she has also written numerous award-winning contemporary romances.

Susan Wiggs, author of *The Mist and the Magic, Circle in the Water,* and other bestselling romances, has won several awards for her novels, including the RITA Golden Choice Award, voted by members of Romance Writers of America, for their favorite book of the year.

All three authors are members of Novelists Inc., Romance Writers of America, and the Authors Guild.

Morgan Llywelyn lives in Stillorgan, Ireland, and is the author of many major works of historical fiction, including the New York Times bestseller, *Lion of Ireland, Red Branch, The Druids, and Finn Mac Cool.*

Put a Little Romance in Your Life With
Fern Michaels

__Dear Emily	0-8217-5676-1	$6.99US/$8.50CAN
__Sara's Song	0-8217-5856-X	$6.99US/$8.50CAN
__Wish List	0-8217-5228-6	$6.99US/$7.99CAN
__Vegas Rich	0-8217-5594-3	$6.99US/$8.50CAN
__Vegas Heat	0-8217-5758-X	$6.99US/$8.50CAN
__Vegas Sunrise	1-55817-5983-3	$6.99US/$8.50CAN
__Whitefire	0-8217-5638-9	$6.99US/$8.50CAN

Put a Little Romance in Your Life With
Janelle Taylor